For Topsfield

Muskets & Minuets

LINDSEY S. FERA

ZENITH PUBLISHING

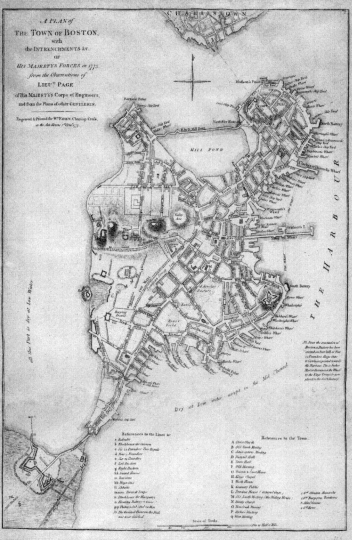

A PLAN of THE TOWN OF BOSTON, with the INTRENCHMENTS &c. OF HIS MAJESTY'S FORCES in 1775, from the Observations of LIEUT. PAGE of His Majesty's Corps of Engineers, and from the Plans of other GENTLEMEN.

Engraved & Printed for Wm. FADEN, Charing-Cross, as the Act directs 1st Octr. 1777.

CHARLESTOWN

MILL POND

THE HARBOUR

References to the Lines &c
a Redoubt
b Blockhouse &c Guns
c the 12 Pounder Two Royals
d Four 9 Pounders
e Six 12 Pounders
f Got the dam
g Right Bastion
hh Guard House
i Barriers
kk Magazine
ll Abbatis
mmm Tents & Traps
n Blockhouse &c Marquees
o Floating Battery 9 Guns
ppp Points &c
* The Arms'd Vessels the Scale was never settled

References to the Town.
A Christ Church
B Old North Meeting
C Anabaptists Meeting
D Fanueil Hall
E Town Hall
F Old Meeting
G Prison & Court House
H Kings Chapel
I Work House
K Granary Public
L Province House (General's House)
M Old South Meeting (the Riding House)
N Trinity Church
O New South Meeting
P Hollis Meeting
Q West Meeting

R etc etc
1 etc Hospital etc
2 etc Barracks
3 etc Barracks
4 etc Store

Scale of Yards.

PART ONE

1769 – 1774

ANNALISA

TOPSFIELD, THE PROVINCE OF
MASSACHUSETTS BAY, OCTOBER 1769

THE ROAD ANNALISA STARED down was a narrow one, just wide enough for two horses to pass through on a chilled evening when snow thickly covered all things. Last night the first snow had fallen, frosting the sloped roof of her family's large saltbox house. From the central chimney, thick smoke swirled into the unseasonably chilled October air. Surely, a considerable fire lapped the iron kettle swinging in its great kitchen hearth.

Annalisa returned her gaze to the road. Snow drifts constricted the lane, and red and orange trees now white-capped and bent, spoiled her view. She stared anxiously through the branches for her older brother, George. He was due home in Topsfield from Ipswich an hour ago.

"Annalisa!" Mamma's shrill voice carried on the breeze.

She froze. Expected in the drawing room with her sisters, Annalisa scrambled over the stone wall and shrank beside the road, her shallow breath puffing into misty clouds.

Tlot-tlot, tlot-tlot.

Tlot-tlot, tlot-tlot.

Horses' hooves clopped around the bend, and a rider appeared. His long black hair, tied in a queue, flapped wildly beneath his cocked hat.

Annalisa's teeth chattered as she lifted from the ground to meet the rider.

Her brother, George, slowed Frederick to a trot, reached for her, and helped her onto his horse.

"Have you the tow?"

Annalisa felt for the fuzzy wad of flax in her pocket. "Yes." She clutched his wool greatcoat. "I thought you'd forgotten. How was Ipswich?"

"Zounds," George guffawed. "I'd not forget. And the gunsmith was able to remedy Bixby's steel." He gestured to his fowling piece strapped snugly over his shoulder.

Annalisa studied the steel, the part of the firelock onto which flint would strike, cause spark, and ignite the gunpowder in the priming pan.

"He looks to have fixed it competently. But quick, Mamma looks for me."

George laughed again, kicked his brown steed, and they galloped away to the east.

Their family's farmland spread nearly twenty acres until it reached woods. At the forest's edge grew an ancient oak, whose uneven and heavy boughs sprawled to touch the earth. Behind this venerable tree rose a steep hill and at its base, a footpath.

George jumped from Frederick and held out his hand to her, but Annalisa slid from the horse without him. Her brother smirked, tied Frederick to the oak, and followed Annalisa up the path, pushing aside snow-covered branches and brush. In less than ten minutes, at the top of this glacial hill, a small field opened before them, where golden grass poked through sparkling snow.

George lifted the fowling piece from over his shoulder and turned to her. "Time to load her up." He squinted against the sunlight glinting off the crystalline snow and adjusted the tip of his cocked hat over his left eye. He set the fowler into her hands. "Come. You know what to do."

Annalisa's fingers molded around its frame with familiarity, as they had these past six months. Each time, it felt as though she was always meant to cradle Bixby. Her confidence surged as she quickly half-cocked the piece and dribbled gunpowder into the priming pan.

"No, too much." George's high, angular cheeks reddened.

"La. I know what I'm doing. I've been practicing since April."

"And I've been loading firelocks since you were in swaddlings," George barked.

Annalisa's hand flew to her hip. "Since you were five?"

His jaw stiffened. "Trust me, you'll cause too great a flare."

Ignoring him, she snapped back the newly repaired steel, then bunched up the flax. When she tried sticking it into the barrel, George groaned.

"That is far too much." He grabbed the wad and compressed it into a smaller ball. "Like this."

She snatched the tow from him, shoved it down the barrel, and plunged it home with the ramrod. Annalisa poured in more gunpowder then held out her hand for a lead round.

George shook his head. "Can't waste balls today, Little One. We must conserve them for hunting." His nose wrinkled. "That bloody tax on lead." He pulled his spatter-dashes over his knee and knelt behind her. "Now, fully cock it—"

"I remember." She rolled her eyes.

"And you've still much to learn." George's dark brows furrowed. "A well-trained soldier or militiaman can load and fire three volleys a minute, Little One." He lifted Bixby to her shoulder. "You're to aim at that birch. The same as before."

Annalisa's left arm shuddered under the firelock's weight, but she settled her shoes into the snow. Her first finger poised to fire, she peered down the barrel. With a final breath, she pulled the trigger.

Crack-boom!

From the priming pan, spark flared into a great flame. The sulfur stung her nose, but not as harshly as her face. Below her right eye, her cheek burned as though she'd pressed it to embers. Misty, grey smoke wafted from the fowler as she dropped it into the snow. Though her eyes watered, she held back her tears. Shaking, she looked to George.

Her brother's square jaw slackened, and his narrow, green eyes rounded. He reached out and touched her cheek. When his hand recoiled, blood coated his fingertips.

2

ANNALISA
TOPSFIELD, OCTOBER 1769

"WHAT WERE YOU THINKING?" Mamma paced the foyer. "No man of Society will marry her now!"

"You regard your daughter with such harsh words." George gestured to Annalisa. "She's hardly an owl in an ivy bush."

"Enough with the vulgar language." Mamma pointed a finger at Annalisa. "And you—you should have been inside practicing needlepoint with Jane. You'll never make a proper wife if you continue to shirk your lessons. Why can't you behave more like your sisters?"

"I try." Annalisa frowned. "I play the spinet better than any in town. But one of us girls must learn to use a firelock. What will we do if Papa, and George, and William, and Henry are gone and we're attacked? Jane will hardly touch a firelock, and Mary is still too young—"

"Silence!" Mamma's pale face glowed red. "You echo your brother like his own shadow. At thirteen, 'tis more important you learn your lessons than practice musketry.

I've told you time and again there's little money for you and Mary after Jane weds. Unless you wish to dig your own potatoes and cook your own meals, you will study French, you will practice needlepoint, and you will learn to dance the minuet. And you shall do it all well as Jane does."

Annalisa ground her teeth. "Why must I marry at all?"

Mamma grabbed her shoulders and squeezed. "To be taken care of. A gentleman of good breeding may have overlooked your complexion if you were diligent about remaining indoors, but this scar may now well prevent you from ever being introduced to higher society."

"And she would be lucky to avoid such a fate." George crossed his arms. "No good can come from those plums."

Annalisa shrugged off Mamma's hands and glanced into the looking glass. Behind her, Mamma and George argued, but before her, a bright red patch beneath her right eye swelled with small, fluid-filled blisters. Dried blood speckled her cheek, still bronzed from summertime. She touched her face and winced.

"Oh, Annie." Her younger sister, Mary, shuffled into the foyer. "Your cheek." She burst into tears.

Annalisa's throat clogged and she knelt, holding Mary close. "I'm quite all right." She smoothed the girl's silky, walnut hair. "I promise."

"Mamma." Jane's honeyed soprano lilted from the parlor and her fifteen-year-old sister glided toward her. Annalisa smelled the sweet lavender wafting from Jane's perfectly porcelain skin. "Addy will know how to treat this." Her robin's-egg-blue eyes examined the wound. "Worry not. A man of modest means might still find you agreeable. Maybe a vicar, or gentleman farmer from Boxford."

"Mary, come here." Mamma took Mary from Annalisa and looked to their beloved housemaid, defeated. "Addy, please clean Miss Annalisa's face at once."

Streaks of grey peeked out from Addy's white linen cap, framing her rich, umber complexion. Her ebony eyes offered a gentle warmth that Mamma's frozen glare lacked.

She tugged Annalisa into an affectionate embrace.

"Come, Miss Annie."

Annalisa cast George one final look of apprehension and followed Addy down the steep staircase into the basement pantry, below the kitchen. With its stone floor and forest of dried herbs dangling from the ceiling's wide beams, the cellar was a cool, crisp refuge in the summer months. But today the large brick hearth rustled with a crackling fire that warmed the stale, smoky air.

Addy placed her hands on Annalisa's shoulders. "What were you thinking, child? You best listen to your momma and Miss Janey."

Annalisa fisted her hands. "Why must everything I do be for finding a husband? Shouldn't a man wish to marry me as I am, and not because I'm akin to every other lady? There are hundreds of girls like Jane. What sort of example is that for poor Mary?"

"A husband will protect and care for you." Addy dabbed away the dried blood with a moist muslin cloth. "And this wound will heal just fine. I promise."

"How?"

"Magick." Addy winked. "I learned from my grand-momma." Her experienced hands picked through the mysterious herbs and roots hanging from the ceiling.

Addy mumbled to herself as she crushed them in her mortar and pestle. After adding several drops of oil, she mixed it into a paste and dabbed the mixture onto Annalisa's cheek. Soothing mint overpowered the lingering bits of gunpowder on Annalisa's clothes and hair. Her skin tightened and tingled under the poultice, and the burn settled with invigorating coolness.

Annalisa unclenched her fists. "I'm afraid."

Addy cocked her head. "Afraid of what, Miss Annie?"

"Of higher society. Of finding a husband among them." She hesitated. "Society is too...they care only for appearances, Addy." She hugged herself. "And I needn't a husband to protect me. I can protect myself."

"Oh, Miss Annie." Addy held her. "Someday, you'll meet a nice, rich man and you'll change your mind. You'll see."

Annalisa smirked into Addy's shoulder. "Or maybe I'll change his."

※

THAT EVENING, ANNALISA SAT WITH A THROBBING cheek at the spinet. Though her fingers played Bach's fugue, *Contrapunctus 1,* she lifted her gaze from a pamphlet she read, and watched Addy light the drawing room candles.

Jane, who sat in a chair nearest the spinet, set down the French book she'd received from her tutor in Salem. Her delicate pink lips upturned into a cat-like smile. She reached over and, with slight finger, picked a bit of dried poultice from Annalisa's opposite cheek.

"Why don't you study French with me?"

"Look." Annalisa stopped playing and showed Jane the page in her pamphlet she'd read. "George and I couldn't practice with a round this afternoon because of the tax on lead from the Townshend Acts. It says here King George imposed these levies without our representation in Parliament. Who knows what else might be taxed without our consent?" Exasperated, she looked up and shifted her gaze toward their father. "Papa, how can they do such a thing?"

"Annalisa, enough." Papa cleared his throat and curled his thin lips around his white clay pipe. A small puff of smoke wafted into the air, its sweet scent familiar, lingering. "You will not speak against the king."

Annalisa sat forward on the spinet bench. "But Papa—"

"Hush it." Mamma looked up from her stitching. "Eligible gentlemen rarely wish to discuss politics with young ladies. You had best learn to hold your tongue."

Annalisa bit her cheek and tucked the pamphlet into her pocket while Jane opened the French book and spread it across her lap. As Jane uttered French beside her, Annalisa resumed the fugue, but studied her eleven-year-old brother, William. He sprawled across the wide, pine floor and arranged an army of lead Redcoat soldiers. He placed toy natives behind the leg of a wooden table, hiding them from the army. The seven-year-old twins, Mary and Henry, watched him set up the trap.

In an armchair facing the fire, George read a pamphlet he'd procured from Mr. Gould at the meetinghouse. Annalisa's mouth twisted with amusement. Mr. Gould often spoke out against the king, to Papa's dismay.

"George." Papa's voice severed the silence and all eyes looked up at once. "A courier came today with a letter from your Aunt Elizabeth in Boston. She's requested you visit."

George sat forward. "My Aunt Elizabeth?"

Jane closed the French book. "You mean Lady Perkins, Papa? The wife of the magistrate?"

Papa nodded. "Aye, Captain Bixby's sister."

Annalisa looked at Mamma. A shadow crossed her face at the mention of her first love, whose ship had carried him to the bed of the ocean. Mamma and Papa seldom mentioned Captain Bixby. He was Mamma's late first husband, and George's natural father.

"She invites you to visit their home." Papa handed George the letter but gave a regard of warning. "That means staying out of trouble with the king's army, no gallivanting about with those rebel Sons of Liberty, no reading Patriot newspapers, or speaking your vulgar tavern speech. You will behave as a gentleman. Is that understood?"

George smirked. "Aye, Pa."

Jane scoffed. "Papa, you mean for George to visit such important family alone? I heard from Mrs. Andrews that Lord Perkins is acquaintance to Mr. Hancock." She smoothed her skirts and smiled amiably. "Papa, couldn't we visit, too? Surely they've sons to meet, and I've learned enough from my lessons—"

"Jane, please." Papa's brown eyes flickered toward George. "'Tis George's aunt, and his invitation. Not ours."

George met Jane's glare with triumph and bellowed a deep-seated howl.

Jane's face bloomed a shade of pink that only made her appear more agreeable. She set aside the French book and crossed her arms.

"Well I'll be damned." George's laughter subsided as he scanned the letter. He looked up and held Annalisa's gaze, a gaze so exact to her own she often dreamt they shared the mysterious Captain Bixby as a father—though she alone boasted Papa's bronzed skin.

"What is it?" Annalisa jumped from the bench and scurried behind him.

William crawled to George's feet and rested his elbows on George's knees. "Let me see."

"Nein, Wilhelmina." George chuckled at his younger brother, then handed Annalisa the letter. "My aunt discovered something about my father—something she could not write."

3

GEORGE
BOSTON, OCTOBER 1769

G EORGE FROWNED AT THE man in the looking glass. He'd been in Boston only two days and already, his middlin' class misfortune glared like the sun off his rich aunt's shiny silver teapot. Even the freed brown-skinned housekeepers wore finer coats than his best wool one. He had no use for formal dinners, or aristocracy, but tonight he would dine with wealthy Mr. Hancock, and learn why he'd been summoned to Boston.

His aunt's pungent, rose-scented perfume encircled him.

"George, darling." Lady Perkins, robed in a blue silk gown, touched his shoulder. "We'll be late if you dawdle."

He threw on his old black wool greatcoat and trailed behind her out the front door with his cousins. George followed Lord and Lady Perkins into the carriage. His cousin Jack, smelling of amber and wearing a finely spun navy wool greatcoat, sat beside him.

The door closed.

"What of Abigail, Ollie, and Andrew?" George pulled

back the indigo velvet curtain to look out the window at the raw, grey day.

His aunt smoothed her skirts. "They're in the second carriage, Dear."

Zounds, a second carriage? Jane would be jealous indeed. The clop of horses' hooves sounded from the cobbled road, and the carriage juddered into the street.

Lord Perkins swayed with the movement, and scratched a ruddy scalp beneath his ashen wig. "Mr. Hancock is Boston's premier merchant, and the most respected of Boston's Whigs." The magistrate peered at George from over his round spectacles. "Though now, many call the Whigs *Patriots*."

George itched his ear and glanced at Jack. His seventeen-year-old cousin's cheek dimpled with a crooked, mischievous grin. "Hancock has been accused several times of smuggling undocumented imports into the harbor aboard his ships."

"Oh, Jack." Lady Perkins placed a gloved hand to her breast.

"Well, he speaks true, madam," Lord Perkins replied.

She frowned. "Enough gossip about poor Mr. Hancock."

Lord Perkins, the magistrate, can't possibly sympathize with the Patriots, can he? Annalisa would love to hear such political musings.

The carriage stopped outside Hancock's manor, and the door opened. George stepped from the coach.

"Well I'll be damned."

Three stories, comprised entirely of granite, berthed two stone chimneys which flanked the house at either end, and a great stone balcony hung above the entryway. He followed his cousins inside.

An imposing staircase, which rose toward the back of the house, paused at a landing before it twisted up to the second floor. The landing, with a large window and seat, overlooked the rear of the property. George pictured Mr. Hancock delayed there each morning to monitor his acreage before continuing his descent to the ground floor.

A native dressed in teal silk ushered them into the parlor. There, amidst the rustling fire and white wainscoting, an agreeable-looking man with skin to match his well-placed white wig, stood and bowed.

Lord Perkins gestured to George. "Mr. Hancock, may I present my nephew, Mr. George Bixby Howlett. He visits from Topsfield, a small farming town twenty-five miles to the north."

"Mr.—Howlett. I'm glad to make your acquaintance." Hancock smiled and his coffee eyes narrowed with minimal creasing.

"Sir, the pleasure is all mine." George flushed, feeling foolish amidst such well-bred men. Next to his cousins in fine brocaded silks, his humble wool coat glared of inferiority. If not for Abigail's generosity, he would have been without clean stockings. The girl had been kind enough to insist he take a pair from Jack's trunk.

"Pray tell, Mr. Howlett, what is your age?"

"I've just made eighteen, sir."

Mr. Hancock nodded. "A man grown." He grinned, then gestured toward a doorway. "Let's into the dining room."

Savory roast meat, salty cod cakes, boiled potatoes, and an assortment of puddings and pies decorated the long, mahogany dining table. A large chandelier gleamed and dangled from the ceiling, while the scrutinizing eyes of Hancock's family portraits lined the walls. They seemed to pay George particular attention—the low-born at the table.

George set his jaw. Rather than eat, he listened over the clatter of silver on porcelain to Mr. Hancock and Lord Perkins.

"'Tis not bad enough the king's army plagues our streets. The king will not repeal the Townshend Acts," Hancock said.

Lord Perkins grunted. "You and every other merchant sailor in this town have felt the effects of those ridiculous regulations. Sir, you are right to be frustrated, but I cannot attest to its constituents who have been blinded in Parliament."

Jack set down his fork. "Sir, it burdens *most* men in town, not just the merchant sailors. These acts are tyrannical."

George studied his cousin. Jack's cool reserve hardly echoed the sentiment he spoke.

Is the dandy a Whig? Nay, a Patriot?

"Yes, but—" Lord Perkins lifted a solitary finger "—the ransacking of lieutenant governor Hutchinson's house in protestation of the Stamp Act was entirely uncalled for. Such riots are disturbances to our good town and are no better than the army's presence itself."

George picked at a loose thread on his coat.

Lord Perkins must be in a precarious situation, caught between loyalty to the king, and the people of Boston. If Pa saw both sides with as much clarity, we could discuss such things at home.

A gust of wind sighed into the fireplace from the chimney, and Mr. Hancock set his gaze on George.

"Mr. Howlett, I must confess." Hancock sipped his wine. "'Twas my late uncle who contracted a business partnership with your father, Captain Bixby, and his ship, *The Preamble*. While I know such storms are the effect of divine Providence, I feel great consternation, responsibility even, for your father's death."

"There's no need to feel guilty, sir." George swallowed, his mouth suddenly dry. "I never had the chance to know him, and he's been at rest many years now."

"Quite." Mr. Hancock grinned at Lord Perkins. "My financial adviser has come across my uncle's dispatches, and from the looks of it, you're owed a sum of money."

"Zounds," George laughed. "How is that possible, sir? My father was a captain who died at sea, in debt, and not having had the chance to work for your uncle."

"Peace, Nephew." Lord Perkins held up his hand. "Hancock uncovered a life insurance policy your father signed prior to leaving England. He took it to me for verification, and judging by the dates listed from customs—both the Old Standard and New Standard—the document arrived here a month before his ship sank."

"Which," Mr. Hancock added, "according to my advisor—and confirmed by your capable uncle, the magistrate, after all debts were paid—has a remaining compensation that is considered legal. I've taken the liberty of corresponding with the insurer, and I'm right heartily glad to offer you that recompense. A sum of fifteen-hundred pounds per annum."

George held his breath.

Fifteen-hundred pounds per annum.

He turned to his aunt, uncle, and cousins seated about the table. Abigail clasped her hands joyously and Jack grinned. Oliver didn't quite scowl but rather looked indifferent, and young Andrew's smile, missing a childhood tooth or two, mimicked Jack's impeccable grin.

"Aunt Elizabeth, is this true?" Sweat gathered beneath George's cravat. "Is this why you summoned me here?"

"Dear Nephew, it is." Lady Perkins smiled. "Mr. Hancock wished to deliver the information himself. I couldn't have written such marvelous news. I daresay, you never would have believed it."

"Well I'll be damned." George wiped his perspiring palms on his breeches. "Am I to give this to my mother? Or Pa? Where should I put it, and who should manage it for me? How shall I receive it?"

Mr. Hancock and Lord Perkins chuckled.

"My dear boy. We'll discuss these matters in detail after dinner. For now—" Lord Perkins lifted his glass "—let's celebrate your good fortune."

Jack raised his glass for a toast. "Cousin, join Ollie and me at Harvard."

"Harvard?" George frowned. "What would I do with an education? I must return to the farm."

They all chuckled.

"George, my boy." Lord Perkins set down his goblet. "You could hire at least eight men to work the farm for fifteen-hundred pounds per annum."

"Better yet." Mr. Hancock lifted a brow. "What if you remained in Boston to be my apprentice?"

Leave the farm for an apprenticeship with Mr. Hancock? I'll have to write home immediately.

4

JACK
BOSTON, NOVEMBER 1769

J ACK LAY IN BED fully dressed. He tapped his foot
against the bedpost in rhythm to the first violin part
of Bach's fugue, *Contrapunctus 1*. The canopy curtains
wavered with each beat. When assured of everyone's
repose, he leapt from the bed and snuck down the hall,
chamberstick in hand, and rapped on George's chamber
door.

"Cousin, wake and dress yourself."

The door creaked open and candlelight spilled upon
George's form as he stepped into the hallway; his tall build
filled the doorframe.

"What for?"

"'Tis Pope Night. We're going to the Green Dragon."

"Pope Night?"

"Aye." Jack smirked. "Tonight, men from the north
and south ends of town parade the streets, knock on
doors, and ask for money or a kiss from the eldest
daughter. The night concludes with the burning of effigies of the Pope in a great bonfire." He lowered his

voice. "This year, 'tis rumored we'll burn the king as well."

"Well I'll be damned." George's face lit up. "Let's make haste."

They slipped from the house through the servants' back door and into the murky street. A raw sea breeze settled into Jack's greatcoat from a light fog rolling in from the harbor. Misty droplets clung to his cheeks, and high tide's briny aroma caressed his senses. With George beside him, they crept through town like wraiths toward their coveted destination—the Green Dragon Tavern—a few streets away in the North End, set between Union and Hanover-street.

A copper dragon statue, weathered to antique jade, hung above the door and lured them closer. Wisps of fog encircled the dragon and lanterns, dimming their flicker of light.

Jack grinned at George as they entered.

"The king continues to throttle us—first with his taxes, and now with his *army*," a man shouted.

The smoky room smelled of body odor and fermented hops. Shadowy figures of men bent over their tables cascaded upward, and danced on the walls. Flames spilled a golden glow onto the wide pine floor from a large, brick hearth.

"Down with King George!" another man chanted.

Jack tugged his hat low upon his brow and led them to a table in the darkest corner, where sat a tawny native. "George, may I present my friend, Quinnapin."

"The pleasure is mine, sir." George lifted his hat to Quinnapin and sat.

Quinnapin gave a reserved nod. "Likewise, sir."

A potboy approached and George ordered three pints. When the boy departed, he cracked a smile. "Relax, Cousin. No one is going to recognize you as Lord Perkins' son."

"Boston is a small town," Quinnapin murmured.

Jack peered at George from under his cocked hat. "All faces are familiar here."

The potboy returned with three tankards of cider, set them on the wobbly table, and hurried away.

Quinnapin lifted his drink. "To Pope Night, and burning the king."

"Sluice your gob, rogues," George said.

They saluted and drank.

Jack set down his tankard. "'Twas good news from the courier today, your pa allowing you to stay in Boston."

"Aye." George nodded. "My mother wrote she would like to visit sometime after Twelfth Night. It has been many years since she's last seen your mother."

"Your family is always welcome." Jack lifted his mug to salute. "To many tavern nights together, and your apprenticeship with Hancock."

Angry hisses and "fies" drowned out the rattle of mugs upon rickety tables, and from a table nearest the hearth, two gentlemen stood.

"We want freedom!" The chant grew louder.

Quinnapin finished his drink and slid his mug to the table's edge. "So, it begins."

Jack craned his neck to look at the standing men, then returned his gaze to George. "Dr. Warren is the younger gentleman, a widower and sole caregiver to his children. He still practices medicine from his house in the North End. The other is John Adams' cousin, Samuel."

Dr. Warren lifted onto a chair. "Gentlemen, please." His voice rose above the clamor. "You talk of freedom. Freedom from the king's army. Freedom from King George himself. Well, *natural* freedom is the birthright of every man. When such a notion is threatened, shaken from existence, we must react with vigilance and tenacity." He jumped from the chair and walked through the tavern, pausing beside Jack's table.

Jack peered up at the doctor with reverence.

A true Patriot all should admire.

Dr. Warren met his gaze before continuing through the room. "There is no man, or army of men, that can claim right to those liberties without being guilty of the most sinister of injustices. Such men are cruel, unreasonable, and act with flagrant, undue purpose. Of course, gentlemen, I speak of King George and his army of regulars."

A series of hisses surrounded shouts of, "hear, hear!"

Jack drew himself to the end of his chair.

"A standing army represents the oppression of liberty. The people fear they will be enslaved. And now, His Majesty's regulars roam our streets, and have encamped upon our Boston common." Dr. Warren lifted his hand to silence the jeers. "But to the army, they are sent to squelch a rebellion. Such propensities, such discrepancies, plagued on both sides, may lead to the most disagreeable of conflicts. Especially this Pope Night. I say to you, gentlemen, tread with ease."

A noble intent, especially tonight.

Jack finished his cider, then stood. "Enough of this place. Let's join the festivities."

They left the rowdy tavern as an ocean gust nearly blew Jack's hat from his head. He clutched it low on his forehead and stepped into the street. Already, the North End crowd had formed with a cart, toting effigies of the Pope and King George. While they marched the street, natives and black freedmen shouted alongside white sailors and fishermen, "down with the king!"

Jack, George, and Quinnapin slipped in with the parade. Men knocked on doors and demanded money, or a kiss from the family's eldest daughter.

"Mr. G, knock on the next one." Quinnapin winked.

"Aye." George laughed. "I'll go to the Flucker's."

Jack lifted a brow. "Thomas Flucker works with my father and Hutchinson at the Towne House. He's loyal to King George—a Tory."

"All the more reason to kiss his daughter." George strode toward the Flucker house as the parade marched past. He knocked, and Lucy Flucker appeared in the entryway. From her frantic eyes, Jack could tell she wasn't meant to open the door to anyone this Pope Night. George kissed her cheek, Lucy giggled, and quickly latched the door.

Jack and Quinnapin howled as George returned to the parade.

"Well done." Jack clapped his cousin's shoulder. "Were they not in Milton at this time, I would kiss Hutchinson's eldest daughter."

George's infectious guffaw drowned out the Pope Night cheers. "The lieutenant governor's daughter?"

"Aye."

They reached Cornhill and met with men from the South End, who had paraded their own cart with effigies to burn.

"Onward to the Liberty Tree," cried one of the freedmen leading the parade.

"Is that the Perkins boy?" another called.

"He must spy for the magistrate. Grab him!"

"Zounds." Jack turned to Quinnapin and George. "Follow me. And run."

He sprinted up King-street—George and Quinnapin trailing behind—and turned into Long Wharf, where they dashed toward the docked ships. They hopped aboard one of the merchant sloops and crouched low.

George huffed. "Who could be chasing us?"

"I know not, but they could have followed us home." Jack's heart pounded as though native drums echoed behind him. They waited in blackness until nothing sounded but the gentle lap of high tide against the docks, and Pope Night cheers in the distance. Jack peered over the rail. "I think we've lost them."

"Proceed slowly." Quinnapin's fists clenched as he emerged from the sloop. Jack and George followed, and met a still, quiet Long Wharf.

Midway up the pier, Jack saw no face as burly arms subdued him from the darkness, the stench of ale, undeniable. He struggled, but the man was stronger.

"Zounds." George strained against two men. "I'll rip your arms off."

"Be still, you gollumpus." A man, who crept over the rails of another docked sloop, set down his lantern. "Else we'll toss you into the harbor."

"Shut your potato trap and give your tongue a holiday," George snapped.

Jack looked to Quinnapin. "Quinn, run."

"Grab the savage," another cried, and the man with the lantern detained Quinnapin.

"The only savage here is you, reptile." George spat at the man but his spittle splattered onto the dock.

Quinnapin wrestled free, unsheathed a pocket knife, and held it to the man's neck who'd captured him. "Another move and I slice your throat."

"Leave the native be."

A man garbed in a red cloak stepped forward through the thick, harbor fog. A hideous mask disguised his face and muffled his voice. "We got the Perkins boy."

Recognizing Boston's infamous masked rogue, Joyce Junior, Jack thrashed, desperate to escape. But his captor's arms whipped him around.

"Ye'll sit still for me, bawdy basket Perkins, won't ye, love?"

Jack spit in his face. "I'd rather be tossed into the harbor."

"Unhand me at once." Another gentleman had also been seized.

"Shut your potato trap, Chatham."

Mr. Chatham? He works for lieutenant governor Hutchinson with Father.

In the lantern light, Mr. Chatham's arms stretched behind his back, his banyan torn at the sleeves.

Chatham's pant rasped in shallow gasps. "I'll have you all jailed and hanged for this."

Behind George, two other men snickered. One rested his elbows on an oak barrel, the other held a large, canvas sack.

"If you release me, I'll not speak of this to my father." Jack's arms wrenched behind him, and a rope bound about his wrists. He looked to George, whose square jaw was set, and Quinnapin, who surveyed the group—and possibly a way to escape.

The others scoffed. "The eldest and most cherished of Lord Perkins' sons?"

"And his nephew," said one of the men holding George.

"Whatever should we do with them?" The man bent over the oak barrel cackled.

The man clutching the sack snickered. "Ye ever see a rat with wings?"

Jack squirmed and eyed Mr. Chatham, whose cap had fallen onto the dock.

They must have dragged him from his bed.

"Gentlemen, we've come from Pope Night. I know your faces. I've seen you at the Green Dragon. I assure you, my cousin, friend, and I abhor His Majesty's army as much as you."

Joyce Junior crossed his arms. "But why should we spare *you*, Perkins?"

"Because…I'm one of you. *Patriot.*" Jack cringed. *How childish I sound.*

Mr. Chatham cleared his throat. "And your father knows this, Mr. Perkins?"

"Such ideals oppose the very nature of your father's work." The voice rose again from behind Joyce Junior's mask.

The man holding Jack loosened his grasp, and Jack wrestled free. "Yes, sir. I'm a Patriot." He straightened his coat. "And so is my cousin. Now release him at once."

"Why should we listen to you, little cock robin?"

George heaved his brawny shoulders. "Let me go, you dilberries." He strained against the men and broke free.

Jack caught Mr. Chatham's scrutinizing glare. A
Loyalist from Nantucket, and proponent of the taxation
laws, Jack had met him only once at the Towne House. But
now Chatham caught him out on Pope Night—Boston's
most notorious holiday.

I'll be in for it with Father when he finds out.

"And what of you, Chatham?" Joyce Junior grunted
behind his mask. "You rotten Tory."

"I'll confess to nothing." Mr. Chatham puffed his chest.
"And I suppose Mr. Perkins here is quite pleased with
himself, pretending to be one of you hooligans. I daresay,
your father must be proud to have a rebel for an eldest
son. You'll never inherit his estate."

George spit in Mr. Chatham's direction. "You squeeze
crab."

Joyce Junior gestured to Mr. Chatham and, without
warning, his captors kicked him to the ground. His head
smashed against the wooden dock like a feeble egg. Blood
trickled down his forehead, and his voice cracked as he
cried out in pain.

"Stop it! That's enough," Jack shouted.

Like a pack of famished, wild dogs, the men tore at
Chatham's nightshirt, exposing his bare chest to the sea
air. They hoisted the barrel high, and a black, stinking
liquid poured over him. An agonizing shriek pierced the
night as hot tar scalded Chatham's face and chest.

"A proper bird, this one." The man raised his sack.

"No, don't!"

Jack lunged at the men but George restrained him.

"Cousin, let's make haste."

Feathers cascaded down in a blizzard of white and grey,
coating the sticky, blackened man. Chatham's screams

turned to whimpers, drowned out in uproarious laughter and Pope Night cheers in the distance.

"Come, quickly." Quinnapin had already started back up the wharf, away from the hostilities.

"Go on. Report to the magistrate the fate you so narrowly escaped." Joyce Junior's masked words sounded inhuman behind that frightful visage.

They sprinted back to the bonfire, the cold, briny air stinging Jack's lungs.

❦

THE CROWD OF MEN WHO HAD PARADED BOSTON'S streets now gathered around conical flames, lapping at least two stories into the dark sea above them. Embers floated and cascaded about, an ashy snow that dusted their hats and coats. Jack paced, gasping, when George and Quinnapin rushed beside him.

"Joyce Junior, the mighty chairman of the committee of tarring and feathering." George clapped Jack's back. His giddy face glowed red in the light of the soaring fire. "I'd only read about him in Boston's pamphlets. I never thought I'd bear witness to him administering the modern punishment. A privilege, indeed!"

Jack spun around. "Is that what you have to say after all we've seen? I cannot believe you held me back." His fingers curled into a fist. "'Tis one thing to resent taxation and His Majesty's regulars, but to administer the modern punishment on an old man? Come, now. Yes, Chatham is a proper Tory cad, but he's an old man, George. An old man!"

"Peace, Friend." Quinnapin rested his hand on Jack's shoulder.

"Cousin, how else can they command fear from Loyalists?" George used his sleeve to wipe the sweat on his brow. "They sent quite a message, did they not?"

"'Tis not right, Cousin." Jack held George's gaze. "And you know it."

"Burn the king," a man yelled.

Several sailors, natives, and freedmen hoisted the straw effigies of King George and the Pope into the blistering fire. Smoke and embers swirled in the sea breeze as King George caught flame, blackened, and turned to ash.

"I see Redcoats." Quinnapin stood on his toes. "They're headed this way."

Jack followed Quinnapin's gaze. Torches marched from the common toward the blaze. It would be a matter of minutes before the Bloodybacks doused the flames. Such an act would instigate a brawl—or worse. But as Dr. Warren had preached, they must abstain from violence. Even if the Sons of Liberty were tarring and feathering Loyalists.

"We should return home." Jack bit his lip. There'd been far too many antics for one night—and they were lucky to have escaped the last.

"You there." A private gesticulated toward them. "Remain where you are." The bonfire's light illuminated his dark red coat with yellow cuffs and collar, and a bayonet scar across his pasty left cheek.

"Cousin, run," George murmured.

Jack turned to flee, but the private grabbed him.

"I told you to stay where you are, whelp."

Jack struggled against the soldier. "Private, please unhand me."

The private's grip tightened around Jack's bicep. "Are you accomplices to this madness?"

"Aye." George's strong, square chin jutted. "I gladly watched the king burn."

"You shall address me as Private White, scoundrel." His vile, onion-scented spittle landed at George's feet. "You are guilty of treason if you celebrate burning our king." He looked to the other regulars approaching. "Seize him."

George bared his teeth. "Try and seize me, you Lobsterback bastard."

The bayonet scar on Private White's face took on the shape of a snake's fang. "You shall all hang for such an act against our sovereign."

"There's no treason here, you Bloodybacks," a man shouted.

Jack recognized the advancing men as Sons of Liberty. They carried their clubs from the docks.

There will certainly be a brawl, now.

"Please you, unhand those men, good sirs."

Jack turned at the familiar voice.

Dr. Warren emerged from the mob, his countenance calm and reasonable. "I know this man here and his cousin. They belong to Lord Perkins the magistrate, and mean to abide by the law, so much as the army grants us the freedom to act in accordance with our charter set forth by the good town of Boston in this Province of Massachusetts Bay."

Private White's eyes narrowed. "General Gage would hardly agree, sir."

"But Captain Preston might." Dr. Warren regarded Jack and George. "Go home Mr. Perkins, Mr. Howlett. There's nothing here that would please your father, your uncle."

"Yes. Get on home." Private White's iron first released Jack. "And if I see you in the streets again, I'll not be so obliging."

5

ANNALISA
BOSTON, MARCH 1770

ANNALISA STOOD ON THE cobblestone walkway outside a grand, two-story brick house with a teal front door. *Perkins House*. She shivered with anticipation. For the next fortnight, she'd reside here with her family. Weary from four hours of travel, and anxious to meet George's cousins, she sucked in the rejuvenating ocean air. Such a fresh, salty scent compared to Topsfield's lush country breezes. She pulled her red wool cloak around her and approached the front door.

"Wait for your papa." Mamma hurried forward with William.

Jane drifted to her side, her shoes clacking on stone. "Remember to put on your finest airs, Annie." Jane smoothed her skirts like Mamma. "This could be our chance to marry well."

The front door opened, and a servant escorted them inside. Scents of cinnamon and clove wafted in the warm air. The foyer gleamed with white wainscoting and shiny cherry tables. Annalisa slinked toward a large, rectangular looking glass hung by the stairs. She peered at herself. The scar beneath her right eye had mostly faded—thanks to Addy—but would always be there.

"No one will notice it." Jane tugged her from the mirror. "I promise."

A tall, thirty-hour longcase clock chimed half-three, and a woman with flaxen hair, finely robed in evergreen silk, emerged from the parlor. Her gaze locked on Mamma, and her amber eyes misted.

"Oh, Peggy."

"Bette." Mamma glided toward Lady Perkins and they embraced. "'Tis been far too long."

"Come." Lady Perkins wiped her tears. "George is waiting in the parlor with his cousins."

"It would be our pleasure," Papa said.

Annalisa hesitated, watching the housekeeper collect their travel cloaks and hats while two other servants hauled their trunks up the stairs. At home, they had only Addy and their indentured Irish girl, Liza, to help with housekeeping and cooking.

"Annie, don't gawk." Jane linked their arms and guided them into the parlor.

In the turquoise-papered room, George sat by the fire, across from three unfamiliar gentlemen, and a young lady with a small child in her lap. He rose to his full height, seemingly taller than before he left the farm.

"George." Annalisa hurried toward him.

He scooped her into a tight embrace. "Little One." He kissed her cheek then set her down, quickly swiping a finger beneath her right eye. "I see 'tis healed well."

"It has. And I've kept up my practice—"

"Annalisa, please," Mamma hissed. "Your manners."

Lady Perkins smiled. "She's clearly missed her brother."

Annalisa's neck warmed, and she stepped back beside Jane.

"This is my eldest son, John Jackson Perkins III." Lady Perkins gestured to a handsome young man in an indigo velvet coat. "We call him Jack."

Jack gave a polite bow, and his smooth chestnut hair, tied at his nape, briefly swept over his shoulder.

Annalisa gaped. His lean and fit figure held the most agreeable air of any gentleman she'd ever seen—or could have imagined—notwithstanding the alluring blue of his eyes, which captivated her senses and dulled her sensibilities. A crooked grin dimpled his cheeks as he acknowledged her, and her breath caught. To her shocking dismay, he held hostage her audience with the greatest of ease, unlike the young men of Topsfield she'd known before now.

His smile...his eyes....

"Close your mouth." Jane's whisper severed the tie between them, and Jack's attention shifted to Jane. Her sister's cheeks flushed pink as a peony.

The second eldest, Oliver, stood as though an iron rod had been welded to his back. His nose in the air, his fleeting glances upon her family were cold. Except when he regarded Jane. With his covetous eye upon her elder sister, Annalisa's hair stood on end.

Andrew—ten or so—must have decided from a young age he would learn his lessons from Jack. He gave a similar, polite bow and held himself like his eldest brother.

A victimless crime for a third son.

Lady Perkins lifted her youngest daughter, Susan, who was no older than two, from the arms of her eldest daughter, Abigail. Both girls' flaxen hair matched their mother's, and a light array of freckles peppered their noses and cheeks.

Abigail, who appeared about fourteen, between she and Jane in age, curtsied. "I'm so glad to finally make your acquaintances." Her doting hazel eyes twinkled when she looked upon George. She left her spot between Oliver and Jack, and approached Annalisa. "I've heard so much about you."

⚜

AFTER A SUMPTUOUS DINNER OF OYSTER PIE, COD CAKES, roast turkey, and dried apple tarts, the servants entered the dining room with a bottle of port.

Lord Perkins took his glass. "Boston's finest." He looked to Papa. "At last, let us toast the repeal of the Townshend Acts. 'Twas a long three years."

Lady Perkins rose from her chair and led the way for the ladies toward the drawing room.

Annalisa lingered before standing. "But my lord, I heard there is still a tax on tea. Think you Lord North and Parliament shall repeal that duty as well?"

Beside George, William cleared his throat. "Annie."

The gentlemen all turned toward her, and she cowered from Papa's dark, disappointed stare.

"Miss Annalisa, you are correct." Lord Perkins chuckled, and the rest of the gentlemen returned to their port. "But I know not what Lord North shall do with the tea tax."

"Always a curious mind, my Annalisa." Mamma reached

for her and whispered, "What have I told you about discussing politics?"

"George, is your sister well-read on such matters?" Jack's whisper was just loud enough for Annalisa to hear as Mamma pulled her toward the drawing room.

Oliver chortled. "If she hopes to be as cultured as your sister Jane, her time should be spent at the loom, stitching delicate flowers into her handkerchief."

The door closed behind her, leaving the gentlemen to their own gossip.

"Your outspokenness will hinder your ability to secure a worthy husband." Mamma nudged her into the room. "Now go and sit beside your sister."

Jane sat on an evergreen damask sofa with hands clasped in her lap. From the spinet, set between two windows, Corelli's *Sarabande* floated from Abigail's capable fingers. Annalisa settled beside Jane, and her temples throbbed with indignance.

How dare Oliver Perkins speak of me thus. Why can I not be cultured as a lady but also knowledgeable in politics?

When Abigail finished the piece, she turned on the bench. "Miss Annalisa, George boasted much of your playing. You must entertain us."

Expecting Jane to play next, Annalisa looked to Mamma, who nodded. Annalisa stood and made her way to the only place she truly sat in any drawing room. At home upon the bench, she set her fingers upon the keys, and the ladies faded away. Her hands sprung about, each trill and cadence of Scarlatti's *Sonata in E Major, K. 216* played with meticulousness, and not a solitary mistake.

At the song's end, an eruption of applause turned her

head. The gentlemen crowded into the drawing room, wafting in sweet tobacco smoke.

George went to her and winked. "You've played well, Little One."

Lady Perkins clapped. "You are most accomplished, Miss Annalisa. I must have the name of your tutor—"

"Bravo, Miss Annalisa." Jack's soft baritone, the most melodious of sounds. He brushed past Oliver and knelt at Annalisa's hems. "Miss, if I closed my eyes, I could have believed Scarlatti himself played for us."

Annalisa's face heated, but she reeled in her senses.

He may be handsome, but can his sincerity be believed?

"Thank you, Mr. Perkins."

"Miss Howlett, do you play or sing?" Lady Perkins directed the question to Jane.

"I do, marm, but I couldn't possibly play now." Jane bowed her head. "Annalisa has established herself as the accomplished musician among us."

Mamma clicked her tongue. "Nonsense, Janey. You've learned your lessons well."

"Please play for us, Miss Howlett, and dazzle us with your talents," Oliver said.

Jane rose from the sofa and overtook the spinet bench. Annalisa joined George and William on a settee by the window.

Jane's delicate soprano soon accompanied the crackling fire. Jack lingered behind her as though reading music that wasn't there. When she neared the end of the song, his light baritone harmonized with hers:

> *"And ask for a like favor from me*
> *And then she'll be a true love of mine."*

Jack's eyes sparkled, but before he could bestow Jane a compliment, Oliver slithered beside Jane, lifted her hand, and kissed it.

"Miss Howlett, the loveliness of your voice has given me new meaning in enjoying the sound of music." Oliver glanced at Annalisa. "Miss, do you *sing* as well as your sister?"

"No, sir. Only Jane has lessons in Salem, and my affinity for music has been found in spinet-playing." Agitated, Annalisa leaned into George and whispered, "Pray tell, is your cousin Oliver always this arrogant? And his brother Jack, is he as much of a dandy as he seems?"

George chuckled. "We'll speak later." His breath smelled strongly of port.

Abigail plopped into a chair on the other side of George. "Miss Annalisa, you play so very well. I think you've impressed my brothers." She reached for Annalisa's hand. "I do hope we can be great friends."

Jack held his violin by the spinet, and the instrument sang Corelli's *Gigue,* as if the music came from within Jack himself. Each cadence flourished, executed exactly as Corelli had written it. His capable fingers not only played with precision and proficiency, but with passion. Annalisa closed her eyes and memorized the sound.

I'd know it anywhere.

She'd hardly meant to impress George's cousins, but the thought of capturing Jack Perkins' attention was hardly intolerable. She opened her eyes and studied Jack's furrowed, concentrated brow, the slight pout upon his lips.

Annalisa chewed her thumbnail to hide her smile. He may be a dandy, but he was the most agreeable, well-bred, handsome man she'd ever seen. Perhaps marriage to such a man wouldn't be as insufferable as she'd assumed.

⚜

ANNALISA'S HAND GLIDED DOWN THE BANNISTER AS SHE tip-toed downstairs, eager and full of anticipation. The household had retired for the night, and she had much to discuss with George.

And perhaps garner more information about Jack.

She rounded the corner and peeked into the parlor. Oliver sat by the fire. He glanced up from his book. Annalisa gasped and hid against the foyer wall. She held her breath, hoping he hadn't seen her.

"Miss Annalisa?" Oliver's voice sounded oily.

"My apologies, sir." Her breathing burst in shallow waves as she emerged. "I meant to see if George was here."

"Come." Oliver closed his book and set it on a table. "Join me by the fire."

Annalisa wavered, deflated his presence was not Jack's, then stepped into the parlor. When she neared him, Oliver grabbed her wrist and pulled her to the sofa.

"Sit."

She settled beside him, though maintained an appropriate distance. Her gaze on the crackling fire, she sensed his adroit study.

"No, you're certainly not your sister." Oliver ran a hand through his dark blond hair, which he'd let loose from its tie. "But I daresay, you're tolerable. Even with that scar and your beige skin."

Her throat tightened. "I beg your pardon, sir?"

"Oh, come now." He chuckled. "You didn't think such

would go unnoticed beside your beautiful, accomplished sister, did you?"

"An old kitchen accident..." She touched the scar, then met his scrutinizing stare. "As for my complexion, sir," her voice cracked, "though I was not raised Agawam and make no claims as such, my grandmama was, and I'm the one in my family who most resembles her. Proudly." Trembling, Annalisa stood. "I know I am unlike Jane. Good-night, sir." She turned to leave, but he leapt from the sofa and found her wrist again.

"I meant no offense." He spun her around and gripped her shoulders. "Miss Annalisa, you're quite the pert lass. Would you indulge my curiosity?"

She wriggled in his grasp. "Sir, you're hurting me."

"A girl from the country who taught herself to play the spinet because her family cannot afford to send three daughters to Salem for lessons." He inched her backward until the corner of the windowsill jutted into her side. "Let me guess, you also seek to marry above your station, yes?"

"Mr. Oliver, please unhand me." Her nose crinkled from the stale port upon his breath. "Mamma and Papa have tried their best..."

"Time for another lesson." Oliver slid his lips over hers, and with one hand, gathered her skirts and grabbed between her legs.

"You cur!" Annalisa shoved him away with a force that seemed to surprise even him. "You...beast!"

"What's this?" Jack's voice sounded from the parlor doorway. "Ollie, is that you...and Miss Annalisa?" A look of horror spread across his face and Annalisa covered her eyes.

"Clearly, the young Miss can't handle being alone with a gentleman." Oliver straightened his coat.

"A gentleman, say you?" Annalisa gasped, fixing her skirts.

"I care not how you think the lady should behave, but you shall act as a gentleman." Jack rushed to Annalisa, his marine eyes rippling with alarm. "I heard a shriek. Are you all right—"

"I've never been...I've never..." Annalisa sucked in air, and when Jack searched for her hand, she swatted him away. "Don't touch me." She ran past him to the doorway. "Either of you." She hurried from the parlor and up the stairs, tarnished like a piece of neglected silver.

Annalisa fumbled with the door latch and slid inside the bedchamber. Mary, who'd been consigned to the nursery with Henry and Susan Perkins after dinner, had long since drifted to sleep. But Jane sat upright in her narrow bed.

"I heard a cry and found you gone. Are you poorly?"

Annalisa paced. "I'm fine. I...was downstairs looking for George...and Oliv—"

"I daresay, Oliver Perkins is quite agreeable." Jane rested against the pillows and sighed. "As is his brother, Jack." She yawned and pulled the covers up to her chin. "I'd marry either of them if they asked."

Annalisa remained silent for a moment, brooding. "I'm not sure they're what you think they are."

"The well-bred sons of the magistrate?" Jane giggled. "We should be lucky to marry such men."

Her heart sank. *Yes, the magistrate's sons. If I tell Jane, or anyone, who will believe me? Except George. He would challenge Oliver to a duel.*

Sickened, Annalisa crawled into her own bed—a luxury she lacked at home—and faced the wall. A queasiness lurked in her stomach and seeped into her throat. She sniffled and buried her face into the pillow.

George would kill Oliver. He must never find out.

❧ 6 ❧

ANNALISA
BOSTON, MARCH 5, 1770

DESPITE THE UNSEASONABLY WARM days that accompanied them to Boston, New-England's unpredictable weather birthed a nor'easter that covered the town in slick, icy snow.

Annalisa was trapped. Trapped inside Perkins House with the offender, Oliver, and Jack—who must now think her some kind of hussy—and the secret shame she must hide.

I must get out of here. I must leave this house.

By afternoon, the snow had stopped, and Annalisa crept from the drawing room, up to the dim chamber she shared with Mary and Jane. She lingered outside the door, then turned toward the room her brothers shared.

"Miss Annalisa?"

She jumped.

Below, Abigail clutched the bannister. "What are you doing?"

"I'm...looking for my book."

"I must have it in the library." Abigail advanced up the stairs with a bright smile. "What are you reading?"

"Margaret Cavendish—"

"I have all of Mad Madge's poetry books." When she reached the top stair, Abigail offered her hand. "Come, I'll show you to the library, and we can recite for our brothers."

Her spirits lifted for a moment. "I'd love that." *Jane never likes reciting, and George never wants to listen.* But Annalisa wavered, wary of reading to Abigail's brothers. "I'd like to take a walk outside first. I'm feeling quite warm."

"Warm?" Abigail shivered. "'Tis so cold, and growing dark. I suppose my brothers could escort you—"

"No, 'tis quite all right. I'll be fine by myself."

Abigail placed a hand to her breast. "Alone?"

"I won't go far. I promise." Annalisa slinked down the hall. "Tell my mamma I'm resting. And not to check on me."

Abigail's smile turned mischievous. "Of course."

Annalisa waited until she had gone before sneaking into her brothers' guest chamber. There, she rustled through William's trunk and gathered his extra clothes. She tip-toed to her room and discarded her dress for the menswear. She peered into the looking glass and blushed, suddenly aware of her legs, now exposed in breeches.

A strange freedom.

After tying her hair in a queue, Annalisa slid from the room and crept downstairs, snatching the first cocked hat she saw at the entry.

Outside, her shoes slipped against the icy cobblestone, but she was free. Free from her petticoats and tight,

binding stays. Free from womanhood. Free from Oliver
Perkins.

In the twilight, she recognized enough to get from
Beacon Hill to the Faneuil market docks. From there, she
could find the Green Dragon Tavern George had written
about in his letters.

Her teeth chattered against the biting cold. She
gripped her brown coat and skidded across the slippery
road toward King-street, the main thoroughfare through
Boston. Without even trying to find the tavern, the jade-
colored dragon out front summoned her to its door. Her
toes already frozen inside her shoes, she pushed open the
door and stepped inside.

ANNALISA
BOSTON, MARCH 5, 1770

A MAN SHOUTED, "I say we descend upon Castle Island and blow it to pieces!"

"Let's light the common a-flame and burn every last regular who occupies it," cried another.

"Hear, hear!"

Annalisa sat with her head bowed low, but clutched her tankard of cider with excitement. After two ciders, she hardly noticed the pungent air, thick with the scent of body odor and stale hops.

Oh, to have such freedom, to expend my own ideals with as much fervent passion as these men. How can any man, or woman, deny that something greater than the sum of each colony is at stake?

She released her mug, ready to ask the potboy for another, when the tavern door swung open.

Jack Perkins stepped inside with George. Annalisa pulled down her hat, but it took only a moment before George recognized her and marched to her table.

"By the devil's cock." George seized her arm and

yanked her from the chair. "With me, young...*lad*." He
lifted her over his shoulder, knocking the air from her
belly, and carried her outside into the March night.

George set her down in the frozen street and paced.
"This...this is..." His lip curled over his teeth. "Have you
any idea what would happen if you were discovered? You're
dressed as a man!" His hands flew about, and Annalisa
winced. "And you stink of ale."

"Cider." She hadn't realized how many she'd had, or
how late the hour had grown. The town was dark, and
stars speckled the night sky.

"Easy, Cousin." Jack set a gentle hand on George's arm.
"Nothing's been discovered...yet. But we must head
home."

In the distance, alarm bells tolled and shouts of "fire!"
echoed up the street.

George pulled Annalisa toward him. "If ever someone
uncovered your identity, you would be arrested, assaulted,
or both." His voice softened and he cupped her shoulders.
"Do you understand? This is dangerous—and with the
king's army about, no less. I know you have an insatiable
interest in this rebellion, but you must keep to your own,
Little One. 'Tis not safe for women."

"George is right, Miss Annalisa." Jack's gaze wandered,
despite his address. "This town is amiss, and I suspect rife
for a brawl. Let's get home."

Annalisa licked her cracking lips. She hardly knew Jack
Perkins, but there was a distinct change in how he
regarded her, or rather, how he avoided eye contact.
George held her under his arm and they walked from the
tavern into King-street. An angry mob of Bostonians filled

the road. They surrounded a Redcoat outside the Guard Station.

"This way." Jack turned them away from the crowd when another Redcoat with a dour scowl upon his scarred face blocked their path.

"We're on our way home, sir." Jack tipped his hat.

"'Tis Private White, if you've forgotten." His red coat burned against the snow.

"Aye," George said. "I remember your hideous face from Pope Night. My cousin is courteous, like the gentleman he is. But I'll not extend you such civility, reptile."

Annalisa bristled. *What sort of trouble had George been in? Papa would be furious if he found out.*

Private White spit at Jack's shoes. "You're nothing but lowly dogs in your godforsaken town."

"That's enough, sir. Good day to you, Private." Jack turned to George. "Come, let's get *Master Howlett* home."

Annalisa detected a commanding urgency in Jack's voice she didn't realize he could summon, much unlike the hotheaded vulgarities that flew from George's wanton tongue. Her shoulders eased, a sense of safety overcoming her in Jack's presence.

The icy snow crunched beneath their shoes, but the click of a cocked musket stopped them. Annalisa turned and stared into the blackened barrel. A second soldier joined and knocked George's hands from her with the butt of his musket.

"You may take your leave. After I've confiscated this young lad here for questioning."

Jack stepped forward. "For what purpose?"

"Let him go," George snarled.

Annalisa strained in the second soldier's grasp. The crowd that had surrounded the Redcoat from the Guard Station had grown and migrated toward them.

"Fire? Where's the fire?" a man called, looking about him.

Several must have been Sons of Liberty and merchant sailors. They jeered at the soldiers and carried clubs from the docks.

"Fire? They won't fire. Have at them, boys!"

"Grab that stone," a young man shouted.

A few boys picked up pieces of ice and rocks and flung them at the soldiers. The private holding her ducked, but a rock struck his face.

Her sensibilities dulled from the cider, Annalisa scurried from his grip, bent over and picked up a chunk of ice. She threw it. "For taking me hostage, you spineless cur."

"Stop throwing ice." George reached for her, but already the number of men and boys had doubled, and two more Redcoats rushed into the mob.

Mad with the crowd, Annalisa lifted another chunk of ice and threw it at the soldiers. "That is for overtaking this city."

"Stay back, the lot of you," an officer ordered.

"Get back here." George pulled Annalisa's arm and held her.

"Let me go." She wriggled in his grasp. "They deserve to be struck."

"This is madness." Jack turned to George. "We must get home. Now."

The emergency bells tolled over the town like a death knell, and more ice and rocks, and now oysters, hurtled through the air. The soldiers ducked and dodged, and the captain was hit. He fell to the ground.

"This is our town," a man cried.

Jeers and shouts drowned out the bells, and four more Redcoats barged into the mob. "Steady, men."

The number of Bostonians had multiplied, and men from the Green Dragon, Sons of Liberty, held up their clubs as weapons.

"Why don't ye fire?"

Ice and oysters flew at the king's men, and three Redcoats aimed their muskets. A man fell into George, knocking Annalisa from his arms. She skidded onto the ground, her knees scraping the ice.

"George?" She looked up. "George!"

The mob had swallowed him.

"Anna—look out!" Jack lifted her as the stock of Private White's musket missed her, and slammed into his face.

"Jack!"

He flew backward into the angry crowd and landed on his rear.

"Lobsterback bastards," a native yelled. "You've assaulted Lord Perkins' son."

"You dogs, check yourselves." Private White pointed his bayonet at Jack. "I told you to take care when next you met me in the streets."

"You foul excuse for a soldier. Your superior, Captain Preston, has dined at my house at least thrice since your regiment's arrival." Jack held the private's frozen stare as blood trickled down his lip. Gripping Annalisa in one arm, he leapt to his feet, and clenched the fist of his other.

"Where is the fire?" a man shouted.

Jack's free arm recoiled, ready to strike Private White. "I challenge—"

"Fire!"

Crack-boom!

Annalisa started at the rotten sulfur and buried her face in Jack's coat. When the musket-fire ceased, she turned her head.

"Don't look." Jack held her face to his chest, but she resisted.

Smoke wafted from a soldier's musket, and a brown man lay dead in the snow.

"George." Annalisa pointed to her brother in the crowd. "He's there."

Jack held Annalisa and reached for George. "Cousin, this way."

"Zounds." George gripped Jack's arm. "They've fired on us."

Two more shots rang out.

"Quick." Jack pulled Annalisa through the throng, and George followed as two more men fell, staining the snow red.

They ran from the scene as more patrons shouted into the street. Annalisa peered behind her. The bells still tolled, drowning out the chaos.

When they reached Perkins House, they paced outside. Her hands on her hips, Annalisa gasped and panted against the biting cold.

"Get inside and do so as quietly as you can." George clenched her shoulders. "You're wrapped in warm flannel. Say nothing."

Ashamed of her errant behavior and drunkenness, Annalisa nodded and ran her sleeve beneath her dripping nose. She snuck into the house, rushed up the stairs, and into her chamber.

Below, Abigail cried, "I heard the alarm bells and gunshots. My God, Jack, what happened? Mercy, some fresh towels and water."

Annalisa tugged her brothers' clothes from her chilled body and piled them into her trunk. With trembling hands, she pulled on her petticoat, and fumbled to pin on her day dress. She ran down the stairs and entered the parlor. Lord and Lady Perkins burst into the room behind her with Andrew and Oliver at their heels, and the indentured maid with a porcelain bowl in pale, shaking hands.

"Jack, why are you so disheveled?" Lady Perkins hastened to his side.

Jack sat upon the sofa. Blood still trickled from his lip, which had begun to swell.

Annalisa lurched for the basin. "Let me." She wet the muslin cloth and dabbed the corner of Jack's mouth.

He winced and grabbed the towel from her. "I'll do it."

"Annalisa." Jane pulled her from Jack and wrinkled her nose. "Where have you been?"

"You had us worried." Mamma took her into her arms. "Are you ill?"

Annalisa shrugged her mother's hands from her. "I'm fine. Just cold, really."

"Were you attacked, or did you provoke the king's army?" Oliver regarded Jack with obsequious leer.

Jack squeezed his fist. "There was no provocation from me, I assure you."

"What of you, George?" Papa crossed his arms. "Were you at this altercation? You were to be checking on Annalisa."

"Annie is well, as you can see." George gestured to her. "Though others are not."

Abigail reached for Annalisa and pulled her from the group. "You were there, weren't you?"

Annalisa held her tongue, unwilling to confirm or deny her allegation.

"I'll not be made a fool, John Jackson." Lord Perkins' grey eyes peered over his round spectacles. "You are heir to this estate. I won't have you gallivanting about with those Sons of Liberty, engaging in disagreeable matters, oblivious to my position as magistrate. You know Captain Preston's been a welcome guest in our home for several months."

"Hardly, sir." Jack threw the cloth into the basin, splashing water onto the wooden floor. "Preston's men opened fire on a crowd."

The ladies, save for Annalisa, gasped.

William tugged George's coat. "They opened fire?"

"On whom?" Andrew asked.

Oliver crossed his arms. "Surely, there was some kind of aggravation for them to have done something so deplorable."

"Silence." Lord Perkins held up a hand. "I want to hear Jack's account."

Jack recounted the chaos that ensued in King-street. "And now, at least three men lay dead."

"'Tis preposterous." His lips taut, Lord Perkins paced the room.

Annalisa studied Jack and George to see if they would divulge information about her being with them, but Jack dabbed his lip as though she hadn't been there at all. As though she weren't even in the room. And yet...he'd saved her.

"This assault on you was unprovoked, for certain," Lord Perkins said. "But from the sound of it, responsibility for this *massacre* lies on both sides. The regulars should never have opened fire on unarmed citizens, but neither should those boys have taunted His Majesty's men. You must understand the impossible position in which you've placed me." He stopped at the window and peered into the bleak March night.

"Sir." Jack followed his father to the window. "'Twas never my intent to cause you such troubles."

Annalisa watched Jack, his bruised cheek and swollen, bloody lip. Her mind dizzy, and her heart heavy with grief and humiliation, she broke from Abigail's arms and quit the room.

THE THICK, WIDE LIMBS of the ancient oak grew low enough to provide effortless entry into the tree itself. Several boughs above the ground, the vast trunk of the tree flattened enough between branches to seat at least two human figures. Settled in this cove, Annalisa took refuge with her Margaret Cavendish poetry book and a pamphlet from Boston about the massacre. Below, she left George's firelock propped against the trunk. Three months had passed since their return from Boston, but images of the massacre persisted, and the poor man who'd first been shot, a half-African, half-native man, Crispus Attucks.

Annalisa closed the pamphlet. The soldiers would be on trial for the massacre in October. She rested her head against the trunk and closed her eyes, wondering if Jack Perkins would be involved in the case. In his last letter to George, he'd written of his apprenticeship with John Adams, one of the lawyers summoned to represent the soldiers.

Would I have behaved as I did had Oliver never touched me?

The unsavory memory had haunted her these three months, worse than the chaos of the massacre. Yet in the streets of Boston, hidden in breeches and drunk on cider, she'd uncovered another version of herself. One emboldened enough to throw ice at the king's soldiers. She never could have behaved so in a dress.

In the margin of her poetry book, she scribbled *"notes on Benjamin Cavendish. A man."* A man she could pretend to be. If she could only join the militia.

"Miss Anna, I found you."

Startled, she looked down.

Quinnapin, one of the new farm-hands George had hired with his inheritance—and an old friend of Jack's—peered up with soft, russet eyes set above high, angular cheeks. His tawny skin glowed in the lacy shade of the tree. He brushed glossy obsidian hair over one shoulder; the other side was entirely shaved.

"Good-day, Quinnapin."

"*Wuneekeesuq*—it means good-day."

"*Wuneekeesuq.*" Annalisa smiled.

"Miss Jane's returned from Salem. She's looking for you."

Annalisa rolled her eyes, tucked the pamphlet and book into her pocket, then slid from the cove and onto the sturdy bough. This she did until she reached the ground limb, and sat on its wide surface.

"How are you getting on here? Do you like Topsfield?"

"I do, Miss Anna. Your brother pays me more than twice what I made fishing in Boston, but I miss making *wampum* beads."

"*Wampum?*"

Quinnapin gestured to a small, white and purple beaded belt at his waist. "This is *wampum,* made from a quahog clam shell. We carve them and turn them into beads." Quinnapin eyed the forest behind them, then leaned on one of the large branches. "Sun sets, Miss Anna. Careful here after dark. *Puk-wudjie* live in these woods."

Annalisa cocked her head. "Is that an Agawam creature you speak of?"

He shook his head. "I'm not Agawam. I'm Wampanoag. Our nation is south of here and *Shawmut,* near the sea."

"Shawmut?"

"Boston."

She warmed. "My apologies. I knew not Boston's original name." She paused. "I know the Agawam used to live nearby...my grandmama was Agawam. Though I know little about her, I'm told I resemble her well."

Quinnapin grinned. *"Puk-wudjie* are forest creatures everywhere." He knelt beside her and lowered his voice. "Lures man into the woods. Means to kill."

"I've not heard the stories." She glanced at the forest. "Pray tell, have you seen one?"

"Yes, in Hockomock Swamp, long before I came here to *Shenewemedy.* He was small, this high." He flattened his hand to his broad chest. "Grey skin and big nose, evil eyes. I threw a tomahawk at him, but he vanished into nothing."

An evening breeze rustled the leaves overhead and Annalisa shivered. Rarely had native folklore rattled her, but Quinnapin's concern struck her as unaffected.

"I'll go inside."

He offered her his hand and she slid from the branch.

A strange tingling ebbed through her as she lifted Bixby from the ground, and slung the firelock over her shoulder.

Quinnapin stopped her. "Let me return it."

She handed him the piece. "Thank you, Quinnapin."

"Call me Quinn."

Annalisa smiled. "Thank you, Quinn."

When she entered her house, Annalisa wandered down the hall and into the drawing room, laden with Jane's lavender perfume.

"Annie." Jane closed her book and set it on the table beside where she sat. "Why must you fire that fowler? You know Mamma insists I teach you what I've learned in Salem."

"To speak French? Or dance the minuet?" Annalisa settled at the spinet and leafed through her music. "I desire to learn neither, as I find them both a grievous waste of time."

Jane stood and met her at the instrument. "You haven't been the same since Boston." She tucked a piece of Annalisa's hair into her cap. "What happened? You were at least somewhat tolerant to our lessons, but now, 'tis been months since you even tried."

Annalisa set the music in her lap. "You know what Mamma says. No gentleman of good breeding will take me seriously, and she won't allow me to attend the public balls in Ipswich until I'm fifteen next May."

"La. There are eligible men who will have you." Jane smirked. "And there's always George's handsome cousins to consider—whenever we meet them again." Her face glowed. "I have a feeling they might pay us particular attention at a ball."

"Us? They were besotted by *you*. But they won't visit

the country." Annalisa pursed her lips so they would not quiver. She hadn't found the courage to tell Jane what had happened with Oliver.

Jane is so eager to marry well, such information will devastate her. And with Lord Perkins as magistrate, who will believe me?

Annalisa thumbed through her music to calm her nerves. The likelihood of Oliver and Jack moving from Boston was improbable at best. She would never have to see Oliver Perkins again if she didn't wish to. And if George's cousins did show interest in Jane, perhaps Annalisa could encourage Jack to court her sister.

Mamma would be glad for such an advantageous marriage for Jane, though I can hardly suppose him for myself. A man as well-bred and handsome as Jack Perkins would never consider me over Jane after my charade in Boston.

"I'll have Addy bring us some tea, and you can play Mozart for me. I know how much you enjoy his sonatas." Jane opened all the shutters and a lovely breeze fragrant of lilac and honeysuckle overtook the suffocating lavender.

The cool evening air slipped into Annalisa's chest. "No. We can dance."

She found a minuet, placed her fingers to the keys, and played. Jane's feet moved in time to the formal dance, her graceful body following each delicate stride, as though she were born into higher society.

The drawing room door burst open and George entered, accompanied by his best friend, Samuel Wildes, and Quinnapin.

George sat on the sofa and stretched his long legs. "I have good news."

Annalisa swiveled on the bench. "Pray tell?"

"Th' best kind o' news, Miss Anna," Samuel said, his Irish accent thick.

"Better than George abandoning his apprenticeship with Mr. Hancock?" Jane crossed her arms.

George's brows creased. "You know I would have stayed in Boston if my uncle would have allowed it. The massacre caused much havoc in town—"

"I think you will be proud of this, Miss Howlett." Quinnapin regarded Jane.

George leaned forward and rested his forearms on his thighs. "You know the old Treadwell?"

"Right off the king's highway?" Jane's nose wrinkled.

"Aye." He leaned back. "I put a down payment on it. I'm going to turn it into a tavern."

"Oh, George." Annalisa jumped from the spinet bench and onto his lap. "That is wonderful news." She kissed his cheek. "You'll be the best tavern-keep in town."

George guffawed. "I'll damn near try."

"What about the lot across from Witch Hill?" Jane asked. "You could build your tavern rather than renovate."

"Mr. Wellman already has a bid on it." Quinnapin brushed a piece of hay from his buckskin breeches.

George tossed Annalisa from his lap and onto the couch. He then pulled the deed from his pocket and handed it to her. "I've decided to call it the Peat Moss Inn."

"Well done." Annalisa read the deed. "I know how much you wished to study under Mr. Hancock, but this seems much more like something you'd enjoy."

He crossed one leg and wrapped an arm around her. "Now when my cousins come from Boston, I'll have something to show for myself."

"Are they planning to visit?" Jane smoothed her skirts and settled into the chair.

"No." A wide grin spread across George's angular face. "They're moving to town. My uncle is leaving his post as magistrate."

Annalisa gasped. "Why? And why move to Topsfield? There are other towns—"

"No town be better'n Topsfield, Miss Anna." Samuel winked.

George laughed. "Boston is better, but they must leave. 'Tis not safe since the massacre, and my uncle refuses to preside over the trial. Stephen Perkins and the town treasurer, David Perkins, are my uncle's relations."

Jane's face bloomed, and Annalisa knew her sister was pleased. "Pray tell, where will they build?"

"Jack wrote that my uncle purchased a large acreage two miles down the lane."

"I'm going to help build it," Quinnapin said. "The foundation and framing will be done this summer, and by autumn, we hope to paint and furnish it."

"There are always delays, so I anticipate their arrival a year from now," George added, no doubt sensing Annalisa's unease.

She picked at her thumbnail. An hour ago, such disagreeable news seemed far and unlikely. Now, Oliver and Jack Perkins were moving to town. Two miles down the lane, no less. They'd be at every public ball, the meetinghouse every Sunday, the Strawberry Festival in June, the corn husking in October—there would be no escaping them. Or the secret she kept.

9

JACK
BOSTON, AUTUMN 1770

B OOKS, PAPERS, AND MAPS covered the grainy wooden desk in John Adams' office, infusing the stale air with the scent of printed pages. Jack, a Harvard graduate and law apprentice since spring, sat in a chair across from Adams himself. He locked his fingers as they rested in his lap.

"I only hope I might be able to continue working with you, sir."

Mr. Adams leaned back in his chair and swiped the wig from his head, revealing a shiny, egg-shaped skull. He set the old wig atop a tower of books.

"So, you were there that fateful day, Mr. Perkins." He sucked in an imposing lungful and held it for several seconds, so long that Jack held his. "But it matters not."

Jack exhaled. "Thank you, sir. I can—"

"Whether you identify as Loyalist or Patriot is of little concern to me. I ask only that you take notes, and learn to practice law without bias. We shall interpret what the

witnesses tell us, and use their accounts to posit exactly
what happened—"

"Sir, I can tell you what hap—"

"Silence. Are you on trial, Mr. Perkins?"

Jack gripped his chair, startled. "No, sir."

"Are you an apprentice of the law?"

"Yes, sir."

"You are studying under my tutelage and shall henceforth proceed to behave as such. I'll not tolerate any inso-
lence, or budding fascinations during this case. Is that
understood?"

Jack tightened his grip on the wooden Windsor chair.
"Yes, sir."

Adams stood, meandered to his bookcase, and
removed several titles. When he returned to the desk, he
offered the small stack to Jack.

"You shall read each of these accounts; Cicero, Cato,
Plato and Aristotle, and Marcus Aurelius." He paused as
though waiting for Jack to object. "I understand you were
admitted to Harvard at fourteen, yes? You've undoubtedly
read the classics."

"Yes, sir. 'Tis been four years since I read them."

"Precisely. You're eighteen now. I want you to read
them again and find yourself anew."

Jack ground his teeth. He'd read the classics, and he'd
studied them well. In fact, he knew more about Cato and
Cicero than his own father. But Adams spoke with reason.
Jack was not the young man he was at fourteen. He'd
oblige.

His haversack heavy over his shoulder, he left the
Adams' Braintree home and caught the coach back to
Boston. By the end of this two-year apprenticeship, hope-

fully he'd be a better lawyer for it. He rested his face in his hands. Partaking in the massacre case would prove most difficult. How could he put aside his own experience that day; the torment, the turmoil, the rage and anger of Boston's people? The incensed ferocity of the king's army?

And Annalisa Howlett's wild green eyes as she chucked ice at Private White. She is reckless, that girl, like George, and yet so unlike her lovely sister, Jane. Jane Howlett was the fairest creature he'd ever seen. And yet, as shocked as he'd been by Annalisa's behavior, he could hardly fault her. They had all gone a bit mad that day. Now as Adams' apprentice, he was expected to deliver a formidable approach to the defense of poor Captain Preston and the king's army, including that dour-faced cad, Private White.

FROM MID-SEPTEMBER UNTIL THE FIRST DAY OF CAPTAIN Preston's trial, Jack lived at the Adams' house in Braintree. Red-eyed and bleary, he dedicated every wakeful moment to Mr. Adams and his defense arguments.

Preston's trial came and went, lasting a tedious six days, and resulted in a victory for the defense. However, it was the second trial Jack dreaded; the one in which his mentor aspired to acquit the soldiers, including Private White.

The night before opening statements, Jack and Mr. Adams convened in his cramped study, gathering all manner of papers they would need for the trial. A fire rustled and snapped, warming the room to sweltering summer temperatures. Jack plunged two fingers against his neck and pulled forward his white silk stock.

A clock chimed midnight.

"Mr. Perkins." Candlelight flickered off Adams' bald head as he slid across the floor in his chair. "The jury must decide if the soldiers of the twenty-nineth regiment committed homicide—was it justifiable, excusable, or felonious?"

Jack looked up from his page. "I would say it was felonious, sir."

"Indeed. But there are two types of felonious homicide. Murder and manslaughter. Which do you think the king's men committed?"

Jack hesitated, and swallowed through the dryness in his mouth. "I suppose it would be manslaughter because there was hardly an aforethought of malice."

Adams nodded with apparent approval, and skidded his chair back to his desk. "You're quite right, Mr. Perkins." A tiny smirk escaped his lips, as quick and fleeting as a snowflake landed upon warm skin.

Jack rested in his chair.

The following day, the 27th of November, Jack perched on the edge of his seat in the stuffy Queen-street courthouse. His head throbbed, but his senses heightened when the prisoners marched before them. He recognized each charged soldier of the twenty-nineth regiment, and Private White's bayonetted face. The soldier glared at him from across the room. Jack's neckpiece choked him, but he would not give Private White the satisfaction of such a suffocation. Jack held his stare until the private averted his.

The judges entered and everyone stood for their address. Jack sighed, glad his father had stepped down as magistrate. He could hardly imagine Father presiding over these cases, especially when he'd been so accommodating to Captain Preston.

After three full, tiresome days of witnesses presenting their versions of what had happened, Jack's bottom lip might have split with the contention of remaining silent.

On the final day, Mr. Adams approached the jury.

"May it please your Honors, and you, Gentlemen of the Jury. I am for the prisoners at the bar, and shall apologize for it in the words of the Marquis Beccaria, *'If I can but be the instrument of preserving one life'...*"

Adams was an orator, a man of philosophy and reason, if nothing else. Jack would learn much from him in the remainder of his tutelage, but these soldiers—Private White—must hang.

"We are to look upon it as more beneficial, that many guilty persons should escape unpunished than one innocent person should suffer." Mr. Adams cleared his throat. "*Quod dubitas ne feceris*—where you are doubtful, never act; that is, if you doubt the prisoner's guilt, never declare him guilty. This is always the rule, especially in cases pertaining to life."

When the time came to reveal the soldiers' sentencing, Jack locked eyes with Private White.

He should hang from the Liberty Tree—no, better yet, Boston Neck, where his body may rot for all to see who enter the town from the south end.

Jack tightened his fists until his fingers numbed. All those long nights and early mornings working with Adams would surmount to this very moment. He should wish for his mentor to be victorious, but would such a victory feel vindicated?

Justice Oliver stood. "Gentlemen of the Jury, this is the most solemn trial I ever sat in judgement upon."

Jack held his breath.

10

ANNALISA
TOPSFIELD, JANUARY 1771

NEWS OF THE MASSACRE trials reached the country before Christmastide, and Topsfield buzzed with gossip. Most of whom Annalisa overheard spoke with Loyalist or moderate sentiments, and were quite pleased by the rulings.

On the eve of Epiphany, Annalisa and George followed their family through the snow-shoveled path and into the meetinghouse across from Topsfield's common. Today, Reverend Emerson would give a particularly long sermon.

"By the devil's cock." George turned to Annalisa as they entered. "I still can't believe the jury found those dilberries not guilty."

"'Tis disagreeable on all accounts." She clutched his arm. "I'm certain you can thank your perfidious cousin and his mentor, Mr. Adams."

"Don't dawdle," Mamma hissed, turning around.

They slid into their family pew on the right side of the congregation, and awaited Reverend Emerson.

George leaned in. "Jack must feel conflicted about it.

He was there with us. He knows those men were not innocent."

"And yet his tutor saved them from the gallows."

"All but two. Montgomery and Killroy were charged with manslaughter but they pled Benefit of Clergy. Now they must walk through life with a branded *M* on their thumbs."

Annalisa bit her tongue. "How thoughtful." She slid closer to him. "Let's brand your cousin with a *D* upon his thumb, for deceitful. For being the true Patriot that he is."

"Fie." George frowned. "Jack *is* Patriot."

"Well, I doubt Oliver is. Perhaps he's had influence over Jack's sensibilities."

Reverend Emerson climbed the pulpit. "Ladies and Gentlemen of our blessed congregation, before we begin, I must introduce the newest members of our church and town." He gestured to one of the family pew boxes at the front of the meetinghouse, nearest the pulpit—where the wealthiest families sat. "Lord and Lady Perkins, and their children, hail from Boston and now call Topsfield home. Let us welcome them as God would have us do."

Annalisa glared at George. "You said June. They're five months early"

George shook his head. "I knew not. I wrote Jack after the trials but have yet to receive his reply. They must've been busy moving."

Annalisa shivered, wound her cloak about her, and settled in for the long service. When the reverend finally offered music to honor this Twelfth Night, Jack Perkins volunteered. Before the entire town, he tuned the communal violin and played Bach's *Jesu, Joy of Man's Desiring*.

Of course he would play. He must think his playing the only tolerable music on the North Shore of Boston.

She'd heard the song countless times, having played it herself every year during Christmastide. But with Jack's swift, precise fingers, each note washed over her as the angels themselves sang through the violin. Annalisa's eyes welled. She yearned to weep, but could not. Rather, she sat stunned with wonderment as the beautiful, godly hymn flowed from the hands of this most agreeable man.

When Jack finished, silence invaded the meetinghouse. Annalisa gasped as though her very life had been sucked from her. She blinked several times and looked into her lap.

George leaned in once more. "I bet Mother invites them to our house for dinner."

Annalisa clutched the pew, pulling herself back into the meetinghouse. "How inconvenient."

❧

THEIR FARMHOUSE, HOWEVER HUMBLE IT MIGHT HAVE seemed to Lord and Lady Perkins, was quite large, and Addy and Liza had decorated it for the season. Not every family in town celebrated Christmastide—those with Puritan roots, like Papa, did not—but most acknowledged Epiphany. Since Mamma was raised in England as a Protestant who celebrated Christmas, she always put forth a grand spread at Twelfth Night.

Pine and cedar wreaths, and garland dotted with mulberries and pinecones hung from walls and doorways. A bundle of mistletoe dangled above the entryway. Evergreen mingled with clove and cinnamon, and the large brick hearth roared with a great fire. Even Jane floated about, at ease hosting their gentry guests.

Mamma embraced Lady Perkins and led her into the warm parlor. "Bette, it is so wonderful to see you again. We do hope you will be happy in town."

Lady Perkins kissed Mamma's cheek. "We cannot thank you enough for hosting us this evening. Our move to the country has been a thrilling adventure."

Lord Perkins and Papa exchanged pleasantries by the fire, each with a brandy in one hand, and a pipe in the other. Jane settled herself on the blue damask sofa with Mamma and Lady Perkins, nearest where Jack and Oliver stood. William escorted Andrew and Susan Perkins, and Mary and Henry into the drawing room.

Annalisa lingered by the casement. The glass frosted from her delicate breath.

Abigail approached. "Miss Annalisa, you have a lovely home. I just adore this little town. 'Tis everything I could hope for."

Strange, Abigail finds such a mundane farming town to her liking.

But Annalisa smiled, comforted by her kind words. "I'm glad you find it agreeable. I do hope we can be great friends."

"Me, too." Abigail squeezed Annalisa's hands.

"Wassail, wassail, all over the town," George's bass sang as he entered the parlor with a large wassailing bowl.

"Our toast it is white, and our ale it is brown," Jack sang with a laugh.

"Come, let's try the wassail." Annalisa pulled Abigail across the room to sniff the warm, spiced wine.

"That smells delicious, George." Abigail lifted her face from the bowl. "Did you make it yourself?"

"Hardly." He chortled, clearly already drunk. "Addy, God love her, is the best cook and housekeeper there is."

Indeed, she was. Addy—with Liza—had cooked a feast of roast turkey, fish and cheese pudding, custard, figgy pudding, and mincemeat pie. Annalisa's mouth watered at the savory, buttery aromas wafting from the kitchen. She ladled spiced wine into two glasses and handed one to Abigail.

"Here's to Twelfth Night, and the coming of the spring season," Abigail squealed.

Annalisa giggled. "We've a way to go before spring. 'Tis only January."

"La." Abigail clanked her glass to Annalisa's. "Let's into your drawing room. You must play for me."

An image of Jack's violin singing Bach this morning gave Annalisa pause. She gulped the warm wine and guided Abigail from the parlor, and into the more intimate drawing room. Henry, Susan upon Mary's lap, Andrew, and William sat about the gaming table playing cards.

"Andrew's taught us to play Whilst." Mary gave a wide, toothless grin.

"Whist," Henry corrected her.

Annalisa grinned, sat at the spinet, and lifted the cover. She played *Greensleeves*, and within minutes, the floor creaked as Jane, Oliver, and Jack entered the room. Her stomach wrenched at the mere sight of Oliver Perkins; the dread and anxiety of this very moment sent the room wavering. In her brief agitation, Annalisa avoided his black stare and focused on her hands at the keys.

"This day would have been incomplete without Miss

Annalisa's accomplished playing." Jack's blue-eyed gaze sparkled for a moment in her direction. He then followed Jane to the sofa, his fingertips gliding the edge of her dress. George and Abigail joined them, but Oliver slinked by the spinet. The churlish dog wore a velvet evergreen coat embroidered with silver threads and announced his presence with thick, musk perfume that overtook her senses before he even leaned against the instrument.

"Miss Annalisa, play a song for me."

She ground her teeth. "I most certainly will not."

Oliver's dark eyes scrutinized her, his blond hair hanging over his shoulder in a tidy queue. His hands dug into the spinet when he shifted his weight. "I beg your pardon?"

"No, sir. I will not delight you with a song." She continued *Greensleeves* while watching his jaw set. Thankfully, nobody seemed to listen.

Oliver leaned down, his scent settling over her as it had the night he'd grabbed her. She pushed away the memory.

"Miss Annalisa, I was out of turn when I kissed you—"

"And forced yourself on me, and touched me in unspeakable places." Her heart galloped. There was no turning back. "You humiliated me."

His face reddened. "And you have my word as a gentleman, it shan't happen again."

"I suppose that isn't much of a promise, had you behaved as one," she hissed. "If you swear on George as a gentleman, I may consider your apology."

Oliver crossed his arms. "George? A gentleman?"

"Yes, George." Her lip curled. "He may be a farmer, but he holds more integrity than you'll ever have."

He blinked several times. "Very well. As George is a gentleman, it shan't happen again."

"I should hope not. Now, please leave me before I announce to both our families of what passed between—"

"Perkins, what of this verdict," George boomed.

Annalisa stopped playing and Oliver held out his hand to her. She stood without his help and rushed to her brother's side.

Abigail frowned. "Jack hates speaking of it."

Jack cast Jane an apologizing glance. "I'm sorry, Miss Howlett. I know I promised no talk of politics."

Annalisa scrunched her nose. *Since when are they acquainted enough for Jane to dictate what he talks about?*

"Worry not." Jane smiled demurely. "I know how much my brother wishes to hear."

"Cousin, there's not much to say, except I worked countless hours with Adams." Jack lifted Jane's hands. "While it sickened me to see those men acquitted, I daresay I wouldn't have slept a wink had they been hanged."

"The trial was fair, as was the verdict." Oliver picked a loose thread from his coat.

"Fie." George growled. "Those soldiers shot five men who lost their lives. Five innocent men. And you say they should not hang?"

Jack held up a hand. "*Quod dubitas ne feceris*—where you may be doubtful, do not act. If there is doubt over the accused's guilt, it is best to never pronounce him thus. 'Tis always better to see twenty guilty men go, than have one innocent man punished capitally."

"But those men were hardly innocent," Annalisa cried. "And to receive Benefit of Clergy? Some punishment, to walk around with an *M* branded on one's thumb when they should have hanged."

Jane gasped. "Annalisa."

"Annie, please." William rose from the card table and ushered the children from the drawing room with Andrew.

When they had gone, Annalisa added, "'Tis true. I was th—I was disheartened to hear the verdict. As was George." She caught herself, having almost divulged she had been there.

"A simple thought from a simple mind," Oliver replied.

Jack's eyes narrowed. "Ollie, shut it. Miss Annalisa is entitled to her opinion."

My opinion? Since when does anyone wish to hear what I have to say?

"Come, Miss Howlett." Oliver held out his hand to Jane. "Let's find some of that wassail."

Jane obliged, and they left the room, leaving Jack to stare after them.

He shifted his gaze to George, his face mostly blank. "I do empathize with your feelings, Cousin." Jack paused. "I admit I had my own demons to conquer during the trial... I, too, wished them to hang." He locked eyes with Annalisa. "But one must learn to practice and exercise restraint, and behave with *reason*." Jack jumped from the sofa and gave a quick bow. "By your leave," and followed after Jane and Oliver.

Annalisa fisted her tingling hands. *Behave with reason. Exercise restraint? Of all the insulting, degrading, pompous things to say.*

"I sense a competition for Miss Howlett's attention." Abigail's gaze shifted to the door. "Pray tell, Miss Annalisa, have you had your debut yet?"

"Annie? Debut?" George guffawed. "She'd rather shoot a firelock than dance a minuet."

"Is this true?" Abigail lifted a hand to her breast.

"It is." Annalisa glanced at the doorway through which Jack had followed Jane and Oliver. "But Mamma says I may have my debut come springtime."

The same as when I join the militia.

"Marvelous." Abigail clapped her hands. "I had a wonderful tutor in Boston. We shall work on that minuet from now until then."

11

ANNALISA
DANVERS, MARCH 1771

ANNALISA TIED HER MARE to a wooden fence and adjusted the cocked hat upon her head. With a quick shift of her coat and tug upon Bixby over her shoulder, she trudged up the hill toward the captain of the Danvers militia.

"Sir, my name's Benjamin Cavendish." She deepened her voice. "I'm a relation of the Howlett family of Topsfield. I wish to join the militia."

The captain crossed an arm over the other and studied her. "Master Cavendish, why have you not joined your relation's militia?"

"Topsfield's militia would not accept me, sir," she lied. "The captain said my shot was not accurate enough."

"A curious refusal." He scratched his neck, then sighed. "Load your firelock and demonstrate your accuracy, Master Cavendish."

She wiped her sweating palms on her breeches, then swung the fowler over her shoulder.

I can do this.

She reached into her brother's cartridge box and removed a cartridge, ripped the paper with her teeth, and spit the litter to the ground. After dribbling the gunpowder into the priming pan, she slammed forward the steel, then poured the remaining gunpowder, with lead round, into the barrel of the firelock. With the ramrod, she packed it all home, then replaced it into the channel.

"My target, sir?"

"The elm." The captain pointed.

Annalisa half-cocked the fowler, lifted the stock to her shoulder, narrowed one eye, fully cocked it, and pulled the trigger.

Snap-crack!

Splinters flew from the trunk.

"You're proficient at forty-yards." The captain nodded. "Let's see you strike that oak."

The oak was considerably farther. She wiped her arm beneath her nose and proceeded to load the firelock as she had before. Her teeth sunk into her bottom lip as she closed one eye, fully cocked Bixby, and pulled the trigger.

Crack-boom!

The sulfur burned her nose, and she barked a deep cough. When the smoke cleared, it was difficult to see if she'd met her mark. She hurried after the captain who advanced toward the oak.

"You've skimmed the trunk." His fingers glided over a bit of upturned bark. He turned from the tree to face her. "But 'tis nothing you couldn't improve upon. I see you've got a keen eye." The captain scrutinized her for only a moment, as if assessing her identity. Annalisa didn't dare breathe.

"Come with me. I'll have you sign on. Better to have too many men than not enough."

She exhaled. "Oh, thank you, sir." Taking care to disguise the inflection in her voice, she added, "I'll not disappoint you sir, I swear it."

Her whole body tingled as she followed Captain Foster to his office, where she would make her mark upon the page, enlisting her to the Danvers militia. Now she must be certain of her identity. No one could discover her in this charade, but being a town away from her own, she should have little trouble in concealing herself.

NOT A QUARTER-HOUR AFTER ANNALISA SNUCK HOME, Jane called out for her.

"Annie, we're late."

Annalisa rushed down the stairs, her fingers frantically tying a black ribbon about her neck from which dangled a small, pewter pineapple; a gift from George on her eleventh birthday.

"Where have you been?" Jane tightened the bow on her straw hat. "I've been looking for you all morning. You know I hate to be late."

Annalisa followed her sister out the front door and into the chaise with Quinnapin, who would drive them two miles down the lane. He glanced at Annalisa and rolled his eyes as Jane stepped into the chaise. Annalisa stifled a chuckle as he handed her inside behind Jane.

The Perkins' new house sat on a small hill facing the road, and was much larger than their Boston home had been. Two chimneys flanked the yellow structure on other either end, all of which piped wispy, white smoke into the dank, March air.

Inside the parlor, a new coat of white paint covered the wainscoting, and lavish teal wallpaper decorated with yellow pineapples decked the walls. Marine brocaded silk curtains, and shiny new furniture completed the room.

Jane and Annalisa joined Abigail by the fire, and removed their needlepoint canvases. Annalisa dipped her needle into the canvas several times.

Jane peered up from her canvas. "Annie, we must continue working on your minuet."

"Yes." Abigail removed a bag full of silk threads in every color imaginable. "And how well your minuet is coming, Miss Annalisa."

"Annie has devoted an hour each evening to practicing the steps with me." Jane eyed Abigail's threads with envy.

"I try, but Janey, you're lucky enough to practice in Salem with a tutor." Annalisa lowered her gaze to her canvas. The little rose appeared oblong. Frustrated, she ripped out the stitches.

A waste of time, same as that horrid minuet.

"Worry not, dear friend. Your sister and I are devoted to teaching you the steps. By the first ball this spring, you'll be proficient." The front door opened and closed, and Abigail turned her head in the direction of the foyer. "I think they've arrived."

Mercy ushered Martha Perley, Lizzie Balch, Hannah French, and Fannie Shepard into the parlor.

"Every time we come here I am in awe at the splendor." Hannah French's pink petticoats swished from side-to-side as she bustled into the room.

"It is so kind of you to have started this club, Miss Perkins." Martha Perley sat beside Jane.

"Yes." Fannie Shepard sighed, her plump face already glowing red. "Lord knows what else we would have been doing all winter."

Annalisa held back her smile. All winter, she'd been firing Bixby in the clearing that overlooked their farm, anticipating today. Her disbelief she was a part of the Danvers militia still confounded her, yet she could hardly share the good news with the ladies.

Mercy re-entered the room with a large silver tray full of tea and biscuits, and set it upon a round, mahogany table.

Abigail gestured to the tea. "Do help yourselves."

"I am famished." Fannie tossed aside her needlepoint for a cup of tea and two biscuits smothered with honey.

"I saw Samuel Wildes at the milliner's in Ipswich yesterday." Hannah daintily dipped her biscuit into her tea. "Miss Howlett, he says George is in Boston."

"Yes." Jane hardly looked up from her canvas. "He's observing the anniversary of the massacre with Abigail's brothers."

Lizzie Balch threaded her needle. "I heard George was there the day it happened."

"Yes." Annalisa set aside her canvas, remembering that chaotic yet profound day. "So was Jack Perkins."

Hannah dropped her half-eaten biscuit onto the plate, then fanned herself as though Jack had walked into the room. "Miss Perkins, your brothers are the most handsome, well-bred, agreeable men I've ever seen."

Abigail's cheeks pinked, and Annalisa frowned. Her

poor friend could hardly escape the fanciful stares and
dotes upon her elder brothers.

If only they knew the truth about Oliver.

Fannie bit into a third biscuit, chewed, and swallowed.
"I'd give anything to dance with one of them at the Strawberry Festival."

Annalisa crossed her arms. "You're making Abigail
uncomfortable."

Hannah snickered. "'Tis but the truth. I ne'er saw a
man as agreeable as Jack. I daresay, he is what it means to
be called a gentleman."

Annalisa rolled her eyes and glanced at Abigail. "And he
knows it, too."

Abigail giggled. "They do know it. Particularly Ollie.
Though, Jack is hardly conceited. He is kind, compassion-
ate, and reliable." She regarded Annalisa with an impish
smirk. "I daresay, he will make a fine husband one day."

Martha Perley snipped a thread. "I quite like a humble
man."

"Like who?" Lizzie asked.

Martha looked down, then peered at Annalisa. "Like
William Howlett."

Annalisa and Jane exchanged a bemused giggle. Their
younger brother—now thirteen—certainly boasted agreeable features, but he was so shy. Annalisa never imagined
him courting anyone, let alone fourteen-year-old Martha
Perley—who was just as shy as he.

"William would be thrilled to know you fancy him."
Jane winked. "Shall I hint?"

Martha gasped. "Heavens, no."

When the laughter dispersed, Hannah French cast a
sidelong glance at Jane. "I think Miss Howlett shall find

out soon enough what a courtship with Oliver or Jack might be like."

"Yes. You are so beautiful, Jane." Fannie licked the honey from her fingers. "Beauty must stick together. Am I right, Miss French?"

Hannah smirked. "Indeed."

"Yes." Lizzie stuck a needle in her canvas. "I think of all the ladies in town, Miss Howlett would make the best choice. We'll have to divine it at the husking in October."

Jane shifted and smoothed her skirts, and Annalisa scowled. "You're making my sister uncomfortable."

Jane's face colored like the peonies that would bloom in Annalisa's garden come June. "You flatter me. While I do find Miss Perkins' brothers to be everything a young lady should fancy, I will not flatter myself with the hope that either of them will choose me as a wife."

"I think Miss Annalisa is quite the contender." Abigail grabbed her hand. "She'll be having her debut this spring. Just look at her dazzling green eyes, her curling, honey-brown hair. What man could resist her?"

Annalisa chewed her cheek. She might find a young man to court her, a neighboring farmer or a vicar's son, according to Mamma.

"You're too tall. I bet you haven't even gotten your flux yet." Hannah French gave a close-lipped smile. "And you're too tanned. Do you not cover your face when outside?"

"Miss French is right," Fannie said. "Have you gotten your menses? You're as tall as William.

"And Ezra Kimball, and Josiah Averill," Lizzie added. "And you really must wear a hat."

Annalisa's chest heated. Jane had gotten the morbid flux at fourteen. *At fifteen, I should have gotten it by now.* She crossed her arms. "My mamma is always trying to make me look pale in summer, but I bronze easily. But, because I'm tall, that means I cannot attract a man of good breeding?" Annalisa's brows furrowed. "I'm shorter than Jack Perkins, and he's mentioned nothing of my height, complexion, nor the scar on my face. Perhaps *he* will ask me to dance."

"Peace, Miss Annie, we meant no offense." Fannie frowned. "I think men find you...intimidating."

"Fie," Abigail scoffed. "Any man who decides Miss Annalisa is intimidating deserves her not."

Annalisa blinked away the sting of tears. She'd never considered her late entry into womanhood a reason why men might not find her agreeable. It was always her summer tan. Then it was the scar beneath her right eye. Perhaps neither was noticeable when compared to her five-foot-seven stature. Each of the ladies about the parlor were at or below five-foot-four, Lizzie being shortest, at under five-foot.

Perhaps that was reason enough she hardly fit in among her sex. She recalled this morning, satisfied she'd fooled the Danvers militia. At least she could delight in fitting in somewhere. Had she been anything less than five-foot-five, she never would have been convincing enough as a man.

If she could only endure her debut come spring.

12

ANNALISA
TOPSFIELD, JUNE 1771

A NNALISA HELD BIXBY TO her shoulder, closed one eye, and pulled the trigger.

Snap-crack!

The maple shook, and splinters flew from the trunk. Gunpowder stung her nose as she trudged toward the tree, retrieved her musket round, and loaded the firelock again. This time, she aimed at a more distant ash.

Crack-boom!

The ash shook, but no woody shards flew about. She rushed to the tree and saw the ball lodged into the trunk.

"That was at least sixty yards."

Satisfied, Annalisa pried the round from the tree, stuck it into her linen coat pocket, and slung Bixby over her shoulder. Burrs buried into her petticoats and dress. She tried brushing them away, but far too many told of where she'd been.

Mamma will chide me. I'll have to start wearing William's old breeches when I practice in the clearing.

Annalisa walked toward the path where field met

woods, and looked out over her family's farm in the distance below. Honeysuckle perfumed the air, a distraction from the lingering traces of gunpowder. She would take the longer, less steep trail home. She slipped from George's old coat, stuffed it into her haversack, and stepped onto the path. As she walked, chickadees sang in the trees overhead, and a gentle breeze rustled the leaves.

"Miss Annalisa?"

She stopped and turned.

Jack Perkins, finely dressed in cobalt silk and with cane in hand, navigated the woods beyond the path. There was no way for her to hide the firelock and cartridge box she carried. She lowered her head and glided along the trail.

"Miss Annalisa." Jack stumbled over a twisted root. "Miss Annalisa, please wait. I seem to have lost my way to your house."

At his urgency, she hesitated and studied his attractive figure as he tumbled over a large branch. To hide her chuckle, she bit her lip. She'd almost forgotten his insulting words at Twelfth Night.

When he made it to the path, Jack gave a good-humored laugh as his fingers flew to pick the burrs on his stockings. "I'm clearly unprepared for such an adventure. This is quite the hill!"

"I take it you're adjusting well to life in the country, sir." She bobbed a curtsy.

His eyes lit up at her banter. "Quite."

She started. When last they'd spoken, he'd lectured her. *Has he forgotten the encounter?*

Though, being alone with him in the middle of the woods tickled her stomach. The ladies would be jealous if they knew. *Nay, incredulous. But I won't be so eager to forgive him like that awful Hannah French would.*

"I should return. 'Tis hardly proper for me to be in your presence without a chaperone."

"And do the rules of Society apply to these woods?" Jack arched a brow and leaned on his cane. His gaze fell on Bixby. "Pray tell, have you plans to hunt with us, Miss Annalisa?"

"Of course not." Heat rose up her back. "And my uses of Bixby are of no concern of yours, sir." She curtsied. "Good-day."

"Miss Annalisa, wait." He rushed after her, his gaze apologetic beneath his beaver-felt cocked hat. "I meant no offense. Please, allow me to accompany you. I can hardly call myself a gentleman if I let you continue alone."

"Then you consider yourself a gentleman?"

Jack's brows furrowed. "Miss, have I offended you in some way?"

"*'One must learn to practice and exercise restraint, and behave with reason.'* You could not have reproached me in a worse way." She curtsied again. "By your leave, sir."

Jack lunged after her. "Miss Annalisa, that was not directed toward you." His azure stare held hers. "Please forgive me. It would be my greatest honor to accompany you home."

She smirked. "I know the way better than you, sir."

"That is true." He cracked a smile. "Can you forgive a fool?"

Annalisa relaxed her grin. "If you can accept friendship in a woman who shoots firelocks for sport."

"I daresay I can." He offered his arm, and she took it without reservation. He smelled of amber and pipe tobacco, an amalgamation of scents she'd not yet appreciated of a man.

They walked down the hill until the trees parted and they were greeted by the ancient oak.

"What a sage tree," Jack said as they passed by, and headed toward her family's farming fields.

"'Tis my favorite place in all the world."

Annalisa waved to Dane and Zeke. Their shining faces peered up from under straw hats. "I'll be out to pick strawberries soon," she called.

"Strawberry picking?" Jack cocked his head.

"Yes, for Addy's pies for the festival tonight."

His smile lines creased. "I look forward to trying them. I hear they're the best in town."

They approached the barn and already the horses grunted in their stalls.

Quinn must be inside.

Jack slid open the door, and they entered. To her surprise, the barn was empty. Annalisa reached up and slid Bixby onto the nails, her palm grazing the dry, splintered wood.

"Zounds!"

The fowler fell, and she clasped her hand. A large shard of wood lodged into her left palm.

Jack rushed to her. "I bet that's sore. May I?" His stare shifted, the serene calm where ocean meets sky. The nearness of his warmth overwhelmed her as he reached for her hand. He pinched the splinter. "This may hurt."

The smoothness of his touch and intoxicating perfume were more than enough to disguise the pain. In one swift motion, he plucked the wooden shard, and blood pooled in her hand.

"How foolish of me."

Jack removed a small, white linen handkerchief from his waistcoat and dabbed away the droplet. "That should do."

"But your handkerchief—'tis ruined."

"Nonsense." He wrapped it around her hand. "'Tis yours now."

With a loud creak the barn door opened, and Annalisa spun around. Jack stepped away from her and focused on plucking burrs from his coat.

George stepped inside. "Cousin, what's this?" He eyed the fowler. "Annie, what did you do?"

She held out her hand. "I got a splinter. But Mr. Perkins removed it."

George crossed the barn in four great strides. He peeked under the linen and chuckled. "I think you'll live." He picked up Bixby and leaned it against his hip. "The Perkins gentlemen have come to hunt this morning before the festival. Mary's waiting to pick strawberries with you."

Jack stopped her. "Miss Annalisa, I hear 'tis your debut tonight. Will you honor me with a dance?"

She beamed. "I look forward to it."

Annalisa left the barn as Oliver, William, and Andrew entered.

"A rather unlikely place for a young lady," Oliver said.

Upon hearing his snide, Annalisa slipped around the side of the barn to listen.

"Annie's in the barn all the time," William replied. "George taught her to use his firelock."

Oliver laughed. "Cousin, you *willingly* taught a girl to use a firelock? This will certainly be the death of you.

What sort of young lady wishes to spend her time with weaponry?"

"Plenty of women in town are more than capable of manipulating a fowler," George said. "Life is different in the country. You'll do well to keep with the pace of your new town, Cousin."

Annalisa hurried from the barn and made her way to the strawberry field, where Mary sat with a large basket amidst a row of plants.

"Why are you smiling?" Mary plucked a ruby jewel from its emerald swing. Her delightful, hazel eyes peered up at Annalisa.

Annalisa settled beside her. "I secured a dance tonight at the festival."

"I knew it," Mary squealed. "With whom?"

"Jack Perkins."

13

ANNALISA
TOPSFIELD, JUNE 1771

TOPSFIELD's COMMON GLEAMED GOLD in the late setting sun. An early evening breeze rippled through the trees, casting delicate shadows across the grass. Ladies in straw hats and gentlemen farmers in their finest linen coats gathered. Sugary aromas of baked strawberry treats tantalized Annalisa's stomach. She tingled at the familiar sounds of fifes, fiddles, and guitars.

"I can hardly wait for them to play *Flowers of Edinburgh*."

"They do every year." Jane laughed. "Usually more than once." She adjusted the bow on Annalisa's straw hat and linked their arms. "You look beautiful, and ready for your debut."

Jane had helped her prepare for the festival—and even allowed her to borrow her blue petticoat. With care, she'd fastened every flower to Annalisa's hat, and tied the bow with precision.

"This is remarkable. How splendid!" Abigail emerged from the crowd. "Are you ready to dance? Though I can hardly imagine they'd play a minuet here." She took Annalisa's other arm and grinned crookedly. "Let's find the gentlemen."

They twirled and weaved through the congregation of townspeople. Already, a set of dancers lined up before the musicians.

Abigail clapped her hands. "A country dance, how lovely." Tonight, she seemed far from the high society in which she'd been raised, and the respectable balls she'd attended in Boston.

At the narrow end of the common, the gentlemen encircled Mr. Gould and his kegs of cider and ale. Nearby, Hannah French, Fannie Shepard, and Lizzie Balch gawked at Jack.

"For shame." Abigail clicked her tongue. "Look at them. You'd think they'd never seen a handsome gentleman."

"Rogues, I am utterly disguised," George bellowed. The others hooted and clanked their pewter mugs.

Abigail turned to Annalisa. "What's George saying?"

"He's drunk." Annalisa laughed. "And that's Mr. Gould. He's famous in town for fighting in the French war."

"My offer still stands." Mr. Gould poured George another mugful of ale, then wiped his hands on a leather apron. "Ye need cider and ale. I'll offer mine if I can be yer innkeeper at the Peat Moss."

"You really mean that?" George sipped from the tankard. "I could use your experience—and your libations."

"Aye. When d'ye open?"

"Next month." George held out his hand. "The position is yours."

"Miss Howlett."

Jane and Annalisa turned at the sound of Jack's voice. He glided past Hannah, Fannie, and Lizzie, and tipped his hat.

"Miss Howlett, Miss Annalisa." He glanced at his sister "—Abby—" and returned his gaze to Jane. "Miss Howlett, will you do me the honor of the next dance?"

"Of course, sir."

Abigail giggled. "Jack, when have you danced anything but a minuet or allemande?"

"I know a cotillion." He chortled. "And I've just danced three reels with three different ladies. I think I shall manage with Miss Howlett."

Jack whisked Jane into the set of dancers and Annalisa stared after them.

Abigail must have seen the disappointment on her face. She turned Annalisa from the set. "Come, let's try some pie."

Once her taste-buds savored the buttery crust and tart filling of Addy's famous pie, Samuel Wildes approached with George and Quinnapin.

Samuel lifted his hat. "Miss Anna, will ye dance th' next with me?"

Annalisa curtsied. "Of course, sir."

They danced the reel, and Abigail with George. For the second, Annalisa paired with Quinnapin, and for the third, Ezra Kimball.

When the cotillion ended, Annalisa scanned the set for Jack.

He stood across from Jane.

Forlorn, she turned away. Perhaps she would not dance with him after all. Jane, at seventeen, had been formally educated in Salem, been *out* for the past two years, and was now ripe for courting. It was no surprise Jack favored her.

And thank God it isn't Oliver.

But Annalisa could hardly shake the bitter sting of disappointment, and an opportunity lost.

She slipped away from the set of dancers and wandered toward the common's edge. Near a large boulder—the Common Rock, as it was known in town—Annalisa sprawled upon the cool, damp grass and lifted her face to the sky. The heavens glittered with a million tiny stars, and the yellow glow of lightning bugs hovered over the field in a thousand flickering lights. The brisk evening air, full of dew and lilac, set her with peaceful ease.

Annalisa reached into her pocket and removed Jack's linen handkerchief. Holding it to her nose, she sniffed his amber perfume and closed her eyes. She imagined his hands upon her as they twirled beneath the night sky.

"Miss Annalisa, there you are." Jack's voice interrupted her fantasy.

Startled, she peered up at him.

"They've done the last dance already. I apologize. I'm afraid we'll have to dance next year."

Flowers of Edinburgh played one final time in the distance. Amidst the fireflies and sparkling skies, all she noticed were his eyes, glassy from too much ale. She replaced the handkerchief into her pocket.

"Sir, that is foul news indeed." She sat up. "I've never seen so many lightning bugs."

Jack peered about. "I've not seen anything like it myself. Topsfield is agreeable."

"'Tis home." She sighed, ready to lift from the ground. "I suppose I should find my parents."

Jack assumed a recumbent position beside her on the grass. "Just a moment more—to atone for missing our dance." He held his hat to his chest and looked into her eyes. "Nights like these are rare."

"You're right, Mr. Perkins."

"Call me Jack." He paused and licked his bottom lip. "Annalisa."

The impropriety of hearing him utter only her Christian name stole her breath. Giddy, she lay back, and together they watched the stars.

"Adams keeps me too busy. I rarely have the chance to star-gaze in Boston."

"George and I used to lie out in the western field for hours, watching for shooting stars. Quinn tells us to beware the *Puk-wudjies* in the woods late at night. I hardly believe in ghost stories, but I'm curious of his tales."

"Good old Quinn. Wampanoag lore is fascinating, though. After he told me about *Puk-wudjies* I thought I saw one in Cambridge. Turns out it had been the ale I'd been drinking!" Jack laughed. "I wish I had someone like George growing up. Your brother loves you very much. He spoke of you countless times when he stayed with us." He paused. "I felt as though I already knew you before we met."

"I felt the same about you. George wrote of you in nearly every one of his letters." She ground her teeth, hating herself for having harbored ill feelings toward him. "You must be a good man if he had only good things to say."

From the corner of her eye, she caught him staring. She turned and smiled.

"I've never known a lady so willing to lie in the grass

like this."

"I'm no ordinary lady."

Jack's cheeks dimpled. "I can see that."

This is most inconvenient. Every girl in town holds a dalliance for Jack, including Jane.

She bit her lip, wishing she weren't on that long list herself, especially when her own sister fancied him.

"Annalisa." Jane's voice struck like lightning. "Papa and Mamma are waiting."

Jack sprung up and held out his hand to her. Annalisa grasped it and scrambled to her feet.

"Mr. Perkins." Jane gave a brief curtsy.

Jack offered her his arm. "Miss Howlett, 'tis always a pleasure."

Annalisa trailed behind them until they met with George, his eyes glassy and frown upturned. He dashed to her side and wrapped an arm over her.

"'Tis getting cool, Little One." George's breath smelled of stale cider.

She eased against him and relaxed her shoulders. "Tomorrow, let me show you how well I've been shooting. You owe me a lesson with Bixby."

Her brother guffawed and stumbled as they walked. "I like the sound of that."

In front of her, Jane held Jack's arm. They beamed at one another, impervious to Annalisa and George behind them.

Annalisa squeezed George's hand. "I've still much to learn."

And much to forget.

She pulled Jack's handkerchief from her pocket, crumpled it into a ball, and dropped it onto the common.

14

ANNALISA
TOPSFIELD AND DANVERS, OCTOBER 1771

WHEN THE PUNGENT SMOKE cleared, Annalisa set down her brother's fowling piece. She'd been drilling with the militia since dawn.

"Well done, Cav." Nathaniel Hitchcock clapped her shoulder. "I think you've met your mark."

"I've been practicing with my cousin." Annalisa wiped her brow.

"Shall we to the tavern, then?" Ebenezer Goldthwait suggested.

"Aye."

As the men started to pack up their cartridge boxes, Annalisa turned and headed toward her horse.

"Why don't you ever join us, Cav?" Nathaniel asked.

"The corn husking is tonight. My aunt and uncle have been preparing for it for weeks, since the harvest."

Annalisa hurried to Dinah and rode north, home to Topsfield.

⚛

"COME, ANNIE, PEOPLE ARE ARRIVING," JANE CALLED from the front doorway.

Annalisa rushed downstairs and outside to join her sister. The sky had darkened to twilight, and down the hill, a soft glow seeped from the barn. Together, they walked from their house.

"Where's George?"

"He's in the barn barking orders at William and Henry." Jane's hand rested on her hip. "He thinks he's running his tavern."

"When I find that red ear of corn, I'm going straight for Jack Perkins." Hannah French bustled up the path with Lizzie, Fannie, and Martha. Hannah gasped. "Oh, good-evening Miss Howlett, Miss Annalisa. Thank you for hosting the frolics this year."

"Of course." Jane smirked. "Our farm is the largest."

Hannah's cheeks flushed, and she followed the other ladies down the path to the barn.

Punched tin lanterns hung from the beams, casting delicate patterns of light into the floors and walls. George and Mr. Gould had set up large kegs of cider, while Papa and William organized chairs for everyone. Of course, the great pile of corn to be husked loomed in the corner.

"For my favorite sister." George handed Annalisa a mugful of cider and slung his arm about her. "And this year, if you find that red ear, I think you should just hand it over to me."

"La!" Annalisa threw his arm from her. "That ear is mine."

George bellowed a boisterous howl, and his gaze flew to the door. "Jack! Ollie."

Jack, with fiddle and bow poking from his haversack,

approached them. "Cousin. Miss Annalisa." He bowed. "This is my first husking. I hope you don't mind I've brought my fiddle."

"'Tis always welcome." George clapped his shoulder. "Mr. Averill and his son, Josiah, will play as well."

The crowd in the barn grew as Quinnapin, Samuel Wildes, Ezra Kimball, and Josiah Averill joined. Lord and Lady Perkins with Steven Perkins and his wife, and David and Eunice Perkins, Mamma and Papa, Mr. and Mrs. Andrews, and Mr. Averill stood near the back, as the older generation tended to do at such frolics.

Papa clapped his hands and the murmurs dulled to a quiet. "Welcome and good-evening ladies and gentlemen. Thank you all for attending this year's husking. Afterward, we've ample food and drink. Let's get the task underway."

The young men cheered, the ladies clapped, and everyone found seats around the big circle. Annalisa settled beside Abigail.

"Think you I'll find a red ear?" Abigail asked. "Martha says 'tis good luck."

"I found one last year, but George chased me into the fields until I gave it up to him." Annalisa leaned in and whispered, "I was supposed to get a kiss from Samuel."

Abigail squealed with delight. "Is that the prize? A kiss for whoever finds a red ear?"

Annalisa smirked and took an armful of corn into her lap. She slid the silken husk from the first few.

Yellow.

She tossed them into a wooden barrel beside her.

Abigail murmured, "Pray tell, who should you like to kiss this year?"

Annalisa warmed. *How can I tell Abigail I want to kiss Jack? She loathes the other girls who ogle him.*

"Perhaps...Quinn. Or Samuel."

Abigail gave a cheeky grin. "I do like Quinn very much. Samuel is handsome, too."

Mr. Averill's guitar overtook the hushed murmurs and Annalisa glanced about the circle. Hannah French glared at Jane, who sat between Oliver and Jack. Martha gave fleeting glances toward William, and George drank cider with Quinn and Mr. Gould. Lizzie sat upon Ezra Kimball's lap, and Samuel sang to Mr. Averill's guitar. Fannie and Josiah tore through their corn in silence.

Annalisa reached into her pile and husked. Yellow again. She tossed them into the bucket. The husking felt to endure ages, though many hands made light work; but it was the anticipation of finding that pin the haystack which made it all the more insufferable. Annalisa sat back and finished her cider. She stood and found her way to George and Mr. Gould, who readily served her more drink. When she returned to her place by Abigail, her pile had diminished to nothing.

"Miss Annalisa."

Jack Perkins held up his last two ears of corn and tossed one to her. He handed the other to Jane.

Annalisa caught it readily, her heart racing.

"Let's see if they're red." Fannie's plump cheeks glistened in the dim lanternlight.

"Both? Highly unlikely." Hannah crossed her arms. Her pile was husked, without a red ear.

Annalisa locked her stare with Jane. "One...two... three!" They tore into the corn, and Annalisa's innards contorted. "Yellow."

Jane peered at Jack. "Red."

"That is half red, Miss Howlett." Oliver pointed. "Does that count?"

"Of course it counts," Ezra cried from across the circle.

Jack grinned at Jane. "If you'd like a kiss, Miss Howlett, I'm happy to oblige."

The gentlemen—save for Oliver—hooted and whistled. Annalisa wanted to look away, but found herself gaping as Jack kissed Jane. A pang of regret surfaced as she looked down at the yellow ear of corn in her lap.

Is this Jane's first kiss? Will they begin a courtship after tonight?

Annalisa finished her cider in two gulps and removed herself from the circle. At least it wasn't Oliver who kissed Jane.

As the husking came to a close, Mamma and Papa helped Addy and Liza bring out the platters of apple pies, fresh new-skimmed milk cheese with hot biscuits, and pumpkin. Hannah, Fannie, and Lizzie surrounded Jane, and Jack joined Mr. Averill and Josiah with his fiddle.

George pulled Annalisa to the keg. "Next year, Little One."

"You think I wanted to kiss Jack?" Annalisa laughed. "Hardly."

"That comes as a surprise." George scratched his ear. "It seems every girl here, save for Abby of course, wants to marry him. You don't find the same of yourself?"

"La! No." Annalisa crossed her arms. "No, not in the least. I don't wish to marry at all..."

"Jane, you must look into the well. Perhaps you'll see Jack's face!" Fannie cried.

"No, that never works." Lizzie, the self-professed

fortune-teller of the ladies, stepped forward. "We must roast nuts over the fire."

Annalisa looked to George. "Of all the husking traditions that are ridiculous. Divination never works."

George laughed. "Come, Little One. If 'tis so ridiculous, you can hardly deny yourself the amusement."

"George is right." Abigail sidled up beside her. "Let's have Lizzie read our fortunes."

When most of the food had been eaten, and the adults returned to the house to tell their own stories, they all ambled outside behind the barn. Giddy, the girls chattered about their fortunes, while George and Quinn started a fire.

"Think you Lizzie has any ability to foretell the future?" Jack carried a small bucket of apples.

Annalisa turned from Abigail and met his dubious stare.

"I think she has as much ability in telling the future as I do of being a man."

Jack chuckled. "Fair enough. Will you come sit by the fire with us?"

Annalisa shook her head. "I'm quite well here. I'd rather not disturb the fortune-telling with my disbelief."

"Nonsense, Annie." Abigail pulled her into the circle. "Sit by me."

Annalisa sighed, and settled beside her friend. She watched as Lizzie roasted her few nuts over the fire, and assigned couples among them.

"Oh, look!" Abigail leapt from her seat. "The nuts jumped apart."

"That means you and Samuel will not end up together," Lizzie said.

Several more nuts were roasted, some burned and some jumped apart.

"Let's read Annie's," Fannie cried.

Annalisa sat forward and gripped her skirts. "Me? No, please."

"Aye." George rumbled with laughter. "Miss I-Don't-Wish-To-Marry. Let's see what the future has in store for you."

"All will be well," Abigail whispered, but Annalisa turned from the fire.

She stared into the fields that had been swallowed by night. Above, the glittering heavens promised the unknown, though behind her, friends thought they could foretell fate.

Laughter erupted from the circle and she turned.

"What is it? Has something happened?"

Lizzie reached into the barrel of apples. "Miss Annalisa, peel this." She tossed her the piece of fruit.

Annalisa caught it, and George handed her his pocket knife. "Just humor us, Little One."

She gritted her teeth and peeled the apple in one solid ribbon of skin.

The ladies clapped, and Lizzie stepped forward. "Now, toss the peel behind you."

Annalisa did as she was told, and Lizzie rushed from the circle to read the apple peel. "'Tis as I predicted. The letter 'J'."

Annalisa crossed her arms. "And what does that mean?"

"That you'll marry Jack Perkins."

Hannah and Fannie giggled.

"Josiah is also present. Could it not also be him?" She searched for Josiah's gaze, but he avoided her stare.

"No." Lizzie returned to the fire and smirked. "When we tossed the hazelnuts into the flames, yours and Jack's burned steadily together. Yours and Josiah's leapt away from one another."

George howled, and several others joined in his laughter. "What say you to marriage now, Little One?"

Her face and neck hot, Annalisa knew not if she should laugh with them, or cry. She turned from the circle but Jane's hand found her wrist.

"'Tis just a silly lark, Annie."

Jack jumped from the circle and soon, his light baritone and fiddle filled the void.

Mid-song, he snickered jovially and said, "Miss Annalisa, for you, my future bride.

At the harvest fair, she'll be surely there
So I'll dress in my Sunday clothes,
With my shoes shone bright and my hat cocked right
for a smile of a nut brown rose..."

She tingled at the address, though she knew it was in jest. Jack, too, seemed cynical of Lizzie's fortune-telling. Everyone about the circle found it amusing that she and Jack should wed. A twinge of pain wrenched her insides.

Is it that ridiculous a thought?

Annalisa forced a smile. "Well done, sir."

"Really, Jack?" Oliver scowled. "You're Father's heir. Must you continue like this? This whole corn husking frolic charade—whatever you call it—'tis a bunch of foolish games for children." He stood. "You'll hardly behave this way when we are in Europe."

Annalisa's throat closed and she glared at Abigail.

Europe? For how long? Why didn't Abigail say anything?

With not a second thought for her role in the militia, coldness slipped into her breast. She shared an attachment for the same man her sister fancied, this same man who would be leaving to cross the Atlantic.

ANNALISA
IPSWICH, MAY 1772

ANNALISA LACED HER JUMP, tied on her petticoats and pockets, and pinned closed her gown. She hurried down the garret ladder, lifted a bucket of pig feed, and hauled it to the pigpen.

"*Wuneekeesuq!*"

Quinnapin, kneeling by the trough, peered up and grinned. "*Wuneekeesuq.* I'll take the bucket, Miss Anna." He stood, took the heavy pail, and tossed the stinking pig feed into the trough.

"Thank you. I was supposed to feed them earlier, but was detained this morning in Danvers." She faltered, afraid she'd said too much.

He nodded. "No need to explain to me, Miss Anna."

For some reason, he could be trusted. "I've been—"

"Annalisa." Mamma stepped from the house. "I don't wish to keep Lady Perkins waiting."

Annalisa wiped her sweaty, calloused palms on her bodice then brushed hay from her skirts. "My apologies, Quinn. I'm being summoned." She rolled her eyes. They shared a brief chuckle, and Annalisa dashed toward her house.

She met her mother and Jane along the path.

"Where have you been?" Mamma sniffed. "Your skirts are in disarray, and where is your hat?"

"I was helping Quinnapin feed the hogs, marm," she half-lied.

I must manage my time better in this militia.

She followed Jane down the path and into the chaise. Zeke pulled the reins and drove them down the lane.

On this particular day, Ipswich bustled with all manner of patrons, no doubt readying for the first public ball on Friday. Annalisa, holding a bag of new ribbons, walked arm-in-arm with Jane and Abigail over the Choate Bridge. A gentle gust blew off the brackish Ipswich River. When they reached the milliner's shop, Lady Perkins stopped.

"Lord Essex, a prominent Whig and member of Parliament, is in Cambridge this summer. I heard he will be attending the ball on Saturday."

"The ball is Saturday?" Annalisa pursed her lip.

I thought it was Friday! I have drill practice Saturday morning. Mamma will never let me miss such a ball if gentry will be present.

"A lord attending a public ball?" Mamma fanned herself.

"He's friends with my father, Mrs. Howlett," Abigail said. "Papa plans to facilitate an acquaintance."

Jane adjusted her hat. "And will your brothers be there as well, Miss Perkins?"

"Of course. 'Twill be our last chance to see them before they sail for England."

"Quite." Jane poked her head in the window of the

milliner's shop then faced Annalisa. "Annie, you must dance the minuet. Perhaps Mr. Oliver will ask you."

Annalisa fingered the pineapple necklace at her throat. She'd escaped dancing the minuet last season, but it was a matter of time before she'd have to dance it. "Only if I'm asked."

I'd rather be shot by a round.

"You've been practicing well, my darling." Mamma picked a piece of hay from Annalisa's shoulder. "I'm sure plenty of...gentlemen...will ask you to dance."

"You must ready yourself, Miss Annalisa." Lady Perkins slipped inside the shop behind Abigail. "With a peer in attendance, a minuet will be played."

⚜

ON SATURDAY MORNING, ANNALISA'S EYES WATERED AS Dinah galloped the road to Danvers. There wasn't a chance she'd miss drill practice, but she must leave in time to ready for the ball.

Nathaniel approached with his musket and cartridge box. "Cav, how good to see you."

Annalisa dismounted and tied Dinah to a fence. "Good-day, Nat. Is Captain Foster here yet? I'm on a bit of a time constraint."

"The Ipswich Ball. Are you going, too?"

She startled. "Oh, la. That ridiculousness? No. But my cousins are. I promised to see them off."

"I see." Nathaniel lifted his musket and wiped soot from the barrel with a handkerchief. "I'll be there with my sister, Sarah. I couldn't convince her otherwise. Apparently, some fancy lord will be present."

Annalisa shrugged, pretending she hadn't heard about Lord Essex.

But now I must take care in seeing Nathaniel at the ball. Hopefully, he won't recognize me in a gown—

Captain Foster approached, jarring her from her thoughts. "All right, gentlemen, let's begin."

Annalisa followed to her line and stood at attention, her fowling piece propped beside her.

"Shoulder your firelock."

She lifted the fowler.

"Join your right hand to your firelock. Recover your arms."

Annalisa brought the fowler in front of her, then cradled it in the crook of her left arm.

"Come to your priming position. Half-cock your firelock. Handle cartridge."

She held the piece and half-cocked the hammer. With her right hand, she reached into her cartridge box and removed the paper filled with gunpowder and musket round.

"Open cartridge."

She bit off the tail end of paper and spit it to the ground.

"Prime pan."

Thinking of George, she dribbled a small amount of gunpowder into the priming pan, something she wished she'd done the day she'd burned her cheek.

"Shut pan. Load with cartridge."

Annalisa pushed forward the steel to close the priming pan, then brought her fowler to her left side. From this position, she poured the bulk of the cartridge into the muzzle, followed by the lead round, still wrapped in paper.

"Draw your rammer. Ram down your charge."

She withdrew the ramrod and inserted it down the barrel, packing it all home.

"Return rammers. Shoulder your firelock," Captain Foster shouted. "Make ready. Cock your firelock."

Annalisa brought the stock of the fowler to her shoulder, the lock level with her chin, and fully cocked.

"Pree-sent. Fire!"

The crack of over thirty fowlers and muskets was akin to a fierce summer storm without rain, with only clouds of gun smoke to clog the air. They continued to practice this dance of death for another hour, until Captain Foster adjourned practice.

Annalisa plucked her linen handkerchief from her coat pocket. "When my brother taught me, there was still a bloody tax on lead." She wiped Bixby clean. "He made me shoot blanks, which made it near impossible to recognize an accurate shot."

Nathaniel cocked his head. "You mean the Townshend Acts?"

"Aye."

"That was repealed what, two years ago?" Ebenezer asked.

"Aye." Annalisa set her jaw. "But they never dissolved the tax on tea. I can't understand why we don't have representation in Parliament. 'Tis not right."

"Hear, hear, Cavendish." Ebenezer slapped her back.

Nathaniel slung his musket over his shoulder. "Bloody tea tax."

Annalisa bit her lip, trying not to smile. These men listened to her. They cared, even agreed with her sentiments.

"Join us at the tavern, Ben." Ebenezer adjusted his strap. "There's a mighty fine flip I'm sure you'll enjoy."

She wavered. "I would, but I'm promised to my cousins this evening."

"Then we'll expect you next time, Master Cavendish." He tipped his hat. "Good evening."

Annalisa rushed to her horse, mounted, and galloped away to the north. She was late.

"ANNALISA HOWLETT, YOU WILL LEAVE ME LIFELESS IN A grave." Mamma's frigid eyes overtook her entire face. "Pray tell, what could be so important to delay your readying for tonight? Speak!"

"Marm, I—"

"Your papa is with Quinnapin, searching for you." She grabbed Annalisa's shoulder and threw her toward the staircase. "He will teach you a lesson when he returns. Now go."

Annalisa ran up the stairs and into the room she shared with her sisters. Jane was already in her gown, and Liza's quick, pasty fingers curled her hair. Mary sat and watched, her face dripping with envy.

"Worry not." Annalisa slid beside Mary on the canopied bed. "You'll attend a ball someday." She whispered, "I'd rather stay here with you."

"No, you do not." Mary snickered. "Janey thinks you both will dance with George's cousins. Don't you want to dance with Jack Perkins?"

Jane applied her lavender perfume, barely looking at Annalisa. "I think you and Oliver would make a lovely pair.

Why don't you wear my blue petticoat with your white dress that has the cornflowers?"

A sinking feeling settled into her stomach. In her haste to pair Jane with Jack, her sister seemed quick in securing a match for her with Oliver. Nothing could be worse.

Now I must avoid two men tonight.

16

ANNALISA
IPSWICH, MAY 1772

ANNALISA LOOKED IN ALL directions for Nathaniel as she crowded into the assembly hall. She crinkled her nose against the thick body odor mingled with perfume. The tallow candles would soon blend their acrid stench to the air. Impervious to the aromas, gentlemen, and ladies with their chaperones, gathered, their chitter rife with hopes for a grand evening.

Abigail, in lovely yellow silk, and escorted by Jack and Oliver, glided toward her and Jane. She reached for Annalisa's hands. "Sweet friend, how lovely you look."

"Thank you, I—" Annalisa spotted Nathaniel across the room with his sister. She spun around and linked arms with Abigail. "Mr. Perkins!"

Jack stood with Oliver, both of whom seemed eager to engage with Jane. "Miss Annalisa." Jack regarded her with gentlemanly candor.

"How strange to hear Handel's *Water Music* at a public ball. I always imagined hearing such at a private ball."

He cocked his head. "Would you prefer Bach, Miss Annalisa?"

"Mozart. I adore him." She grinned impishly. "If you see him when you are in Vienna, do give him my regards."

"Oh, Annie." Jane rolled her eyes with Oliver.

"I shall." Jack laughed. "Have you any message for the maestro?"

"Tell him to write me a sonata."

"A proper request. One he could not refuse." Jack winked, then turned to Jane. "Miss Howlett, would you do me the honor of the first dance?"

"Of course, sir."

Jack whisked Jane away to the set, leaving Annalisa with Oliver, Abigail, and George.

George rubbed his forehead. "I'd rather be at my tavern burning East India Company tea leaves."

"When will they repeal the tea tax?" Annalisa asked.

"La." Abigail peered at George with her round, coffee-colored eyes. "Surely you will dance, Cousin."

George crossed his arms. "Not if I can help it."

Lord Perkins approached with a genteel-looking gentleman in a lavender silk suit with silver embroidery. His manicured white powdered wig suggested wealth and prestige.

"My dear." Lord Perkins gestured to Abigail. "Oliver, Miss Annalisa, and Mr. Howlett, it is my pleasure to present the Viscount Essex."

The viscount gave a short, polite bow. "The pleasure is mine." When he lifted his head, he revealed a row of straight white teeth, and a prominent chin dimple.

Curious such a man has escaped marriage for so long. Perhaps he is widowed.

"Miss Perkins, might I have the pleasure of this first dance?" Lord Essex held out his hand.

Abigail's freckled cheeks rouged. "Of course, my lord." She took his hand and he led her to the set, but not without first glancing back at George.

"A proper dandy, that one." George cackled.

"Fie, Cousin." Oliver glared. "As lord and member of Parliament, he's twice the man you are."

Lord Perkins clicked his tongue. "Ollie, speak to my nephew, your cousin, like that again and you shall find yourself without an inheritance." He turned on his heels and left them forthwith.

"My apologies." Oliver adjusted his crimson coat, then glanced at Annalisa. "Shall we dance?"

Her lip curled, ready to refuse him, when Nathaniel wandered toward her with a curious expression upon his face.

"Aye, sir." Annalisa grabbed Oliver's arm and pulled him toward the set.

"The first is a minuet, you know. I hope you've been practicing. 'Tis not for the fainthearted."

"I've been practicing for months."

Can I do this?

There was no going back. She lined up across from Oliver, and beside Jane. The first strings sounded, and the couples moved their feet in time to a count of six.

Jack danced with such grace, his foot light upon the dance floor, like Jane. Oliver danced well but with an air of pomp. Aloof, and never quite looking at her, he spoke not once.

When nearest Oliver, Annalisa asked, "Is there a rule you may not speak while dancing?"

"No."

She turned her nose up to him. "Your brother seems to converse well enough with my sister. Dare I suggest he means to court her?"

"Try as he may, though I'm not convinced she returns the sentiment."

During the promenade down the center of the room, Annalisa noticed Nathaniel at the outskirts of the assembly. She looked down as she danced by, and lost count of the steps.

"I see you're not talking," Oliver said.

"I must concentrate."

"There are distractions in every assembly room, Miss Annalisa. I suggest you adapt...and learn your place."

Annalisa's foot struck an immovable object and she tumbled forward. The glint of a silver shoe buckle caught her eye as her wrist braced her fall.

Oliver's shoe.

Angry heat flushed her face. Oliver held out his hand to her.

"How dare you."

"You can prove nothing," he whispered.

The violins and cellos paused. She scrambled to her feet and hurried from the set, her chest and neck burning as she passed the giggling spectators.

Near the entryway, Mamma intercepted. "Annalisa, what happened?"

"Please, leave me alone."

Annalisa pushed her way outside. Cool air lapped at her fiery skin. She slid behind the brick building and leaned against the wall. With her trembling hand, she wiped her cheeks.

"Miss Annalisa?" Jack Perkins turned the corner of the building. He reached into his pocket for a handkerchief. "May I?"

She nodded, and let him dry her tears. "Thank you."

He smiled. "Of course."

Jack never would have tripped me. Though, I can hardly prove Oliver did, either.

"Your brother is the worst kind of man."

Jack's brows knitted. "Ollie means well. I assure you. Your sister is quite convinced of a good match between you." His face softened and he cracked a gentle smile. "Perhaps you require a bit more practice, is all."

"A match?" Her stomach heaved. "More practice? You think I need more practice?"

"Like your spinet. You are accomplished, but even with that, there is room for improvement. The minuet is a rather difficult—"

"I beg your pardon." She gritted her teeth. "You think I need to practice the spinet the same way I must practice the minuet?"

"You play exceedingly well, please mistake me not. But when you play, 'tis like a metronome plunking each key in perfect rhythm. There's no...passion." His gaze held hers. "Pray tell, have you ever closed your eyes and let the music flow through you, regardless of what was written upon the page?"

"No. My papa would be displeased by such a display— my grandsire and great grandsire were Puritan." She wiped her face with his handkerchief.

"And that means you cannot play music as though you were to die tomorrow?" His lip puckered as though he would kiss her. "I've seen it in you...the life, the emotion that is hardly Puritan."

She crossed her arms. "What has this to do with my minuet this evening?"

"You know the steps, but you do not dance with passion, Annalisa. What is it you fear?"

"Fear?" She scoffed. "Did not you see what happened?"

"I saw you stumble—"

"Over your brother's foot. He tripped me."

"Ollie would never stoop so low."

"You dare call me a liar?"

"Peace, Annalisa." Jack rested a hand on her shoulder. "Your humiliation is also his. For what purpose would Oliver trip you?"

"To remind me of my place." Her jaw tightened. "My experience with Oliver runs deep...we are hardly a good match. But I don't wish to elaborate to someone who believes my spinet playing to be accomplished but insincere, my dancing intolerable, and my words fabricated." She curtsied. "Good-night, sir."

"No, Miss Annalisa, that's not...wait—"

She darted past him and into the assembly room, knowing very well she would not see him again for eighteen months.

17

JACK
THE NORTH ATLANTIC, JULY 1772

A MONTH AT SEA and several unfinished, crumpled letters to Annalisa Howlett, Jack's conscience still perseverated upon the Ipswich Ball back in May. Sore from the way he'd left her, he finally approached Oliver. His brother sat on a wooden crate, reading Voltaire.

"Ollie, what happened at the ball?"

Oliver looked up, then returned to his book.

"I'm quite serious." Jack crossed his arms.

Oliver peered up again, then slid one leg over the other. A damp sea breeze rustled his hair.

"You think I should admit to something I did not do."

"I continue to be vexed by the way Miss Annalisa behaved." Jack spun his signet ring around his pinky finger. "I can't imagine why she'd fabricate such a tale, and we parted ways in a most disagreeable manner."

"Miss Annalisa is ill-behaved, is she not?" Oliver marked his page and set the book in his lap. He studied

Jack for a moment, then a small smirk lifted his lips. "But what vexes you, dear brother?"

"She said her feelings for you run deep, or something to that effect." Jack sighed ruefully. "Did you, or did you not trip her during the minuet...to *remind her of her place...* as she put it?"

"Fie." Oliver's cheeks pinked. "She fell because of her own incompetent dancing. 'Tis a difficult dance when you haven't the proper tutor...which *is* a statement of her place in Society, whether you agree or not." He paused. "I would like to put this nonsense behind us."

"Quite." Jack bit his lip. "I suspected as much, but I—"

"Let's shake on it, dear brother." Oliver held out his hand. "So, there are no hard feelings between us."

Jack hesitated, unsure of whether he could be believed.

It would be easier to forgive Ollie than begrudge him these next several months.

He gripped Oliver's hand and shook it.

"Now," Oliver grinned, "let us detail the cities we're touring, beginning with London."

SALZBURG, AUSTRIA, APRIL 1773

NINE MONTHS INTO THEIR TOUR OF EUROPE, AND A two-week journey from Rome to Austria, Jack and Oliver entered the royal Austrian theatre, an imperial venue. According to local newspapers, Mozart had just been employed by the Salzburg court, and would conduct his newest symphony tonight. Jack vibrated with anticipation.

Gold filigree and vibrant paintings adorned the ceiling.

Oliver gloated watching Austria's most affluent, with their white powdered wigs and their profuse perfumes.

They moved to their seats in the balcony, alongside the other wealthy patrons. A strange prospect to behold, now that he lived in a humble farming town; a town he adored far more than this royal theatre.

"Miss Annalisa holds Mozart in higher regard to any other composer. I feel guilty sitting here in her absence." Jack frowned, the shame of their exodus haunting him.

Oliver snorted. "Nonsense. She wouldn't know what to do with herself. She may favor Mozart, but we know right well Farinelli won't be his castrato. Bach and Handel were superior to any other." He gave a lamented head-shake. "'Tis a shame they both now play their music for Heaven."

"Farinelli?" Jack scoffed. "He does not even sing anymore, therefore your argument is null. I'm anxious to listen tonight. For Miss Annalisa's sake."

Oliver chuckled. "And no consideration for lovely Miss Twysden in London."

An acrid burn rose into Jack's throat. "I knew not Miss Twysden was married to Lord Jersey. Had I known, I never would have strummed her in the dark walk."

"You needed to strum a lady. I merely facilitated the happening. Admit it—'twas better than milking your Thomas."

"Then you knew she was married to Lord Jersey?"

"Of course, I did. Everyone in London takes a lover. Lady Jersey is no different."

"Villain. And you said the corn husking games were childish charades." Jack's jaw set. "You did trip Miss Annalisa at the Ipswich Ball, didn't you?"

Oliver's face matched the scarlet of his coat. "What of

it? I also stole a kiss from Miss Annalisa when she visited Boston three years ago, if you recall. Shall we continue to recount these past pretenses?"

Jack's chest squeezed as though boulders had stacked upon him. He'd forgotten that night in Boston, or perhaps had forced it from his mind. Now, he saw it all—walking in on them in the firelit parlor—as though the scene were presently before him.

"Mean you to court her? Jane believes you to be a good match."

Oliver shrugged. "Sport."

"Sport?" Jack gripped his seat. "Miss Annalisa is as a sister to me, particularly if I marry Jane. I care little for your affairs, but I do ask if you pursue her, you behave as a gentleman. She is a lovely girl, deserving of any man's unrequited attention—"

A short, young man emerged from behind the curtain and stood before his orchestra. The gentleman could be no older than seventeen.

Is this youth the famous Wolfgang Amadeus Mozart?

The German chatter faded to silence, and the strings and horns blazed in triple forte. The hall itself vibrated from the grandiosity of the opening movement, and with the triumphant blares of the horn section, Jack's prejudice against Oliver washed away. Mozart was as gifted as Annalisa said.

18

JACK
VERSAILLES, SEPTEMBER 1773

THEIR APARTMENT AT VERSAILLES was small but boasted all the modern luxuries. Two canopied beds stood at opposite ends of the room, each with claret velvet curtains. A series of bronze sconces emitted golden glows upon ivory paneled walls. Yet, Jack found himself missing the simplicity of his Topsfield home. His family boasted one of the finer houses in town, but when compared to Versailles, such gratuitous extravagance overwhelmed.

Jack sat upon a velveteen settee and sipped a glass of wine. "I'm eager to return to Boston and our fellow Patriots." He lifted the newspaper. "It says here the royal assent of the Tea Act reached America."

"*Your* fellow Patriots." Oliver focused on tying his white linen cravat about his neck. "And the Tea Act is a good thing. The East India Company was near collapse."

Jack looked up. "Are you not Patriot?"

"I would say such rebelliousness from the Sons of Liberty is rather treasonous."

"Then you are a Tory."

"'Tis no matter. There will be no war between our allegiances." Oliver returned to the mirror and finished tying his cravat. "I plan on gaining several acquaintances of notable rank tonight. Perhaps we'll even catch a glimpse of the beautiful Madame du Barry."

Jack pursed his lips. With Oliver's admission and tensions swelling at home, he could hardly consider the ball tonight.

❧

JACK AND OLIVER ENTERED A GREAT HALL OF GILT AND mirrors. Vivaldi's orchestrations carried over French banter and ladies' giggles, all of whom were dressed to the nines. Jack peered at Oliver, who strutted through the luminescent space making eyes at any lady who would have him. One in particular gained Oliver's explicit attention.

"Bonjour, ma petite fleur." Oliver kissed her hand.

The Marquise du Cheney introduced herself, then proceeded to float beside Oliver like a little purple dove, decorated in shades of lavender from her hair to her silk-embroidered shoes. Many more ladies, several of them countesses, duchesses, and marquesses, flocked to Jack's side, eager to make his acquaintance, and more.

When he'd declined the twelfth lady to introduce herself and coax him into her bed—despite her husband's watchful stare—Jack excused himself to make water.

On his return to the hall, a gentleman approached and bowed.

"Ah, *Monsieur* Perkins, delighted."

Jack bowed. *"Bonsoir, Monsieur Beauregard."*

"I've just received a letter from your esteemed friend in London, Dr. Franklin. His sentiments of the impending revolt in Boston were quite rousing. I daresay, your colony has King Louis' attention."

Jack grinned. "Sir, that is good news." He turned. Oliver stood behind him with the marquise.

"You speak of Dr. Franklin," she said. "What an odd fellow. I believe he spent a week in the favor of my dear friend the *Comtesse de Boulainvilliers*. But you didn't hear such gossip from me, *monsieur*." She placed a gloved hand to her pouty painted lips, and winked.

The gentlemen chuckled and Monsieur Beauregard took her hand. "A pleasure, *madame, monsieurs*. Enjoy the ball. I hope we shall speak further, *Monsieur* Perkins. By your leave."

When he'd departed, Oliver's lip curled. "How could you speak of the rebellion to these Frenchmen? Lord Cornwallis, the British general, lingers yonder."

Jack shook his head. "We hardly spoke of it. And Beauregard initiated the intercourse."

"Forget the rebellion." Oliver threw his hand to his hip. "Can you not see the room is bursting with beautiful, eager ladies?"

"This is true, *monsieur.* I can introduce you to any lady you please." The marquise licked her lips.

"I daresay, such a sight is lost on me, my lady." Jack leaned toward Oliver. "We are on the brink of war."

Oliver stepped back. "You astound me. We are at Versailles—the center of the world—and you speak of war. Look you. Cornwallis mingles with not a care upon his face. War seems far from his mind, as it should be of yours. Come, let the marquise find you a lady."

Jack studied the dame on Oliver's arm. She babbled absentmindedly to a friend beside her. "Are you so willing to forfeit Miss Annalisa for some unsuspecting lady with a title?"

"Miss Annalisa?" Oliver's eyes widened. "I've not once proclaimed an attachment for her, and I'll certainly not hinder my enjoyment tonight for the mere possibility of courting Miss Howlett upon our arrival home."

Jack clenched his fists. "*Jane?* You know I would like to court Jane Howlett. And might I remind you, you kissed Miss Annalisa—most violently."

"I told you my interest is merely for sport."

"Then you admit to exploiting the young lady in a most vile way."

"I'll admit nothing."

Jack held his gaze. "I had thought twice about gifting Miss Annalisa the music I bought her in Salzburg. I feared it might impede upon your budding romance. Now, I daresay I shall most heartily give it to her. Hopefully, it will act as a peacemaker between us when we return. I owe her a heartfelt apology. And you owe her far more than that." He turned to leave. "Enjoy your marquess."

☙❧

THE FOLLOWING AFTERNOON, JACK BURST INTO THEIR apartment, and tripped over a set of panniers in front of the door. He steadied himself and straightened his velvet coat.

Oliver lay in bed, the blankets strewn about, and clothing peppered the floor. Jack banged a fist upon the mantle to stir the couple in bed.

The marquise rolled onto her stomach. "All this noise at so early an hour."

"Ollie, I suggest you get the chambermaid to start packing your things."

Oliver sat up. "What for?"

"There's a rebellion I wish to be a part of. You may have aligned yourself with the Loyalists, but I have not." Jack turned to the door. "I've taken the liberty of booking us on an earlier vessel. We depart tomorrow."

19

ANNALISA
TOPSFIELD, NOVEMBER 30, 1773

H ER STOMACH IN KNOTS and her lower
abdomen cramping, Annalisa awoke. The black
shroud of early morning obscured much of the room she
shared with her sisters. Her knees to her chest, she curled
into a ball and a trickle, followed by a greater gush, flowed
between her legs.

Have I made water?

She jumped from the bed.

"Annie?" Mary's sleepy voice filled the darkness.

"Annie, what's wrong?" Jane asked.

Annalisa fumbled with a paper spill and held it to the
banked embers in the fireplace. "I've made water, but I
cannot understand why." She lit a chamberstick and held it
aloft, bathing the room in gold. She grabbed her wet shift.
It stained red. "'Tis blood!"

Addy rushed into the room. "I heard a cry. Everything
well with you girls?"

Jane sat up and pulled back the coverlet. The bed, too,
was stained. "Oh, Addy, Annalisa's gotten her menses." She

looked to Annalisa. "Have you not experienced your courses before now? Surely, you've taken notice each month of dark staining in your shift..."

"Oh, the morbid flux," Annalisa cried. "I've had some dark discharge since my sixteenth birthday this past spring, but it was infrequent. I assumed that was the extent of it." Agitated, she paced the room.

Mary hugged her knees. "I don't ever wish to have the morbid flux."

"If only it could be so, Miss Mary." Addy smiled ruefully. "But you're eleven, and I've seen most girls get it much younger than Miss Annie. It could be coming for you soon." She turned to Annalisa. "Here, let's get you a flux apron to wear beneath your shift."

"I've got one she can use." Jane shuffled from the bed and rummaged through her trunk. She handed the linen apron to Addy.

Addy tugged at the linen. "This will do. And I'll stitch you two aprons to alternate out."

"Why has Mamma never taught me thus?" Annalisa sat on the bed and massaged her forehead.

"Mamma never told me either until I came to her with that ruined silk petticoat, remember?" Jane rubbed Annalisa's arm. "Then she gave me a flux apron to wear."

"Your momma is a busy woman." Addy sat beside Annalisa. "Here, Miss Annie. Put this on." She handed her Jane's apron.

Annalisa stood, lifted up her shift and tied the apron about her waist, then twisted it so the fabric hung over her rear. She gathered it between her legs, and pulled it up and through the tie in front, as she'd seen Jane do over the years.

"You're truly a woman, now." Jane smiled. "And no one will know, I promise."

Annalisa pulled down her shift over the flux apron, and sat on the bed beside Mary. "Stay a young girl as long as possible. Womanhood is cruel."

Mary's eyes rounded with melancholic fear. "I'll try."

"'Tis not so bad, Annie. I promise." Jane's soothing reminder did quell her initial anxiety. And she was right, no one would notice the flux apron beneath all her layers of clothes. But the agitation of militia drill practice later today loomed like a grey storm cloud blotting out all traces of sunlight.

Annalisa chewed her bottom lip. *Men have no courses to worry about. How will I conceal this in breeches?*

THAT AFTERNOON, ANNALISA SNUCK INTO THE BARN. She retrieved her menswear from beneath a crate in the loft and doffed her day dress, petticoats, and stays. With care, she tucked, smoothed and folded the diaper linen between her legs and over her rear and pulled up the breeches over the extra fabric.

A tad bulky, but my waistcoat and coat should hide it.

Annalisa finished dressing, climbed down the ladder, and mounted her mare for Danvers.

Drill practice ended early, thankfully, at the behest of Mr. Proctor, who'd demanded a meeting at the local tavern. He led the way, and Annalisa followed with Nathaniel and Ebenezer. Carefully, she stepped inside the small, smoky tavern and sat across from her friends. Nathaniel ordered a pitcher of flip.

"Gentlemen." Mr. Proctor stood from his chair. "The Tea Act has been sanctioned since May. We've done all we can boycotting British tea and smuggling it from the Dutch, but now *The Dartmouth* has docked in Boston Harbor, carrying East India Company Tea. 'Tis legal, and far cheaper than the smuggled Dutch stuff."

"We must continue to boycott." Annalisa tingled, surprised by her outspokenness. But when the room quieted, she stood. "Gentlemen, the East India Company's monopoly on the tea trade will not only put smugglers out of business, but also legal merchants who aren't consignees of the East India Company."

"Hear, hear." Ebenezer raised his mug.

"Furthermore," she added, "what's to stop Parliament from issuing monopolies on other goods?"

"Aye," Nathanial said.

"Hear, hear!"

Annalisa slammed a fist onto the table. "And it stands to be said, gentlemen, we still have no representation in Parliament, a grave concern for us all."

"Aye. Cav is right." Ebenezer rose. "The law states *The Dartmouth* must be unloaded of its cargo, and duties paid within twenty days. I heard Samuel Adams suggested at a town meeting in Boston yesterday, the ship be sent back to England with its cargo so we may avoid paying import duties."

"Aye!"

"Send back the ship!"

The room filled with "huzzahs" and "hear, hears," and Annalisa hid her grin behind her mug. Her voice was heard —and valued. If only she could attend George's tavern as openly, without fear of being recognized.

Satisfied by her disguise, she leaned back in her chair and finished the bitter flip. The alcohol did wonders for her menstrual cramps, which had mostly subsided once she had started drill practice. Her mind wandered to Jack and Oliver, and if they were in the middle of the cold North Atlantic.

What would Jack say of the Tea Act? Might he indulge me upon his return?

She stiffened in her seat. The disagreeable way they'd parted eighteen months ago left her doubting his consideration to debate with her. Though now, she was a woman.

$\mathcal{H}$ 20 $\mathcal{H}$

JACK
BOSTON, DECEMBER 16, 1773

THE SKY OVER BOSTON faded to twilight, and Jack stood with Oliver on the dock at South Battery with their travel trunks. The town seemed almost deserted, save for a couple of sailors' wives lurking nearby. Rather than follow Ollie to Aunt Catherine's coach parked in Milk-street, Jack approached one of the women.

"Pray tell, madam, where are all the gentlemen?"

The lady regarded him with desperation. "Sir, they're at the body of the people."

Jack turned his head. "Which meetinghouse?"

"Old South," the woman replied. "They've been debating the tea tax all day. They are awaiting Mr. Rotch's return from Milton. He's paid Governor Hutchinson a visit."

"Thank you, madam." Jack faced Oliver. "Shall we venture to the meeting?"

Oliver groaned. "Are you daft? You'll have me attend some town meeting after I've endured an eight-week crossing of the Atlantic? I'd like a nice brandy and the comforts of Aunt Catherine's fire. If you wish to attend, you'll have to go without me." He followed Mr. Scott and Mr. Henley, their aunt's coachmen, who hauled their trunks.

Jack called after him, "Tell Aunt I'll return when the meeting's adjourned." With a steady pace, he marched up Milk-street to Old South Meetinghouse.

A group of men, assembled in the doorway and outside of the large brick building, pushed their way inside.

"Good sirs, I beg your pardon—"

"Come, come. Mr. Rotch has just arrived." A man ushered Jack into the crowded meetinghouse.

The great hall smelled of musk and oak, and every pew and balcony seat occupied. Shouts and ravings echoed off the white walls with clamor.

At the pulpit, Mr. Salvage, with stern countenance, rapped his gavel. "Silence, silence. Let Mr. Rotch speak."

Samuel Adams stood, and the assembly dulled to murmurs. "Mr. Rotch, what say you of the governor? Will Hutchinson allow you to send your ships back to London with their cargo?"

Though Jack stood in the back he noticed Dr. Warren in a pew near the front. The doctor's face distorted and his brows furrowed.

Mr. Rotch walked before the assembly, his shoulders rounded and face sullen. With fumbling hands, he gripped his hat. "Hutchinson has...denied...the request."

An eruption of hisses and "fies" heated the meeting-house, drowning out the force of Salvage's gavel.

A man shouted, "Who knows how tea mingles with sea water?"

"Boston Harbor, a teapot tonight!"

They mean to destroy the tea. But how can they enact such a scandalous plot?

"Gentlemen." Samuel Adams' voice rose above the jeers. "Gentlemen, please. At midnight, we must pay the levy. We've appealed to Hutchinson now for twenty days. There is nothing else we can do to save the country."

"Mohawks are coming," a voice called from the balcony.

"To Griffin's Wharf."

"Huzzah!"

Jack followed the hoard of men outside. The cold, salty air nipped his face. He held onto his hat and weaved through the crowd. Frantic, he sought anyone willing to make eye contact.

"What is happening? Where are we going?"

A man in his middle thirties paused before entering a brick rowhouse. He looked both ways and pulled Jack aside. "We're headed to Griffin's Wharf. We're operating with the Sons of Liberty."

"May I join you?"

The man grunted. "Not dressed like that." He pushed Jack inside and, in the darkness, grabbed two wool blankets from a wooden chest. "We're costuming as Mohawks. Ye need to put this on and conceal yer face." He handed a lantern to Jack.

Jack swiped his fingers into the soot and smudged the greasy lampblack onto his forehead and cheeks, far better paint than the stuff worn by the ladies at Versailles.

"Have ye a weapon?"

"No, sir." Jack started. "Mean we to fight?"

"Nay. I'll lend ye me hatchet."

Jack took the tool. "Thank you, sir. And what might you be called?"

The man shook his head. "No names tonight, sir. We operate without identity."

"Of course." Jack's throat tightened. Such an act was treason, and to be caught meant being tried and imprisoned. *What will Father say if he finds out?*

With not a moment to reconsider, the man cackled, and shoved Jack outside into the street. "Tonight, we purge the ships *Dartmouth*, *Eleanor,* and *Beaver* of their tea."

"Rally Mohawks, and bring your axes, and tell King George we'll pay no taxes on his foreign tea."

The chant echoed up and down Milk-street as they marched to the wharf.

The beckoning rhyme stood Jack's hair on end. "You mean to jettison all the tea crates?" He exhaled his anxiety. It sounded like the town had appealed to Hutchinson several times with little effect. They had no option but to engage in this act of defiance. Or pay the hefty tax.

If only George and Quinn were here.

"His threats are vain, and vain to think, to force our girls and wives to drink his vile Bohea."

Engulfed by the chanting, the man pushed Jack along, where they slipped among the sea of lanterns to Griffin's Wharf.

When they forced themselves onboard the creaking *Dartmouth*, an anonymous man spoke to the captain. "Sir, if you go to your cabin without a fuss, we'll not hurt the remaining goods. 'Tis the tea we want, and the tea we'll have."

To Jack's surprise, the captain acquiesced and ordered his sailors, "Below deck, the lot of you. Else, lend a hand." He then escaped down the stairs to his quarters.

"To the brig, gentlemen," a man in disguise shouted. "Carefully remove the inoffensive cargo, then we haul the crates of tea."

৩১৩

AN HOUR INTO THE RAID, JACK HACKED THROUGH THE tea crates' rough canvas. With his sleeves rolled to his elbows, he and his new friend lifted a hundred-pound crate of bohea over the rail. A flurry of black leaves cascaded down onto the mudflat.

"Too bad the tide's gone out." Jack wiped his perspiring brow. "I don't think I've ever seen it so low."

Below, several men scurried to spread the heaping piles of tea leaves into the shallow water, but the mudflat only created a mess.

"Aye. Looks like the harbor will be a teapot come morning. That arse Hutchinson demanded these ships be unloaded. Well, they're being unloaded...into the harbor!" His friend echoed a throaty chortle into the December night.

Jack hoisted a smaller box of bohea and emptied it overboard, then tossed the wooden container after it. "And when we've finished?"

For the first time all night, his friend's jovial countenance melted into grim sobriety. "We retreat quietly to our homes and dare not speak to *anyone* of this night, lest we condemn ourselves to treachery."

Jack wiped his soiled palms on his breeches, and

tucked loose strands of hair behind his ear. In all this turmoil, there was no way for his identity to be uncovered.

But what can I say when Father hears the news? Surely, he will suspect my participation if he sees me return to Aunt Catherine's in such a disheveled state, with soot upon my face.

"I swear I'll not speak of it to anyone."

His friend glanced into the inky harbor beyond the brig. "Admiral Montagu's marines float in their vessels yonder."

The British loomed like an impending blizzard just offshore, their ships' strongholds threatening with huge guns.

Jack furrowed his brows. "I wonder they haven't stopped us."

"They won't fire on us—the proximity be much too close to town."

It was true. The cannonade from such guns would send Boston into a flurry of flames.

When the last tea crate was emptied and disposed of, Jack lifted his hat and shook any rogue tea leaves overboard.

"And your shoes, gentlemen," a man cried from the helm as he swept debris from the deck.

Jack unbuckled his shoes and clapped them over the rail, spilling bits of tea leaves onto the mudflats below. Not a single piece of evidence could be found on him.

As they marched back down Griffin's Wharf to the musical flouting of a fife, Admiral Montagu stuck his head out a window.

When they passed, Montagu yelled, "Well boys, you have had a fine, pleasant evening for your Indian caper, haven't you? But mind, you have got to pay the fiddler yet!"

৩৯৫৬

THE FOLLOWING NIGHT, JACK SAT IN AUNT CATHERINE'S parlor on Tory Row in Cambridge. Oliver sat silently sipping his brandy, but Father's round face glowed redder than a boiled beet as he stood by the fireplace.

"Three-hundred-forty-two crates of tea into the harbor. The *Gazette* is calling it *'the late transaction in Boston'*."

News of the ransack had spread like smallpox. Father paced before the hearth and puffed his pipe, while Aunt Catherine and Oliver looked on, their faces twisted with grievous doubt.

Jack stood tall. "I hear it was organized, sir. A peaceful protest."

"Peaceful or not, 'twas an act of treason. I hardly agree with the Tea Act, or the control Parliament and the East India Company have imparted on tea. But I daresay, we may end up paying the duty anyhow. The ruffians, those Sons of Liberty."

"But sir, it was said not a single item else on board those ships was so much as touched."

"How could you know such information?" Oliver's eyes narrowed. "Were you there? Did you partake in this traitorous event?"

Jack fisted his hands under the scrutiny. "I was not."

"You were," Oliver jeered. "I found a hatchet in your trunk last night, covered in soot. And you still bear the remnant of lampblack under your fingernails. Are you entirely determined to sully our family name at all cost?"

Jack glanced at his hands. He'd taken great care to clip

and clean his nails when he returned from the raid, but the soot was embedded.

Father's nostrils flared and he grabbed Jack's hands. "You didn't."

"No. Of course not." Jack pulled free and crossed his arms. "Ollie, you dare accuse me of treason?"

"Admit your treachery, you rebellious lout. You humiliated our family enough while we were in France."

"You lie."

"Ollie, for shame." Aunt Catherine frowned.

Father set down his pipe. "Jack, is this true?"

Oliver faced Father. "Sir, Jack made no attempt to conceal his connection with the rebels. He sought any Frenchman at Versailles who would hear his plights for freedom in the colonies. And this was all in the presence of Lord General Cornwallis. I am sure the gentleman overheard the nature of his treasonous tongue."

Father's forehead vein bulged. "Jack, I know where your principles lie, but to engage in such topics of discussion at a ball?"

"No, sir, he lies." Jack ground his teeth. "Ollie, that account is false. I spoke with one gentleman by the name of Beauregard, who sought *me* out. The exchange was brief and cordial. That was exactly how the intercourse went, and your rotten Tory self knows it."

"Enough." Father slammed his fist against the fireplace mantel. A small reverberating wave rattled the clock and wavered the candle flames. Jack and Oliver stood at attention. "Tory, Patriot. These are mere words. Remember, you are brothers above these." He regarded Jack, his face no longer red with anger. "I want to believe you. And Ollie,

I'll be damned if you slander your brother with indecency. I'm no Tory. You both know that. But neither am I radical. Jack, you must look to gentlemanly ways of dissent. I'll not have one son gallivanting about with the Sons of Liberty while the other accuses his own brother of treason."

21

ANNALISA
TOPSFIELD, DECEMBER 1773

A NNALISA SAT WITH HER needlepoint canvas
in Martha Perley's parlor with Jane, Hannah French,
Fannie Shepard, and Lizzie Balch.

"Jack and Oliver Perkins have returned." Hannah
giggled. "'Tis why Abigail declined the invitation today."

Annalisa looked up from her canvas. It had been a long
eighteen months of waiting, wondering, hoping she could
make amends with Jack Perkins. Her anxiety heightened,
but something about the news relieved her. They'd
returned in good health and unharmed.

Jane blushed, but kept her head lowered, her little
needle pointing upward and outward. "Lady Perkins
invited us to spend Twelfth Night dinner at their estate. I
can hardly wait to see how cultured they must be from
spending so much time in Europe."

"How lucky you are to see them so soon, and that your
families are so close." Fannie's round face glowed.

"'Tis because of George." Annalisa pushed aside her
canvas. "He is their cousin, after all." Her nerves gnawed

her insides at the thought of seeing Oliver again. He so often left her feeling humiliated. But in their time apart, she'd found her voice within the militia—a voice she meant to carry into her newfound womanhood.

"Miss Howlett, perhaps you'll finally receive an offer from Jack Perkins." Fannie heaved a dreamy sigh. "He's the handsomest man I've ever seen."

Annalisa laughed. "If Abigail was here, she'd reproach you for such talk."

"That is why I say it in her absence," Fannie replied, her plump fingers hard at work.

"Do you all still find him this agreeable?" Annalisa surveyed their faces. They each nodded.

"Annalisa, must you ask something so absurd? He's the finest gentleman in town, if not the province." Hannah made a knot in her thread. "I bet he'd make an excellent lover. Quite the lobcock I've noticed."

"Miss French." Martha gasped. "How can you tell?"

Hannah smirked. "He and Oliver are the only men in town who wear silk breeches with nary a wrinkle. 'Tis impossible not to wonder what's beneath them."

The other ladies tittered, but Annalisa looked to Jane. Her sister's porcelain cheeks flushed a delicate rouge.

Does Jane, too, ponder these things about Jack Perkins, or any man for that matter?

"I disagree," said Lizzie. "I think Jack would be a selfish lover. He knows how handsome he is. Why would he bother being considerate when so many of us would do anything to see what's beneath those breeches?"

Jane fanned herself. "I cannot continue with this conversation."

"I agree with Jane. We should cease this intercourse."

Annalisa's temples throbbed. All this ladies' chatter was enough to dizzy her. "If I may change the subject, George mentioned a motion came to pass with the tea tax—"

"Oh, Miss Annalisa, nothing about that silly tea." Hannah clasped her hands to her bosom.

"'Tis all I hear about from my papa and brothers," Fannie complained.

Jane gave her a look as though she knew the ladies would react this way.

Annalisa bit her lip and returned to her needlepoint. *There must be more to know about what became of those ships and the tea on board.*

❧

THE FOLLOWING NIGHT, LONG AFTER HER SISTERS FELL asleep, Annalisa crept from their freezing bedchamber, and snuck outside to the barn with naught but a lantern and her wool cloak. There, she donned her Benjamin Cavendish clothes and rode to George's tavern.

From down the road, she made out the dim, flickering light of the Peat Moss Inn. On dark winter nights, when snow blew about, its faint glow was barely recognizable. Chilled, she dismounted, tied Dinah to the maple, and hurried down the lane.

As soon as she opened the rear door, Mr. Gould's earthy libations struck her senses, and the smoky, roaring hearth warmed her. Seeing George and his friends at their usual table, she snuck into the keg chamber and poured herself a cider.

"...which is why we must ban British textiles." Mr. Averill slammed his fist upon the table.

Ban British textiles. A wondrous idea. Perhaps I could get the ladies' group to join in the ban. But banning textiles would mean more time at the loom.

Annalisa nibbled the mug with disdain.

The front tavern door opened, and a gust of cold winter air swept the room, and into the keg chamber. Annalisa shuddered.

"Cousin," George bellowed.

Her heart trembled, and she peered into the main tavern room. Jack's agreeable face beamed at George's warm welcome. His tall stature and muscular calves beneath fine silk stockings; his finely sculpted chin and nose; he was as handsome as she'd remembered. Cider sloshed within the tin tankard from her quivering hands, but the sourness in her stomach returned.

How could such a man have spoken to me so poorly?

"Then 'tis true. You and Oliver have returned," Mr. Averill said.

George filled a tankard for Jack, then lifted his own. "To the return of Jack Perkins. Sluice your gob, abrams."

Several others raised their mugs for the salute. Annalisa inched backwards into the keg room, her view of the main tavern restricted to only Quinnapin and Jack.

"Jack, heard you the news?" Quinnapin sipped his drink. "While you were away, it was printed in the *Boston Gazette*—your mentor, Dr. Franklin, leaked letters from Hutchinson."

"No." Jack frowned. "Franklin never mentioned them—"

"'Twas printed mid-June. Hutchinson had apparently written to the king asking to further oppress Boston's liberties," George said with repulsion. "I ran the news out here."

Jack sat in a chair and stretched his legs. "I imagine Franklin betrayed such letters with good reason."

"Your Dr. Franklin is a good-hearted Patriot who won't remain in England much longer." George's tall build spoiled her view of Jack as he grabbed a dirty mug and walked it to the bar. "Boston has been in an uproar."

Annalisa picked her thumbnail until Jack was no longer obstructed by George. Her brother spoke of nothing but those letters all summer, until *The Dartmouth* docked in Boston Harbor with its crates of tea.

"Have you heard about the tea?" Jack raised a quizzical brow.

Quinnapin leaned forward. "You mean the Tea Act."

"What do you know?" George asked.

Annalisa gripped the keg beneath her.

"Our fellow Patriots disguised themselves as Mohawks and snuck aboard the three ships carrying East India Company tea. They disposed of it into the harbor." Jack smirked. "I can hardly believe you weren't a part of it."

Quinnapin snorted and shook his head. "Mohawks?"

"Were you?" George must have slammed his hand on the table because a loud bang echoed into the keg room. Annalisa jumped.

Jack laughed. "Hardly."

Intrigue pulled her closer to the chamber doorway, and the room came into full view.

"Gentlemen." George faced the room. "We've news from Boston and the Sons of Liberty." The tavern quieted to a lull of murmurs. "Go on, Cousin."

Each man looked up from his drink. From behind the

bar, Mr. Gould ran a hand over the ashy stubble of his unshaven face.

Jack stood. *"Rally Mohawks and bring your axes, and tell King George we'll pay no taxes'* were the assembling cries of our fellow Patriots. Three nights ago, they jettisoned crates of British tea into the harbor in protestation of the Tea Act. We will not pay a levy on textiles, and nor should we on tea. As gentlemen of this great town, we must join with our brothers in Boston."

"Hear, hear!"

"Huzzah!"

Annalisa finished her mug of cider. The room spun, but she neither felt sick, nor dizzy. If her small town was willing to ban British textiles, surely tea would follow— and they'd have Jack Perkins to thank for it.

22

ANNALISA
TOPSFIELD, JANUARY 1774

O N THE LAST DAY of Christmastide, two hours after church, Annalisa arrived with her family to the Perkins' stately home. The large yellow house boasted an elegant design for the season. Each wreath and hemlock garland smelled of fresh pine and cedar, every holly berry and pinecone a cheery reminder of winter's delicate grace.

Jack Perkins sat by the crackling parlor hearth, puffing his pipe. Though she'd spied him at the tavern two weeks ago, Annalisa's heart skipped like a stone across still waters. His eyes, a majestic marine, glimmered in the fire's glow, and his cheeks dimpled with each sip of the pipe. He wore a coat of blue velvet, and beneath his chin, a cascade of ivory linen.

How cultured he'd be after visiting so many European cities. At one-and-twenty, and a lawyer, such a man could hardly remain unmarried much longer. She wondered if he would finally ask Jane.

Abigail, in her claret chintz gown, took Annalisa's hand. "Come, sit by me, dear friend."

As she joined Abigail on the sofa, Jack set down his pipe. "Miss Annalisa, it does me good to see you. You look well in that evergreen dress. It matches your eyes."

"Thank you. Though I hadn't meant to wear it. It forces me to lace my stays too tightly."

Jack's eyes rounded and he looked away.

Mamma gasped. "What a vulgar thing to say, Annalisa. Where are your manners?"

Lady Perkins placed a hand over her swelling, pregnant belly. "Jack, why don't you sit by Miss Howlett and tell her of your travels."

"Oh, yes," Mamma said. "Jane's been looking forward to hearing all about Versailles."

Jack hesitated, his gaze locked with Annalisa's as though he wished to speak with her instead. "Of course." He stood, then made his way to Jane.

Abigail leaned in close. "Apparently, Ollie proclaimed himself a Loyalist."

"What?" Annalisa fisted her skirts. "When?"

George slid beside Abigail, wedging her between him and Annalisa. "Jack told me Oliver is a bloody Tory." He nearly spat his disgust upon Annalisa's petticoat.

Abigail's mouth curled. "I know nothing, except Jack is in terrible distress. I can hardly imagine the strain it bears upon my papa. No one will speak of it—not even my poor mamma. Jack only told me out of utter despondency, but I think he, too, has some bold secret he's keeping."

"Yes, the tea," Annalisa blurted, then held her breath.

George's eyes narrowed. "How do you know about the tea?"

"I...heard you speaking about it to William. How lucky

Jack was to have stumbled across such madness at that body of the people."

"And what madness it was," Abigail whispered. "My father was not pleased he attended."

George leaned closer to Abigail. "Think you Jack partook in the destruction—"

"I have a gift for you, Miss Howlett," Oliver announced.

They each turned to find Oliver standing boldly in the middle of the room before Jack and Jane.

"Ollie, what have you?" Abigail rose and rushed to her brother's side. "What is this?"

Oliver reached into his waistcoat pocket and revealed a gift wrapped in gold decorative paper, the finest Annalisa had ever seen. With an air of pomp, he handed the present to Jane.

"Miss Howlett, I must bestow upon you a gift most deserving of a lady."

Jack's face paled, but Jane's tinted the color of roses. She unwrapped the gold paper while maintaining a demure and refined poise, then opened a rectangular pewter box.

From it, she lifted matching pearl earrings and a necklace. "Oh, heavens, they're beautiful."

"Ollie, how generous," Andrew said.

Five-year-old Susan left Henry and Mary, and glided to Jane with hands outstretched. "Let me see, Miss Howlett."

"Pearls all the way from Paris, Susie." Oliver beamed, then looked to Jane. "I saw them and immediately thought of no other beauty rare enough to wear something so elegant."

George snorted, then whispered to Annalisa, "Jack

wishes to court Jane, and that cock robin undermines him before us all." He shook his head. "The squeeze crab."

A lump formed in Annalisa's throat, wondering if now Oliver, too, would pursue Jane.

Mamma fussed with the pearls until they draped perfectly about Jane's neck. "Oh, Mr. Oliver, what a thoughtful gift for my Janey. Clearly, she is speechless and full of gratitude. Jane, what a vision."

"Let us celebrate with a carol." Abigail, with a look of perplexity, glided to the spinet, and grabbed George and William along the way.

The *Gloucestershire Wassail* erupted from her fingers, and Annalisa inched toward the window, relieved for the distraction. Jane could no more be the center of such a display of impropriety than could Jack's humiliation. For Oliver to challenge him before both their families was nearly an act of treason itself.

Jack, with arms folded and brows knitted, stood by the fireplace. He took up his pipe, sucked on the end, and exhaled an endless cloud of smoke. With one glance in Annalisa's direction, he scooped up his dram of brandy and joined her by the window.

"The likes of him." He peered out the icy casement. "Damn all propriety." In one swallow, he finished the liquor and set the glass on the windowsill with a clash. His amber perfume peeked through the smoky tobacco and brandy on his breath. "Miss Annalisa, if you permit me, I would like a private audience with you. Meet me in the carriage house?"

His proposition, nearly drowned out by George and William bellowing the *Gloucestershire Wassail*, gave her pause; the indecency of being alone with him swirled her insides with excitement.

"How shall I excuse myself?"

Jack grinned. "Say you're feeling unwell, that you require some fresh air. Do it now, while there's still some light—and your brothers to distract with their wassailing." He winked.

❈

OUTSIDE, ALL GLISTENED IN THE CIVIL TWILIGHT AND sparkling, undisturbed snow. The crisp air nipped her cheeks, and the smell of freshly fallen flakes mingled with heady smoke from the chimneys. She clutched Jack's strong arm, cloaked in the navy wool of his greatcoat. Next to him in the fresh outdoors, her spirits lifted.

Jack held steady a barn lantern as he guided them down the shoveled pathway toward the carriage house, their shoes squeaking as they walked. Once inside, he hung the tin lantern on a hook. Golden sunbursts and dots splayed about, filling the space between them. He turned, his face full of apprehension. He seemed nervous, though doffed his cocked hat with confidence.

"I want to apologize for that bit of...elaboration between your sister and Ollie. I, too, was flabbergasted. Surely, you must know my intentions for your sister are honorable."

Annalisa looked down. "Yours *and* Ollie's intentions are quite obvious. Jane is much desired."

He sighed. "Oliver has made his ambition rather clear —and before both our families." Jack hung his head. "I know not where I may place myself in that charade. I never thought I'd be confronted with such competition, let alone from my own brother."

"There's little need to explain yourself, sir." She shuddered against the chill and wrapped her cherry-red cloak around her. She paced about the carriage house and examined the Perkins' fine coaches. *One day Jane may call these her own.*

Jack intercepted her. "Let's into the carriage. It may warm you some."

She nodded and allowed him to hand her inside. Once settled onto the velvet seat, Jack closed the door. The coach felt warmer, but was probably his closeness. In the dim light between their cloudy breaths, she made out the attractive features of his face.

"I've been meaning to speak with you since my return." He studied her briefly and grinned. "You've grown much since last I saw you. It does me good to see you." He spun the signet ring upon his little finger. "But perhaps you, too, are still haunted by the way we parted...I daresay, there's no way for me to atone for mine and my brother's actions that night. If you can find it in your heart to forgive me, I would be forever in your debt."

"Speak not of it. 'Tis in the past, and I am well over it."

Jack reached into his haversack and presented a small glass bottle. "I found this in Paris. For you."

Annalisa lifted the cork and placed the jar to her nose. The flowery scent of May met her with agreeable familiarity. "Lilac." She smiled. "My favorite flower. You really shouldn't have troubled yourself, sir. 'Tis absolutely perfect."

"I've one more." He reached into his haversack again and handed her a thick roll of paper. Jack sucked in a breath as though to calm his nerves. "I think not even this is enough to apologize for my behavior, but I pray you like it, and we may continue our journey as friends."

Across the front page, Jack's immaculate pen read,

For a dear friend, always near, no matter how far—J. Perkins.

She thumbed through the pages and gasped. "Mozart's Piano Sonata Number Two...in the key of F major." She looked up at him reverently, the world beginning to blur. "Oh, Jack..." Overwhelmed by his kindness, she choked back her tears. "This must have cost you a fortune. Wherever did you find this?"

"I tried to commission a sonata for you from the maestro himself, but as it turns out, he'd just written this one." He winked. "But in actuality, 'tis off the printing press in Salzburg. Just for you. I know of no other musician who could play such a composition."

"Save for yourself." She chuckled, but almost as quickly as she'd laughed, she fought back her tears once more. "This is...this...Jack, I am so deeply in your debt. How can I ever thank you?"

He lifted her hand and she recoiled, afraid he would despise her callouses. But his palm felt surprisingly rough and similar. "There's no need to thank me, and there's certainly no debt. I only ask you play it for me once you've learned it. I've not yet heard it myself...and it would be an honor."

Her shoulders relaxed, and she let him hold her hand. "Yes, of course, I shall." She held his gaze. "I'll make sure I play it passionately."

They sat in silence for a moment, his thumb rippling across her knuckles. "While we're alone, I'd like to share something with you." He cleared his throat. "When we returned to Boston, I was involved in some...questionable pursuits. I was sworn never to discuss it with anyone. But —" He drew in a deep, rendering breath. "I would like to tell you, to confirm myself to you." An impish grin parted his lips. "Because I know you can keep a secret, my little rebellious rogue."

She started, knowing he alluded to the massacre. "What have you done?"

Jack lifted a brow. "You may have heard about the tea?"

"I have." She held back her smirk.

"I knew you would." He exhaled. "I was there. I helped commit the treasonous act. Heaven knows I would be disbarred and lose my partnership with Adams if ever he found out." He tapped his fingers on the seat. "But I regret it not...and I had to tell you...you who I witnessed that day at the massacre, unafraid of anything. I suppose...I'm much different than you may have perceived me." Through his wry smile, he added, "An heir. The son of a lord. But I daresay, we may be more alike than you might've thought when first we met."

Her lips twisted with amusement. *The son of a lord who plays a rough country fiddle and engages in treasonous acts with the Sons of Liberty.*

"My good opinion of you is not altered, though it had been tainted from the way we parted eighteen months ago. But tonight, you've reaffirmed yourself as goodly man, and an honorable gentleman—perhaps we're now even in our antics."

His countenance softened. "I feel I can trust you,

Annalisa. I've always felt that way about you." He reached for her hands once more. "I should have told you before I left for Europe, but you're like a sister to me." He paused. "No. You're more than that. The ease I feel when we're together...I can't explain it. I find our intercourse natural and unforced. You're a...a confidante in this confusing, disorderly world, and I am forever grateful for you, and your forgiveness. I'm undeserving of it."

If only Fannie and Hannah could hear this.

Her confidence surging, she squeezed his hand. "Then perhaps I can sufficiently admit to you something equally scandalous of myself."

Jack leaned forward and cocked a mischievous brow. "Oh?"

Her mouth parted, ready to tell him about Benjamin Cavendish and the Danvers militia, when the carriage house door swung open.

"Jack? Miss Annalisa?" Andrew's charming young voice echoed into the darkness.

Jack ducked and pulled Annalisa to the coach floor. Their noses nearly touching, he whispered, "Don't move, else they'll think we're consorting."

Annalisa giggled. "What a scandal. The whole town will talk. What shall we say on our return?"

He snickered. "We'll say I walked you down the lane to your house."

"You're daft. That is near two miles in the snow. Surely they will see our footprints."

They tittered in the stillness until Andrew's voice sounded once more. "I don't see them, Father."

The carriage house door closed with a bang. She

remained motionless for what felt like hours before Jack sat upright and helped her onto the seat across from him.

"I leave for Boston in two days." He sounded glum.

"You will be sorely missed."

"I have plenty of reasons to return." Jack winked. "You shan't miss me too much."

23

JACK
CAMBRIDGE, APRIL 1774

F ROM AUNT CATHERINE'S TALL parlor window, Jack peered out at Tory Row, his foot tapping against the wooden floor. His aunt, a Patriot, was one of the few families remaining on this street of Loyalists. Most others had retreated across the river to Boston. He expelled a tendril of smoke from his pipe and turned to face the room.

Aunt Catherine, seated in a chair by the fire, hardly peered up from her canvas. "Your father should be here any moment. His meeting with Mr. Hancock must have been delayed."

No sooner had she finished speaking than did the *tlot-tlot* of hooves sound from the lane.

Father barged inside in a huff, and Jack hurried into the foyer.

"Sir?"

His father flung his hat and greatcoat into the arms of the waiting housemaid. "A brandy, Dot."

"Yes, sir." The maid's mobcap bobbed with her curtsy, and she departed.

Father waved a dispatch and hastened toward the parlor. "Hancock notified me of something most odious, Jack. Most odious, indeed."

"What is it, sir?" Jack followed him.

Aunt Catherine set down her embroidery. "John, whatever's the matter?"

Dot hurried in with the brandy. Without so much as a 'thank you', Father took it and downed a good measure of the liquor. After a quick adjustment of his spectacles, he unfolded the dispatch.

"Britain has issued the Coercive Acts...the Boston Port Act, the Massachusetts Government Act—" He stopped as if something had choked him. With a single hand, he crumpled the paper and tossed it toward the fire. "Our king is a tyrant."

Jack lunged after the dispatch before it wasted to embers. Eager to read Hancock's script, he smoothed the page.

"The act closes Boston Harbor until Britain is compensated for the tea." Father finished his brandy. "What's more, the act has taken away Massachusetts' charter, which means all government officials shall now be appointed by our governor, Parliament, or King George."

"Fie." The paper crushed inside Jack's fist. "Close the harbor? The despot has condemned Boston's trade and livelihood!"

Father lifted his spectacles and rubbed his eyes. "It could be as simple as repayment of the tea, but I fear John Adams' exuberant cousin, Samuel, and his Committee of Correspondence, will answer the bill with temerity." He turned to Aunt Catherine. "Kit, have you heard from your husband?"

"No. Lord Brunswick sails to Boston as we speak." She set her needle into the canvas. "He was due to leave London three weeks ago."

"Good. I should very much like to speak with him when he arrives." Father lit his pipe. "No doubt he'll have information from Parliament Whigs, and that Tory bastard, Lord North."

Jack swiped his sweating palms over his breeches. He hadn't seen Father this incensed since the massacre. "I must return to Mr. Adams."

Father frowned. "Jack. The gratuitous destruction of private property by mob violence is not the answer. I know you align yourself with the rebels, but do be reasonable."

"If I leave straightaway, I'll make it to Mr. Adams' office—"

"Heed my warning. You're now Adams' partner. You're to work for him in the trade of law, not participate in riots and protests. I'll not hear of you engaging in such charades. I know Oliver's loyalty to the king distresses you, but there are far more judicious ways of rendering our king intolerable. I know Adams would agree."

Jack turned. "But, sir, the king is mad."

Father held up his hand. "Do I believe King George and Parliament have acted unjustly? I most certainly do. The province can govern itself, and has for over a hundred years. But do I wish to sever ties with England? Most certainly not. And to consider such is treason. I'll not have my first-born tried and imprisoned for treachery."

"But, sir—"

"John Jackson, I know you were involved with those buffoons the night they emptied tea into the harbor."

Aunt Catherine gasped. "Jack, is it true?"

Jack straightened his coat. "I'll neither confirm nor deny your allegation. 'Twas an organized protest of proper men who tried everything within their means to refute the tax. 'Tis all I'll say of the matter."

Father clasped his shoulder. "We may create change through the law. Altering the law. Creating new law. Keep yourself immersed in your work, hmm? I promise, Hancock and I shall be the voices of this town, and for the province. We'll not stop until a concession has been made, and Parliament in agreement with our terms. You have my solemn word."

Jack gritted his teeth. "Yes, sir."

❧

A WEEK LATER, JACK SAT INSIDE MR. ADAMS' BRICK Boston office in Queen-street, engulfed by the stale scent of books. Mr. Adams paced, reading Jack's latest proceeding.

"No." Adams grunted. "No, no, no." He tossed the pages into the fire and slammed his fist upon the desk, nearly toppling a stack of books onto the inkwell.

Jack straightened in his seat. That proceeding had taken him nearly two weeks. Dejected, he awaited Adams' unabated scorn.

"Remember the massacre trial, Mr. Perkins? *Quod dubitas ne feceris*—where you may be doubtful, do not act."

Jack exhaled. "Yes, sir. That is understood."

"Good. Please resume the case while I step out. I've a

meeting in King-street with Mr. Otis." He turned to leave, then hesitated. With a sudden twinkle in his eye, he added, "If Mrs. Adams stops by, give her my regards. God willing, I'll return in an hour."

Jack nodded. "Yes, sir."

The door slammed shut, and Jack groaned. He slid from the desk, the chair squealing across the wooden floor. Leaning back, he rubbed his temples, then stood and walked to the window. Water dribbled down the dirty pane from melting snow.

There came a rap on the door and he started. *He couldn't have returned so soon...*

Jack adjusted his cravat and moved to open the door. A rush of tepid air blew in from the street, drenched in the smell of slush mixed with dirt.

Abigail Adams, a kindly woman of thirty years, stepped inside and untied the ribbon on her red cloak. Despite the muddy snow outside, she smiled. "How are things, Mr. Perkins?"

The fresh April air shook Jack from his charge as he closed the door and returned her smile. "I'm well, ma'am. Your husband left not ten minutes ago for a meeting with Mr. Otis. He should return in an hour or so. He gives his regards."

"And he hasn't taken you with him? For shame. I hope he isn't working you too hard." She held out a sealed envelope. "A letter was delivered at the house for you."

"Thank you, ma'am." Jack took the note and returned to his desk. "Mr. Adams is quite the lawyer. I'm undeserving of his partnership." He turned the envelope over and made out George Howlett's script. His heart thumped; he yearned for his small country town. In two months, he was scheduled to venture home for a sabbatical when the Adams' moved back to Braintree.

Mrs. Adams set her cloak near the fire. "Would you like a cup of coffee, sir? 'Tis John's favorite. He always drinks it when hard at work."

"That would be lovely, ma'am." Jack fingered the seal, eager to learn why George had written.

With a genteel nod, she left him. How kind Mrs. Adams was, and how her eyes lit up at the mention of her husband. Despite Mr. Adams' less than agreeable temperament, it was no secret he sought his wife's advice in all things. Theirs seemed a close and affectionate friendship, one Jack deeply envied and wished for himself.

Would Jane offer me such counsel? She seems to care little for politics.

He broke the seal and discovered two letters within the one. The first was from George—his cousin was purchasing another tavern in Portsmouth, in the Province of New Hampshire. *Wondrous news. Surely, it will be a tavern for Patriots to gather.*

The other was from Annalisa. He smiled, recalling her at Twelfth Night. His interest piqued at her unfamiliar script:

TOPSFIELD

APRIL 9*TH*, 1774

DEAR SIR,

I HOPE THIS LETTER FINDES YOU WELL, AND YOU HAVE BEEN IN GOODE HEALTH SINCE TWELFTH NIGHT. I AM REMISS TO SAY I HAD A TERRIBLE COLDE IN FEBRUARY BUT AM NOW WELL RECOVER'D.

George asked me to write because he thinks it will put you in a goode humour, and because his letter is so shorte. He's been buzy finalyzing the deede to his new tavern in Portsmoth. He says he will call it the Black Watter Inn.

I've keppt my promise and have been stedfast in learning Mozart's sonnata. I find it quite challenging, but verry agree-able. I should be able to play it for you when you are againe in Towne, though without the graces of Mozart himselff.

If you finde time, do read Margritt Cavendish. Her poetrey is physick for the Soul.

Mamma has assign'd to me the tasck of planting a new Flower garden this spring. I believe I shall enjoy that verry much. You are sorely missed.

Respecktfully yours &c,

Annalisa Howlett.

Something about her note felt familiar, like he'd received countless before now. He folded the page. As he tucked it into his pocket, he smelled lilac.

"Ah, lilac." Mrs. Adams returned with a steaming mug of coffee. "A note from your beloved?" She winked.

"No, no." His neck warmed. "Just an old friend."

"La." She laughed. "My dearest John looks at me like that. With such an air of esteem, Mr. Perkins, I daresay that letter is from no friend."

Eager to dispel the heat in his face, he looked down, but grinned. *Could my admiration for Annalisa be the beginning of an attachment?*

He hadn't seriously considered the thought until now,

though it had certainly crossed his mind, particularly after Lizzie's fortune-telling the night of the corn husking two years ago. But he'd always been far too deep in admiring Jane to notice. In the light of Mrs. Adams' observation, he could hardly deny his happiness in receiving Annalisa's letter.

But what of my lovely Miss Howlett? She is truly the image of what every well-bred young lady should be...

When he looked up, Mrs. Adams' face had twisted with mortification. "Oh, dear, I've outspoken my turn. Truly, Jack, I meant no harm."

"No, not at all, ma'am. Your perceptiveness has taken me by surprise, but perhaps...it shouldn't have." To make such a remark upon catching him at the end of a solitary moment was bold but not without cause; Mrs. Adams had now known him for years.

I'll have to pay closer attention when next I meet Miss Annalisa Howlett.

24

JACK
TOPSFIELD, JUNE 1774

DESPITE JACK'S PROMISE TO Mr. Adams that he'd work diligently during his time in Topsfield, the fine, sunlit beauty of the day called. He dressed in his riding clothes, mounted his mare, and rode down the narrow lane to the Howlett farm. Their vast, verdant acreage sprawled, the fields separated by rock walls. Furthest from the house, Zeke and Dane trailed behind two oxen. Much nearer, Quinnapin left the barn with a large pail in hand.

Jack dismounted and led his horse down the path toward the stable. A chickadee's simple melody filled the air, but as he approached, the distinct hum of a voice carried on the breeze, drowning out the tiny bird's solo.

Miss Annalisa crouched in the garden adjacent to the barn, planting flowers and singing a familiar tune.

Exhilarated, Jack tied his horse to the wood fence and snuck up behind her. "I see you're making good on your mother's request for a garden."

Annalisa jumped and wiped her hands on her apron. At

eighteen, she stood tall, only a few inches shorter than he. Small curling wisps of hair peeked out from her ivory cap, framing her tanned face. With high cheekbones, and a prominent jawline, her countenance no longer held the roundness of childhood. She had blossomed, an irony not lost on him as he admired her amidst the flowers.

"Mr. Perkins, you're home!" Her warm, contralto voice resounded a deep elegance. "It does me good to see you. Are you here to call on George? He's in the barn, I believe—"

"Miss Annalisa, I am your most obedient servant." He bowed to her playfully and stripped from his jacket. "May I assist you?"

"The well-bred son of a lord dirtying himself in the garden? I couldn't possibly let you. But if you insist, I won't refuse you." She winked.

"Then I insist." He rolled his sleeves and, disregarding the fine weave of his silk stockings, knelt with her to the ground. "What blooms have we here?"

"Those are peonies. I planted them years ago with the rose bushes and lilacs..."

As she spoke, the sunlight glinted overhead, highlighting the evergreen of her eyes. He blinked several times as if to rid a speck of dust.

"What is it?" she asked.

"The sun shines so luminously today."

She gave a hearty laugh—the essence of her brother, George. "Why, you're smitten by Mother Earth herself."

Heat rose up his neck. "I could hardly deny it. She's blessed your garden with all assortments of beauty."

Annalisa's smile waned. She must have expected him to extoll such compliments upon her sister, who remained dutifully indoors. Jane was as lovely as their garden's most precious rose, and he was eager to see her, too. But such exquisiteness paled when next to Annalisa. A curious observation.

"Have you yet read Margaret Cavendish?"

"I've not, but I shall."

Annalisa reached into her pocket and retrieved a small, tattered book. Without opening its pages, she clutched it to her bosom and recited: *"Beauty, you cannot long devotion keep; The Mind grows weary, senses fall asleep...but if they kneel an hour-long to pray, their Zeal grows cold, nor they know what they say. So, admiration last not very long, after nine days the greatest wonder's gone.'* Her poem is called *'a dialogue betwixt Wit and Beauty.'* Beauty fades, much like these flowers. I like to think we should appreciate the hardiness of wit— much like the herbs in our kitchen garden. Whether fresh or dried, they faithfully keep to their uses."

"How well you recite. And of course, Mad Madge speaks true. I'll oblige you and read her, if you but lend me your book." He held out his palm.

With a hint of mischief in her eyes, she recoiled her hand and with the other, lifted the cocked hat from his head. "Pray, how do I look in your hat?"

He chuckled. "You'd best remove your dormeuse first."

She dropped the book, pulled the linen cap from her head, and replaced it with his hat. A long lock of plaited, honey-brown hair flowed over her shoulder. "Now I may join you in your fight against the Lobsterbacks."

"You'll have to wear it like this if you wish to use your musket properly." He adjusted it so the front corner angled over her left eye. "Now you may aim and shoot your Lobsterback with ease."

George appeared from the barn in his leather apron with Quinnapin. They jogged to them.

"*Wuneekeesuq!* Good-day to you both."

"*Wuneekeesuq*, Quinn," Annalisa replied.

George clapped Jack's back. "Cousin." Looking down, he grabbed Annalisa's book. "Mad Madge?" He thumbed through the pages and read aloud: "'Notes on Benjamin Cavendish.' Annie, what is this?"

Her cheeks reddened and she jumped. "Give it back."

George's dark howl filled the garden as he held the book above his head. "Only if you catch me." He pulled off the apron and sprinted from the garden.

"Come back here, George Howlett! I'll poison your patrons for this." Annalisa ran from the garden, and Jack's hat flew from her head.

Quinnapin clicked his tongue. "She's pert today."

Jack snickered, watching George and Annalisa squabble into the fields. "Let's follow them."

Retrieving his hat, he dusted off the corners and continued to the edge of the woods with Quinnapin. When they met George and Annalisa by the ancient oak, she jumped for the book he held above her head.

"Higher, Miss Anna," Quinnapin called. "You're nearly as tall as he!"

"A bit more and you've got it." George guffawed. "Or perhaps we could strike a bargain." He glanced at Jack and an impish smirk curled his mouth. "I'll return your notes if you show Jack and Quinn how well I've taught you to manipulate a firelock."

"You mean that?" Annalisa appeared tense, eager to have her poetry book.

"Aye. I think the fruits of my tutelage should be admired by those with as fine a shot as my own."

"Very well." She huffed. "If you retrieve Bixby, I'll meet you in the clearing."

Jack escorted her up the steep wooded path with Quinnapin, and into the clearing overlooking their farm.

Annalisa took Jack's hat and placed it on her head. "Have you seen a woman fire a piece before?"

"No. But when I see your capable eye, I'll be sure to tell the men at the tavern." He winked at Quinnapin. "I've doubted George for years, but I'm ready to see for myself."

She raised an eyebrow. "Oh, you have? You, too, Quinn? I suppose I'll have to rise to the occasion and prove this scar was well worth it."

Jack stopped himself from touching her cheek. He'd never quite focused on the silvery scar that was just a shade or two lighter than her complexion, as it was nicely healed, but he'd always wondered how she'd come to boast such a feature.

George appeared with fowler and cartridge box, and set them before his sister. "Try not to humiliate me."

Annalisa knelt and squinted up at him. "If I make my mark, I suppose you could afford me a seat at the tavern tonight."

Jack bit his lower lip to hide the affection in his smile. "Indeed, we shall." With interest, he studied her.

She loaded the fowler as quickly and proficiently as a militiaman, as though she'd been firing muskets since childhood. When she returned the ramrod to its channel, Annalisa faced George. "Are you satisfied, sir?"

"Aye." He nodded. "That tree." George pointed to a birch at thirty yards.

She scoffed. "The birch is the easiest one. How about... that one." She gestured to a smooth, grey beech tucked amidst a series of oaks and maples at near seventy yards.

George choked on his laughter. "Very well."

Jack's eyes widened. "Miss Annalisa, you needn't exceed yourself for me. I'm already impressed."

"I'm not here to impress you, Mr. Perkins. I'm here to show you I'm the best shot in town."

Quinnapin sidled up beside her. "I think you could probably strike a tree at even greater range, Miss Anna." His hand to his forehead to shield the sunlight, he scoured the tree line of the clearing. "How about that one?" He pointed to an elm at well over seventy yards.

Annalisa nodded. "Yes, Quinn. I daresay, you're right."

Jack swelled at her shift in confidence, and focused on her as she lifted the firelock to her shoulder. "Wait." He adjusted the front corner of his hat over her left eye. "There you are."

George shouted orders. "Make ready. Pre-sent...Fire!"

The familiar *snap-crack* ignited the quiet day with spark. The tree shivered, and shards of splinters flew off. Jack's nose burned from the sulfuric gunpowder, and his ears rang. Stunned and titillating, he shifted sideways.

Quinnapin cried out with excitement. "Aiee! Well done, Miss Anna."

"Thank you, sir." She curtsied. "And I think you do well to beg my pardon, Mr. Perkins."

"Yes. I do," Jack stammered, focused on hiding the unanticipated arousal within his breeches. *Perhaps Mrs. Adams was right. Society's standard of beauty, be damned!*

He looked on Annalisa Howlett not as Jane's younger sister, but as a lovely woman—a woman capable of making a man feel more than the platonic compassion of friendship.

"I daresay that should be enough to get my book back, Brother. And perhaps a drink at the Peat Moss tonight?" She grabbed the book from George and kissed his cheek.

"Aye. Then I must take Jack to my new tavern, aye Quinn?" George clapped Jack's shoulder. "She's in Straw-bery Banke of Portsmouth, and much larger. I've dubbed her the Black Water Inn."

"Might you sell the Peat Moss?" Jack asked.

"I may." George rubbed his sideburns. "If I get an offer at the right price."

They left the clearing, descended the hill, and trudged across the western field. As they approached the house, Mrs. Howlett opened the front door. Annalisa removed Jack's hat and thrust it back to him.

"Annalisa." Her mother's voice rang shrill and Jack stepped back as Mrs. Howlett marched outside. "Annalisa Howlett, cover your face this instant. You'll turn as swarthy as Addy. And where has your cap gone?"

"Yes, marm." She reached into her pocket.

With a genteel swish of her skirts, the lady of the house greeted him. "Why, Jack, what a pleasant surprise." She gave a quick sniff. "Do I smell gunpowder? George, were you and Quinnapin hunting?" She narrowed her eyes at Annalisa. "Or were you two shooting that firelock?"

Disconcerted by the change in Mrs. Howlett's voice, Jack forced a smile and tipped his hat. "Madam, I am your obedient servant. I was calling and saw Miss Annalisa in the garden. I thought I'd offer my assistance."

Mrs. Howlett clicked her tongue. "Jack, dear, you mustn't dirty yourself. Though I must say, the flowers are looking lovely, Annie my sweet. Do come inside. My Jane is seated in the parlor and would very much like to hear of your work with Mr. Adams. How wonderful he was to make you a partner. When do you think you might open a practice here in town? Janey is always much obliged to your calling, you know."

Jack hesitated. "Of course, ma'am. I've learned quite a bit from Adams, but there is still much to know."

Annalisa curtsied and handed him his coat. "Thank you for your help, Mr. Perkins. Your conversation and company were most stimulating."

"'Twas a pleasure, as always." Jack tipped his hat to them and followed Mrs. Howlett indoors.

Jane's lavender perfume filled the parlor. She looked as lovely as ever in her white dress and pink petticoat; her ample, milky white bosom heaved upward with each breath. *An angel from heaven.*

Jane lifted her gaze to him. "Mr. Perkins."

"Miss Howlett." He rushed to her side and kissed her hand.

"Do sit down," Mrs. Howlett said. "I'll have Addy bring us some tea and toast."

"Tea, ma'am?" Jack turned. "Have you any?"

"Oh, certainly. Mr. Howlett keeps the usual bohea. 'Tis quite agreeable, I assure you."

A Loyalist home.

He sat beside Jane and watched her delicate fingers embroider a perfect daisy. Her glances were fleeting but flirtatious. *An unrelentingly cultured and tantalizing creature!*

Yet he found himself glancing out the window.

Jane faced him when her mother had gone. "Mamma tells me you've moved back to Topsfield. What splendid news. I do hope you and Mr. Oliver will be able to attend the midsummer ball in Ipswich on Saturday next."

"I'm only in town for two months," Jack said. "And I must make myself useful to Adams. But I cannot see why not."

"Please, sir, don't work yourself too hard." Jane smiled and set down her needle. "This is such a fine time of year, especially for dancing."

His head spun with the dizziness of a dalliance. *To earn Jane Howlett's love, in spite of Oliver and his tawdry gift at Twelfth Night would be sweet, sweet indeed.*

🦋 25 🦋

ANNALISA
TOPSFIELD, JUNE 1774

A NNALISA POISED HER FINGERS upon the spinet keys and closed her eyes. The *allegro* in Mozart's new *Piano Sonata No. 2 in F Major, K. 280* was quick, complete with plenty of trills and syncopation. Until today, she'd practiced unrelentingly with the music, but now, she played from memory. When she reached the end of the first movement, she opened her eyes and wiped her moistened palms over her linen skirts. Had it been passionate enough? She'd played from memory countless times, but to play from the heart, from her soul, felt different.

She closed her eyes once more, and imagined Jack Perkins as she started the second movement, the much slower, languid *adagio*. Each plunk of the ivory keys, each note and cadence flowed with as much yearning and passion she felt for him; the graciousness of his generous gift, and the pain of unrequited attachment to which she knew she could never succumb. Her fingers elaborated improvisation, playing extra notes and trills that were absent from the pages of her memory, but free-flowing from within, until the fullness of the music overtook her.

"Annie, why are you crying?"

Annalisa spun around on the bench.

Jane stood in the doorway, her hands on her hips.

She wiped her tears. "I was moved, 'tis all."

Jane glided into the room and sat upon the sofa. "'Tis a beautiful piece. Would that I could play it for Mr. Oliver."

"Mr. Oliver?" Annalisa lost her breath. "I thought you fancied Jack."

"I did." Jane smoothed her skirts. "But Mr. Oliver was so kind to have given me these pearls at Twelfth Night. How could I refuse his advancements? And besides, Jack seems...distracted."

"I understand the propriety of accepting such a gift from Oliver, but you must refuse him."

"'Tis not correct." Jane chuckled. "You know that. I can love him well enough. He is unrelentingly cultured."

"And Jack is not?" Annalisa's brows furrowed. "He is to inherit the Perkins' estate. That is what you wish for, is it not?"

"I told you I would accept whoever offers me marriage, and Oliver has proven his attachment with greater conviction. I should be lucky to marry a man with that sort of ambition and devotion."

Annalisa rose from the spinet bench and hurried to the sofa, where she sat beside Jane and took up her sister's hands. "Please. If you love me at all, you will not accept Oliver. You must accept Jack if he asks."

"Annie, whatever's gotten into you?" Jane pulled her hands away. "Why do you not approve of Oliver?"

"He's...not suitable. Not for you to marry."

Jane crossed her arms. "Whyever is he not? Because he is Loyalist?"

"No. Because...because he...he's..." Annalisa swallowed over her closing throat. "He put his hands on me, Jane. He grabbed me. When we were in Boston—before the massacre."

Jane was silent for several moments, then her eyes narrowed. "Why should he do such a thing to you?"

Annalisa's chest squeezed. "Perhaps he's a scoundrel?"

"No." Jane's full lips pressed into a tight line. "He's indescribably well-bred. He'd never do such a thing."

"Janey." Annalisa stood. "He did grab me. Between my legs. He's not the man you believe him to be."

"You lie." Jane rose and paced between the sofa and spinet. "He'd never touch you, Annie. Oliver would never consider you, so why would he dare put his hands on you?"

"I beg your pardon? You who've claimed Oliver and I would make a fine match, yet he would never consider me?" She gripped Jane's shoulders. "I cannot change what happened, though I wish I could. I've suffered enough for it—and now my own sister believes me not?"

"Oh, please Annalisa." Jane swatted away her hands. "And even if 'tis true, can't you accept it? How many years have passed since? Four? And you waited this long to tell me?" She looked as though she would cry. "We are women, destined to one day be but a man's property. 'Tis time you realized our place in the world."

"No." Annalisa's face tingled and she backed toward the drawing room door. "I'll never accept being treated thus. Not by Oliver, or any man. I'd rather die a spinster." She fled the room.

THAT NIGHT, ANNALISA SNUCK INTO THE STABLE WITH George, her head pounding, and her spirit laden with grief.

Surely, George doesn't view women as lowly or severely as Jane views our own sex?

Saddled behind him, they rode from the farm. Annalisa buried her face in George's coat, sickened, and unable to bring herself to ask him.

Under moonbeams, the Peat Moss Inn's yellow clapboard appeared silvery. From the lane, rowdy laughter, shouts, and voices bellowing song echoed into the shadowy night. When George opened the door, the familiar musky odor and fermented hops welcomed her. Nearest the hearth, Jack played his fiddle. In his light baritone, he sang with Mr. Averill.

Jack caught her stare and grinned, singing,

"When came riding over a knough, I met with a farmer's daughter; Rosie cheeks and bonny brow. Good faith made my mouth to water."

Annalisa's face flushed. Before her altercation with Jane, such a charming look from Jack would have kindled her budding fascination, but she followed George, disgusted, to his table at the rear of the tavern.

Mr. Gould approached with a large pitcher of ale and dispatches. He slapped George across the back. "Ye ole whipjacket, bringing this nice lady here after dark."

"Sir, you know I would be here any night if my mamma allowed me. If you don't tell her, I certainly won't." Annalisa winked.

Mr. Gould gave a throaty chortle and handed her a

glass of madeira. He turned to George. "I saw a discrepancy in this ledger."

George scanned the document. "We paid too much for that."

"Not that. That." Mr. Gould pointed at the page.

George's thick brows knitted. "'Tis no discrepancy. That's the going price." He shook his head, defeated. "I can't afford to keep this tavern open with my new one."

"Why don't you sell the tavern you just purchased?" Annalisa asked.

"The Black Water was cheaper than this." George handed the papers back to Mr. Gould. "The tavern itself is bigger and is located in the seaport. I'll have far more patrons in Portsmouth than I have here. I'd be better to sell this one."

Mr. Gould scratched his scruffy chin. "Give me a fair price, and I'll buy this one from ye."

George's eyes rounded. "You mean that, Gould?"

"Aye. I been wantin' a tavern of me own. Nothin' too big. This be perfect in me old age."

"Zounds." George jumped from his seat. "I'll gather my paperwork, and we can talk tomorrow."

At the song's end, Jack set down the fiddle and joined them at the table. "Miss Annalisa, I was most impressed this morning."

"Indeed." She hid her frown behind her glass of madeira. "My skill would be well-placed with any militia or minuteman band."

George choked on his drink. "Annie—"

"A lady she is." Mr. Gould spit into an empty tankard.

Jack cocked his head. "You wish to be a minuteman?"

As the men at the table remained silent, Annalisa clenched her fingers and released them. "Permit me an observation, gentlemen. Is it daft to have as fine a shot as my own amongst yours when you are in need? Or shall you keep us women—your property—indoors while you fight for freedoms we have not?"

Mr. Gould grunted. "A woman can't fight."

"Property?" George leaned forward. "Annie, no."

"How could I live if you were to die at the hands of a Redcoat?" Jack frowned. "I'd surely die myself."

She shivered at his words, and Mr. Gould left the table with a shake of his head, muttering something about doxies from New York being hardly less trifling than the women of town.

George slammed his hand on the table. "Are you satisfied? You've offended Gould. There's no place for women at the tavern who—"

"There's no place for women anywhere!" She crossed her arms. "I meant no harm in my conjecture, but what have I if I cannot fight?"

"There's a place for you, here." Jack reached for her hand. His thumb slid across her knuckles. "And you have plenty of talents—"

"In the ladies' needlepoint circle? With Lizzie and her ridiculous fortune-telling?" Annalisa pulled her hand from his. "I can hardly withstand the chatter of such idled minds. You must mean to use me as sport amongst your friends. I am a bit of gossip, some silly girl who fires a fowling piece. It makes no difference whether or not I do it well, or if I may put it to use—to fight for what I believe in—not that what I believe matters to any of you."

Jack's gaze softened. "Annalisa, you are no joke. You must know how I delight in your wit, and your opinions. But it saddens me you cannot enjoy your time with the ladies. Surely, their minds are not as idle as you propose."

"The ladies cannot afford me the kind of conversation I have with either of you. They lament each time I bring up the rebellion. And Hannah French. With her rude, degrading—"

"Annie, you lose yourself." George's jaw stiffened. "I've taught you to use a firelock to safeguard our home as a last resort. I know we've practiced with quite a shocking bit of liberty between us, but I don't think we ever considered you might become so proficient. 'Tis most unnatural."

"*Unnatural?*" Her fingers dug into the table. "It surprises you a woman can fire a weapon as well as a man. Why not accept it and—"

"Zounds. You're persistent. What's gotten into you? You're lucky I've allowed you to come here tonight against Mother's wishes."

Jack squeezed George's shoulder. "Cousin, Miss Annalisa is always welcome."

She stood. "George Howlett, you haven't allowed me."

"Sit down."

"I will not."

George rose from the bench and pulled her aside. "I'll not have you make a fool of yourself—not before me, not before Gould, and especially not before Jack."

She ripped her arm from his grasp. "You try to control me like Mamma. I'm just some burden you're waiting to marry off."

"That is a lie." George tugged her from the bustle of

the tavern and into the keg room. He sat on a large barrel. "Come, you know I cannot abide by what Mother says. She treats you far more unfairly. I speak with reason. It would behoove you to listen for once in your life...else you never would have gotten that scar."

His words stung, but it was true. Her heart in the trenches of her stomach, Annalisa leaned against two oak kegs stacked on top of one another and massaged her temples. Jane thought she should accept her place in Society as a demure lady; George seemed to believe it, too.

George rubbed the side-whiskers that extended to his jaw. "I'm no doxie, nor am I a member of your ladies' circle. I can't fathom the depths of your frustration, so I can only assume how you feel is correct. You know I love to discuss politics with you. But as your brother, and someone who loves you deeply, I can't allow you to speak such folly about the militia, nor can I entertain your ridiculous thoughts about minutemen. Know you anything about them?"

"I—"

"A minuteman must be ready at a moment's notice to engage in imminent battle." He held her stare. "You're braver than most rogues I've seen wielding a firelock, but that doesn't change the fact you're a mort. I don't understand how you can be so fearless, but I like to think I had something to do with it." He scratched the nape of his neck. "Were you a rogue, I'd have you join in an instant."

"George, I can—"

"Stop." He held up a hand. "'Tis nothing to do with me believing your capability, because I know you'd be famous in any militia. But you don't realize the repercussions for a

woman masquerading as a man in the military, do you?"
His bass voice deepened. "You will be charged with imper-
sonation—and jailed. At worst, hanged, if you're found by
the enemy. And I along with you for knowing."

The tavern musings from beyond the small room reverberated between them before he spoke again. "You're
lucky you weren't found out the day of the massacre."

Annalisa swallowed the lump in her throat. She'd
fooled her Danvers militia quite readily—and they liked
her, even respected her—as Benjamin Cavendish. *But will
they be harsh with me if they discover my true self? Will
Nathaniel or Ebenezer listen to me if they know I'm a woman in
disguise?*

Goosepimples spread over her arms, and she shivered.
How could she be a woman in a world that didn't
value her?

When they returned to the table, Annalisa finished her
madeira, determined to prove her worth. She considered
Jane's hope of marrying Oliver and was inspired with an
ingenious plan.

*I can teach Jane a thing or two about being useful as a
woman. Using wit over beauty...*

"Jack...Jane and I have been talking." She ran a finger
around the rim of her glass. "If you'll permit us, we would
like to help the militia. We heard from...Mr. Smith...the
importance of a minuteman band. Perhaps we should go to
the door of every Patriot in town and urge them to vote
for an alarm band for Topsfield's militia. Surely, other
towns have voted for them."

George gave a dubious glare, but Jack looked on her
with tenderness. "A grand idea. I think the men of town
may require some persuading, perhaps even an ordinance,

but we could never begin too soon. It would be an honor to accompany you."

"Jane will be thrilled." Annalisa smirked at George, then returned her attention to Jack. "With you there, I assure you, the rest of our ladies' circle will help."

26

ANNALISA
TOPSFIELD, JULY 1774

ANNALISA RETURNED FROM DANVERS dripping with sweat, and with a burning to reconcile with Jane. It had been two weeks since their quarrel. Her sister had mostly repented in her own way, offering her favorite petticoats to Annalisa.

She hurried inside the barn, lifted Bixby, and propped the piece onto its nails.

"Miss Anna?"

She spun around and gasped. "Quinn."

He squinted with curiosity.

"Please, Quinn, you mustn't tell anyone you've seen me here like this." She rushed toward him. "Please. Especially not George. I'll...I'll do anything you ask of me."

Quinnapin chuckled. "No need, Miss Anna. Do you often sneak off in the early morning dressed like this?"

She fisted her trembling hands. "Yes. I'm part of the Danvers militia."

Quinnapin studied her with thoughtfulness. "And will you fight?"

"I will if I must."

He nodded. "I suspected as much. Will you accept protection?"

She started at his kind reply, when George and Jack had so recently rebuked her. "Of course. But I cannot be worthy."

From a leather sachet at his waist, Quinnapin revealed a purple and white carved feather made of *wampum*. He uttered something in his native Wampanoag, then closed her hand around the *wampum*. "Keep this on your person always. And you are worthy, Miss Anna. Remember that."

The glossy, grooved surface felt warm and energized against her palm. She wanted to hug him, to thank him for believing in her when it felt like no one else did, but she resisted. Instead, she simply looked him in the eye.

"Thank you, Quinn."

"Perhaps we will fight beside one another in battles to come."

"You'd be willing? After what our people did to yours?"

"That is a complicated answer, Miss Anna." Quinnapin ran his thumb over the *wampum* belt around his waist. "I've carried it as a wound in my heart, as my people have for over a hundred years. Everything that was given us by the Creator was taken." He paused. "We're blending in, for the balance of everything...the equality of nature, of Mother Earth and Father Sky. But we want our land back. And maybe fighting against the people who took it will allow us the opportunity to have lost lands returned. I have a Mohican friend out west. He told me the Mohicans have decided to ally with the Patriots. Others have aligned with the British."

Annalisa reached for Quinnapin. "If nothing else

comes of war with England, I pray at least your lands are returned to you." She looked down. "Though I cannot understand your heartache, I do know what it feels like to have to blend in...to pretend to be someone you're not."

Quinnapin squeezed her hand. "Thank you, Miss Anna."

⚜

THAT AFTERNOON, ANNALISA SAT WITH JANE BY THE unlit kitchen hearth, running her fingers over the *wampum* in her pocket. "It will impress Jack if you lead with him today. And remember, a minuteman band is not the same as the militia."

"I know." Jane slid her hands over her petticoat. "You've been educating me since Sunday." She lifted her gaze with gratitude. "I don't deserve this, Annie."

"You do." Annalisa reached for her hand. "You're my sister."

Jane's smile was small. "Is there anything else I must know?"

"No." Annalisa cleared her throat. "Only...don't shy from political talk. Jack will enjoy it."

"Mamma would be livid—"

"Mamma won't be there to listen." Annalisa tucked a piece of Jane's hair into her cap. "You're more than just a beautiful face. Remember that."

Jane and Annalisa met Hannah French at her house, where they joined with Lizzie Balch and Fannie Shepard, then Martha Perley, along their way into town.

Hannah swatted a bug with her fan. "Why are we doing this again?"

The girls walked from the milliner's shop toward the common, where Jack and Abigail would meet them. The air was thick with humidity. From their pink, shining faces, Annalisa knew the ladies were less than enthused to be outdoors today.

"Topsfield's militia needs minutemen. We must get the men in town to vote in favor of them." Annalisa eyed her sister. "Jane?"

"What good would that do for us?" Fannie asked, her chubby face already perspiring beneath her straw hat.

"Annie has explained it quite well," Jane said. Her sister looked beautiful beneath her large straw hat decorated with roses. Perhaps she stood a chance at relearning her self-worth—if Jack Perkins married her.

"I think 'tis a lovely idea," Martha said. "But think you our men will vote for something so radical?"

Annalisa wavered. She, too, was unsure of the idea. Jack was probably right—they'd need an ordinance from the Provincial Congress. But he also said it was never too soon to propagate the idea. "We'll see. I have a good feeling about it."

"I'm shocked it was Jane's proposition." Hannah tossed her head back. "Anna is always spouting off about politics. What a bore."

When they reached the common, Jack and Abigail stood by the Common Rock.

"How handsome he looks in that cream linen coat." Hannah fanned herself.

Annalisa studied Jane for her reaction. Her sister remained silent and poised; the model of a well-bred lady.

"Good-day, ladies." Jack tipped his hat and gave a slight bow. But for Jane, he kissed her hand. "Miss Howlett."

"Mr. Perkins, pray tell, how much longer will you be in town?" Hannah batted her long eyelashes.

"I leave tomorrow for Boston," he replied, without a hint of curiosity in his tone. Hannah turned from him, probably aware of his disinterest.

Abigail linked arms with Annalisa. "Jack will be glad to be far from Hannah French."

Annalisa chewed her nail to hide her giggle. Abigail never liked Hannah—or Lizzie, or Fannie. But for Martha Perley, who had eyes for dear William, Abigail held out her other arm.

"Come, Miss Perley. Let's to the Andrews' first."

Mr. Andrews answered the door himself, probably having heard the giggle of silly girls at his doorstep. His round face and portly belly took up most of the door frame.

"What can I do for you fine ladies and young gentleman?"

Jane hesitated. "Mr. Andrews, we're here to propose a minuteman band for Topsfield's militia. It would require volunteers..."

Annalisa added, "Due to the time commitment to drilling and always being ready to take up arms, Mr. David Perkins, our town treasurer, has proposed the town can offer to pay one shilling per drill."

"We'd like to hold a vote at the next town meeting, sir." Jack stepped forward. "We're hoping to get the voice of every man in town."

Mr. Andrews cleared his throat. "I understand your motives, Mr. Perkins, but I cannot agree with the idea of minutemen in this town. 'Tis far too close to rebellion for my taste. Good-day, sir." He promptly closed the door.

"If anything, Andrews is somewhere between Loyalist and Patriot, like much of town." Jack offered his arm to Jane. "But I'm certain we can sway the lot of them."

They knocked on five more doors, with only one promise to vote in favor of the motion—Mr. Gould. After Mr. Gould, they received six more votes, and two they'd swayed in their favor, thanks to Jack's reminder of the Intolerable Acts and Boston's closed harbor.

Jane glided beside him, her arm around his. "How wonderfully you persuaded Mr. Hill." She still showed no sign of discomfort, despite the suffocating heat.

Jack's pride to have her on his arm gleamed like the beating sun. "Miss Howlett, if I had no skill in the art of persuasion, I'd make a terrible lawyer."

By the time they reached the Averill farm, a good mile from the center of town, even Annalisa lagged from the heat. Fannie dragged behind with Hannah and Lizzie, while Martha kept up with Abigail. They all trailed behind Jane and Jack.

Agitated, Annalisa squeezed her swollen hands. Jane didn't support the Patriots, yet thanks to her coaching, she stuck to Jack's side as though her life depended on the minutemen. Annalisa frowned at her jealousy. *It was my grand design to get Jack and Jane together on this plan. I should feel nothing but grateful they're getting on so well. Jane's probably forgotten all about Oliver...*

Jack stopped and turned, releasing Jane's arm. "Miss Annalisa, would you knock on Mr. Averill's door with me?"

Annalisa marched up to the Averill house with Jack and knocked. Mr. Averill appeared in the doorway, much like Mr. Andrews had.

"My word. What a sight, all these lovely ladies, and a

fine young gentleman." Mr. Averill buttoned his waistcoat and pulled up his stockings. He looked as though he'd been catching a cross breeze in the summer kitchen. "To what do I owe the pleasure?"

Annalisa explained the purpose of their visit, and Mr. Averill nodded.

"Of course. I think 'tis a splendid idea. I heartily give my consent. And I suspect Josiah will vote in favor as well." He nodded again. "A brilliant idea. I'm mighty impressed. Our town needs more ladies like you, Miss Annalisa." He chuckled, then murmured, "I won't tell your father."

When he closed the door, Annalisa jumped from the stone step. "I think we've swayed enough men in our favor."

The ladies clapped, then returned to fanning themselves.

Jack detained Annalisa at the bottom of Mr. Averill's front-door steps. "We could not have done this without you."

"Pardon?"

His smile lines creased. "I have a feeling this was your grand scheme."

"No." Annalisa pointed. "Jane—"

"Is Loyalist, and cares little for the rebellion." Jack held her gaze and kissed her hand, lingering a moment too long for propriety. "Thank you, Annalisa."

She bit her lip. *He saw right thought my plan. Should I feel this relief?*

When they joined the others, her friends looked sweaty and miserable.

"Ladies, each of you has helped the cause, and I can

speak for the other men in town relaying our gratitude."
Jack bowed. "If the vote passes, on my honor, I swear to
offer myself to the band to protect this town at a
moment's notice. None of you need fear the regulars as I
fight alongside your fathers and brothers."

Annalisa swelled with Jack's gallant promise. Lost in
his sincerity, she took Jane's arm. "See how glad he is?"
They lingered behind for a moment until Jack and Abigail
were beyond earshot.

"I do." Jane squeezed her hand. "Are you happy?"

Annalisa furrowed her brows, confused. "Yes."

Jane faced Annalisa. "I never should have let you
convince me to partake in this. If the vote passes, we've
ensured Jack will risk his life for this rebellion at a
moment's notice. What if he dies in battle? I can hardly
marry him, then."

27

ANNALISA
SEPTEMBER 1, 1774

DRESSED AS BENJAMIN, ANNALISA sat across from Nathaniel and Ebenezer at the tavern in Danvers. Mr. Proctor had summoned them after drill practice this afternoon with urgent news.

She leaned forward. "When will he speak?"

"I think he hopes for more men to join." Ebenezer looked about the tavern.

"Gentlemen." Mr. Proctor's voice rumbled like thunder. "The Bloodybacks are marching."

Annalisa's skin prickled, and Ebenezer's eyes rounded.

Nathaniel jumped. "From where?"

"Boston. I heard from the cobbler in Salem they mean to engage in battle. This is cause for alarm. We could be at war."

It had been two months since their efforts in Topsfield, and the militia had yet to enact a minuteman alarm band. Annalisa rose from her seat and hurried to the door.

"Where are you going, Cav?" Nathaniel asked.

"To warn the men of Topsfield."

Annalisa rode Dinah hard and fast, northward home. But it wasn't her farm she meant to go. She arrived outside the Peat Moss Inn, tied her horse to the usual maple, and ran to the road. As she approached the tavern, shouts resonated through the quiet September evening.

A gallop sounded behind her, and a man hastily dismounted. She lowered her head, seeing only shapely legs covered in white silk stockings and fitted black breeches. The man made his way toward her, his black frock coat flapping behind him.

He touched her shoulder as he passed. "Pardon me, good lad."

She'd know that genteel voice anywhere.

Jack.

He hadn't recognized her. She reached into her coat and fingered Quinnapin's *wampum* feather. *Could it be magick?*

Her spirits lifted for only a moment, then a cold sweat broke under her hat. *If Jack had ridden from Boston, Mr. Proctor's news must be true.*

Annalisa dashed behind the building, pushed open the rear door, and entered the tavern. Quickly, she slipped into the keg chamber. The salty stink of sweat settled around her as she sat upon an oak barrel. Shadows flickered against the walls and passionate vulgarities flew from the mouths of even the genteelest of men.

"Gentlemen, please," Mr. Averill shouted, but no one paid him heed.

"Those Lobsterback bastards dare to march on us," George exclaimed.

When had George returned from Portsmouth?

"How can we sit here and do nothing?" Her brother

slammed his fist on the table and stood. "I say we march to Boston at once."

Mr. Andrews' round face turned purple as he stood by the fire. "Peace, Mr. Howlett. You come here after being absent for weeks. How quick you are to throw us into the fire. We must learn more of what's happened before we march."

"Nonsense, Andrews." Quinnapin slammed his tankard on the table. "Mr. G hears news quickly in Portsmouth by way of water—we are lucky he rides here tonight. I, too, heard Boston is being blasted by British ships."

"What do you care if we march, *savage?*" Mr. Andrews scorned. "Last I heard, your tribes have been neutral in these conflicts."

"Shut your potato trap, Andrews," George barked. "Quinn is a devout Patriot—"

"Savage?" Quinnapin rose and flew toward Mr. Andrews. He gripped the portly man by his coat, his face inches from Mr. Andrews'. "Your *savage* people would have us sit here and hold a vote if your own meetinghouse were ablaze."

"Gentlemen, please," Ezra Kimball pleaded.

"War be at hand." Samuel jumped. "We must act."

"Jack Perkins." Mr. Gould's voice resonated near the chamber, and Annalisa froze in place. Gould's tall, thin frame came into view as he wiped clean a pewter mug and tossed a muslin towel over his shoulder. "Ye just returned from Boston. What have ye heard?" He chuckled. "Ye rushed in here with your arse afire."

Annalisa studied Jack from across the room, and her stomach knotted. His tranquil, blue eyes appeared dark and uneasy in the candlelight.

Jack spun his signet ring—a tick she'd noticed when he was nervous. "I'm on borrowed time, Gould." His voice was even, but rushed. "I must make the last Winnisimmet ferry...Adams expects me in Boston by morning. But I heard the regulars were marching, and people were killed. We must do something. If Stephen would please read aloud the letter I've given him from my father..."

A chorus of shouts raged, and Annalisa hugged herself. The town's militia could very well vote to march to Boston tonight and engage His Majesty's soldiers. Her own militia may be voting similarly.

And I left them.

"Gentlemen." Stephen Perkins held up the dispatch. He waved the note until the clamor faded. "Jack, you may find this pleasing. 'Tis from the Provincial Congress at Cambridge." He read, "*'It has been decided the town of Tops-field, in accordance with the Province of Massachusetts Bay, shall enlist volunteer Minutemen from the militia, should the need arise. Furthermore'*—"

"This is an outrage." Mr. Andrews loosened the colored cravat choking his thick neck. "This is treason."

Cheers erupted, drowning out Mr. Andrews.

"We will have volunteer men always at the ready," Stephen said. "Given a moment's notice, these minutemen will march—should there be reasonable cause." He tilted his chin and gave Mr. Andrews a smug grin. "Tell me, gentlemen, is this news tonight reasonable cause to march?"

"Aye." George straightened his coat. "I'll do it. And any one of us who joins the minutemen tonight should ride to Boston at once."

She'd always known George would join, but in the

reality of the moment, she could hardly contain her disquiet.

"Me, too." William sprang from his chair.

Annalisa gripped the keg. *No, not William, too. He will surely die if wounded in battle.* Her sixteen-year-old brother was not nearly as strong as George.

Samuel and Quinnapin offered themselves, along with Ezra Kimball, Mr. Averill and his son Josiah, David and Stephen Perkins, and Mr. Gould.

"I volunteer as well," Jack spoke, and the room quieted.

"Ye plan on joining the minutemen." Mr. Gould gave a throaty chortle. "Some lawyer ye be."

Jack held up a hand and eyed his father's cousins, David and Stephen. "I made a promise I mean to keep, and I'm my own man, gentlemen—no matter my father's station, no matter Mr. Adams. We must act, lest we find ourselves at the whim of King George and his fools in Parliament. The punishment the Intolerable Acts laid upon Boston Harbor and Massachusetts' charter is tyranny. We must be prepared, should the other colonies follow our lead. I only hope they rally behind us, and not see us as an example of failed resistance."

I must return to Danvers and the militia. Her grip on the keg loosened, and she lost her balance. She tumbled and knocked over a table of pewter mugs that clashed onto to the dusty floor.

"What was that?" Ezra Kimball asked.

"Redcoat spies," Samuel cried.

Annalisa scrambled to her feet, fled the chamber, and pushed herself outside. She clutched her bosom as though a musket ball had trapped itself within her. Dinah was too far. She must hide in the woods. Annalisa snuck into the forest behind the tavern and hid around a tree.

The gentlemen emerged.

"Was it Redcoats?" Ezra asked.

Mr. Averill held a lantern in front of him. "I see not a soul."

She stood motionless in the darkness for several minutes. The danger, the unrest, the uncertainty—all of it was real.

A snap of twigs and rustle of leaves jarred her.

"Kmea, kmea."

Her throat closed, and she narrowed her eyes in the darkness. A creature with grey skin, no taller than three-foot, stared at her. It lured her with a single, pointed finger.

"Kmea."

Annalisa darted from the woods and sprinted up the road a quarter-mile until she reached Dinah. Panting, she mounted her horse and galloped down the lane toward home.

28

ANNALISA

PORTSMOUTH, THE PROVINCE OF NEW
HAMPSHIRE, SEPTEMBER 1774

TWO WEEKS HAD PASSED, and George spoke
nothing of what transpired that night at the Peat
Moss. All Annalisa knew, by admission from Quinnapin,
was they decided not to march to Boston. Anxiously, she
followed George from one room to another inside his new
tavern, the Black Water Inn. She hadn't been there but
once since he'd purchased and opened it, but she had to
admit, the Black Water Inn—near the seaport in Straw-
bery Banke—was a much finer establishment than the
Peat Moss; it's location a hub where news and gossip
could easily spread. The three-story building boasted
several rooms on the ground floor to host guests wishing
to drink, gamble, or discuss politics. The upper two floors
harbored rooms for rent for the weary traveler, as George
put it.

"Look at this, Little One."

Little One—he must know I am taller than I once was?
Bemused, Annalisa followed her brother into a smaller
room with a large gaming table. Already, men sat around it

with cards in hand, their noses and cheeks ruddy with brandy.

"I acquired it from the previous owner." George pulled her into the largest room at the front of the tavern. "Come, I want you to meet Elisha Porter, my tavern-keep for when I'm away in Topsfield."

Behind the bar stood a well-kept freedman in his early thirties, his kind eyes deep brown, like Addy's. He peered at them with a twinkle.

"Mr. Porter, this is my sister, Miss Annalisa." George gestured to her.

Annalisa curtsied. "Sir, how good you are to work for my daft brother."

"Zounds." George chortled. "You demean me in front of my employee?"

Mr. Porter cracked a smile. "He is a fair owner, Miss Annalisa. And I insist you call me Elisha."

"Very well, Elisha. I daresay, we shall meet again."

Annalisa followed George to a vacant table near a window, and Elisha brought them libations; a tankard of flip for George, and a glass of madeira for Annalisa.

When he'd gone, she leaned across the table. "How much longer must I wait before you tell me about the night of September the first?"

George was sipping his warm, frothy beverage when he spit the liquid back into the tankard. "The devil's cock! Annie, what's there to know?"

She crossed her arms. "Tell me what happened."

He cleared his throat and drank from his mug once more. When he set it down, he folded his arms. "There were rumors Boston was being bombarded by warships, people had been killed, and the Lobsterbacks were marching. Truth was, General Gage of the king's army stole gunpowder from the magazine in Charlestown. Seems he'd been planning to raid other arsenals and storehouses throughout New-England." He gulped more of the steaming liquid.

"I did read that in the *Gazette*. But what do we do now?" Annalisa leaned over her drink, nearly spilling it.

"Topsfield has done its duty, as have other towns. A third of all militias now have organized minutemen who will be ready at a moment's notice to engage." He sighed. "Now we wait and see."

Annalisa sipped her sweet wine, wishing it was the flip George drank. "Was Jack there?"

"Why do you ask?" He smirked. "Have you an attachment for him? You know it is *Princess* Jane he seeks."

"I've no attachment." She circled the rim of her glass with her forefinger. "Has he told you he fancies Jane?"

"Nay." George shook his head. "He never speaks to me about such information. I only suspect it." He finished his drink and set it aside. "Pray tell, what of you? Will you, too, try and marry one of my cousins?" He laughed. "Oliver is a bachelor the same as Jack."

"I'll never marry Oliver Perkins."

"Can't say I blame you." George sat back in his chair and locked his fingers behind his head. "He's an insufferable Loyalist cad."

Annalisa bit her tongue, debating whether or not to tell him about Oliver's assault. George would track Oliver down and have him dragged to Portsmouth behind his plow, or worse—a duel. She shivered.

I must prevent bloodshed no matter the cost.

"Jane still wears his pearls. I've instructed her to remove them, but she will not."

"She's a bawdy basket." George's evergreen gaze flickered to Annalisa's neck. "Pray tell, what is that feather you wear? Did it belong to Pa's Agawam mother?"

She shook her head. "No, Quinn gave it to me. He blessed it to keep me safe."

"You believe his Wampanoag fables?"

"I didn't at first, but—" She recalled the night of the gunpowder alarm with feverish clarity, and the creature that had caused her to run. *A Puk-wudjie. I know it was.* "I do believe him."

"He's a true, reliable stable-hand, friend, and Patriot. I cannot fault him that, though his superstitions are just stories."

"You wait." Annalisa smirked. "One day, a *Puk-wudjie* is going to lure you into the forest, and we'll never see you again. Then you'll see."

George cackled. "I'll keep that in mind when next I'm in the woods at night." He winked. "Or I'll call for your help, Little One." He scratched his chin. "You're a special young lady. I hope you know that."

Annalisa reached for his hand. "Only because you taught me to be different than Jane."

"And how different you are." He peered into his empty tankard. When his gaze shifted, mischief twisted his face like she'd never seen from him. "You do have an attachment for Jack."

Heat rose up her neck, and she averted her gaze.

George guffawed. "When next he is in town, play that music for him he bought you in Austria. I bet you Jane's run goods he will fall in love with you."

"You bet Jane's virginity?" Annalisa chuckled, then looked down. "No. How could I do that to Jane?"

"Of course, you can. Then she can marry Prince Oliver and go live her Loyalist life with him."

Jane *had* crossed her terribly back in June. *Do I owe it to myself to pursue Jack when my own sister treated me so cruelly? I would be condemning her to life with a brute. But what if Jack could love me, instead?*

2929

JACK
TOPSFIELD, EARLY DECEMBER 1774

"WHOA, HEY." JACK PULLED the reins of his mare and glanced behind him. "You couldn't wait, could you?" He dismounted, careful to sidestep the horse's fresh pile of dung. He scrunched his nose and rubbed the animal's muzzle. "For shame, Morgaine. Now we must clean this before we make ourselves unwelcome."

"Jack."

His pulse quickened. He'd know that voice anywhere. Annalisa Howlett bounded toward him, her grey wool petticoats tucked between her legs as she ran.

"Good-day, Miss Annalisa." He lifted his cocked hat.

She performed a deep, mocking curtsy. "Mr. Perkins. I'm right heartily glad for your call. You know to call me Annalisa. In fact, with no one else to hear you, I may even permit you to call me Annie."

He warmed. "That is bold."

"La. We are close, are we not? Near as kin?"

"We are." He smiled. "I recall myself saying something of the like at one time." She twirled about and her emerald eyes left him breathless, as they had the day of the massacre. "Annalisa, watch out." Jack reached and pulled her from the horse's dung. "You've stepped in Morgaine's..." He laughed.

She peered at her shoe and her face brightened to the color of cranberries. "Oh, so I have."

He helped her onto the mare and held her ankle while he unbuckled her shoe.

Annalisa jerked her foot. "Someone will see."

He shot her a mischievous glance and led the horse inside the stable. All was dim and quiet, with not even Quinnapin to see them. "Now may I?"

"Jack Perkins, I can't allow you such a thing."

"What sort of gentleman would I be to let a lady clean horse dung?" He slipped off her shoe and left her protestations inside the barn.

Outside, the icy wind whipped his hair into his face as he knelt at the iron scraper. When he finished, he returned to her. Annalisa sat atop Morgaine, curling and un-curling her toes incased in wool stockings.

He waved the shoe at her and grinned. "May I?"

She nodded.

He held her foot, and burned with the fleeting thought of her bare leg. A hasty glance about the barn, he noticed they were alone, save for Morgaine and the other horses snuffling in their stalls. With the fragrant hay, now an aphrodisiac, the warm and out-of-sight loft beckoned.

Remembering Jane, he shook his head, slid on the shoe, and fastened the buckle. Annalisa had always been dear to him as his cousin's sister. But since springtime, when Mrs. Adams had planted the seed, he'd wrestled with a blossoming attachment. Now it was December, and well past the harvest.

His heart skipped.

The harvest...and Lizzie's fortune-telling at the corn husking those years ago we'd both ridiculed. Could it be true?

"Jack, what is it?"

He blinked, still holding her ankle, then released her. "I know not what came over me. I—"

"Was lost in thought?" Annalisa tilted her head. "No need to apologize. I'm often lost to my own dreams. I like to think it a lesser offense to what I might do otherwise."

"What would you do instead?"

"Of that, I cannot speak. Especially not to you."

Jack grinned. "I hope 'tis nothing that would hinder your reputation."

She giggled. "Heavens, no."

His hands secured about her slim waist, he lifted her from the horse. Once on the ground, Annalisa lingered, her fingers gripping his arms.

"That is...so long as no one catches me in the act."

Jack bit his bottom lip. He'd never be so bold as to take her here in the stable. She deserved far better than that. He wouldn't be like Oliver, the scoundrel.

Annalisa glanced sideways. "You do follow, yes?"

Did she peer at the loft? She must mean it, then.

Jack laughed as though he were at the tavern. "Please, tell the gentleman of offense to keep his boots on, lest someone interrupts and he must make a quick getaway."

Annalisa's cheeks flared to scarlet. "I beg your pardon?"

One look at her and his smile vanished. "My God. I've spoken out of turn. I cannot believe I said that to you."

"You think I take men with me into the loft?"

He shifted his weight. "I suppose I thought it was the garret you glanced at. Was it not?"

"I allude to musketry. I glanced at Bixby." She crossed her arms. "Jack Perkins, you think of me as some bawdy basket. Surely 'tis from the night Oliver assaulted me at your house in Boston."

"Assaulted?" His throat closed. "I knew not what happened. Beloved friend, if 'tis not too painful to recount, please tell."

Her jaw set as she averted her gaze. "I came downstairs searching for George, but Oliver was alone in the parlor. He beckoned I sit with him, so I obliged. He cornered me...your brother kissed me and..." She placed the heels of her hands to her eyes, perhaps not anticipating the difficulty of relaying such a memory. "He cornered me, lifted my skirts, and..."

Jack clenched his fists, and anger burned his neck. "I saw he kissed you, which was offense enough. But he—touched you?"

"He did grab me," Annalisa cried. "Between my legs. I swear to you, I didn't want him. I never wanted him—I barely knew him at all. And now you think I wish to take men into the garret."

"Oh, Annalisa." Jack took her into his arms, and she heaved against his chest. He pressed his nose to her cap and smelled delicate lilac. His tender friend, what horror she endured at the hands of his own beast of a brother. His ire swarmed like a hornet's nest. "I'll challenge him."

"No." She pulled from him and swiped her tears.

"The scoundrel behaved as a beast. 'Tis uncouth, and... and a defamation to your good reputation. And mine."

"You mustn't. Then George will find out."

Everything screeched to a halt. "George knows not?"

Annalisa shook her head. "If he finds out, he will kill Oliver."

Jack cupped his mouth and paced for several moments. *She is right. If George discovers what Ollie did, there will be a duel. But can I keep this terrible secret from my beloved cousin?* He faced her. "What can I do to avenge your good character?"

"You can promise me one thing." She hesitated. "It comes at a high price."

"Go on."

She rubbed Morgaine's snout. "I know you volunteered to be a minuteman for Topsfield's alarm band…"

"There is little reason to worry. I know the gunpowder alarm had us all affright, but I swear, your brothers and I shall be safe."

"This must be your promise. Can you keep it well?"

"I can." Jack took up her hands. "No Redcoat shall kill me so long as you're here for me to come home to."

"Then I'll never leave Topsfield." A frigid breeze blew through the stable door, and Annalisa shuddered.

Jack held out his arm to her. "Let's get indoors."

"Yes. Mamma will be wondering—and Jane. They've been expecting your call." She turned to him before stepping outside. "I have a surprise for you."

He followed her from the barn, up the path, and into the warm farmhouse. Comforting smells of thyme and sage wafted from the kitchen, yet he proceeded to the drawing room with trepidation. He'd nearly forgotten his call was for Jane.

Mrs. Howlett beamed. "How good of you to call, Mr. Perkins."

Annalisa gestured to her sister, who sat diligently at the spinet. "Jane has learned the music you gave me, and would like to play it for you."

He laughed. "This is not the music I stole for you from Mozart when I was in Austria, is it?"

"Stole?" Annalisa's eyes widened.

Jack grinned. "I crept into Mozart's maestro suite, long after his concert ended. There, upon his own luminescent pianoforte, I plucked the pages from his stand and tucked it into my waistcoat. I nearly risked my life to bring you this masterpiece." Though he jested, his heart coiled with melancholy. He'd so hoped Annalisa would play it for him.

Jane rose from the bench. "Annie, you should play it for Mr. Perkins."

"Nonsense." Annalisa touched Jane's shoulder. "You worked hard to learn it." She glanced at Jack. "It was to surprise you, sir."

Jane placed her fingertips to the keys and started the movement, but she stopped after the first page, shaking her head. "I cannot, Annie. Please, this was your gift." She lifted from the bench and joined Jack on the sofa, her lavender scent settling over him.

He leaned back and crossed one leg over the other, and clasped her hand. It drained the warmth from his.

Annalisa sat at the spinet and clutched the music to her breast. "In all your kindness and unaffected generosity that has made me feel worthy of your friendship, this is for you, Mr. Perkins." She straightened herself upon the bench. When she exhaled, her fingers sprang across the keys in a rapid whirlwind of the first movement, the *allegro*.

By the time she reached the slower second movement,

the *adagio,* Jack barely breathed. The room faded, and he lost himself in her passion; her slender frame, her focused eyes, her capable hands.

She played from memory, but with unwritten flourishes and trills that only the purest love of music extracts from the soul. His heart ached as the sad melody drenched his senses. And when her hands repeated the beginning of the movement, Jack returned from his reverie, back into the comfort of the drawing room and the ever-so-quiet Jane beside him.

A deafening silence followed, and Annalisa turned.

Mrs. Howlett clapped. "Well done."

"Yes," Jane said. "I never could have played it so well."

Jack shook himself of his stupor and returned Annalisa's eager smile. A strange tingling edged along his back. *With such grace she played, such resonance.* How profound she was, this young lady whom he had gotten to know so well over the past four years, this lady whom he was now certain he loved—had loved all along. The thought startled as he acknowledged Jane's chilled hand between his. He'd been so blinded by her beauty.

This must be what love—true love—feels like. I am in love with Annalisa Howlett.

He reverberated with the delight and novelty of a child eating sugary molasses candy for the first time.

"Mr. Perkins, say something, please." A look of horror spread across Annalisa's face.

Jack stood and joined her at the spinet. "My dearest friend, you've entranced me. You've come such a way from Scarlatti."

She lowered her gaze. "I hardly believe my playing is worthy of your compliment. You saw Mozart himself."

He blinked several times. "Your playing has moved me beyond anything, or anyone."

"'Tis true," Jane added pleasantly. "You are more accomplished than any other girl in town."

Could I have mistaken Annalisa's favorable attention this past summer as sisterly affection—as I had assumed of myself until this very moment?

He returned to his seat beside Jane, his chest tight with an even greater conviction. Should there be a battle in the coming months, it would be hard enough leaving Annalisa as a dear friend. As a wife, he could never part with her.

30

ANNALISA

PORTSMOUTH, THE PROVINCE OF NEW
HAMPSHIRE, MID-DECEMBER 1774

MAMMA's ICY GLARE CHILLED Annalisa to her core. "Annalisa Howlett, you've gawked at Jack Perkins for the final time. While the gentleman is in town, I'm sending you to Portsmouth with George."

"But Mamma, he called on Jane." Annalisa hurried after her. "I only played for him because Jane insisted. He fancies Jane, I know he does."

Mamma's hand settled on her hip. "He made it quite clear he appreciated your talents. Perhaps too well." Her tone hardened. "As your elder, Jane must marry first. You know the rules."

"An antiquated tradition." Annalisa threw up her hands and followed Mamma into the kitchen. "I assure you I have no attachment for him. He is my brother's cousin, and my friend."

"Your friend, indeed." Mamma whirled around, her eyes wild. "Bette and I have agreed Jane should marry Jack. What say you to that?"

"You have?" Annalisa's face numbed. "Does Jack know? Does Jane?"

"They will soon enough. Now pack your things. George leaves in an hour. I'll not have you delaying him. The weather looks like snow, and your brother has a business to run. That poor Elisha cannot bear the brunt of your brother's lackadaisical management." Mamma pointed to the stairs. "Go."

⚜

ANNALISA SHIVERED AND GRUMBLED BESIDE GEORGE AS he drove the chaise north to New Hampshire.

"Worry not." George glimpsed her. "Jack won't call while we're away. He's far too busy with his work."

She grunted. "'Tis no matter. Mamma will have Jane married to him before next year's husking."

By the time they reached Portsmouth, the snow flurries had turned to thick white flakes that obscured the road. Their wobbling chaise arrived at the Black Water Inn just as the wheels had begun to skid and slide upon the road.

George carried Annalisa's trunk up the stairs to her usual guest room on the third floor at the tavern's rear. He set her chest at the foot of a narrow bed.

"I could use your help tonight, Little One." He lingered before the open door. "Come down when you've changed and freshened up." He kissed her forehead and latched the door behind him.

Annalisa splashed cold water on her face and cleaned her hands in the washbasin. She peered into the looking glass.

Surely, I'm as agreeable as Jane. Not as pale or beautiful or accomplished, but still handsome despite the scar. Some man other than Jack Perkins might marry me someday. If I marry at all.

She turned from the mirror and quit the room.

At the bottom of the stairs, Elisha greeted her with a kind smile. "Welcome back, Miss Annalisa. If you wouldn't mind serving ale—"

Two gentlemen entered the tavern and snow blew in from the street. A gust of wind whipped around Annalisa's skirts.

"Have you any private tables, sir?" The man who directed his question to Elisha bore dark hair and eyes. He wore a travel cloak and clutched a haversack. Judging from his harried figure, he must have ridden far, and without rest.

Elisha nodded. "We do, sirs. Follow me. Miss Annalisa, the ale."

She hurried after Elisha through the main tavern area —picking up a pitcher along the way—and into a smaller room at the back of the inn. Elisha set down two pewter tankards and retreated from the room.

The dark-haired man took a hasty seat. "Mr. Cutts, I come with news most foul from Boston."

Mr. Cutts nodded. "Go on, Mr. Revere."

Mr. Revere paused and glanced at Annalisa. She quickly poured ale into the tankards and fled the room, but hid behind the door to listen.

"The king's army embarked in secret for Newport, Rhode Island, but it is suspected they travel here to Portsmouth to take possession of Fort William and Mary," Mr. Revere murmured.

Annalisa gripped her bosom. *'Tis like the night of the Powder Alarm in Charlestown.*

"Thank you for your information, sir," Mr. Cutts replied. "I'll gather our fellow Patriots. Surely Langdon will lead our rallied men to the Castle on the morrow."

A chair squealed upon the wooden floor, and Mr. Revere sped through the door, meeting her along the way. Annalisa gave a quick curtsy and followed him to the main entryway. He tipped his hat to her, opened the front door, and stepped into the cold December afternoon, the door slamming behind him.

SHE JERKED AWAKE THE FOLLOWING MORNING TO THE sound of fifes and drums echoing down the streets. Bright light streamed through the window. The clock chimed ten. George had let her sleep quite late.

Or he is not here.

Annalisa jumped from the bed and started to pull on her brothers' garments, now altered to better fit her figure, and noticed blood staining her shift.

The morbid flux!

She rummaged through her trunk and gasped. She hadn't packed her menses apron made of diaper linen. Panicked, she used one of her regular linen aprons. When dressed, she opened the door and lingered atop the stair, listening for George's deep, cavernous voice from the ground floor. *Nothing but the sound of patrons below.* Annalisa snuck down the rear staircase and out the back door.

Cold, winter air slipped into her chest as she meandered through town toward the parade.

"To the castle," men shouted.

"We shall raid the fort of its gunpowder before His Majesty's men arrive!"

The crowd multiplied by the minute as more Patriots gathered in the street.

"Such is treason," a voice boomed over the mob. "Governor Wentworth hath sent me to dissuade you."

"Who is that man?" Annalisa asked a gentleman beside her.

He snarled. "Governor Wentworth's lapdog, Councilor Theodore Atkinson, Jr."

"Gentlemen," Atkinson continued, "it is unlawful to take His Majesty's gunpowder, and to do so is the highest act of treason committed."

Hisses and "fies" erupted from the crowd. Annalisa shivered, recalling the day of the Boston Massacre. Hopefully, this would not end in bloodshed.

"Go back to Wentworth, you Tory reptile," a man cried.

"Aye. To the gundalow."

Annalisa followed the spirited mob down several streets until they reached a body of water, the Piscataqua River, she'd heard them call it. There, a barge would take them to the island that kept Fort William and Mary—the place she'd heard Mr. Revere speak about yesterday.

Nearly fifty men pushed and crowded onto the flatboat.

"Where d'ye think yer headed, young master?" A foul odor of rotting onions huffed down her neck. "There be plenty o' men aboard the gundalow."

Annalisa squinted at his beady eyes. "Shut your potato trap, you reptile."

He chuckled. "Yer an awful pretty boy, ain't ye?" He knocked off her hat and yanked her from the pier.

She ripped her arm from his grimy grip. "My name is Benjamin—"

"Shut it." He grasped her shoulder and glanced down at her breeches. "Looks like yer bleedin', *Miss Benjamin*. I suggest ye get back t'yer husband. Or I'll take ye home with me."

Her skin bristled at the scent of his acrid breath, and she looked down. Blood had seeped through her apron and stained between her legs. "I'd rather die." Annalisa's arm recoiled and swung. Her fist collided with his cheek, and he stumbled backward.

The man, stunned, shook his head and held his face. "I'll...I'll have ye arrested!"

Her knuckles pounding, Annalisa snatched her hat and hurried from the pier as the barge bobbed down the icy river toward New Castle Island.

When she returned to the tavern, Annalisa dashed up the back stairs, into her room, and latched the door behind her. She closed and opened her throbbing fist. Dark purple already spread across the knuckles.

It mattered little that she'd taken such care disguising her appearance. Without a proper period apron, she could hardly disguise her sex during the morbid flux. She paced before the small fire, still fisting her hand. At least he hadn't turned her in to the authorities.

How unlucky, how humiliating. Will my militia, too, eventually discover my identity?

The thought clogged her nose and throat, and she rubbed her eyes. Composed, she stripped from her menswear, changed out of her apron, and donned her jump, petticoats, and work-dress. It didn't seem George or Elisha looked for her, so she removed a few books from the bookcase, eager to quell her troubled thoughts.

Annalisa opened an old book of poems. Her eyes fell upon one by Saint John of the Cross, and she read,

"In darkness and concealment, my house being now at rest. In that happy night, in secret, seen of none, seeing nought myself, without other light or guide save that which in my heart was burning."

She fingered the *wampum* at her neck and closed the book.

How many secrets do I keep? The militia, Oliver's assault, my love for Jack...how much longer can I masquerade in the militia before they realize my identity? How long before Jane spills my secret to George, and when will Jane and Jack wed?

Turning toward the fire, she released the necklace. The flames flickering and dancing illuminated a light inside her that could hardly be snuffed, the same burning desire which guided Saint John of the Cross in his poem.

I've come too far, fought too hard. I will persist, for, if I do not, what else have I worth living?

Part Two

1775

31

GEORGE
TOPSFIELD, APRIL 1775

A RMED WITH BIXBY AND his cartridge box, George walked through the main room of the Black Water Inn, and past William, who bent over a ledger at the bar.

William jumped from behind the bar and chased after him.

"You can't leave now. We've inventory to check."

"I'm promised to Topsfield's minutemen." George turned. "I will not abandon them now."

William's arms crossed. "Then you leave me to do all of it with Elisha."

George adjusted the haversack over his shoulder. He'd had this argument with William since his brother started working for him in March, every other week. "*Wilhelmina*, you'd be attending with me had you not changed your decision to join."

William's blue eyes pierced like their mother's. "I had to. Your tavern would never make it through the season with both of us engaged. You know I wish to join. You needn't salt the wound of my pride with yours."

"Will, these are the times which define us. You're seventeen now, and can do one of three things: stay here and cower from the fight, return to Topsfield and sit idly in Pa's Loyalist shadow, or you can pull up your breeches and join us. No one is going to force you. 'Tis your decision, Brother. Not mine."

George quit the tavern as William shouted after him, "'Tis your tavern, not mine!"

DRILL PRACTICE ON TOPSFIELD'S COMMON LASTED several hours, and George could hardly wait to slake his thirst with Gould's strong ale. Gould, their newly appointed captain, rallied the minutemen and led them to his Whispering Willow tavern—George's old Peat Moss Inn—where the smoky, bitter aroma of hearth and liquor lingered like a welcome lover.

Invigorated, George slid onto the bench at his usual table. "I'll maim the first Redcoat that crosses my path."

Jack, having returned from Boston, sat beside him. "'Tis good to hear your Lobsterback rhetoric, Cousin."

George smirked. "And when will you open a law office here in town, Perkins?"

Jack's cheek dimpled. "As soon as I find a wife."

"Ye mean ye haven't asked Jane t' marry ye yet?" Samuel howled. "What're ye waitin' fer?"

"Easy, Sam." Quinnapin pushed a frothing mug of flip before George. "George, we're all grateful you've decided to remain in the minutemen, but how does your tavern fare while you're gone?"

"It does well enough. Elisha is an honorable inn-keep in my stead. But since William's started working every other week, he scolds me like some doxie each time I leave for town." George's jaw tightened. "He is Patriot, but needs to think—and act—for himself."

Samuel leaned across the table. "Will any o' ye enlist in a proper army if th' time comes fer such measure?"

"I am committed to the minutemen." George drank the warm, bitter flip, then wiped his mouth with the back of his hand. "Rogues, I'm a wayward farer, and the Sons of Liberty are my compass. Blood pulses through my veins for one purpose alone, and 'tis to bring King George to his knees."

The others snickered, and Samuel's hand landed upon the table. "The only person ye bring t' such a position be Dolly Smith o' Andover."

George chuckled. He'd had his share of women, including Dolly. But now, only one woman occupied his thoughts: Abigail. The other reason he frequented Topsfield.

"What? Miss Smith?" Jack's brows arched. "I thought she was a girl of propriety."

Samuel snorted. "A decent girl at takin' t' th' hayloft."

"She's a rather eager girl," George replied. "But that was years ago."

"I heard she been t' Mr. Whipple's hayloft now, twice. Won't be long 'til she has a full belly," Samuel cried.

Quinnapin leaned forward. "Twice in one week, or twice in a month?"

His friends' voices faded as George peered about the

room. All this talk of Miss Smith drifted his thoughts to Abigail. He rose from the bench. "To the necessary."

"Always makin' water, ye are," Samuel bellowed.

George left the tavern through the back door. Outside, he untied Frederick and rode into the April twilight. He traveled two miles from town, past his family's farm, and farther yet, until he reached the Perkins Estate.

The gentle chirp of peeper frogs stirred the evening air from a bog across the lane. He lifted from Frederick and tied him to a fence. In the light of the rising moon, he glimpsed the Perkins' large house perched on its small hill. Dim, yellow glows flickered from windows at both levels. He waited several moments, staring at the second story, before he snuck up to the house.

A woman's silhouette appeared in full form as she passed by a window. He reached for a pebble and tossed it up to tap against the glass.

The lady stopped and threw open the sash. Abigail poked out her head.

George crept below the casement. "Abigail, 'tis me."

"George?" She peered back inside, then stuck her neck out once more. "I thought you in Portsmouth."

"I returned for drill practice, and to see you. I want to take you somewhere."

"You're daft. Ollie is in the parlor. I'll never be able to sneak out. Beatrice has Susie and me tucked in for the night. I must wait at least until she falls asleep."

"I'll wait."

"Go behind the carriage house. I'll be down in twenty minutes."

George disappeared down the hill, across the drive, and slipped behind the carriage house. He waited, gazing at the sky. Thousands of stars glittered, though paled by the waxing moon. He looked at his pocket watch. Nine o'clock.

Twenty minutes had passed, and Abigail scurried around the side of the building. She looked beautiful in the moonlight, and all sense of uncertainty vanished. He reached for her hand and placed her palm to his mouth.

Abigail recoiled. "I won't be taken for some doxie, George Howlett."

"You're no doxie." He chuckled at her bear-garden jaw. "I've told you, 'tis been at least a year since I've last considered another." He brushed her cheek. "You occupy my thoughts, and you alone."

"Do you promise to behave as a gentleman?"

George grinned. "Of course, my lady. This way." He led her to Frederick, and they rode from the estate.

When they neared town, George trotted his horse down a narrow trail, where dark forest surrounded them.

Abigail shuddered against him. "Where are you taking me?"

"The Capen Barn."

She gasped. "'Tis haunted."

"Not while I'm there." George snickered. "'Tis an old relic."

She gripped his arm. "Was it not used for witchcraft?"

Amused, he bellowed. "The rumor is the old barn was a haven for accused witches in 1692." In a low, eerie voice, he added, "'Twas nearly burnt to the ground by the accusers with the defendants trapped inside."

Abigail squeezed him tighter, and he wrapped a protective arm about her. At once, her rigid form eased.

The barn, illuminated by scattered moonbeams,

appeared against the blackened forest. George dismounted and lifted Abigail from his horse. The entryway seemed an ominous tomb. As they drew nearer, silvery rays spilled down from holes in the roof onto the old, wooden floor. He led her inside.

"What a derelict place," Abigail whispered, as though afraid to rouse lingering spirits.

George crinkled his nose against the musky mildew. "Josiah Averill claims his distant cousin, Sarah Averill Wildes, was trapped in this barn as an accused witch." He turned to her. "She did hang, you know."

Abigail slapped his chest. "Stop it, George Howlett. You frighten me so. Do you tell that to every girl you bring here?"

"Peace, Abby. I've never so much as witnessed a chipmunk or squirrel, let alone a wraith, or visage of the deceased. I jest. This barn played no part in the witch trials." They moved slowly, avoiding holes in the floor and cobwebs dangling from the ceiling. "I've not taken any other lady here."

She faced him. "Truthfully?"

"Upon my word—as a gentleman."

"I always thought I'd dread such a place, but with you here, I fear not a thing in this world." She paused, seeming to debate whether or not to speak further. "I've always favored you, you know."

He ached at her fine words, and his desire pulled her into a strong embrace. They stood in the murky quiet, the dankness engulfing them with her cheek pressed to his chest. George kissed the top of her head.

Abigail lifted her face, and their lips met. He drank her entirely, her soft mouth quenching the thirst he'd long endured. George tugged free of his coat and placed it onto the floor. He lay her atop, only considering for a moment he could get her with child.

She unbuttoned his waistcoat. "George Howlett, I wish for you to strum me here, this instant." Moonbeams slid across her face to reveal her smile. "I wouldn't be here with you if I didn't favor you above all others."

"Even more than that dandy Lord Essex?"

"La. I've met him but once. You've grown to mean so much to me."

He held her close. "I wouldn't have you like this if I didn't feel the same."

"What if you get me with child?"

"Then I'd be a father."

Abigail slapped his chest. "You would marry me, George Howlett."

"Of course, I'd marry you. I'd marry you even if I don't get you in the family way." His heart quickened. He hadn't yet admitted these feelings to himself, and now he relayed them to her.

George kissed her again, this time for several moments, when beyond the barn, he heard a crunching of leaves.

It is probably a squirrel or a deer. Or a Puk-wudjie. Damn Annalisa and Quinn's lore.

Footsteps echoed in the darkness, and an intruder held out a lantern.

"For the love of God!"

Oliver emerged in a crimson coat, a beacon of Tory loyalty. George pulled Abigail to her feet. She brushed leaves from her hair, and he adjusted his cravat.

Oliver stormed inside and grabbed Abigail's arm. "The act of a whore."

She jerked. "We only kissed, I swear it. How did you find me?"

"Susie was awake and has a rather fast tongue." Oliver glowered at George. "I only guessed where he might take you."

George glared at Oliver, but pulled Abigail close. "I love her, most violently."

"You mean it?" Abigail faced him. "Because I love you, too."

Oliver, lingering near the doorway, lowered the lantern and crossed one arm over the other. The light, now below his chin, cast a devilish shadow upon his face. "Abby, you're a fool to think Mother and Father might allow you two to marry. You're the daughter of a lord. You must marry a lord. Think you they will be proud to have their daughter the wife of a tavern owner?"

"You speak cruelly," she cried. "George has an inheritance. If he is not worthy of me, no man is."

"You know Society will never accept such folly." Oliver huffed. "You should be glad Mother and Father know nothing of your sneaking out." He spat at George's shoes. "I must protect Abigail's reputation."

"Reputation be damned." George bared his teeth. "I'd do nothing to hurt her, or your family."

"Fie. You'd better keep a sharp eye, *Cousin*. I'll not forget this. And you'll not say a word of this." Oliver tugged Abigail from his embrace. "Especially not to Annalisa."

George stared after them as they quit the barn and the glow of lanternlight disappeared down the path.

That Tory bastard.

༺✿༻

A WHITE MIST DRIFTED OVER THE FARM THE FOLLOWING day. Despite the chill of morning, sweat dripped from George's brow. His head spun with weariness as he lagged behind two oxen pulling his plow.

Will Oliver relay last night's charade to Jack?

His stomach heaved.

"With some energy, George," Pa called from under his straw hat.

George grumbled. Already, Quinnapin, Zeke, and Dane had covered twice as much field as he.

Horse's hooves sounded from the road, and George looked up. A rider galloped wildly down the narrow lane, then cantered up the path to their farm. "There are engagements at Lexington! Redcoats have fired on us!"

George stopped mid-furrow, all thought of last night vanishing from his mind. He sprinted toward the barn with Quinnapin close behind him.

"George, wait!" Annalisa ran from the house. "Engagements? What sort of engagements?"

"Annalisa Howlett, back inside." Mother stepped from the house, blocking her from chasing him.

Despite his huffing breath and racing heart, George focused his thoughts. "Let's ride, Quinn."

He and Quinnapin retrieved their effects, saddled and mounted horses, and hurtled from the farm. They galloped hard and fast toward the common, where the minutemen were to assemble.

32

JACK
CONCORD, APRIL *19, 1775*

J ACK MARCHED THE LONG road to Concord
beside Samuel, and Topsfield's minutemen. He could
only surmise what they'd encounter when they
arrived. It was possible the king's army opened fire on
civilians as they had in Boston five years ago. Or, it was
false information as the powder alarm had been last
September.

He bit his cheek, wondering where George and Quinnapin were. Surely, his cousin hadn't returned to
Portsmouth last night.

Several hours into the march, Jack's feet throbbed and
swelled inside his stiff, leather shoes. It made little difference that the day was particularly cool; droplets beaded at
his temples and dripped down his cheek. Perhaps his
cousin and Quinn had ridden this long way to Lexington.

Ahead, clouds of smoke rose up from the land, the air
smelling faintly sulfuric.

Gunpowder.

When they reached a junction in the road, the crack of

musket-fire rang out from the west.

"The Lobsterbacks retreat," a rider shouted. Grime and sweat covered the man's face, his eyelids dropping from apparent weariness. Jack gripped his musket and looked to his captain—Father's cousin, Stephen—for orders.

Stephen squinted. "Are there other militia along the road, sir?"

"Aye." The rider wiped his brow. "The Bedford and Billerica militias arrived not but a quarter hour ago. They are up the road, waiting in ambush."

Stephen looked to Gould, their second captain. "It seems this is no drill."

Gould nodded. "Aye, gents, we march on."

They continued until they reached a mildly-forested area where the highway sharply curved.

"Sir, the other militia." Jack gestured to the men gathered on either side of the lane. They crouched behind trees and a stone wall.

"Make haste from the road," a man shouted from behind a tree. "The regulars are coming."

Stephen motioned for his band to gather on one side, while Gould's took the other. "Gentlemen, cover yourselves well, and make ready."

Using the stone wall as a refuge, Jack crouched with Samuel and loaded his musket. His body pulsated like a native drum, an anxiety he must share with the others beside him. For a moment, he studied Stephen. His captain's face remained calm, steady as stone—like Father. Did Stephen tremble with anticipation? Samuel, too, held a serene countenance, but behind those light grey eyes, did he fear?

Jack lifted his gaze to the highway. Neither voices nor the chirping of birds sounded. The world remained in awful stillness, like the trepidation that precedes a great nor'easter. While he watched the road, two panting men rushed to his side.

"Well I'll be damned."

Startled, Jack turned.

"Howlett!" Samuel clapped his back. "Quinn."

Relief washed over Jack at the sight of his cousin and Quinnapin. They appeared unharmed, a feat he marveled.

"You're both well." Jack gripped George's arm, and his cousin squatted behind the stone wall. Jack's gaze darted between them and the road, expecting the regulars to march into view any minute. "Came you from Lexington?"

"What've ye seen?" Samuel's knuckles whitened around his musket. "How long they be fightin'?"

George looked to the lane. "There was an assault at the North Bridge, now they retreat. We heard from a rider Topsfield's minute came this way."

"We arrived after Lexington's boys pursued the Redcoats to North Bridge." Quinnapin sipped from his canteen. "I heard from another militiaman the first shot rang out a bit before dawn."

George wiped the sweat under his hat. "I'm certain the Bloodybacks fired first." He looked past Jack and his face hardened. "Are you ready, Perkins?"

Jack turned. From the winding curve in the road, a sea of red emerged. His breath staggered at the glint of gold buttons and steel bayonets.

A crack of musket-fire resonated from the Billerica and Bedford militias, and a large plume of gun-smoke billowed toward his position. The sulfur burned his nose.

"Fire!" Stephen shouted.

Jack knelt, peered over the rock wall, aimed, and fired. He missed, and ducked to pour more gunpowder into his priming pan on the reload. A ball whizzed past and ricocheted off a boulder. It skimmed Jack's shin, just below the knee.

"Damn." He dropped his musket and clutched his leg. Blood dribbled through his ripped stocking and between his fingers. The wound seared like fire and throbbed viciously. Hidden behind the wall, he leaned onto his side and rolled down the stocking. A piece of flesh flapped over the gash. It bled much, but would heal better than if it still held the round.

Behind him, a shot fired, and a charging Redcoat fell forward, his bayonet fixed and aimed, even in death.

"Keep a sharp eye, Mr. J." Quinnapin had fired the fatal round from behind a tree.

An ominous mist of gun-smoke clouded the area. Jack flipped onto his stomach. His body pulsed against the cool, damp leaves. Resolve surged, and he reached for his musket and reloaded.

A few yards away Stephen knelt behind the rock wall, loading. From the road, a British officer took aim. Jack knelt, held the stock to his shoulder, aimed, and fired.

The officer caught the round in his neck. His musket fell as he slapped a hand to his throat. Heaving and choking, the officer staggered toward the rock wall. Desperation flooded his eyes, and he tumbled over the barrier.

Jack crawled toward him, the dead leaves and twigs scraping his knees. He pulled the officer from the barricade and onto the ground. Up close, the Redcoat appeared only a little older than he. Perhaps a man with a wife and children. The man exhaled finality with a sputter of crimson.

"Lord God, be with him," Jack whispered. He shuddered at the thick gurgle of blood-soaked lungs. *I've killed a man.* The officer twitched, then lay still. *Children now fatherless, a wife now widowed. Could I do this to Annalisa?*

Sickened, he suppressed the urge to retch. Jack wiped his face and, with bounding heart, hastened toward Stephen.

"Jack, you saved my life." Stephen's eyes glistened with appreciation as he grabbed Jack's arm.

Musket rounds flew across the road, and Jack ducked. He may have saved Stephen, but Quinn had saved him only moments prior. He peered at his leg. A sizable clot stained his white stockings. He grimaced at the searing pain.

George scurried to meet them.

Crack-boom.

"Cousin, look out!"

"Zounds!" George flew backward and clutched his arm. "Bloodyback bastards." He scooted toward a tree and rested his back against the trunk.

Jack dashed to his side. Blood flowed from George's left bicep and through his fingers. "This is sizeable. You need a surgeon at once."

"'Tis but a scratch." George bellowed with laughter, though he grimaced.

Musket-fire had ceased, and Quinnapin, Stephen, and Samuel joined them by the tree.

"Howlett, ye hulking gollumpus, stand up at once." Though he jested, Samuel's nervous laughter melted into an apprehensive frown.

Quinnapin glanced at the road. "The Billerica militia's already gone. Do we pursue the Lobsterbacks with them, sir?"

They all looked to the lane. The Redcoats continued their march toward Boston. From the look of it, eight Bloodybacks lay dead.

Jack bit his lip. "George needs a doctor. He cannot continue like this."

"We'll follow the regiment until we reach Menotomy," Stephen ordered. "There, we'll rest the night at Cooper Tavern. Mr. Perkins, you will take Mr. Howlett to get the care he needs—"

"Take me home, Perkins." George ground his teeth against the pain. "I can withstand the ride, I swear it."

Stephen pursed his lips. "Mr. Perkins, if you do return to Topsfield, you must relay to our family, and the town, that hostilities between sides have caused imminent battle. Is that understood?"

"Yes, sir."

"Frederick is at Hartwell Tavern." George's pale face glistened with a light sheen of sweat. "We'll make it. I swear."

"Let me help." Quinn scooped his arm beneath George's good shoulder, and Jack braced George's left elbow, just beneath the wound. They lifted him to his feet. "If you manage to make it back to Topsfield, there is yarrow in Miss Anna's garden. Ask her for it. And have Miss Addy prepare a tea of willow bark."

Jack nodded. "Thank you, Quinn."

Before they turned to leave, Quinnapin gripped Jack's hand. "Ride steady, old friend. The road is long but the ride will be quick."

33

ANNALISA
TOPSFIELD, APRIL 19, 1775

I N THE DIMMED TWILIGHT, Annalisa paced the
foyer of her house. The old clock chimed half-eight.
George had left the farm mid-morning. *When will he
return? Will he return?*

A boulder overtook her stomach. She would have
joined her own militia had Mamma not held her hostage
with her sisters.

Certainly, the Danvers minute marched...

Galloping hooves sounded from the lane and Annalisa
ran outside with a lantern. When she met the path, she
gasped.

Jack rode Frederick, and George, looking rather limp,
held onto his waist. All air left her lungs.

"What's happened to George?" Briny tears dripped
onto her neck and chest.

Jack dismounted. "He's been wounded. We need a
doctor."

She ran toward them, and a sudden terror paralyzed
her from touching George. "Was there a battle?" The

lantern rattled in her hands, and she threw her arms around Jack. "Tell me George will live." She inhaled the gunpowder on his clothes and the salty sweat from his neck.

"Dear heart." Jack held her. "Please, we must get him a doctor. And yes, there was a battle."

"Yes. Of course." She reluctantly pulled from him and her mind cleared. "This way. I'll have Henry call on Dr. Brown."

They led Frederick up to the house, whereupon Jack aided George from the horse's mount.

"Annie? 'Tis but a scratch." George's head slowly lifted and he grinned, but his vacant stare chilled her.

Annalisa squeezed his bloodied hand. "This is far more than a scratch, dear brother." She helped Jack, who walked with a considerable limp, haul George indoors. "Henry! Come quick."

Her youngest brother appeared from the parlor with Mary. "My God, what's happened?"

"You must ride to Dr. Brown's at once. George is wounded from battle. Frederick is right outside but he's ridden a long way. Perhaps take Dinah."

"Of course." Henry rushed past them and out the front door.

"Into the drawing room." Mary led the way and cleared off the pillows from the sofa.

Annalisa and Jack helped lay George on the sofa. "You foolish oaf." She pulled off his shoes and threw them to the floor, then knelt by his head. "You fool. How could you sustain an injury like this? What sort of minuteman are you?" Her hand collected the perspiration at his brows and a lump formed at her throat.

He cannot die. He cannot leave me. Not George, God. Please, do not take my George.

George chuckled darkly. "The kind who will bear his scars with pride."

"The kind who nearly lost consciousness just outside of Danvers. I didn't think we'd make it." Jack tightened a cravat tied about George's bicep. "He's bled much since Concord.

Mamma and Papa rushed into the drawing room with Jane, Addy, and Liza.

"What's happened?" Jane asked.

"Henry's gone for Dr. Brown," Mary said.

"I'll retrieve some yarrow while we await Dr. Brown." Addy fled the drawing room.

"My dearest Georgie!" Mamma flung herself to his side, and Annalisa stood and backed into Jack. He tugged her hand and pulled her near the spinet.

Papa approached Annalisa. "Annie, why don't you see to Mr. Perkins. Get him a horse to take him home. No doubt Lord and Lady Perkins are anxious to see him."

She shook her head and forced away the tears in her eyes. "I cannot. Not until Dr. Brown's arrived. I must know George is being cared for—"

"Nonsense, young lady. Cared for!" Mamma cried. "Imagine what she means by such a statement. *Cared for*. Of course, George is being cared for. Now listen to your Papa and go to. Go to!"

Annalisa and Jack left the house. She drew up her lantern and led him down the path to the barn. Before entering, she stopped and turned.

"'Tis finally happened."

"It has. The minuteman band is unharmed...mostly.

They're spending tonight at Cooper Tavern outside Meno-tomy. I expect they'll return either tomorrow or the next." He brushed her tears with his gunpowder-stained thumb. "And I know George will survive this. He's a sturdy minuteman."

The lantern rattled in her quivering hands. Jack took the light and set it on the ground, and embraced her. Quelled by the chorus of spring peepers from the bog across the lane, she rested her head upon his chest and listened to the rhythmic beating of his heart.

Guilt overtook her. *I should have been there with my militia. What will I do if there are injuries among them?*

"I cannot believe it has really happened." Annalisa sniffled. "But you kept your promise. You returned."

"I did." He stepped back. "I hate to leave you in such a state, but I must see to my family."

"Yes." She looked down. "Your leg."

He forced a smile. "It will heal."

"Let me tend to it. You cannot ride home like that."

"I've already ridden the longest way. To go a bit farther is nothing compared to Concord."

"You're still bleeding."

With the lantern, she hurried to her garden, plucked a handful of yarrow, then scurried behind the barn where she pumped water into a pail.

Inside the barn, Jack sat upon a large wooden crate. She knelt, and place the lantern and bucket before him. Annalisa unbuckled and kicked off one shoe, and lifted her petticoats. She untied the ribbon above her knee and rolled down the stocking, removing it entirely.

"I'll be quick. I can't keep you from your family any longer."

"It would hardly be a terrible way to spend my night, considering what I've seen today." Jack smiled, though she suspected his heart ached.

She plunged the sock into the fresh pail of water and wrung it out. With nimble fingers, she rolled down his stocking and washed away the blood. "'Tis not too deep. Did a ball do this?"

He nodded. "It looks worse than it is."

Annalisa held the yarrow leaves and flowers to his wound and wrapped her damp stocking around his leg. "Next time, you must return without injury. You and my brother."

"I'll try." Jack chuckled. "But I will not make promises I cannot keep."

She finished tying the bandage and stood with hands on her hips. "I suppose that will suffice if it means you can be here alive."

"I should hope so."

She wiped her hands on her apron. "Please, ride Frederick home. Henry will retrieve him tomorrow."

"Thank you. My leg will be better for your care." He paused. "I fear the worst is yet to come." Before leading her from the barn, he lifted her hand and kissed it, his lips lingering long enough to signify he'd rather remain with her. "*Adieu,* my dearest friend."

She twisted her petticoats with apprehension as he mounted George's horse and rode into the deepening night.

34

JACK

TOPSFIELD, APRIL *19*, *1775*

WHEN JACK ARRIVED HOME, he found Father pacing the parlor, his pipe smoke spewing into the air. He looked up, set down his piece, and lunged toward Jack in the doorway.

"God answered my prayers at last." Father stepped back after a long embrace and eyed him from head to foot. "My God, look at you."

"Oh, Jack." Mother hurried forth with her thirteen-month-old babe, Charlotte, in her arms, and kissed his face.

"Thank God you're alive." Abigail hugged his waist. "Tell me George lives."

"Your leg," Andrew shouted.

"George was wounded, but he will live," Jack replied. "And my leg will heal."

"Mercy, some clean water, towels, and ointment," Father ordered.

Mercy nodded and took Jack's hat and coat. He

followed his father to the set of chairs nearest the fireplace and saw Oliver remained on a settee by the window.

Father took up his pipe, drew in a breath, and exhaled a long tendril of smoke. "While I'm displeased by your decision to fight, I admire your bravery. You've certainly proven your character is dependable."

His breeches and ripped stockings coated in gunpower and dirt, he hardly looked like the lawyer his father should be proud of. "Thank you, sir."

Mercy returned with the requested items.

"I'll do it. Thank you, Mercy." Jack rolled down Annalisa's bloodied dressing. As he dampened the towel in the basin, he looked at Oliver. "We were victorious."

Oliver stood. "I can't believe such a vice."

"Ollie, peace." Father turned to Jack. "You bring inspiring news. Though I can't help but feel apprehensive. Pray tell, how were the aggressions between sides?"

"Yes, what is to come now?" Andrew asked. "Does the king's army continue to march? Shall we all take up arms?"

"No, Andrew, you're fifteen," Father snapped. "When you're seventeen, you may join—"

"We should leave town at once." Abigail's hands shook as she clutched Susan's shoulders. "Surely the regulars will march north..."

"I cannot speak of such brutality before the ladies." Jack looked to his mother and sisters. "But the regulars were in retreat from Concord when we ambushed them along the road to Boston."

Oliver shook his head. "A dishonorable way to fight."

Father sucked on his pipe for several minutes in contemplative silence. "I must go to Mr. Hancock at once."

Mother rocked Charlotte. "My darling, you can't mean it."

Father went to her and kissed the top of her golden head. "Yes, my dear, I must. Hancock must hear of the barbarity. I don't doubt there will be many testimonies written in the days to come, and I wish to be sure he has a truthful account."

"Sir, let me go with you." Jack jumped from the chair, nearly forgetting his injured leg. He grimaced. "I will recount mine."

Abigail hastened to Jack's side and pulled his arm. "I think it must be unsafe for either of you to travel thither."

"Perhaps, but Aunt Catherine and Lord Brunswick know to expect me on Tory Row at any time." Father turned to Jack. "Write your account, and I'll bring it to Hancock. You must remain here and heal."

"But Mr. Adams needs me," Jack protested.

Father lifted his hand. "I'll relay your condition to him, though given the gravity of the hostilities, I'm certain he already knows." A shadow of foreboding crossed Father's face. "I've a feeling you may need to remain in town. It may be many weeks before I return. I leave you in charge."

❧

JACK'S CHAMBER DOOR BANGED, AND HE AWOKE WITH A start. He sat upright in his canopied bed, his neck and chest damp with perspiration. Daylight spilled into his room from the window beside the escritoire.

"Jack." Abigail's voice cried from the other side of the door, her fists pounding incessantly.

He swung his legs from beneath the coverlet and

pulled on his breeches and waistcoat. Jack opened the door.

"What is it, Abby?" He rubbed his face and limped to the chair by his desk. There, he retrieved his cravat. "Pray tell, what is the time?"

"Half-ten." Abigail flung herself into his chamber. "The British have landed in Ipswich. We must leave town at once."

Jack lifted his gaze from buttoning his waistcoat. "How have you come by such information?" He sat in the chair, dejected. "Is it reliable?"

He thought she would burst to tears. "'Tis from Mr. Averill's farmhand. He was returned from Ipswich this morn and made it known immediately to Mr. Averill, who notified Papa. Apparently, a ship has landed in Ipswich." Her hands trembled. "I knew they would come north. I knew we had to leave last night—"

"Peace Abby." Jack reached for her quaking hand. "We know little about this farmhand's account and for what reason the ship has landed in Ipswich." He bit his lower lip. "Is Father yet gone?"

Abigail's frown quivered. "Yes. He left for Mr. Hancock early this morning. He said he would write, but I think we must leave town. I know Ollie will protest, but we cannot stay. We must go north...to New Hampshire, or Newbury-port...or perhaps west, away from the coast—"

"Peace."

If the regulars have landed in Ipswich, what is their purpose? Will they so soon engage us in battle with all the militia still surrounding Boston from yesterday?

Without washing his face or brushing his hair, Jack lifted from the chair and ambled from the room, Abigail trailing behind him. He hobbled down the steps and stood in the parlor doorway. Andrew and Oliver sat in silence with Susan; Charlotte fussed at Mother's bosom.

Oliver met Jack's stare. "We're not leaving town." He rose from the settee and glared at Abigail. "'Tis a rebel's action to flee. It would only alert His Majesty's men to our treachery. Let you remember, we are a respectable family."

Jack held up his hand to quiet his brother. "While I'm inclined to agree with you, I hardly believe it treachery to abscond from town after such hostilities yesterday." He swallowed through the tightening in his throat and considered Annalisa and her family. Their fears were probably rampant by these circulating rumors, and magnified by George's injury. "I must go to the Howlett's."

Mother's hand covered her breast. "Whatever for?"

"George is recovering from his wound...but if they are planning to escape town, perhaps so should we—"

"Fie." Oliver slinked across the room, his dark eyes narrow. "Mr. Howlett is a Loyalist, and will henceforth remain in Topsfield. It matters not whether George or Miss Annalisa are Patriot. We should all stay put." His lip curled. "This too, shall pass."

Jack's jaw set. "You were absent from yesterday's battle. You saw not the brutality and disdain of His Majesty's men. If fleeing town will keep our ladies safe, whyever should we not?" He crossed his arms. "You forget, as Father's heir, I'm in charge while he's gone, as is Father's wish."

"A mistake from our rebel father," Oliver chided.

"Ollie, enough." Mother looked to Jack. "Darling, if you think we must go, we'll leave at once for Exeter."

"I'll to the Howlett's before I decide. I'd like to remain

close to them, if possible." He turned and limped into the foyer as a knock sounded from the front door.

Mercy quickly glided past him and opened it.

Henry Howlett removed his hat and bowed. The boy stepped inside, and Mercy closed the door behind him. She offered to take his hat, but he declined.

"I'll only be a moment, marm. I've come for my brother's horse."

"Of course. I'll join you at the stable." Jack led Henry back outside, down the hill, and along the winding path to the stable. "Is your family planning to flee town?"

"Nay." Henry frowned. "Father is Loyalist and requires us to remain."

"I see."

It would be preferable to leave, even if for a little while, until the truth of these rumors is determined. If only to protect Mother and my sisters...if only to protect Annalisa.

"My father thinks we are safe in Topsfield, that the regulars will not march on us here." Henry stepped into the stable.

Jack fisted his cold hands. The gruesome image of the officer he'd killed flashed before him. He rubbed his eyes and lingered in the doorway. "Are you inclined to believe him?"

"I know not what to believe," Henry called from within. "But George has yet to awaken and give us his account of what happened. I daresay, I'm at ill-ease." Henry paused. "As is Annalisa. She gives her regards."

Tender creature.

Jack opened his eyes and followed after Henry, who'd already saddled Frederick. Together, they left the stable. Outside, the bright April day was no one's fool.

Chilled winds gusted, nearly blowing Jack's hat from his head.

"I pray George wakes soon. Is he with fever?"

"No. Annie's been by his side all night with Addy. It seems they've kept him well."

"Thank God." Relief washed over Jack. "Do me the honor of telling Miss Annalisa, as long as your family remains in town, so shall we."

Henry nodded and mounted Frederick. "I shall. God-speed, old friend."

Jack stood in the path and watched Henry disappear down the narrow lane, a precariousness surrounding them in the wild April winds.

☙✲❧

DESPITE THE IPSWICH FRIGHT THAT HAD MOST OF THE county in an uproar, nothing became of the king's army in Topsfield. Their small, secluded town remained mostly quiet, though not without the looming trepidation of impending war twenty-five miles to the south surrounding the small peninsula town of Boston.

And two weeks later, in the first week of May, a letter arrived post-marked from Philadelphia. Jack took the note to his family that evening and read aloud,

"...It is my only regret, beloved family, I must remain in Philadelphia with Mr. Hancock and Mr. Adams. The Second Continental Congress convenes, and my invitation could not go Unanswered. Though I shall be Parted from you at this time, know my devotion runs deep. Neither Time nor distance may alter my Affecktions. God be with you in my Absence and may He keep you. As instructed, Jack shall continue as master of the Estate *untill further notice. Should War Break out, I expect for you to keep true to your duties. —Yours &c, J. Per—"*

Oliver snatched the letter and returned to the settee. "Our own father, consorting with the likes of Congress—a traitor he's become." He crumpled the note and tossed it toward the fire. "I suppose 'tis fitting you assume his place."

Abigail rose from the sofa. "Ollie, you owe Jack far more respect—"

"Respect? Don't start with me on respect," Oliver snapped. "Does no one in this family wish to uphold our good name?"

Abigail's face and neck flushed, and she moved beside Mother, who sat by the fire with Charlotte and Susan.

"A traitor, say you?" Jack studied Oliver with an adroit eye. "You forget yourself, Brother. Father convenes with great men who neither wish for war, nor to sever ties with England. Our good name is secure. I'll accept your harsh feelings without reservation, but I will not tolerate your disrespect of Father."

"Father's mere presence at such a convention is treason. You both condemn our family to treachery." Oliver looked down for a moment, but when he lifted his gaze, his glare chilled Jack's core. "I don't wish to hang. I'll continue to proclaim loyalty, no matter yours and Father's allegiances."

The Tory dog. Jack stood. "Your scruples astound me. Wipe that smirk from your face at once, or I'll wipe it away for you."

"Are those the words of a gentleman?" Oliver lifted from the settee.

Hot rage flooded Jack like a broken dam. "You dare

question my intentions as a gentleman." He fisted his hands. "Pray tell, what say you about how you treated Miss Annalisa when she visited us at Boston? Or when you tripped her at the ball? Shall you continue to hide behind your cool reserve and our family name and call yourself *gentleman?*"

Oliver's nostrils flared. "What has she told you?"

Abigail glided toward them. "Ollie, what did you do to Annie?"

"Nothing to concern you," Oliver snapped.

"Boys, please." Mother rose from her rocking chair, Charlotte at her breast.

"Nonsense." Jack advanced toward Oliver. "I was there, if you've forgotten. And I saw more than enough. Annalisa only elaborated on what I could not see—and what she told me was more than I could bear."

Oliver crossed his arms. "And you wish to relay these details before the ladies?"

Jack ground his teeth. "Never."

"Annalisa Howlett is unruly. She's merely the ill-bred, younger sister of our vulgar, low-born cousin."

Abigail gasped, "Oliver—"

Jack made a fist. "Insult her again and I shall challenge you."

"Boys," Mother's voice lifted once more.

Andrew inched toward them. "Brothers stop it."

Oliver stepped closer to Jack. "She is a graceless, disfigured wretch."

"Cur." Jack lunged at Oliver, gripped him by his frock coat, and flung him toward the fireplace. Oliver toppled to the floor, landing against the wall with a thud. The candles rattled in their sconces.

"John Jackson," Mother screeched.

Jack's baby sister wailed, but he paid no mind. He jumped onto Oliver and threw a fist at his face. "That was for Annalisa." He punched him again. "And this is for your insult of Father."

"Stop it, Jack," Mother shrieked.

Andrew and Abigail grabbed him from Oliver.

"Jack," Abigail cried.

He let her pull him back, but when he turned to protest, Abigail's pink cheeks glistened and her eyes welled with tears. His throat squeezed. *Has the battle unleashed this beastly fury, or have I housed this disdain for Oliver far too long?*

Frustrated he'd been unable to maintain his composure, Jack straightened his coat and waistcoat, and ran a hand over his disheveled hair. He made his way toward Oliver and held out his palm.

Oliver spit at Jack's shoes, then gripped Andrew's wrist and stood. With the back of his hand, he wiped a dribble of blood from the corner of his mouth. "Find yourself in my presence again and I'll have you jailed a traitor." Oliver turned and quit the room, glaring at Abigail as he left.

❦ 35 ❦

ANNALISA

PORTSMOUTH, THE PROVINCE OF NEW
HAMPSHIRE, LATE MAY 1775

ANNALISA SAT IN GEORGE'S smoky tavern, her cocked hat low upon her forehead. George, who was in Topsfield recovering from his wound, and William, who had gone to bed, held no notion of her spying. For this, she sat quite comfortably at her table, ruminating about her fallen friends of the Danvers militia. She rubbed her arms against the hairs standing on end. As if George's injury hadn't frightened her enough, she'd learned of several from her militia who had fallen at the hands of the British that fateful day in Concord. Though weeks had passed since, the truth stung as fiercely as a thousand bees within her bosom. Her eyes burned, and she pinched them shut.

I should have been with them...should have marched with them. If I had been there, perhaps I could have saved Ebenezer from falling...

Even George, a fearless, well-trained minuteman, had been wounded in battle. *I have little chance of surviving such a conflict, no matter my skill with a musket.* The thought settled heavily, and she fought back her dejected tears.

A glass crashed to the floor, startling her. She looked up at the crowded room.

"The Second Continental Congress has elected John Hancock president," a man announced to his table.

George's old mentor from Boston. Fitting he should be appointed to such a position.

She sipped her ale and turned her attention to the table beside hers, where two gentlemen sat with heads bowed low.

"With so many militias surrounding Boston, how can the Redcoats possibly escape?" a portly man asked.

Something about these men seemed amiss. She lowered her head and listened.

Portly Man continued, "think you General Gage will hold them off long enough?"

"Word has it, reinforcements will arrive in Boston any day now," his ruddy-faced friend replied.

Reinforcements? For whom?

Annalisa bit the side of her pewter mug as she finished her ale.

"Who did they send?" Portly Man asked.

"Howe, Burgoyne, and Clinton," Ruddy Face muttered.

Portly Man sighed. "Then this siege may end, and Boston returned to a goodly town."

These men are Loyalists. When the men had finished talking, she rose from her table and slinked out of the room. She climbed the stairs to her chamber and quickly wrote down the three names. She was returning to Topsfield tomorrow and could relay the information.

TOPSFIELD, EARLY JUNE 1775

A WEEK AFTER ANNALISA ARRIVED HOME, SHE TRUDGED through the foggy morning with Mary. Together, they glided across dew-covered fields toward the strawberry patch. Even the dazzling sunrise over her misty farm couldn't chase the wariness that beset her. Each time she stepped outside, she wondered if the ominous *snap-crack* of British musket-fire would send her family running.

Is it my farm's destiny to become a battlefield as it had been for Tabitha Nelson's in Lexington? Will the regulars find their way to Topsfield and set our house afire?

The skirmish at Chelsea Creek had been only a week and a half ago. It seemed the hostilities moved ever north. *If only Papa weren't Loyalist, if only he let us relocate to New Hampshire...*

George ran toward her, his left arm in a sling, and Bixby slung over his good shoulder. "You were right. Those Bloodyback generals were exactly the reinforcements sent to Boston."

Annalisa grinned. "I'm glad I could be of service. But pray tell, where did you take such information?"

He smirked. "Pray tell, how did you come by such information?"

"I'll not divulge my secret if you will not divulge yours."

He tsked and shook his head. "Little One, I've never underestimated you." He kissed her forehead.

"What about me, George?" Mary crossed her arms.

He laughed. "You're a clever mort, too. But I must be

off to drill practice. I'll see you both tonight at the festival."

"Take care of that arm, George," Annalisa called after him. His wound healed well, but he still overused his arm.

"I hear things, too, Annie. And I see things."

Annalisa faced Mary. "Pray tell."

Mary narrowed her hazel eyes. "I heard from Mrs. Andrews, who heard from a friend of hers in Danvers—a Mrs. Foster—that a Benjamin Cavendish, nephew to the Howletts of Topsfield, has a keen eye in their militia...who neglected his post the day they marched to Concord. Apparently, he had been detained at home..."

Annalisa's nerves heightened as she pulled Mary further into the field. "What else?"

"Mrs. Andrews said she knew not of a man by that name in town."

Annalisa reached up for her *wampum* necklace. "You know Mrs. Andrews and her wagging tongue—"

"I know not what you do, nor exactly where you go when you sneak away early mornings dressed in breeches, but I daresay, tread with care, Annie. I suspect *Benjamin* will be under scrutiny."

Annalisa gasped, exasperated. "You've seen me in breeches?"

"Aye. More than once I've snuck out to the barn to follow you—"

"Oh, Mary!" She clasped Mary's hands. "'Tis everything I've worked so hard for." Unable to stand, Annalisa sat between the rows of strawberry plants and held her face. "I only ever wished to join a militia and fight, and I hadn't even the chance with Lexington and Concord, and my friends died, Mary." She heaved a sob. "I failed. I failed them all."

Mary knelt beside her and rested her head on Annalisa's shoulder. "I know. But imagine had you been with them. You might have marched and taken a ball to your chest like the others. Or George. I think God was at work to keep you safe."

"But they know me, Mary. Not the woman that Society, Mamma, and Jane expect me to be. They accept the real me." Annalisa wiped her cheeks. "And they were my friends." She lifted her head and through her blurred tears, caught sight of Quinnapin in the western field. She reached again for the *wampum* hanging from her neck.

To keep me safe. Perhaps the wampum's blessing is what kept me from battle—and had delayed me from the barge that day in Portsmouth.

Mary frowned. "I know the real you. I love the real you."

Annalisa smiled through her sadness. Her dear, amiable little sister, now thirteen and at the brink of womanhood. "You do. And I love you, too."

Mary hugged her. "They did not die in vain. But do try to think of happier things." She pulled away and grinned. "We've the Strawberry Festival tonight."

Annalisa nodded, though nothing could quiet her despair. *I must quit the militia, but how can I? 'Tis the one thing I truly earned, the one place my voice is valued and heard.*

For near two hours, Annalisa and Mary picked strawberries for Addy's pies. When they finished, they trudged to the old, gnarled oak and sat in the shade. Annalisa opened her Margaret Cavendish poetry book and read aloud to Mary.

A horse's gallop sounded from the lane, and Annalisa looked up. Her hands tingled, wondering if it was a warning, as there had been for Lexington. Her face relaxed as Jack Perkins, upon his fine brown mare, rode into view. When he'd stabled his horse, he made his way across the field toward the ancient oak.

Annalisa closed her book. "Mary, would you take the strawberries to Addy?"

"I shall." Her sister's gaze darted between them as he approached. "I hope you get to dance with him tonight." Mary lifted the baskets, and trudged back to the house.

Jack lifted his hat to Mary as she passed by, and gave Annalisa an easy smile. He sat on one of the low boughs. "Join me, dear friend." He patted the space beside him.

Annalisa lifted from the ground and sat on the branch. "I see your leg is mostly healed."

His thigh brushed her skirts, and her spirit fluttered like the wings of her garden butterflies. She gripped the bough to steady herself.

"It has. The ache is all but gone, even when I ride." Jack smirked. "I heard from George you were the one who overheard the news about Burgoyne, Howe, and Clinton arriving in Boston."

Annalisa bit her lip. "I was cleaning up at George's tavern one night and overheard a couple of Loyalists speaking in hushed tones. I thought it best to listen."

Jack laughed. "A clever little spy you are." His eyes sparkled in the lacy rays of sunlight shining through the oak canopy. "I should expect no less from you. You're fearless, my dear."

She fought her grin as she studied his profile. His sideburns came to the edge of his freshly shaved jaw, his

smooth, chestnut hair tied loosely with black silk ribbon.
"I'm glad you think so. I can hardly consider anything else,
but Mary's been talking about the festival tonight for
days."

"You must be at ill-ease from the skirmish at Chelsea
Creek." Jack's shapely mouth pressed into a line. "But we
must move forward, including from Concord and Lexington. We can't let it bridle our hearts and minds." He cast
her a sidelong glance and his smile lines creased. "I've
come to tell you there is a ball on Tory Row in
Cambridge on June 16th. You and your family have been
invited."

"A private ball on Tory Row? Are they not all Loyalists
who've fled town?"

"All but two families remain, my aunt included...she
and Brunswick are Patriots."

"I've never been out in higher society. But Jane will be
thrilled. I daresay, she expects a marriage proposal soon."

Jack blushed and averted his gaze.

"Forgive me." She frowned. "That was far too bold. I
mean not to accuse you of waiting too long to ask Jane. I
know you wish to set up a law office in town before you
wed, and with all that has happened—"

"Shh." He lifted her hand as gently as one who cherished a small, delicate bird, and brushed his lips across her
knuckles, the same that had been bruised at midwinter.
For a long moment, he did not move and did not speak.
His majestic, marine eyes held her captive. "Unless my
wife-to-be is as passionate a Patriot as I, how can I
consider marriage?"

Annalisa wondered if her heart would gallop through
her breast. "I...well, of course, Mr. Perkins."

He smiled and dropped her hand. "I owe you a dance tonight. 'Tis been a long five years since I promised you."

36

ANNALISA
TOPSFIELD, EARLY JUNE 1775

A T TWILIGHT, ANNALISA STOOD with Jane and Mary on the common. She bent and fixed the bow on Mary's hat. "There, much better."

Mary blew Annalisa a kiss, and skipped away with Henry.

Annalisa turned to Jane. "When Jack finds you, you must accept his offer to dance, else Oliver will—"

"I know what I'm doing." Jane chuckled. "But, thank you."

Annalisa gave a tight-lipped smile. *How can anyone celebrate the strawberry crop this year?*

Abigail emerged from the throng of townspeople with her brothers and Susan. "Annalisa, Jane." She embraced them.

From the eastern edge of the common, the fiddles, guitars, and fifes played *Flowers of Edinburgh,* and Annalisa caught Jack's twinkling gaze. He seemed eager to speak with her, or perhaps dance. She diverted her stare from his, ready to dutifully push Jane forward, when Oliver offered his arm.

"Miss Howlett, a dance?"

"I'd be delighted." Jane smiled so broadly Annalisa thought her sister must've forgotten what he'd done to her in Boston five years ago.

Jarred, Annalisa dropped her sister's arm, and Oliver whisked Jane into the crowd toward the set.

"I need a private word with you," Abigail whispered.

"I suppose we'll leave you to your confidences." Jack winked. "Come, Susie. We'll get you some of Addy's famous pie."

Annalisa followed her best friend through the crowd of townspeople, avoiding Hannah French and Fannie Shepard along the way. When they arrived at the Common Rock, she settled beside Abigail, who frowned.

"Annie, I am in love."

Relief flushed away her anxiety like a summer rain. "What is so terrible about that?"

Abigail's hands circled her waist. "'Tis an awful feeling to be in love and worry he may not wish to marry you."

"True. May I inquire as to whom? How came you to meet such a gentleman? Is he deserving of you? Will he leave you to fight in battles to come?"

"Yes, I daresay he might." Abigail fidgeted with her bodice pins. "You know the man quite well, and he is most deserving." She inhaled, then released a great breath. "The man I love is...George."

Annalisa squealed and clapped her hands. "That is agreeable news!"

"And we kissed. In the Capen Barn."

Annalisa lost her words. She could hardly imagine her

fierce, hulking brother attempting to woo anyone, never mind Abigail—the wealthiest young lady in town and his cousin, no less.

"Annie, say something. Oh, Lord. Leave it to me to render *you* speechless. It happened the night before Concord. I wished to tell you, but...I feared how you'd react...I know you find courting superfluous given the circumstances of our province, but I swear, I'm not some bawdy basket. I love him."

"Superfluous? No, we need love now more than ever." Annalisa held her friend's hands, saddened Abigail would think her unhappy to hear such wonderful news. "Pray tell, does he love you, too?"

"Yes. It was the most magical of nights." Abigail's blissful smile faded. "Until Ollie discovered us."

"Oliver found you?"

"Yes." Abigail picked a blade of grass. "He was cruel, but I think my mamma will allow George to court me." She looked up and smiled. "I'm glad to hear you don't find me silly for wishing to be courted in these trying times."

Annalisa grinned. "Of course. And I see no reason why your mamma should refuse him. He's your cousin and now owns a rather successful tavern. He can provide for you quite well."

"I pray you're right. Let's find him...and someone for you to dance with." Abigail winked, jumped up, and dragged Annalisa to her feet.

Lanterns lit the green in a subtle glow as the sky darkened from lavender to indigo. As they neared the crowd, George and Jack walked toward them with Samuel and Quinnapin. Their eyes glimmered from too much ale.

Jack exaggerated his bow. "'Tis been four years since I promised you a dance." He slurred his words.

Annalisa chuckled. "Five years, but I appreciate your effort in remembering."

"May I have the honor of the next?" Jack lifted his hat and strands of his long, brown hair fell loose into his face.

Abigail pushed Annalisa forward. "She accepts."

"He's ripe with liquid courage," George bellowed.

Annalisa took Jack's hand and he led her, with an occasional stagger, across the green toward the set of dancers.

He gestured to her and sang, *"The next time I go o'er the moor, she shall a lover find me."*

She giggled. "Sir, you are quite disguised."

"Nonsense, dear heart." He pulled her into the set of dancers.

Dear heart? What a term of endearment!

"My abilities are hardly comparable to Jane's. I must apologize."

Jack's inebriated grin dimpled his cheek. "'Tis been a while since last I danced, too. Regulars be damned." He turned to Ezra Kimball beside him, who stood across from Lizzie. "Good evening, old friend. I daresay, I've the most agreeable lass in all the county before me."

Lizzie's eyes widened and Annalisa knew she thought of her fortune-telling at the corn husking. Gossip would be ripe tomorrow.

The song began, and Jack stumbled over his own foot.

"Have you two left feet tonight?"

"Perhaps I've had a bit too much ale," Jack stammered, trying to hide his laugh. "Come now, I know you know this song. Sing for me."

Despite Lizzie's careful eye, Annalisa sang, *"Oh, John come kiss me now. John, come kiss me by and by…"*

Jack grinned. "Your voice is lovely and quells the nerves."

"Oh, John, come kiss me now—"

He reached for her. "Ask, and you shall receive."

"Sir!" *The ale must have carried his sensibilities far from him.* She heated under Ezra and Lizzie's adroit study. Yet she could hardly deny her wish to steal a kiss, but not in front of all these people—people she would see at the meeting-house tomorrow. Mamma would be displeased and probably send her to Portsmouth until the ball on Tory Row.

And what of Jane?

"Come with me, quickly." Jack locked his fingers with hers and the world blurred as they ran from the set, through the throng of people, to the Common Rock.

Here again.

"Young love." Jack tossed his hat into the air. "How it turns us into fools." The fiddles echoed from the far end of the common, and he turned to her with his arm outstretched. "Let us dance."

His hand upon her waist, they spun across the grass— no minuet or other formal dance to burden her—as though the common was theirs alone, as if the province was not at war, and Annalisa needn't quit the militia. It was as she'd dreamt at the Perkins' first Strawberry Festival.

A satisfaction ran through her she'd never known, and she beamed. "This dance was worth the wait, Mr. Perkins."

He pulled her close. "Dear heart, call me Jack." The scent of ale mixed with tobacco on his breath covered her in gooseflesh. "'Twas here you first asked me to call you Annalisa."

"So I did." She lifted a finger and traced the buttons of his waistcoat. "Our friendship has spanned half a decade. I insist, you must call me Annie."

He lifted a curious brow. "What if I call you my Annalisa dearest?"

"You may call me whatever pleases you." She suppressed a frown as she thought of Jane, and pulled from his embrace. "Though, it sounds like something you may call your wife."

"My wife?" The fiddles started to play *Flowers of Edinburgh* again, and Jack tugged her behind the Common Rock. "Let me hold you a moment longer."

"If it pleases you."

"Does it please *you*, Annalisa?"

She wavered. "It does."

Jack wrapped his arms about her and held her as he did the night he arrived home from Concord. Crickets chirped and the fiddles played on in the distance. He removed her straw hat and brushed his lips against her forehead, humming along with the fiddles. His hand lingered upon her waist, perhaps unwilling to let her go.

"If you permit me, I should like to accompany you home." His voice low and alluring, "There is much I wish to discuss with you, and I can hardly do it here."

Heat rose up her back as she could no longer doubt his advances. *But what of Jane?*

37

JACK

J ACK WALKED ANNALISA UP the path to her house. "I hope you don't find my addresses too forward." His thumb ebbed across hers.

"Not at all."

"I—"

"I'll kill you, you reptile!" George's voice echoed into the night.

"Ollie? Is that Jane?" Abigail's screech followed.

Jack paused midway up the path. "Wait here."

"No." Annalisa dropped his hand. "I'm going with you."

Together, they ran to the barn.

"If I could throw you from this post, I swear upon Captain Bixby's death, I'd do it," George growled.

"George, don't speak, thus," Abigail said. "Please, come down this instant."

"Only if Oliver agrees to a duel," George barked.

"I'll do no such thing," Oliver replied.

"That's my sister you mean to defile," George roared.

"I'm not defiled," Jane said. "I chose to be up here."

"Ollie. George." Jack barged into the barn. "What is the meaning of this?"

Annalisa hurried to Abigail, and they whispered amongst themselves.

"A duel or nothing, you bastard," George said.

"No duel." Jack stood by the hayloft ladder. "'Tis not worth it."

George, up in the garret with Oliver and Jane, peered over the edge. "Cousin, mind yourself and stay below. I'll settle this the way I see fit." He turned back to Oliver. "I have a right mind to throw your Tory arse from here."

"George, enough." Jack stepped onto the ladder. "I'm coming up." He wobbled as he climbed, still limper from too much ale.

Jane lay in the hay, her hair disheveled and gown crumpled. Knowing what had transpired between her and his brother, Jack fought the disgust so surely painted across his face. "Miss Howlett...are you well?"

Jane smoothed her hair, straightened her bodice, and glanced at him with humiliation. "I...was feeling poorly upon our arrival home. Mr. Oliver helped me into the loft, as I was too ill to make it to the house." She forced a smile. "Too much cider at the festival."

Jack glared at his brother, then returned his gaze to Jane. "Are you well enough now, Miss Howlett? Shall I help you inside the house?"

"She needs no help from you," Oliver said. "Away with you."

Jack's lips tightened. "Ollie, I'll assist George in throwing you from this loft if you don't mind yourself."

"Mr. Perkins, no." Jane regarded Oliver. "No, thank you, sir. I will go inside soon."

"Very well. Take care, Miss." He carefully descended the ladder, casting one final scowl at Oliver.

Jack offered his arm to Annalisa. Her face ashen in the moonlight, she took a gentle hold of his arm, and they followed George and Abigail from the barn.

"Abby, I'll take you home," George said.

Jack pulled George's shoulder. "Cousin, we should talk about this—"

"About what?" George shrugged away his hand. "How your cockrobin brother strummed my sister in my family's barn?"

"Please, Jack." Abigail squeezed his hand. "Let's leave it for what it is." She looked to Annalisa and kissed her cheek. "Good-night, sweet friend."

Annalisa remained silent as Abigail followed George to his horse. They fled down the blackened lane with a lantern to guide them.

"To your house, then?" Jack asked.

"No." Annalisa shook her head. "The oak."

Jack grabbed a lantern from the barn and walked with Annalisa, in silence, through the darkened fields to the ancient oak. The massive tree loomed before them, its canopy and low limbs offering shelter from the night.

He set the lantern on the ground. Its gentle glow illuminated the sage tree and Annalisa before him. "I'm sorry you witnessed that. The likes of Oliver. I'll never understand him. He is so...he's such a—"

Annalisa walked up to him, placed her hands on either side of his face, and pressed her lips to his. Startled, he covered her hands with his, and he pulled his mouth from hers.

"Is this what you want, Jack?"

"Yes. I mean, no. Well, yes, I do want to—" Jack forced her hands from his cheeks. "Annalisa, we must talk." Softened by her sad eyes, Jack led her to the bough they sat on earlier that day. "You must be troubled."

Annalisa stared into the lantern's lapping flame. Golden light flickered upon her profile. "I told Jane what your brother did to me in Boston." Her mouth grimaced. "She told me I was lying." Annalisa held her face in her hands. "Like a fool, I forgave her, and now she's..."

"She didn't believe you?" He gripped the tree branch. "How could she not?"

"I am a pitiable fool who knows nothing of love." Her cheeks glistened when she looked up at him.

"What Oliver did to you has nothing to do with love. And you're not a pitiable fool. What happened is not your fault." He lifted her chin with his thumb and forefinger. "Oliver is a villain, and Jane is the fool." He hesitated. "If 'tis any solace, I know Oliver to be rather attached to your sister."

"Once a lady's virtue is gone, 'tis impossible to recover it." Annalisa paused. "What does this mean for you and Jane?"

"I held an intention of courting her once, but I've quit those feelings." Jack cleared his throat. "Last month, I sent for my things to be delivered from Boston. I wrote Adams in Philadelphia. He sends his best."

Her gaze lifted. "You're moving to Topsfield permanently? You mean to open your own law practice?"

"Yes." He fiddled with his ring. "As you so pointedly described to me this afternoon, with my law practice—and my inheritance—I may soon marry." He traced the back of Annalisa's hand with his forefinger. "But impending war dampens the motive...I cannot stand the thought of being parted from you. It seems my heart is divided."

"Me?" She looked at him with reverence.

"Yes, you." Jack smiled. "I feel I can tell you anything, that you are more than just a lovely, dear, old friend. Annalisa, I'm come to see you as my equal, my companion —a most likeminded companion."

"Your companion?" Annalisa stood. "Your equal? You truly mean that?"

"Yes. When I was in Europe, I met with great men from all walks of life who spouted ideals for equality, the abolition of slavery...we cannot assume a civilized world with such barbarity. You, me, Quinn, Addy...we're each so different, but our differences must be celebrated. People should be treated as people, rather than those below, or those above. 'Tis what I hope to be established in this country, should we found a new one, separate from England."

"'Tis what I've imagined for our world my entire life," she said. The lanternlight danced in her eyes like the fire-flies across the common at their first Strawberry Festival. He'd never quite ridded himself of the memory.

I've never heard any man speak like you," she contin-ued. "Not even George.

"Nor I, you." Jack kissed her hand. "'Tis you, Annalisa. 'Tis always been you. My God, you're everything."

"Jack, please." She pulled her hand from his. "You can't mean that."

"I do. Yet everything is so uncertain. Would that I could whisk you away to another time, away from all this madness." Jack swallowed, his mouth dry. "I shot and killed a man at Concord—a man not much older than me.

I took his life as though I had the right to decide whether or not he lived. His dead, black eyes still haunt me."

She sat beside him once more.

"I always dreamt of fighting for our cause, but I cannot forget it. Nor can I rid the memory of you at the massacre." He gave a grim laugh. "Here we are tonight, trying to be merry, and dancing. But in the back of my mind, I'm tormented—we all are, I'm sure of it."

Her hand closed over his. "He could have killed you just the same."

"Aye. And now my father wishes me to join him in Philadelphia."

"But you must set up your law office. Which is more important to you?"

"Neither. I'd rather join the campaign surrounding Boston." Jack sighed. "But someone must run my father's estate while he is gone—and it cannot be Oliver. Have I much choice but to open my practice and remain in town?"

"You are a man. Cannot you make decisions for yourself no matter your father?"

"Yes." Jack chuckled. "But—"

"But nothing." Annalisa held a finger to his lips. "You make your decisions and you follow through. You're a man of integrity. I've seen this in you these past several years."

"Aye, but Lexington and Concord set the stage for what is to come. This rebellion might last years if we put up a fight. If not, all will conclude in the Mother Country's favor, and without pardon."

"George read that Congress petitioned Parliament—perhaps it may manifest and there will be no war at all."

"They wrote an olive branch, but we remain in restless

standstill, possibly till summer's end...at the mercy of King George. I cannot tell you not to fear, Annalisa. I cannot even bestow you a promise the rebellion will end well. But apart from what happens to the province, one thing will remain certain." He sucked in a breath. "My attachment for you will not waver."

Annalisa looked surprised but pleased. "Jack, I cannot be the reason you withhold yourself from something so great."

"'Tis no matter. I wish to court you, properly. But I sense in you some hesitancy. What is it you fear? Or have I misread your favor?" *She must sense the unsteady beating of my heart.* "Have I been too callous, or blunt in my past behaviors?"

"We both know you favored Jane." Annalisa looked down. "And she is not yet engaged. Papa is quite traditional. I doubt he will allow you to call on me, or write, until Jane's fate is secured. I had thought that would be you, sir." She paused and added with hardened spite, "Until tonight."

"Then she may marry Oliver—"

"No. Everything I've done has been for her to marry you instead of Oliver, despite my own feelings." Her cheeks colored in the lanternlight. "That is to say, if you noticed me over her."

He kissed her hand. "Annalisa, I was a fool. I'd been blinded by Society and what's expected of me. But 'tis you, I swear it—"

"Jack..."

"I've made you frown. Have I spoken out of turn?"

"No. 'Tis Oliver."

"You don't wish to see him marry your sister because of what he did."

"Yes. But now Jane pursues him, knowing how I feel about him—and how I tried to get you to favor her. To say I'm wounded by her actions is an understatement." Annalisa bit her lip. "As of this moment, I will no longer discourage you, sir, or your advances."

"Thank heavens." He pressed his forehead to hers. "Dear heart, then you speak true?" His nose brushed the tip of hers, and he inhaled her fresh, lilac perfume.

"I think perhaps I hid my secret better than you, sir."

"It would be an honor to have you beside me."

"Then will you not give me a hasty kiss as I've already given you?"

Jack laughed. "'Twas unexpected, indeed. Though, not unwanted." A spark ignited within him and he lifted her chin. "You've no idea how you've captivated me."

He fused his lips with hers. They were stiff at first, unsure of the task, then softened, parting just enough for him to taste the lingering strawberry pie upon her tongue. She returned his kiss with more assuredness, then pulled away and shivered.

"Did I do that well?"

"Yes." He grinned. "Very well."

"Jack, you mustn't tell anyone—"

"I will but shout it from the meetinghouse pulpit." He clasped her hands and jumped from the bough, pulling her to her feet.

Annalisa giggled. "No, you will not."

"Then I suppose I'll wait until you tell me to ask your parents' permission. I daresay, we needn't much of a courtship." He brushed her cheek. "My darling girl." He wrapped his arms about her. "Were we not in such upheaval, I would in this moment ask you to mar—"

A snap of twigs sounded from the forest beyond the oak. Jack and Annalisa turned, separating themselves.

Annalisa shuddered. "We should return to the house."

"If you're at ill-ease. But I daresay we are protected by this sage tree. Nothing could harm us here."

"Then you've not encountered a *puk-wudjie*."

She gripped his hand and tugged him from the sprawling confines of the ancient oak. Jack smiled to himself, hoping that the tree had witnessed similar declarations of love in centuries' past. Even if the oak, in the years long after they'd been gone from this world, forgot their night beneath its branches, tonight carved itself into the memory of his heart, indefinitely.

❧ 38 ❧

ANNALISA

DANVERS, EARLY JUNE 1775

A NNALISA OPENED HER EYES the following morning to the melodious chatter of birds. The sun had not yet risen, but beyond the casement the springtime sky faded from dark to periwinkle. Beside her in their canopied bed, her sisters slept, but Annalisa's spirit vibrated. Last night beneath the oak, Jack's closeness, his words of affection, had been a dream come true. Yet as she stirred, her thoughts returned to Jane and Oliver. And George—she hadn't heard him return home.

Annalisa slipped from her bed and dressed. Without a sound, she opened the door and glided down the wooden steps. Grey-blue light shone into the house, illuminating the darkness. She made her way into the parlor, where-upon she sat at the corner desk and scribbled a note. She sprinkled sand over the wet ink to prevent smudging, folded the page, and sealed it. A quick tuck of the letter into her pocket, and she ventured outside.

In the silent stable, the smell of sweet hay left her

queasy with the memory of Jane and Oliver. She tacked up Dinah, mounted the animal, and rode from her farm.

Annalisa arrived in Danvers, and the sun was just barely above the horizon. Her militia gathered on the common. She dismounted and tied her horse to a fence.

"May I be of assistance to you, young miss?" Captain Foster's hand rested on his hip.

"Yes, sir. My name is Annalisa Howlett, and my cousin is Benjamin Cavendish." She grazed the *wampum* at her throat. "I'm pained to say he's been quite ill, sir, taken to bed since early April. I've a letter from him, sir."

Captain Foster cocked his head. "Is that so? And he sent...you, a lady, to deliver it?"

She squared her shoulders. "I wished to do it, sir. For him. He's a noble young man, and he is still shamed he could not fight with you at Concord."

His brow lifted. "Pray tell, and what is his illness?"

"Dropsy, sir. He has days where he can hardly breathe walking upstairs, let alone march."

"Quite." He held out his hand for the letter.

She gave it to him, and he started to open it.

"Wait to read it, sir. He wouldn't wish to detract from drill practice. But these are the words of a dying man."

Captain Foster frowned. "I'm deeply troubled by this news, Miss. And even more sorry I thought ill of him after Concord. He's a fine young man, one of the best in our militia." He studied her as though his generous approbation was meant for her and not Benjamin. "Miss, do tell him it was a pleasure knowing him."

"I shall, sir. He will be grateful to know how well you thought of him." Annalisa's spirit swelled. Captain Foster never complimented anyone, yet he'd provided her an opportunity she could only dream of.

He smirked. "I know."

"I beg your pardon, sir?"

Captain Foster winked, turned from her, and walked back into the field, where the rest of the militia waited.

Her throat clogged as she gazed one final time at the men she'd drilled with, week after week, for the last four years; the men who'd helped hone her eye when George could not; the men who'd listened to her when no one else would—save for Jack. But now she'd earned the love of a man who did wish to hear her voice, regardless of whether she wore skirts or breeches. In this she took solace, satisfied enough to leave Danvers, content enough to hang up Benjamin's breeches. For now.

ANNALISA
TOPSFIELD, JUNE 1775

A WEEK AFTER THE Strawberry Festival, Abigail called to help Annalisa practice the minuet. As she guided Abigail into the drawing room, Annalisa's mind burst with questions about George and the events that ensued in the barn.

Abigail sat at the spinet and played a minuet. She counted aloud to six while Annalisa stumbled over herself.

"Annie, you've done it perfectly before now." Abigail frowned and dabbed her breast with a muslin cloth. "Let's take some air." She lifted from the bench. "I've a letter for you from Jack. Perhaps you may use it as inspiration to dance well at the ball." She handed her the note. "I may have read it before he sealed it."

Annalisa broke the wax that had been sealed with the gold signet ring upon his little finger, unfolded the page, and read:

12ᵀᴴ JUNE 1775

FOUR O'CLOCK E'VNG, TOPSFIELD
DEAREST ANNALISA,

IT IS WITH PLEASURABLE IMPATIENCE I AWAIT DANCING WITH YOU AT LORD SUFFOLK'S BALL. THOUGHTS OF YOU FILL MY MINDE WITH ARDENT FELICITY AND YOU MUST KNOW I FINDE YOU THE MOST AMIABLE OF CREATURES. THE DAY I MAY CALL YOU MY DEAREST IS QUITE NEAR, INDEED. I ANTICIPATE OUR NEXT MEETING WITH UNRELENTING ALACKRITY.

AFFECTIONATELY YOURS,
J. PERKINS

"HOW BEAUTIFUL IS HIS WRITING." ANNALISA EXHALED. "Oh, Abby, could I possibly be your sister some day?"

Abigail squealed. "I daresay you shall. I knew Lizzie's fortune at the husking four years ago to be true!" She squeezed Annalisa's hands. "There is no other in all of Massachusetts Bay I find worthy of marrying Jack."

"I'd been so worried you would think ill of me like Hannah or Fannie, or every other girl in town who ogles your dear brother."

"Never. You're the only one I could ever want marrying him."

They left the drawing room and bumped into Jane in the hallway. Annalisa's hands turned cold.

"Janey, I thought you in the parlor."

"I forgot my threads." Jane's face was as blank as a failed artist's canvas. "I understand your minuet is going well?"

Annalisa nodded. "Quite."

Abigail and Annalisa hastened down the hall, out the

front door, and rushed across the fields to the ancient oak. Beneath its great canopy, Annalisa paced.

"Abby, I'm riddled with anxiety." Her innards burned with guilt. "I'm attached to Jack. I have been for years. But I tried, heaven knows I've tried, to secure his fate with Jane's."

"What? Why?" Abigail jumped up from the lowest branch.

"Because she cannot marry Oliver."

"Whyever not? She was caught with Ollie in your barn." Abigail made her way toward Annalisa. "I daresay, he has fancied her for years. He will make her a fine husband. I promise."

Annalisa rubbed her arms. "I should have told you when it happened."

"Told me what?"

"Oliver advanced upon me when we visited you at Boston."

Abigail cupped her mouth. "When?"

"'Twas the night before the massacre." Annalisa relayed the course of action which led to her ultimate shame.

"The cur." Abigail's freckles darkened in a red rush of anger. "I could kill him. To behave as a beast to my very best friend! Does Jane know?"

"Yes, and she believes me not. And since the barn incident, we've barely spoken—"

"She thinks you lied? Oh, I could strangle her beautiful neck with my bare hands—"

"You must keep this to yourself. I've not told George. If ever he finds out, he will challenge Oliver."

A shadow of pain crossed Abigail's face, but she held

Annalisa's hands confidently. "Worry not, sweet friend. Your secret is safe with me."

⚘

THAT AFTERNOON, ANNALISA PICKED WEEDS FROM HER flower beds. Beneath her straw hat, she glimpsed George approaching from the stable.

He stood beside her with Bixby and his cartridge box. "I saw Jack last night. He wishes to call on you today. I told him you'll meet him by the oak at three."

"Thank you." She studied his stance. "When are you headed to Portsmouth? May I join you?"

"I leave tonight." He gave a wry smile. "I doubt Mother will let you skip your minuet lessons before the grand ball next week."

"'Tis hardly anything I care for, only that we shall be in Cambridge where Washington recruits for his army. How ridiculous to host a ball when nearly all of the town is fled. Pray, how is your arm? Will you join the army?"

He flexed his left arm. "'Tis better. And I must ensure the inn is well-cared for in my absence before I make such a commitment."

"William could manage with Elisha. I know he has no inclination of joining."

George chuckled. "Aye, true. Would that you were born a brother. I daresay, we'd be inseparable in that army, you and I." He planted a kiss to her forehead. "I'll see you for the ball next week. Be a good mort. But not too good." He winked and mounted Frederick, and rode from the farm.

Headed to drill practice, no doubt. Annalisa stood and brushed off her skirts. She yearned for her own militia.

Did I do the right thing?

It was nearly three. She made her way across the fields to the venerable tree that stood guard at the outskirts of their property. Jack stood beneath its ample canopy, hidden from view on her family's farm.

He hastened forward, tipped his hat, and gestured to their bough. "Shall we sit?"

"No. Let's climb." Annalisa led him to the series of low-lying limbs that lifted her high into the tree, and onto the widened cove in the trunk between thick boughs. She settled against the trunk and Jack nestled beside her.

How long I've craved to be this close to him.

"I've something for you." He reached into his haversack. "I feel foolish giving you something so intimate—I hope you don't find it too bold." He removed a long, intricately carved wooden busk meant to nestle down the front of her stays. "'Tis wood from this tree...I started making it after Concord, and finished it after our night beneath these branches. I hoped you might do me the honor of wearing it."

"Oh, Jack." The thought of him carving something that would settle beneath her breast warmed her. She held the busk and studied it. The top was rounded to mimic the shape of a heart, and the year, *1775*, was carved into each curved edge. Beneath the heart, a pattern of stars, and below that—she could hardly mistake his artistry—the ancient oak.

Her vision blurred. "What a beautiful, thoughtful gift." She kissed his cheek. "I will wear it, and it will sit close to my heart." She pulled her dress forward and started to slide the busk down the front of her stays, then stopped. "I would be honored for you to do it."

His brows arched. "Are you certain?"

"I insist." Annalisa leaned back and lifted her face. Golden rays of sunlight dribbled down through the canopy, warming her. Beside her, Jack placed his hand on the tip of the busk and slowly slid it into place within her stays, his hand at her bosom for only a moment. When he finished, he rested his hand upon her stomach and sighed.

"Upon my word." He laughed.

Annalisa exhaled and caught his stare. "There's not a man in the world with whom I'd rather share such closeness."

"I've thought of you—of a moment like this—for quite some time. I apologize..." He glanced down sheepishly, and she followed his gaze. The front of his breeches had tightened against him, and Annalisa felt her own lifeblood awaken.

"Whyever would you apologize?"

Jack gave an impish grin. "Do you wish for a green gown?"

She traced the buttons of his waistcoat. "Mr. Perkins, if you're quite able, you might wish to enjoy the pleasure of my garden—perhaps now, or later this evening?"

He chuckled. "Eloquently put." He licked his lower lip. "I'd be lying if I denied my own titillating thoughts. But I want you to know I respect you. I don't wish for you to think I'm like my brother..."

"Jack." She gripped his coat and pulled him closer. "You're nothing like Oliver."

He peered at her bosom and touched the tip of the busk. "Annalisa," he whispered, "I would have you every day for the rest of my life." He tossed his hat below, and pulled her onto his lap. Jack closed his eyes, his lips inches from hers. She inhaled his amber scent and shivered.

"Annalisa." Mary's voice echoed into the tree.

She slid from his lap. "Oh, for the love of heaven."

Jack steadied her hands. "Next time, my dear."

Mary ran to the base of the oak. Huffing, she lifted her shiny, reddened face and stared into the branches. "Mr. Perkins...I'm sorry to interrupt...my mamma sent me looking...for Annie. Mamma wishes to see you...in the drawing room. Please come with us, Mr. Perkins. Addy will make some coffee. Maybe you can stay for dinner?"

Jack called down to her, "If your lovely sister insists, I cannot refuse her."

Annalisa returned his smile. "Then I insist."

They climbed down the tree and met Mary on the ground.

Her sister jumped and clapped her hands. "I think Addy is preparing roast quail. But maybe she will bake a strawberry pie for you."

They followed Mary from the tree and into the fields. The girl chattered endlessly, but Annalisa neither heard nor acknowledged her sister's rapid questioning. She only saw Jack, his face full of felicity, his hand warm as his fingers entwined with hers.

"Leave a candle by your window," he whispered. "If you'll have me, I'll come for you tomorrow night."

JACK
TOPSFIELD, JUNE 1775

ALONE IN HIS BEDCHAMBER, Jack stared into his looking glass. He ran a hand over his freshly shaved face and inspected his side-whiskers. Since moving to the country, he'd grown accustomed to keeping them long, as his cousin George wore the same style. Satisfied, he reached for his cravat and tied it about his neck. Everything had to be perfect for Annalisa tonight. In a couple of hours, after dinner and all turned dark, he'd be well on his way to her house, where a candle burning in her window would guide him.

He hadn't been with a woman since London—Miss Twysden, or Lady Jersey as it was revealed. That had been a horrible charade. Hopefully, tonight would atone for that miserable occasion made in drunken haste. This time would be for love. And after Annalisa's debut at Lord Suffolk's ball, there could be no objection from higher society; he could openly court her.

He dabbed on his amber perfume, slid into his coat, and ambled down the stairs.

"Jack, is that you?" his mother called from the parlor.

Jack paused at the bottom step, recognizing an announcement in her tone.

"Yes." He moved through the foyer and into the parlor.

Mother sat in her chair by the fireplace, rocking Charlotte. "I've some news for you."

Jack sat on the sofa. "Oh?"

"I was going to wait until tomorrow to tell you, but such excitement must be brought to your attention at once." She boasted an enthusiastic smile, reminding him much of Abigail. "Mrs. Howlett accepted my proposal. Your betrothal announcement to Jane will come at Lord Suffolk's ball."

"I beg your pardon?"

"Darling, do look more pleased. I believe thanks are in order for such a smart match, don't you agree? Jane will make a superb wife for you. But say nothing to her, Dear. Mrs. Howlett wishes for it to be a birthday surprise."

"Thanks? A surprise? Of all that is ridiculous!" Jack leapt to his feet. "Madam, I will not abide it. How dare you and Mrs. Howlett conspire to decide whom I shall marry?"

His mother's face distorted. "But you've always fancied Jane."

"I may have been blinded by Jane's beauty, but I am no longer. And Oliver seems to have claimed her for himself."

"I realize that. Those pearls." Mother pressed her lips together. "Ollie knows he may not marry her."

"'Tis no matter. I've decided whom I shall marry, and it is not Jane." He locked his gaze with his mother's. "'Tis Annalisa."

"To think." Mother gripped her neck handkerchief.

"I've been fooled into believing you've been calling on Jane."

"I never made you believe thus. You conjured such images yourself."

She stood. "Jack, Annalisa's second in age to Jane, and yet to have her debut with higher society. You've been educated with manners far better than that. And Mr. Howlett will never allow it."

"Annalisa's to have her debut with our society at Lord Suffolk's ball. What more do you need?" Jack softened and went to her. He rested a hand upon her shoulder. "Mother, Annalisa is kind, generous, and gracious."

Mother frowned. "Mrs. Howlett was so happy when I consented to the arrangement. I couldn't possibly now tell her you are refusing. She's already declined other offers for Jane."

Jack gritted his teeth. "She agreed, or you consented? Which is it? Because it seems you've both been plotting to appease ambitions that have now ruined both Jane's and my prospects, including Annalisa's."

His mother circled the parlor with Charlotte at her bosom. "Do mind your temper. I did as what a mother should for her first-born. You're to inherit all of this when your father dies, and you must marry an upstanding girl who has been accepted by our society. I don't doubt Annalisa's credibility as a life partner, but Jane has already made a respectable reputation for herself. She can enter our society without objection. Aside from that, you know very well Annalisa may not marry before her. 'Tis not correct."

Jack rolled his eyes. "That old adage." In two strides, he met her by the window. "Then I'll court Annalisa until

Jane *does* marry—or becomes engaged. Ollie and Jane favor one another. Why can they not marry?"

"Because Jane is more suited to be the next Lady Perkins. She is accomplished and demure, the very picture of a well-bred lady. There's no gossip surrounding her, and she behaves as a lady should." She sighed. "Annalisa—while proficient in music—is wanting much for the rest of her ladyhood."

"And this is by Society's standards you judge her thus."

"Annalisa's a...hearty girl, Jack." She paused. "She, at times, too closely resembles her native relatives. Surely, she understands her prospects. Mrs. Howlett has been most diligent in her upbringing. She'll marry some...gentleman farmer, or a vicar, but Society will not accept her. She will have heartache, as we all do, when we cannot marry the first man who finds us pretty—"

"First man who finds her pretty?" Jack's jaw tightened. "She's more than some 'pretty girl'." He straightened his coat. "I love her."

Her head jolted toward him. "You *love* her? You've not gotten her with child, have you?"

His conscience thick with their design for tonight, Jack warmed. "No. I have not."

Mother glided back to her chair and sat. "Thank heavens."

"I have not." Jack twisted his signet ring. "But if I had, our child would be beautiful, and there'd be no question as to whom I'd marry. You'd best hope I keep Miss Annalisa's run goods intact."

"Her *run goods?*"

"Her virginity," he snapped.

She huffed. "I see half these country girls with a full

belly at the altar." She adjusted Charlotte at her hip. "You wouldn't dare do something so deplorable."

He adjusted the clock upon the mantle. "I love Annalisa. If it meant I could marry her, why wouldn't I?" He faced his mother, only to meet her fire-filled glare.

"John Jackson, those are neither the words—nor the attitude—of a gentleman who acts in his father's place."

"Quite. But must I remind you, I already quit the minutemen—a duty to which I took great pride—for Father, who, I might add, also refused to let me join the army forming in Cambridge. Now, it has been decided whom I am to marry. What more can you expect of me, a man grown? A marriage is eternal. I'll not enter into one lightly."

"I married your father as an arrangement. We've been together now, happy, four and twenty years. I'd not change a thing about it." She smiled wistfully. "Of course, I was young and frightened. I remember questioning my papa and mamma, how I could possibly marry a man I did not love, how I could marry a man almost twice my age. But they knew better—"

"No—no, no. I will not accept this. Unless you wish to further strain relations with my own brother, I urge you, please arrange for Ollie to marry Jane."

"He knows he cannot. He's been instructed on this."

"Then he is a scoundrel." Jack bitterly recalled Oliver and Jane in the hayloft. "Society be damned. My mind's been made." He turned from his mother and left through the front door.

MR. GOULD'S WHISPERING WILLOW TAVERN WELCOMED
him with libations and a false sense of liberty. Alone, Jack
sat at the table he frequented with his cousin and friends
when it had been George's Peat Moss Inn. His mind
seethed with anger and regret as he drowned himself with
ale and flip.

Can I in good conscience go to Annalisa tonight?

The thought of forsaking her devastated him. She was
expecting his furtive call. What was more, he wanted to
see her—to hold her, kiss her, discover the intimate details
of her—despite the disgusting news from his mother.

Am I, too, a scoundrel, no better than Oliver?

Jack clutched his mug and gulped. To have such a basic
freedom at stake in his own home burned the liquor from
his stomach into his throat.

*As a man of three and twenty, how can I allow such a demand
—and at the design of Mother and Mrs. Howlett. Surely, Father
isn't in agreement.*

He loosened his cravat. The room wobbled in a
drunken haze. Beyond the window, the sky had turned
dark and the old clock chimed nine. He'd been there long
enough. Determined, he stood.

"Gould, I need to borrow your fiddle."

The old man cocked his head with curiosity but
retrieved the instrument.

"I'll return it before we leave for Cambridge on the
morrow. Many thanks, old friend." Jack stuck the fiddle
into his haversack, the bow sticking out of one end, and
dashed from the tavern. He needn't his father's approbation to join the army, and he needn't his mother's permission on whom to marry.

41

JACK
TOPSFIELD, JUNE 1775

A SOLITARY CANDLE FLICKERED from the second-floor window of the Howlett house. Against the inky night, thick with the scent of jasmine, Jack tossed a pebble up to the window. He waited several minutes, poised and ready to throw another, when the basement pantry door opened and closed.

Annalisa dashed toward him holding a small, tin lantern. When she reached him, she adjusted the handkerchief at her neck.

"Let us leave now before someone hears."

Jack took the lantern and kissed her hands. "You're sure?"

"Yes, of course." With a giggle, she added, "You've been to the Willow, have you?"

"Only for a little while." He grinned. "I daresay some liquid courage was in order."

"I've had quite a bit of madeira myself."

He could hardly wait to taste the saccharine wine upon her lips. Jack lifted her onto his horse and they rode down the narrow lane, two miles to his family's estate. If he was to get her with child, it would be on his father's property —his future property with his future wife.

After stabling his horse, Jack led Annalisa down the path to the carriage house. There, they would hardly be heard. Inside, he lit a couple of barn lanterns. Patterns of golden light from the punched tin scattered across the stone floor and onto the oak walls like a blanket of stars. He withdrew Gould's fiddle from his haversack.

"I thought I might play for you." He smirked. "Would you dance for me?" The instrument beneath his chin, he glided the bow across the strings and quickly tuned.

"Only if I choose the song."

"Anything for you."

She bit her thumbnail. *"The Gobby-O."*

He hadn't played the old tune in years, but he knew it well. Jack moved to the rear of the room, behind his family's two carriages. There, no one would hear his playing. With one foot on a wooden crate, he started the familiar jig. Annalisa stepped in time to the melody, her form fluid but modest. Her mischievous glance led her toward him.

"How well you play." She tugged her neck handkerchief and tossed it to the floor.

She certainly had madeira enough for the two of them. And his own consumption of libations dizzied him still.

Annalisa twirled about and slid a pin from her dress. She approached, closer and closer until he backed into, and sat, on the wooden crate. Annalisa slid another pin from her dress, then another. With a smirk, she took the fiddle and bow from him, then sat on his lap. After setting the fiddle on the stone floor, Annalisa removed two more pins until the front of her dress opened, exposing her stays and the gentle curve of a modest bust.

"Is this how we properly do this?"

Jack wound his arms about her slim waist and rested his head upon her bosom. "Yes."

With a lithe finger, Annalisa traced his nose, ending at his lips. "You said you wish to have me. I hope you still do."

The desire for her touch, and the promise she would one day be his, pulsed through him. "Of course, I do." His lips grazed her collarbone. "Come with me."

Jack led her to one of the carriages, opened the door, and handed her inside. He sat close enough to feel her warmth through her skirts. Annalisa's lilac perfume spellbound him. His thumb brushed across the patch of skin beneath her right eye, and she shuddered.

"How beautiful you are."

"'Tis wondrous to hear you speak so kindly of something I've been taught to shame."

He frowned. "Shame? You're so lovely." He wrapped an arm around her shivering body.

Annalisa looked down at her hands. "I understand you've done this before."

His mind dulled with flip; his sensibility lacked. "Yes, I was with two ladies in London—"

"At the same time?" Her fingers dug into her bosom.

"No." Jack warmed, and he chuckled nervously. "No. Not at the same time. 'Twas two different occasions, shortly after we arrived. I regret it terribly." His thumb rippled across her hand. "Lust without love is an empty thing to behold."

The coach fell silent and Annalisa tugged the necklace

at her throat. "I would have doubted you if you claimed to still have your virtues intact at three and twenty."

He lifted her hand to his lips. It quaked in his palm.

How nervous she is.

"You've not been with anyone, but have you...pleased yourself?" Only Gould's flip would give him courage enough to ask something so base.

"Pleased myself?"

"Yes." Jack cleared his throat. He could hardly retract his question now. "When you find yourself alone, caught in a mood, have you ever...?"

Annalisa chuckled. "I'm rarely alone. But one time comes to mind." Her cheeks flushed in the dimness.

Jack settled into the seat. "Would you mind telling me about it?" He kissed the palm of her hand and then her wrist. "So I may learn how to please you."

She turned to hide her smile. "If you wish."

His lips trailed up her arm, and Annalisa rested her head against the seat.

"I was in the barn. All my family had gone to Ipswich —I'd been feeling poorly that morning."

"When was this?"

"Last summer. I suppose I caught myself in a mood— as you put it."

He slipped the sleeve of her gown from her shoulder. "And what did you do?" His mouth swept her skin. She smelled of lilac, yes, but also earthy from the farm. His breeches tightened against him.

"I retreated to the oak and climbed out of sight."

"And?" He kissed her collarbone, up to her neck.

"It was late afternoon. I rested in the tree and lifted my skirts."

"Like this?" He slowly slid his hand up her leg, gathering her petticoats.

"Yes."

His fingertips glided against her thigh. "And what did you imagine?"

"Your hands upon me."

"As they are now?" Jack kissed her neck up to her jawline.

"Yes."

"Shall I kiss you now?"

"As though we were to die tomorrow."

He blended his lips with hers, the only lips meant for him. From Annalisa's full-body shiver, he knew she felt it, too. His tongue slipped into her mouth. She tasted like sweet madeira. Hopefully, she didn't mind the flip certainly lingering on his.

"Is this pleasing for you?"

She shuddered. "Yes."

Perhaps she would allow him to tip the velvet. He stiffened at the prospect of what else she might taste like...

Annalisa slouched. As much as he wished to strum her, he continued to please her with his hand.

"I'll lose myself unless you let me satisfy you. You're so generous with me. Surely you must wish for me to bagpipe you."

He smiled against her mouth. "'Tis pleasing for me to delight you."

"You're certain?"

"Yes." And how he enjoyed delighting her.

When Annalisa's breaths turned to panting, he murmured, "Go off, my darling girl. I want you to let-go."

She gasped, then shivered against him.

At her apex, he cupped her face and kissed her. "You're my heart. Once we're married, I promise I'll strum you all night if you allow it of me."

Annalisa rested her head on his shoulder. "I suppose I should be content to wait till then. Though, I suppose our futures would be the same if you got me in the family way before our wedding, or after."

Jack held her close and his throat tightened at the thought; his conversation with his mother flashed through his mind, pummeling him into soberness. He would never marry Jane. But if Annalisa were to be his wife, he could never go to war, particularly if he left her with their child.

Annalisa wrapped her arm around him. "I wish you didn't have to take me home—that I could awaken to you like this each morning."

"One day." He pressed his face into her hair. He loved her, more than he could fathom. He had to get himself out of this engagement before Annalisa found out. Else, he'd lose the one thing he held dearest.

❧ 42 ❧

JACK
CAMBRIDGE, JUNE 15, 1775

J ACK SAT WITH HIS family in the very carriage
he'd shared with Annalisa the night before. Her lilac
perfume had long since vanished, leaving only his
mother's orange blossom hair powder to choke him.

He peered out the window. The old bay road to Boston
was as familiar as always, but with his betrothal to Jane at
the foreground of his thoughts, the journey elongated into
an insufferable nuisance. His father awaited them at Aunt
Catherine's.

*Surely, Father could talk some sense into Mother's deter-
mination.*

They neared the road to the Winnisimmet ferry, and
carts and chaises full of women and children passed by.

They must be fleeing the sieged city.

Jack tugged his lower lip. Since Lexington and
Concord, militias had formed a ring around Boston trap-
ping the British—and Boston's people, now mostly Loyalists from Cambridge—on the Boston peninsula.

Abigail tapped her finger on the window. "Think you Lord Suffolk will still host the ball?"

"He would be a fool to cancel." Oliver crossed one leg. "The rebels can hardly do a thing, and the season must go on."

"The season?" Jack's gaze narrowed. "Suffolk is a fool *not* to cancel. Look around you, Ollie. The province is in shambles. Boston is under siege and with dysentery running rampant. Cambridge is mostly abandoned, as is Charlestown."

"Enough of this troubling talk." Mother frowned.

When their juddering carriage arrived in Mystic, the horses snorted and stopped mid-stride at the bridge to Cambridge. Jack jumped from the coach. A tall man armed with a musket stood at the foot of the bridge.

"What's this, good sir?"

The man held his musket in readiness. "Boston be under siege."

"Aye, 'tis common knowledge, sir," Jack replied. "We're to Cambridge for Lord Suffolk's ball to-morrow eve."

I should be with these men. He bit his cheek to withdraw all foolishness from his face.

The man heaved an ugly laugh from the pits of his belly. "The Loyalist fool. It seems Suffolk acknowledges little of the siege." He approached with a quick step. "Where will ye stay in Cambridge?"

"Brunswick House. I assure you, our allegiances lie with you, sir. We are of Patriot-mind."

If only George and I were already in Cambridge, enlisting with General Ward.

"Ah, yes. Lady Catherine Brunswick, a kind gentle-woman. A Patriot." The minuteman paused. "The regulars have completely infiltrated Boston. The people are lucky to leave. Charlestown's been deserted. Cambridge, too. Surely ye can see the situation into which ye ride."

Sweat pooled under Jack's cravat from the humidity. "Aye, sir. Thank you kindly for your information. We'll make haste."

"God-speed. And if ye not with the cause, stay far from the hills."

"Which hills?" Jack recalled the rolling landscapes of Charlestown, Boston, Dorchester Heights, and the harbor islands.

The man squinted as though scrutinizing Jack's motives. "General Ward has ordered Colonel Prescott to secure Bunker Hill." The man stepped closer. "The plan is to fortify before the regulars seize Dorchester Heights."

Jack started at the man's wanton tongue. *But all the better to hear such information.*

"Pray tell, when?"

"Tomorrow, before midnight. About a thousand have already joined. We meet in Cambridge this evenin'. One more night o' recruitment, then we march. Avoid the streets if ye have no interest to partake."

Of all things fortunate! Perhaps George and I can sneak away and join. It would be a lofty price to pay, though they can hardly announce my engagement to Jane if I am absent from the ball.

"Sir, my thanks to you." Jack bowed and returned to the carriage with a lightness of step.

JACK HADN'T SEEN HIS UNCLE, LORD BRUNSWICK, SINCE his trip to Europe. The lord was rarely in Cambridge. In fact, his uncle only graced Tory Row but once a year. Otherwise, he remained in England as a member of the House of Lords, and a Whig Party advocate.

Lord Brunswick stood tall beside the gleaming mahogany longcase clock, but not as tall as Jack remembered. Beneath a pristine, white powdered wig, his grey eyes glimmered within a thin, regal face. Despite his ascetic appearance, Lord Brunswick was a just man, and above all else, a gentleman who doted upon Aunt Catherine.

Aunt Catherine stood behind her husband and alongside Father, who stepped forward. Father's eyes gleamed over the rim of his spectacles. He kissed Abigail's cheeks, shook Oliver's hand, then reached for Mother.

"My dear, it does me good to see you." Father kissed her hand. "You look to be in good health. How does the babe? Is Andrew situated at home with the Howlett twins and Susan?"

"She is well, and growing fast." Mother smiled. "Andrew is conscientious. He's quite well to be on his own with the girls and Henry."

Father nodded with approval then regarded him. "Jack. It seems these few months have looked well upon you."

Jack bowed. "You've been missed, sir. There's much I'd like to discuss with you prior to the ball. If I could but hold your private audience at your earliest convenience, say, now, perhaps?"

"Yes, yes, of course, my dear boy." Father chuckled.

"An eager man you are, young Jack." Lord Brunswick grinned. "Please you, whatever discussion can wait, yes? Your friends, the Howletts, were received. Let's into the parlor and help you relax after a long journey. I've some of the finest pipe tobacco in the province, and my favorite brandy from London."

Jack spun his signet ring. He'd have to wait until after dinner to speak with Father.

The maid, Dot, led them into the parlor. Jack perspired with the anticipation of seeing Annalisa. She sat beside Jane upon a turquoise velvet sofa, and cast him a short, but loving glance, then turned her attention to Abigail.

She is ignorant of the betrothal. There is still time. He heaved a relieved sigh and moved to a chair beside Father, and took the brandy offered.

"Jack, Ollie, it seems your illustrious uncle is leading in the House of Lords with the help of the Duke of Devonshire," Father said.

Oliver swirled his brandy. "Is it true, sir?"

Jack detected much ambition in his brother's stilted countenance. He finished his drink and shifted in his seat. He'd need far more than a single dram to pass this evening.

"My goodness, Lord Brunswick." Mrs. Howlett smoothed her skirts as Jane always did. "What a privilege."

"Indeed, madam." Lord Brunswick's lips pressed into a straight line. "And the Whigs are adamant in opposing Prime Minister, Lord North. We've endless financial support from the Duke of Devonshire. I daresay the Party holds more power and influence than North should like. There may be a chance Congress's olive branch petition is met with merit on the other side of the Atlantic."

"God willing." Father adjusted his spectacles.

"Hear, hear." Mr. Howlett gave a sage nod. "I do not wish to break ties with the Mother Country."

Father sat forward and lit his pipe. "And your sentiment is shared by many in Congress, Howlett."

Jack eyed George across the room and held up his glass
for another pour. "Father, have you any news from
Congress?"

"Indeed." Father sucked his pipe and exhaled a puff of
smoke. "This is fine weed, Brunswick. My thanks to you."
He cleared his throat. "Hancock—our new president of
Congress—has given me leave to attend this ball. I assure
you, this is more than a fine evening of dancing for you
young men and lovely ladies. It is a political event in which
we must show unity, both Loyalist and Patriot alike.
There's been quite a struggle with South and North
Carolina. The southern colonies, and even New York, have
demanded it is not in our interest to sever ties with
England, ergo, their allegiances lie in the petition."

"Things are beyond negotiating, Uncle." George
glanced briefly at William, who remained silent. "Sir, if
they were at Concord, perhaps they'd feel differently.
War's begun."

"George, mind your manners." Mrs. Howlett's voice
cut, but George paid his mother little heed.

"My apologies, my lords. But I cannot lightly acknowledge all my uncle says of Congress. Those fools from the
southern colonies have little understanding of the tribula-
tions our province has endured at the hands of the
Lobsterbacks these several years. The brutality of
Concord still burns in my mind, aye Jack?"

"George." William's soft voice carried from the other
side of Annalisa.

Father held up a hand and nodded. "Peace, George. I,
too, feel your frustration. But we must have a united

Congress if we're to invoke a notion of change. This means reasoning with the more difficult colonies. At this ball, we hope to show the southern provinces our willingness to unite with our Loyalist brethren. We must have Virginia's support."

Jack finished his second dram. "Mr. Hancock is in Philadelphia, as is Adams. Yes, Loyalists and Patriots will attend tomorrow, and we will show unity, but what of the men outside this house and the militias surrounding Boston? The men who only a few weeks ago were engaged at Chelsea Creek? How can we—in good conscience—attend such an event with guiltless reverie when beyond these doors men are burdened by the struggle for power?" He sat forward. "Can we trust this display of accord will prevent the regulars from opening fire on the militia while our heads spin from wine and dance?"

"Jack, please." Mother's amber eyes scrutinized him.

Father rubbed his chin. "You raise fair points. We must trust there won't be further engagements, yes?" He cleared his throat. "But let us not deliberate on these burdensome topics and put politics aside for one night, hmm? Brunswick, this is a most welcome reprieve for my weary mind."

"I'll second that, Perkins." Mr. Howlett raised his dram.

Jack relaxed his shoulders, surprised by Mr. Howlett's display of diplomacy—a Loyalist farmer with Puritan roots and an Agawam mother. *Curious Mr. Howlett is not more willing to abandon England's tyranny.*

Before they assembled in the dining room, Jack lingered behind in the parlor with Annalisa. When they were the only two remaining, he brushed her hand. "I wish for nothing more than to hold your private audience."

"Shh, my mamma will hear." She hid her grin and slowed her step into the next room. "But I daresay, seeing you has brought back all manner of affection from last night."

"Miss, you have no idea." He gave a soft smile. "I only wish to carry you far from this place."

"I wish you would," she whispered. "Perhaps to an encampment where we could leap the sword and you could take up arms."

Jack's eyed widened. "You wish to be a camp-follower."

She winked, and they entered the dining room.

Lord Brunswick rose from his chair. "Before we begin, I've an announcement." He looked to Jack. "As you know, my wife and I have no children, but Jack, you've grown into quite the gentleman. Your father boasts of you in each of his letters, and I find I could not hold a nephew in higher esteem." He turned to Oliver and grinned. "Ollie, we are proud of you, too, but I must have an heir, and I've decided to name you, Jack, as the heir apparent to my estate."

Mother and Mrs. Howlett gasped.

Jack's cravat suddenly squeezed his neck. "Sir, you don't mean it. This is an honor I cannot be worthy of." His uncle owned land in both England and America, and boasted three different homes.

Lord Brunswick gave a small nod. "I do. And you are worthy. I've already discussed the matter with your father and my estate managers. The paperwork has been completed. All you must do is accept." He chuckled. "And sign, of course."

George laughed. "'Tis strange hearing you've an inheritance beyond what you've planned for yourself, is it not, Cousin?"

Lord Perkins grinned. "George, I'll not forget that dinner at Hancock's so long as I'm living."

Beneath the table, Jack rotated his signet ring, and glanced at Oliver. His brother sat with a sour face. "Sir, I know not what to say. I am humbled beyond words."

"There's a good lad. We'll speak more later, yes?" Lord Brunswick sat and the rest of the table followed.

After dinner, while Annalisa's playing Mozart echoed down the hall, Jack and his father disappeared with Lord Brunswick into his private study. They sat in the mahogany office reviewing the estate's paperwork, all of which Jack signed with reticence. By the time they finished, Father's eyelids drooped. Burdensome conversation would have to wait.

ANNALISA
CAMBRIDGE, JUNE 16, 1775

A NNALISA CURLED HER LEGS against the twisting pain in her lower abdomen. She jumped from the bed, recognizing the familiar monthly sensation. *The morbid flux! Of course, it would come the day of the ball...but thank God it didn't the night in Jack's carriage.*

Her face heated at the thought. Or perhaps it was the humidity of the day, already wafting in through the open casement. She rummaged through her travel trunk for her menses apron, and after dressing, she snuck from the room she shared with Abigail and Jane, who still convened with blessed repose.

Voices murmured from the parlor below. She advanced down the staircase and lingered by the longcase clock. Beyond, George and Jack sat in the parlor.

She stepped into the room and Jack stood, his gaze downcast and his face haggard. "You look well-rested, Miss Annalisa."

George held out his hand to her, and she sat beside

him, rubbing her arms. Despite the mugginess, Jack's disagreeable countenance covered her in goosebumps.

"I've slept well these past few nights." She held his stare, hoping he would crack a smile.

"I've been awake most of the night deliberating the fortification of Bunker Hill." Jack glanced at George. "I suspect the regulars may make haste to Charlestown and initiate an attack."

She faced her brother. "George, will you join them?"

"Aye."

"We must do what we can, Miss Annalisa." Jack sat and rested his forearms on his thighs. "Our fellow Patriots are out there for a cause we all believe in. How can we abandon them now?"

"You intend to join, too?" She slid to the edge of her seat, her spirit vibrating with opportunity.

"Annie, you saw the massacre five years ago." George rubbed his cheek. "You know what the Bloodybacks have done to us, and Boston. We're involved, whether we like it or not."

"Of course." A burning crept into her throat, and her sensibility ruptured. She wished to join the fight, but in Jack, she'd secured a bit of womanhood she'd never realized she'd wanted. And tonight's ball was her chance to debut with higher society and gain their approval. Only then could she hope to marry him.

But the freedom of breeches was again within her grasp. Jack and George listened to her, took her more seriously than most. *And Jack believes me to be his equal. They might accept me, now.*

"You know I can fire a musket. Quite readily, in fact. Should you join, I'll be not far behind. I have no fear—"

"No." George slammed his fist into the sofa and Annalisa jumped. "You will not. You're a woman, and you will attend the ball. I'll not be manipulated into staying behind over your idle threat."

"Idle threat?" Annalisa stood. "George, my talents with a firelock would be well-met—"

"If you were a man." George rose, his face inches from hers.

"Men be damned! And yet you still managed to incur injury." She glared at him. "I can fire a fowler better than the both of you combined."

George's face reddened. "Because I taught you, goddammit!"

"Peace." Jack lifted from the chair and placed himself between them. "Please, cease your quarrel." He held a hand to George's chest then turned toward Annalisa. "I empathize with your sentiment, Miss Annalisa. And I admire your courage. But you cannot fight."

All hope sank into the pits of churning belly that now dispelled the unwanted bits of her womanhood. "But I am your equal, am I not?"

"I...yes, but...if you took a ball to your chest, I'd never forgive myself." He glanced defeatedly at George. "I'll remain. And attend the ball." His velvety voice cracked, but he held her hands with reassurance and kissed them. "We both will. We'll do anything to keep you safe."

AGITATED AND INCENSED, ANNALISA STARED OUT THE window. She clutched the frame and dreamt of ways to join the minutemen bustling through the streets below; her decision to remain made for her by the men in her life who so whimsically considered her their equal. She turned from the scene and faced the one behind her. Her sister and Abigail, in their petticoats and stays, underwent the tedious female tasks of readying for the ball.

"How fortunate for Jack, Miss Abigail, your uncle holds him in such high esteem to bequeath him his estate." Jane sat in a chair as the chambermaid curled her long, dark locks. "Fancy, that. Now he may take a wife. He may even choose to stop practicing law." Jane regarded Annalisa. "Are you ready for your debut to higher society?"

Annalisa's stomach coiled like a rope around a capstan. "I think so."

"You'll dance famously." Abigail stuck earrings into her earlobes. "I know it."

After two hours of having her hair curled around a hot iron rod, then pinned, Annalisa stared into the looking glass. A nervous giggle slipped loose; she hardly recognized the girl in the mirror. Her summer tan paled beneath white paint and rouge, and her honey-brown hair towered larger than she'd ever seen it—a high roll, piled atop her head with a long, single curl over her shoulder. The spring green sack-back gown trimmed with ivory lace and ribbon, fit her with nary a wrinkle, the hoops wide at each hip.

"I never imagined myself in so much silk." *A young lady upon the flowery path of female delicacy.*

ANNALISA CLASPED HER RETICULE AND APPROACHED THE third coach. Her parents had already assembled in the second carriage with William and Oliver, and the Perkins' with Lord and Lady Brunswick in the first.

"You're incandescent."

Annalisa jumped and turned. "You startle me."

Jack's index finger flew to his lips, and his crooked smile dimpled his cheeks. He was dressed to the nines in a light blue silk suit in ditto, embroidered with metallic gold threads. He'd probably commissioned it in Europe. Annalisa studied the way he leaned on his cane as he handed Abigail into the carriage. He somehow appeared both sophisticated and understated—fit to be his uncle's heir.

How can this be the same man who knelt in my garden and dirtied his hands beside me; the same man covered in sweat, blood, and gunpowder who'd held me after Concord; the man who pleased me in his family's carriage only two nights ago?

When he turned back toward her, his brown glossy hair, tied with black ribbon, flipped over his shoulder. He handed her into the carriage and followed, settling between her and Jane.

George sat across from them, beside Abigail. He looked well in his fine evergreen coat and breeches. Despite his grim countenance and their quarrel of earlier that morning, George leaned toward Annalisa. "Think you I'm dressed well enough to use Lord Suffolk's remedy critch when making water?"

Annalisa giggled, and he winked. George was rarely cross with her for long, and for that, she was grateful. She'd need him and his droll musings tonight more than anything—so long as he remained at the ball.

If he does abscond from tonight's festivities, I will follow him. I will prove to him and Jack I can do anything they can, no matter my sex.

When they arrived at Lord Suffolk's imposing brick

mansion, George helped Annalisa from the carriage. With three stories and four chimneys, the house was larger than Lord Brunswick's.

She took her brother's arm, and followed their party up the steps.

Inside, they gathered in a large antechamber of white wainscoting and two grand staircases leading up to the assembly room. Violins and cellos resonated the stately trills of Handel's *Water Music* into the foyer. Annalisa clasped George's hand and they walked up the steps.

"You look lovely, Little One," he whispered. "This plum brigade is nothing but a festival of dandy prats and peacocks. Remember, you are fearless." His thumb swiped the scar below her right eye, and he turned to enter the assembly room.

44

ANNALISA
CAMBRIDGE, JUNE 16, 1775

H IGHER SOCIETY, DRESSED TO the nines, met Annalisa with censorious eyes. Several gentlemen boasted powdered wigs and unfeeling glances while their ladies, in copious silk and wide hoops, chattered and whispered amongst themselves. Even the servants bore a regal splendor, all of whom wore gold embroidered scarlet costumes and white wigs. The people of Topsfield seemed so simple and plain by comparison.

I do not belong here.

Annalisa averted her gaze from the swarming gentry and studied the room. The hall, thick with lavender, orange blossom, and musk, glimmered in warm gold and sparkling crystal chandeliers. White paneled ceilings extended down the walls and exquisite wainscoting, affixed with sconces, flickered with beeswax candles. There would be no foul tallow burning tonight.

Abigail glided toward her with a grace she'd never before seen from her dear friend. "Look at this ballroom, Annie."

"'Tis unlike anything I could have imagined."

"Like you." Jack's whisper came from behind, and he offered her a glass of wine.

"What kind words you bestow, sir." She took the glass and sipped the claret.

Jane found her way beside Jack. "Mr. Perkins, would you mind taking a turn about the room? I so wish to admire the splendor."

He glanced at Jane, then replied with gentlemanly candor, "Of course, Miss Howlett."

Jane glided beside him, her ashes-of-rose, sack-back gown swishing from side to side.

Annalisa finished her glass of wine. "I thought she meant to pursue Oliver."

Abigail rolled her eyes. "Since Jack was named my uncle's heir, her motives may have shifted."

"She wouldn't dare."

George shuffled closer and handed her a second glass of claret. "A little more liquid courage for you and your minuet, Little One."

Abigail tugged on her sleeve. "'Tis Lord Essex."

The handsome viscount, with his strong chin divot, approached. His dark eyes glimmered beneath an ample brow and exquisitely manicured hair. His violet silk suit in ditto boasted elaborate silver embroidery.

He bowed. "Ladies. And gentleman."

Abigail curtsied. "Good to see you again, my lord."

Lord Essex grinned and revealed a row of straight, white teeth. He studied George. "I daresay, Mr. Howlett, your figure is rather commanding. You'd make quite a captain in this new provincial army."

Annalisa eyed Abigail with curiosity. *The viscount must be a Whig or rebel sympathizer to make such a remark.*

"I'm no commander, my lord, but I do participate in my town's minute band." George shifted his weight and curled his arms over his chest. "Perhaps I may one day command a militia if ever I enlist with the army."

Lord Essex nodded, then regarded Abigail. "Miss Perkins, I don't make a habit of dancing, but would you do me the honor of the first?"

"I'd be delighted, my lord." She glanced at George before taking Lord Essex's arm, and disappeared into the crowd.

George shrugged. "He's a right cockrobin if ever I saw one."

"It seems he supports the rebels." William joined, sipping a glass of wine. "Perhaps you should try to know him better."

"Nein, Wilhelmina." George took William's wineglass and finished its contents. "I have neither the patience, nor the fortitude, to befriend viscounts and dukes." He scoffed. "I'm no diplomat. And I'll not compete for ladies. If Abigail wishes to spend her time dancing with dandy prats all evening, I'll not chase her."

"Fie, George." Annalisa slapped his arm, her ease fleeting. Guests paraded toward the other end of the ballroom. The minuet loomed ever closer.

"Miss Annalisa." Jack snuck behind her once more and reached for her hand. "They're lining up for the first. Let's to the set."

This was her chance to prove her worth as a lady to higher society, her family, and Jack. She balled her fists. This time, she wouldn't trip.

45

ANNALISA
CAMBRIDGE, JUNE 16, 1775

L ADIES AND GENTLEMEN STOOD across from
one another in the center of the large, rectangular
room. The first sound of strings floated through the air
like feathers, but a stone formed at the base of Annalisa's
stomach. The minuet echoed off the ceiling and she froze,
pummeled back in time to the ill-fated Ipswich ball when
Oliver tripped her.

"Dear heart, follow me." Jack's charm, resplendent in
the ballroom, melted her. She would prove to Jane and
Mamma she was worthy of this debut no matter her
informal lessons, that despite her unruly girlhood she
could be Jack's wife.

Determined, she held up her head and followed,
though one half-step behind, counting to six in time with
the music.

Their hands touched, and they stepped down the hall
in a promenade.

"Shall we take my father's name, or have us called Lord

and Lady Brunswick when my uncle passes?" Jack whispered.

She gasped. "You don't mean it."

Is this an informal marriage proposal?

She flashed an eager smile, but it was enough to distract her counting. Annalisa tripped over her own foot. Her palm met the wooden floor and her wrist bent to catch the brunt of her weight. Jack pulled her up and steadied her, but the blunder had been made. She circled her throbbing wrist, her bosom and neck burning with humiliation as she passed the guests lining the room's perimeter. Several smirked and murmured amongst themselves, her old fears from Ipswich now returned to haunt her.

She gritted her teeth. *No. I will not run. Not this time.*

Annalisa continued the dance, and during the final promenade, held her head up with conviction as she passed ladies who snickered and jeered. Their chastising stares behind her, she made her way back to the line.

When the dance ended, Annalisa bowed to Jack. "I need some air."

"Annalisa, wait."

She glided from the line without waiting for him, and forced her way from the ballroom, onto a small balcony terrace. There, she inhaled the muggy night air.

What a fool I am. Why did I allow myself to be distracted? What a horrid dance. When it comes to muskets and minuets, I will always choose muskets.

"Miss Annalisa." Jack stepped outside. His handsome face gleamed in the evening twilight. "I am so sorry. I—"

"I should have known I would embarrass us with that dance."

"I care not for the minuet—or any dance for that matter." Jack rubbed his thumb across her cheek, wiping away a rogue tear. "I care for you. Everything about you has enamored me." He cupped her cheek. "You astound me in every way, and more."

"Mr. Perkins, there you are." Jane floated onto the balcony. "Oh, Annie." She frowned with spurious disquiet, and Annalisa knew she'd humiliated Jane beyond repair. "I knew we had to practice more."

Annalisa placed a hand to her hip. "One stumble is not enough to deter me."

Jane sighed. "Then you are more resilient than I." Handel's *Larghetto* from his *Concerto Grosso in F Major* drifted onto the balcony, filling the silence between them. "Mr. Perkins, they are lining up again. I was hoping to dance the next with you."

"Where is Oliver?" Annalisa asked.

Jane's gaze flickered downward. "I know not."

Jack looked to Annalisa. "I will stay if you will have me."

"No. Go dance. I will be quite well here, I assure you." Annalisa forced a smile. "Perhaps Jane can send out William or George."

Unease flooded Jack's eyes. "Will you remain here much longer?"

"No. I..." Annalisa peered over the balcony and saw minutemen. "I will return in a few moments. The air is refreshing."

"If you so desire." His lips met the back of her hand. "We shall dance again." He lingered a moment, then left the terrace with Jane on his arm.

Annalisa returned her attention to the street below.

Minutemen gathered by the dozens with lanterns and muskets in hand. Her disgrace quickly vanished in their cocked hats bounding down the lane.

"Abby dances again with that plum Lord Essex."

Annalisa turned to see George fiddling with his coat.

"What befell you two?"

"I told her I could not marry her and then leave for the army." He rested his arms upon the rail, leaned over, and watched the men below. "But I promised I would send for her when the time was right. She agreed, but watching her tonight with Lord Essex has me wondering if she's serious about being a camp-follower."

Annalisa rubbed his arm. "George, I know she loves you. Let her dance. 'Tis hardly a crime. Surely, you saw me dancing with all my graces intact."

George cackled. "I did." He grazed a thread from his coat and flicked it over the balcony. "'Twas the best stumble I ever saw."

They snickered.

"We don't belong here, do we?"

George remained silent, squeezing his bottom lip. "No. We don't."

"Perhaps you could marry Abby before you leave."

He rolled his eyes. "What good would that do?"

"La." Annalisa shoved him. "You know Abby as well as I. She will be glad to marry you no matter the circumstance."

"I suppose."

"Go. Retrieve her from Lord Essex when the dance is done. I have my own gentleman to find."

George grinned. "Jack?"

"Aye." She returned his smile. "Jack."

46

JACK

CAMBRIDGE, JUNE 16, 1775

W HEN THE *ALLEMANDE* ENDED, Jack led Jane from the set to a corner of the ballroom. There, his parents lingered with his aunt and uncle, Oliver, and the Howletts.

"You're quite light of foot, Jack," Lord Brunswick said.

Aunt Catherine clapped. "Lovely, both of you."

"How wonderfully you and my Janey dance." Mrs. Howlett's cheeks glowed rosy from too much claret.

Oliver scowled and excused himself.

"Thank you." Jack's mouth felt like cotton. He cast a wistful glance over his shoulder, eager to return to Annalisa. His mother and Mrs. Howlett tittered, keeping to each other's confidences.

Mrs. Howlett turned to Jane. "'Tis almost time for your birthday surprise, my darling."

Jane tugged on her necklace. "Mamma, you're too kind to have planned a surprise for me on Annie's debut. You know I care little for birthdays, and turning one and twenty is hardly something to be proud of when one remains unmarried."

Jack cleared his throat. "If I may interrupt, I require a private word with my father."

"A private word, now?" Lord Brunswick asked. "'Tis nearly time for Master of Ceremonies to make announcements."

"Aye, sir. I must speak with my father. At once."

Father studied him over the rim of his spectacles. "Yes, Jack, of course. Excuse us."

Jack led him outside to the terrace. Annalisa had gone. *Perhaps she returned to the assembly room with George.*

Balmy, brackish air from the back bay only added to the sweat pooling beneath Jack's clothes. He dipped two fingers beside his neck to loosen his stock.

"Sir, I have reason to believe my betrothal to Miss Howlett has been made in haste, and in vain. I intend to break the engagement...to marry another."

His father, who had appeared solemn, broke into reverential laughter. "My dear boy, is it true? You've found a lady who has caught your eye?"

Jack started. "Yes, sir."

"She must be most esteemed." Father adjusted his spectacles. "And from your manner of speech, it is not Miss Howlett?"

"No, sir. It is not."

"Your mother said you wished to discuss this matter with me." Father wiped his brow with a handkerchief and replaced it into his waistcoat. "Pray tell, why did you not come to me sooner?"

"I tried when we arrived, but Uncle—"

"Yes, yes. I recall." Father paced the balcony. "I daresay, I know the lady."

"You do?" Jack itched the back of his neck. "I never anticipated this happening the way it has. I know it may disappoint Mother and Mrs. Howlett, but I cannot marry Jane when my heart belongs to her sister."

Father straightened his coat. "Then you mean to wed Miss Annalisa?"

Jack fought the smile forming, but his mouth parted with joyous relief. "I do. It has always been her. My heart has been full of her long before I learned of my betrothal to Jane."

"It pleases me to hear. Though, you are meant to announce your engagement tonight." Father sighed. "But I cannot abide by this if you are unwilling. I suppose I could stop the announcement."

Jack held his father's shoulders. "Then you agree to it. I may marry Annalisa?" He hesitated, weary of his father's consent. "You find her a fitting wife?"

Father nodded, his smile small but warm. "Yes, of course. She is a lovely girl."

Jack's shoulders relaxed. "And you'll speak with Mother?"

"I'll handle your mother and the announcement."

No time could be wasted. Jack rushed from the balcony and hurried through the ballroom. He caught sight of Annalisa and William at the outskirts of the set.

"Miss Annalisa." He weaved through a gathering of ladies and reached for her. "I've much to tell you. Will you join me in the foyer?"

"Of course. What is it?" She returned his grin. "You're beaming."

He kissed her hands. "I've spoken with my father and—"

"Annalisa, Jack, William. I need you at once!" Abigail hastened toward them, her eyes wild.

Jack glanced around, feeling others' stares. "Abigail, you forget yourself."

Annalisa's face fell. "Whatever's the matter?"

"You must come with me. Nothing could be more urgent than this." Abigail gulped. "'Tis George and Oliver."

47

JACK
AFTER MIDNIGHT, JUNE 17, 1775

J ACK, ANNALISA, AND WILLIAM followed Abigail through the swarm of gentry toward the antechamber. Shouts resonated from the first-floor foyer. Annalisa clasped Jack's hand as he positioned himself at the banister.

Below, Oliver and George stood across from one another, poised to fight.

"I told you to stay away from my sister," Oliver admonished.

"The same could be said for you, *Cousin*. I'll not forget the night you strummed Jane in our barn."

Already, a gawking crowd had formed. Poor William ran down the stairs. "Off with you now, ladies and gentlemen. Go to. There's nothing to see here." He ushered people up the stairs and into the ballroom, their chatter in waves as they passed by.

Annalisa steadied her glass of wine on the marble railing and looked to Abigail. "What's this?"

Abigail bit her thumbnail but said nothing.

Jack ran down to the antechamber and stood between his brother and cousin. "This is neither the time, nor the place, for an altercation." He turned to George. "You love Abigail, yes?" He faced Oliver. "Brother, you must accept it. There's nothing left to discuss."

Oliver adjusted his waistcoat. "I caught them consorting here not but ten minutes ago. I'll not stand for this ruffian to marry our sister—who, I might add, should use a little discretion. Lord Essex is here and has his eye on you, Abigail."

"I'll worry about my own reputation, Brother." Abigail descended the stairs. "And you're one to talk, Ollie. As if the way you took Jane in the loft wasn't vile enough, what you did to Miss Annalisa was a degrading act of vulgarity. Is that the mark of a gentleman? Fie! I am shamed for what you did."

"Abby, no!" Annalisa shrieked..

Jack's heart nearly stopped at the sound of Annalisa's cry. He glanced at George, who transformed from man to angered beast.

"What did this reptile do to Annie?" George bared his teeth at Oliver. "What did you do to Annalisa?"

"Not here," Annalisa cried. "Not like this."

Abigail looked up with wild indignation. "Nonsense, Annie. He must know." She stood by George but faced Oliver. "You forced yourself on her. Did you not?" She waved a wanton finger. "You kissed her and placed your hands upon her in an ungentlemanly fashion. You should be ashamed. Such is the act of a beast."

Shattered glass left Jack's face cold and tingling. Beside him, claret spread from the broken goblet like blood across the white marble floor. He looked up and saw

Annalisa, ashen as the room around her. She wobbled and clutched the bannister. He went to ascend the steps, to carry her away from the scene, but George tore free of his coat and lunged at Oliver.

"I'll kill you, you Tory bastard. I'll kill you with my bare hands." George punched Oliver's face. "I'll drag you through the streets and have you administered the modern punishment, you Loyalist cur." George threw another blow to Oliver's stomach. "A duel, or nothing!"

Oliver doubled over, but when he looked up, he leered. "A duel it is, you lout."

"No." Jack ran to his cousin and pulled his burly arms. "No duel. You must contain yourself."

Murmurs and shrieks echoed into the foyer from a crowd atop the stairs.

"A pistol, gentlemen," Oliver shouted to the gathering.

"No pistol," William cried.

George hurled himself at Oliver and swung again. He missed, the force of the blow sending him toward the stairs. Oliver pursued George and recoiled his fist.

William lunged and pulled Oliver from George. "You'll never win a fight against my brother, trust me."

"A pistol!" Oliver struggled in William's grasp.

Jack hauled George from the altercation. "You must stop this—if not for me, then for the ladies we love, who are now humiliated." He glared at Abigail, who stood to the side, weeping.

George shrugged Jack from his shoulders. "I'll not spend another moment here, so long as this squeeze crab remains."

Oliver swiped the blood from his lip. "Likewise, you peasant dog."

"A dog, say you?" George sprang forward and swung at Oliver's jaw. He tumbled to the ground and lay there, unconscious.

"Oliver." William shook his shoulders and slapped his face. "Wake up, Ollie."

Jack pulled George up the stairs. "This is madness."

George threw off Jack's hands. "Unhand me."

"I beg of you. Let Oliver be. I've assaulted him for what he did, now you've assaulted him. Perhaps he's learned his lesson without dueling him."

George's menacing eyes narrowed. "You knew what he did to Annie and didn't tell me?"

Jack swallowed. "I would have killed him myself when I found out, but he's my brother. He is cruel and selfish, but with any hope, he's learned a lesson. I thought I could handle him without your knowing. I apologize—"

"You should have told me, and I could have dueled the traitor." George's lip curled. "You wronged me, Cousin."

"No." Jack reached for him. "Listen to me."

"No. Listen to *me*." He swatted Jack's arm with disgust. "You don't get to protect Annalisa. I do. And until you're her rightful husband, I'll take responsibility for her wellbeing." He spat at Jack's shoes, then turned from the stairs. When he reached the door beneath the staircase, he said, "You betrayed me, *Cousin*."

The crowd had dispersed, and Annalisa with them.

Jack looked to William. "Sit with Ollie until he comes to." Frantic, with his coat and stock askew, he seized Abigail. "Return to the ballroom and make amends with Annalisa. I must pursue George."

48

ANNALISA
CAMBRIDGE, JUNE 17, 1775

S ICKENED, ANNALISA PUSHED HER way through the crowd and back into the ballroom, where she searched for Papa. Halfway across the room, Jane, with cheery countenance, stopped her.

"Mamma told me my birthday surprise. I'm to marry Jack. We're engaged."

Engaged?

Jane's words left her cold and numb. "What about Oliver? Does Jack know? He couldn't possibly have agreed to it."

"Of course, Jack agreed. He was speaking with Mr. Perkins. I trust he was learning about it at the same moment. Oh, I can hardly begin to tell you how happy I am." Jane took her hands and squeezed them. "One day, you will have this feeling when you find your future husband."

"But...but you and Oliver strummed in the barn." Annalisa's temples throbbed. "I cannot believe you."

"Strummed?" Jane's face pinked. "We did not strum."

"You lie."

Abigail hurried toward them, her face careworn. "Jack is searching for George, he's nowhere to be found. Your dear brother has left Ollie in a bloody heap on the antechamber floor. William's tending to him."

"A bloody heap?" Jane's face fell. "What happened?"

Annalisa heated. "Abby, why did you tell George what Oliver did to me? I knew this would happen."

"I am so sorry." Abigail reached for her. "I never should have said anything, but Ollie crossed George and me for the last time. I knew not what else I could say that would teach him a lesson—"

"A lesson?" Jane's hand settled on her waist. "For what Oliver did to Annalisa?"

"He treated me cruelly, Jane. And you refuse to believe it." Annalisa rubbed her temples. "Abby, Jack is gone, too, you say?"

"Jack hasn't gone anywhere," Jane snapped. "We are announcing our engagement."

"Engagement?" Abigail slapped Jane. "That's for not supporting your sister." She pointed her finger. "If you're lying about this betrothal because you wish to become the next Lady Brunswick, you're a right doxie. And if you aren't, you must break the engagement at once, else Annie will die of a broken heart."

Jane held her face and looked away.

"Look at your sister, you selfish witch. She's in love with Jack and yet you perseverate upon marrying him!"

More secrets spilled from Abigail's wagging tongue!

"Of all things that are ridiculous." Annalisa slapped

Abigail, then Jane. "Enough. Have not I endured enough humiliation from the two of you tonight? Jane, if I've learned one lesson, 'tis I am no good at being a lady. Society would rather die of plague than accept me among them. You both may bicker about Jane's dubious engagement, but our brothers have left this ball, probably for Bunker Hill. I'll find them. I cannot remain a second longer."

"Bunker Hill?" Abigail reached for her. "Will you go?"

Jane rubbed her other cheek. "Let her go."

Abigail called after her to wait, but Annalisa ignored her.

Tangled in Bach's fugue, she snaked through the ballroom, snuck through a door, and hurried downstairs to open air. An unattended horse was tied to a nearby gate. She loosened the reins, hiked up her skirts, mounted the beast as best she could in hoops, and rode to Brunswick House.

❦

ANNALISA SLIPPED INSIDE THE MANSION THROUGH AN unlatched door beneath the kitchen. In the moonlight, she uncovered a servant passageway and tiptoed up the creaking stairs. Once inside the room she'd shared with Jane and Abigail, she fumbled for a paper spill, lit the chamberstick, and set it on the vanity. In the flickering light, she unpinned her gown with frantic fingers, tore it from her body, and flung it onto the bed.

In shift and stays, she sat beside the crumpled heap of silk and lace. Bach's fugue had long since vanished, leaving a vestige of Jack, and Mozart's *adagio* to haunt her.

Engaged? Jane is mistaken. He would never have agreed to such an arrangement after so candidly declaring himself to me that night beneath the oak.

She yanked the string from her stays and pulled the whale-boned binding until it fell to the floor.

And Abby, to have betrayed my confidence. I'd always imagined it would've been Jane.

Her nose stuffed and throat clogged, she threw open the top of her trunk. Annalisa bound her breasts, then pulled on her shirt, slipped into her breeches—careful to manipulate her flux apron—and buttoned the waistcoat. With quick fingers, she tugged the pins and curls from her head and plaited her hair into a queue. After donning William's old, cocked hat and George's linen coat, she peered at herself in the looking glass.

He calls me his equal and yet I cannot fight.

She wiped the white paint and rouge from her face and smudged her cheeks and forehead with lampblack.

I could have been dirtying myself at Bunker Hill all night with the rest of them.

Only God knew what awaited her on Bunker Hill. With a final glance in the mirror, she removed Quinnapin's *wampum*, and set it atop the escritoire. Nothing was going to prevent her from joining the fight this time. An adjustment of her breeches, and she fled the room.

Below, the longcase clock struck half-three. Lord Brunswick's English musket hung beside it. She lifted the bulky weapon from its hold. It weighed more than George's fowler but would have to do. She slung the musket over her shoulder, along with the cartridge box beside it, and quit the house. The road to Charlestown, a dark ribbon between aubergine fields, lay before her.

Tonight, I walk upon the heroic precipice of feminine perdition.

❦ 49 ❧

JACK

CAMBRIDGE, JUNE 17, 1775

I N HIS SEARCH FOR George, Jack encircled the mansion twice before returning indoors. He ascended the steps to the ballroom, where he found Abigail and Jane.

"Where is Annalisa?"

Abigail gasped. "You're still here." Her mouth bent. "Jane told her about your engagement and—"

"Our engagement." He balled his fists. "We haven't time to discuss this. I must find Annalisa."

"You must stay." Jane grabbed his arm, her lavender perfume overwhelming. "Our engagement is to be announced."

Jack lifted her hand from his arm. "Miss Howlett, I spoke with my father and he's consented to me marrying Annalisa. You'd best quit me and focus your attachment on Oliver."

"I see." Jane's face fell like soft rose petals after the first frost. She smoothed her skirts as if to distract from her disappointment. "A lovely ball this has been for each of us.

I've never been so mortified." Jane dipped into a curtsy and sashayed into the ballroom, not once looking behind her.

William emerged from the crowd, his face contorted. "Oliver's awake."

Part of the heaviness lifted from Jack's chest. "Thank God."

"He's with your father. Needless to say, they're both full of ire. Have you seen George or Annie?"

Abigail held Jack's gaze. "Annie thinks you pursued George to Bunker Hill. She said she'd find you, but I can't believe she'd do something so daft."

"Zounds," Jack cried. "There's no telling when, and if, there will be hostilities between the militia and the Redcoats."

"We should leave now." William's gaze swept the room. "Should we first search Brunswick House? In case they returned there?"

Jack rubbed his face, remembering Annalisa's threat this morning. "We may, but I suspect a darker truth."

☙❧

JACK DASHED INSIDE BRUNSWICK HOUSE. HIS SISTER scurried up the stairs, while William took to the basement. In his search of the first-floor, Jack noticed his uncle's musket, a Brown Bess, missing from its place on the wall. A lump formed in his throat.

William emerged with a lantern, the light flickering upon his wan face. "No one is down there."

Together, they ran upstairs and convened in the ladies'

bedchamber. The air was saturated with foul tallow. The chamberstick had long since been lit.

Abigail sat on Annalisa's bed and gestured to a mound of silk and ribbons. "She was here."

"Then she did follow George?" William asked.

Jack twirled his signet ring. "George and I discussed joining the minutemen at Bunker Hill. Annalisa overheard our plan...she said she'd follow us. I've no doubt George has gone to Charlestown—"

"Fie." William's fist closed. "Annie has little reason to do something so foolish."

Abigail fumbled with Annalisa's ribbons. "'Tis my fault. George never would have left if I hadn't spoken out tonight." She rose from the bed, cradling Annalisa's clothes over her arm.

Jack inched toward the door. "We must scour Cambridge. With any luck, we'll find her in town." He led them down the stairs and gathered a couple of lanterns. "Abby, stay here. Perhaps Annalisa will come to reason and return to the house." He faced William. "A couple of cartridge boxes, Will, and firelocks."

William nodded and left to retrieve the effects.

Abigail lingered by the longcase clock, its hands already at half-four. "I'm mortified. I made a fool of myself and our family."

Jack kissed her forehead. "Love turns us all to fools, does it not?" He opened the front door. Outside, the sky brightened. He and William must make haste.

ANNALISA
CHARLESTOWN, JUNE 17, 1775

THE DIRT ROAD CURVED upward, and Annalisa followed until she reached the top. Beneath the hazy dawn before her, the Charlestown peninsula stretched across shimmering waters, southeast toward Boston. She squinted at the faintly visible slopes of Dorchester Heights far to the south. Steep, green islands were not the only things to speckle the harbor. Three-masted warships littered the inlet with billowing ivory sails, each one crowned with the blue, red, and white flag of Britain.

She shivered. Far nearer, and more visible through the summer smog, sat a large fortification atop one of Charlestown's hills. The king's warships pointed their guns at the rising land—land a thousand minutemen had worked all night to secure.

George and Jack must be there now.

Her throat tightened as she imagined Jack and George clutching muskets behind those ramparts. A thunderclap of artillery shattered the morning calm. At last, she was direct witness to the hostilities. Sweat trickled between her breasts bound in linen, but the fabric wicked all moisture, as did the menses apron between her legs.

I should face no troubles today as I did in Portsmouth.

But the threat of her womanhood in disguise loomed.

A half-mile from Charlestown Neck, Annalisa lingered beneath a wide maple. The cacophony of cannonade washed over her with bitter resonance. Without her militia, she must find a way to safely cross the narrow strip of land.

The clank of metal mixed with a scuffle of marching shoes, and two regiments of what appeared to be provincial militia, gathered across the road. The gentlemen in command, addressed as Colonels Reed and Stark by their subordinates, appeared sullen and stiff. Colonel Stark, a thin, older man who must be in his middle-forties, stood tall and imposing. He wore his cocked hat low over squinted eyes. With a scowl upon his sunken mouth, he held himself in readiness, and lifted his cutlass into the air.

"Gentlemen." Stark's craggy voice severed the eerie silence between cannon fire. "Ready yourselves. We march across the neck."

This was her chance. She gripped her musket. The regiment marched passed at a deliberate pace, and she slipped in.

"Watch yourself." An older man scrutinized her as she stepped on his foot.

Panicked, she lowered her hat, and fell in with the march. She must take extra care to blend in and keep her identity hidden, no matter the cost.

When they reached Charlestown Neck, water glim-

mered on either side of the narrow strip. Gunboats and
warships blasted artillery across, turning the ground to
crumbled wasteland. A blazing cannon screamed forth and
lodged itself into the earth mere feet from her. The
ground quaked and Annalisa lost her footing. She tumbled
and fell, the moist soil inches from her nose. A minuteman
from behind scooped her up and continued the march,
scarcely wasting a step. Shaken, she advanced across the
neck.

Bunker Hill rose before them. It was probably thirty
feet high. Beyond it, a valley, then a smaller rise, Breed's
Hill, she'd heard them call it. There, atop the shorter
mount, minutemen gathered behind six-foot high dirt
walls and ram-shackled rail fences.

Perspiration gathered on her brows and dripped down
her back. Hand trembling, Annalisa wiped her forehead.
The regiment stopped after they descended Bunker Hill.
To her left, the grassy land sloped down toward the banks
of the Mystick River. Colonel Stark crossed in front of the
regiment with another officer.

"My boys." He gestured to the river. "Low tide opened
up this beach. You are to secure it with stones to form a
breastwork to the water's edge. Three ranks of men will
flank you from behind."

Before she could sneak away, Annalisa fell in with a
group descending the bank. They scurried over the edge
and set to building a stone wall that would meet the
brackish river waters.

A young, bright-eyed boy handed her a large stone.
"This is madness, is it not?"

She grabbed the heavy rock from him, and her knees
buckled. Annalisa bit her tongue, unwilling to speak. The

timbre of her voice over cannonade would surely give away her secret—the one secret she had left.

"Stack the stone, lad," an older man barked.

She placed the large rock atop the first row.

"I daresay, we're lucky to have made it this far." The young man handed her another small boulder.

"Nathaniel." She gasped.

He tipped his hat out of habit, then his brows lifted. "Ben Cavendish."

They embraced for only a moment, and Annalisa pulled away, her anxiety pulsating. *Will he ask why I abandoned our militia at Concord?*

Hesitantly, she asked, "What are you doing here? Is Captain Foster here with the militia?"

"No, I left the militia shortly before Concord. My family moved to Exeter in New Hampshire. I enlisted with Colonel Stark's first New Hampshire regiment only a fortnight ago."

Annalisa exhaled, relieved. He didn't know she'd been detained in Topsfield that fateful day Ebenezer fell at Concord.

"Here we are, Cav. Everything we believe in we get to fight for." Nathaniel clapped her back, and his palpable vigor set her at ease—an old friend from her militia beside her in this fight.

51

JACK
CHARLESTOWN, JUNE 17, 1775

S WEAT DRIBBLED DOWN JACK'S temples as they neared Charlestown Neck. He stood atop the knoll. Below, Bloodybacks swarmed Charlestown's guarded hill in organized formations, a storm of angry red wasps with bayonets glinting in sunlight like steel stingers. He choked on the smoke rising in the east.

William heaved and gagged until he retched. "I can't do this. I cannot go on."

"Will." Jack crouched beside him. "We must. We must find Annalisa. And George. This is war."

"Don't be daft." William cleared his throat. "If we manage to cross the neck without getting killed, we'll never find her. Even if we do, they set Charlestown on fire. There's not a chance she's alive. I know not whether I could bear seeing her...dead." He choked on the last word and wiped his face with his sleeve. "Or worse. Without a limb, dying, with blood seeping all which ways from her."

Jack quaked. *If the Bloodybacks take Annalisa's life, I will take my own.*

He pinched the bridge of his nose, closed his eyes, and ran a hand down his face, cupping his mouth. Dust and smoke ebbed across the landscape but parted momentarily.

Bunker Hill, tallest, and rising nearest the neck, was without a primary redoubt. Breed's Hill, shorter and in the middle of the peninsula, was closest to the scorching town. It was there the minutemen made their stand. Warships surrounded on all sides, pounding the land with cannon fire.

"My God." Jack's face tingled as the lifeblood drained from him. "They secured the wrong hill."

"Pardon?"

He pointed. "They were supposed to garrison Bunker Hill because 'tis taller and nearest Charlestown Neck—a better vantage point."

"How could they be so foolish?" William cried. "How can we continue?"

Flustered, Jack stood and paced to clear his mind. "Maybe Annalisa's trapped behind Bunker Hill—near the neck—or between the hills. In that valley." He faced William. "Trapped, but with any luck, alive behind some haycock, or tree." Hopeful, he shook William's shoulders. "We cannot leave her stranded. She went there believing I was with George. I can't desert her now." He wiped his eyes. "I love her. With every bit of my soul, I love her."

"I love her, too." William nodded. "Yes. Of course."

They loaded their muskets and descended the knoll toward the isthmus. Sulfuric gunpowder stung Jack's throat and cannonade deafened his ears. Given the afternoon hour, the minutemen had to be running low on artillery. Jack looked down the road. A regiment marched over the ridge. Joining the militia was the safest way to cross the neck.

The captain's sharp voice severed the cannonade. "We gain on Charlestown Neck, men. Steady and ready yourselves."

"There is no turning back from this." Jack gripped his musket. "Are you with me?"

William was silent. The poor lad had no inclination of joining Topsfield's minutemen and was now about to engage in battle.

"I'm with you."

"When they pass, we slip amongst the others. Make no sound."

They lingered beside a wide maple, and when the militia spanned the width of the road, Jack and William slid in.

52

ANNALISA
BUNKER HILL, JUNE 17, 1775

COLONEL STARK WEAVED THROUGH the line and, several yards from the rock fence, planted a wooden post in the sand.

"Men, you will not open fire upon the Redcoats until they reach this point of entry, and you can see the whites of their eyes. We must conserve our gunpowder. These are the men of our tyrant king, the sycophant who taxes and oppresses us from three-thousand miles away. These men represent King George, and these men we shall defeat. Death is not the worst of evils. Live free or die!"

"Live free or die," the men cheered.

"Live free or die," Stark shouted.

Invigorated by Stark's rally, Annalisa crouched beside Nathaniel behind the stone wall. In a moment of unnatural quiet, she turned.

"Friend, I wish you luck. Once they make their assault, we may never speak again." She clutched her musket as each memory of firing Bixby in the clearing with George, and the Danvers militia, washed over her. "We fight here for Ebenezer."

Nathaniel lowered his gaze. "Aye, I did hear of his death at Concord." His chin jutted and he met her anxious stare. "We fight for him, Cav, and we will speak again when the battle is won." He hoisted his firelock into the air. "For Ebenezer. Live free or die!"

The surrounding men joined, and Annalisa opened her mouth to cheer, when a man behind her shouted, "Gents, Bloodybacks!"

"They're sending the light infantry against us. Howe's Royal Welch Fusiliers—"

"Shut it, man."

The enemy's rowboats floated and bobbed in the waters just beyond their small stretch of beach. Annalisa squinted, blinded by the menacing glare of bayonets. She adjusted the tip of her cocked hat over her left eye. *There, now you may shoot your Lobsterback with ease.* Jack's words rang in her mind.

There was no mistaking it: the province was at war with the Mother Country. Nothing remained of her minuet at the ball, nor her anxiety about marriage, or her fears of womanhood. All vanished in the face of the advancing light infantry.

A burning rage for Oliver Perkins surfaced, followed by her frustration for Jane and her hideous deceit. Annalisa clutched her musket. Though her hands trembled, she loaded her musket with resolve. *I will show them all I can do this.*

"Steady, Cav." Nathaniel gripped her shoulder. "Remember drill practice. You and your Brown Bess will kill many this day."

She startled, the reality now before her. *Can I kill a man?*

Annalisa wiped the sweat from her brows and clung to her musket until her knuckles whitened. The light infantry, now afoot on the beach, advanced past the stake Stark had planted in the sand. A burst of sparks and gun smoke erupted from the men in front of her, directly behind the stone wall. As quickly as they had fired, they reloaded. Pungent clouds of gunpowder wafted in the salty breeze, distorting her view and clogging her throat.

Each man spent less than thirty seconds to reload, as George had instructed. Every crack of the musket symphony took her back to the Danvers common and Captain Foster's orders.

Her hands shook as she half-cocked the musket and pushed forward the steel. She ripped the paper cartridge with her teeth and spat the litter to the ground. Gunpowder spilled about as she dribbled it into the priming pan. After snapping back the steel, she removed the ramrod and held it in one hand as she poured the remaining gunpowder and lead round into the barrel. She wielded the ramrod into her musket, packing it all home, and replaced it into the channel. With the musket to her shoulder, she pulled back the cock, steadied herself, aimed, and fired.

A flame flared from the priming pan, followed by a thick, cloud of smoke and a deafening *crack-boom*. A Redcoat dropped to his knees within eighty yards of the stone wall.

"Good eye." A minuteman in front of her turned and squinted. "But keep up, lad."

Annalisa flushed, and she heard George's voice, *Three*

volleys a minute, Little One. It was one thing to have a keen eye. Speed was quite another. She reloaded, quicker than she'd done before. A Redcoat charged and Annalisa pulled the trigger. The lead ball struck his chest. He staggered toward them and toppled over the rock wall, onto the minuteman in front of her. Under the soldier's dead weight, the minuteman fell into her, and warm blood splashed her face from an open wound. The minuteman, she, and Nathaniel pushed the body away, rolling him back over the wall. Her breath shortened at the scent of iron from the enemy's blood trickling down her cheek and neck.

A queasiness lurked in her throat when she recalled Jack's tale of his first kill. This Redcoat may have had a wife or children. She squeezed her eyes shut and forced the Welch Fusilier's cold, dead stare from her memory.

He earned his death. I executed him as befitting a soldier.

But it was hardly enough to settle her rattling hands.

"Damn the king," Nathaniel wailed beside her, pulling her back into the moment. His face and hands were imbrued with the blood of the enemy. The Royal Welch Fusiliers fell, and one by one, their tall, black hats rained down upon the sand.

Annalisa clenched her musket and watched her innocence wash away with the waves of the oncoming tide.

JACK
BUNKER HILL, JUNE 17, 1775

J ACK AND WILLIAM MARCHED with Captain
Chester and his New Hampshire regiment across
Charlestown Neck. The sharp crack of artillery rang
in Jack's ears and smoke burned his eyes; old torments to
remind him of Concord. To his surprise, many of the dead
watering the grass with bloodshed bore the red coat of
England. Jack lunged up Bunker Hill's steep slope, eager to
see their provincial victory. As they rounded the top,
horrified, disorganized minutemen fled their posts on
Breed's Hill. His skin iced.

A militiaman crouched in the tall grass, behind a large
stack of hay.

"You, man." Captain Chester pointed. "Behind the
haycock. What is the meaning of this?"

Shaken, the man turned. "Sir, we have no artillery left,
and no one to lead us. In such circumstances our lives
cannot be preserved, sir." The man tied a bloodied cravat
around his bleeding thigh.

"It appears Prescott has provided less than inspiring leadership," Captain Chester muttered to his subordinate.

Another minuteman rushed toward Bunker Hill. "The gunpowder's spent. Turn back while you can."

"My God." Jack coughed over the smoke. "This is madness."

William's ruddy cheeks faded to linen white. "Should we turn back as well?"

"No. We came all this way. If we leave the regiment, we may stand a chance of finding Annalisa."

They broke from Chester's troops and scurried through the long grass, and across the field between hills. They crouched behind a rock wall.

Yards away, a Redcoat rushed at them with bayonet fixed. Jack loaded and fired. The soldier lost his weapon, gripped his chest, and stuttered toward them. He toppled onto William as blood pulsed from his wound.

"God in heaven," William shrieked.

Jack pulled him from beneath the soldier, and they darted to an apple tree. Jack opened his cartridge box and reloaded. "Keep your guard. And load quicker."

Charlestown's church steeples blazed in conical flames, billowing black smoke into the air.

"Well I'll be damned."

Jack and William turned.

"Brother!" William's face alighted, though he panted.

Jack grabbed his cousin's wrist. "George, thank God."

George dripped with sweat, his hands, face, and clothing soiled and caked in blood. He tied his filthy cravat around a bayonet wound to his right forearm, then sank to the ground and embraced his brother.

"Fancy seeing you here, *Wilhelmina*." He neither smiled

nor acknowledged Jack's relief. "This way." His long legs vaulted him toward a haphazardly-dug ditch.

Jack followed, his musket aimed and loaded.

George knelt at the base of the trench and loaded his fowler. "What brings you bawdy baskets to the Devil's Den? Found it within yourselves to abandon the plum brigade?" His mouth curved into a frown, but his straight, white teeth appeared menacing as he bellowed a low, deep laugh.

"We're at the brink of death and you tease?" William's eyebrows lowered, but Jack could tell it was hard for him to remain angry.

"Abigail told us Annalisa believes we fled the ball together," Jack said.

"Zounds." George ground his teeth. "I suppose you've no idea why she'd leave such an extravagant evening, hmm?" He spat on Jack's shoes. "When next I meet your reptile brother, I'll have him administered the modern punishment and dragged from Portsmouth to Boston behind my plow."

George's words struck Jack far worse than the cannonade shaking the earth. "You're right. But 'tis hardly the time to debate what befell us at the ball. I love Annalisa, and we know she must be here—I will not return to Cambridge without her."

"That minx." George adjusted the tip of his hat over his left eye and rubbed his stubbled chin. "If Annie's here, she hasn't gotten far. Charlestown is ablaze, and the redoubt has been overtaken by Bloodybacks." He choked on the last word.

Jack started at his cousin's sudden lament.

When George looked up, his eyes glimmered red, full

of sorrow. "I regret to tell you, Cousin...we lost the good Dr. Warren."

Jack's cheeks numbed, and the ground beneath him shifted. "Our Dr. Warren?" A beat of silence passed between them when the thunder of artillery ceased fire in a moment of unnatural quiet.

"His head was struck by musket round, and his body stabbed by bayonet." George's voice gave a slight quake.

"No." His hero, his inspiration for turning Patriot—gone. The Green Dragon, the Sons of Liberty, would never be the same. Tightness encircled his chest and a piece of him vanished with the spirit of the doctor. "He was a good man. The best of us. God be with him."

"God? He's not here." George wiped his face. "This way. I heard Stark's First New Hampshire has been by the Mystick River decimating Howe's Welch Fusiliers. If Annie's crossed the neck, I bet she'd have marched with Stark." He hung his head. "Otherwise..." His gaze shifted toward the blazing town. Smoke soared into the afternoon sky. The world burned around them, a catastrophe of red uniforms and fleeing Patriots.

❧ 54 ❧

ANNALISA
BUNKER HILL, JUNE 17, 1775

"WITHDRAW, MEN. WITHDRAW!" STARK ordered from atop the embankment.

Annalisa turned to Nathaniel. "We must leave."

"Stark is too hasty." Nathaniel replaced his ramrod into the channel. "Did you not see how the King's Own made their retreat? We should be victorious."

"But more regulars approach, and we've little gunpowder." Her voice cracked. She cleared her throat, then squeezed Nathaniel's arm. "If we make it up the bank, we'll have a clear shot at the neck once we round Bunker Hill."

Nathaniel locked his stare with hers. "I trust you, Cav." He glanced over his shoulder. "I'll cover the rear if you lead."

Her loaded musket in hand, Annalisa lunged up the bluff.

"Cav, you're bleeding," Nathaniel shouted.

Incessant musket-fire had crumbled the dry earth beneath her, but she scrambled to the top. Her breeches were stained with menses.

"'Tis from the Fusilier," she lied. Clutching her musket, she slid across the soil and leaned over the edge. "Take my hand."

Nathaniel lifted his arm, and she grabbed his wrist. Her face burned while she tugged him over the top. As he cleared the edge, a musket ball whizzed past and lodged into Nathaniel's thigh. Blood spurted and pulsed, soaking his breeches and stockings.

"Oh, God!"

Annalisa's hair rose at his guttural cry. She whirled around, aimed, and fired at the assailant. The Redcoat grasped his chest and fell over the bank, landing below with a *crack-thud* on the stone wall.

She curled her arms under Nathaniel's shoulders to help him stand. "We must run."

He struggled to his feet, his hand clasped over his leg. "I can't."

"We haven't a choice."

They scurried up Bunker Hill, rounded the top, and Nathaniel stopped. His face paled despite the afternoon heat.

"I can't, Cav."

Annalisa tugged off her cravat and tied the linen around his wound. She tightened the cloth, and searing pain suddenly struck her right shoulder. She fell back with the force and grabbed her shoulder, stifling a scream.

The pain burned worse than her cheek had six years ago. She looked down at the blood ribbing through her fingers, far more than the morbid flux now adorning her breeches. A sharp, shooting agony radiated down her arm as she lifted it. The lead round was stuck inside. There was no time to remove it.

"Come." She gritted her teeth over the throb.

"I think if you help me, I can manage." Nathaniel threw his arm around her neck. Using her left arm, Annalisa helped him to his feet. Together, they bent low and descended the hill toward Charlestown Neck.

A fleet of warships and gunboats still clogged the surrounding waters, but fewer cannon balls shredded the soil. Ahead, several minutemen dashed across to safety.

By the time they reached the strait, Annalisa choked on the smoke. With each cough, her shoulder burned. She limped under Nathaniel's weight across the narrow strip of land, her feet raw with eruptions of blisters. Before her, the road to Cambridge blurred beneath a smoky haze. She blinked her watery eyes. Her knees buckled.

"I can't carry you like this, Nat. I need you to bear some weight."

Battered militiamen ran past and littered the road to Cambridge, their heads hung in defeat. Her heart twisted.

Is Jack among them? George?

The battle behind her, Annalisa pushed forward, dragging her feet against the dirt lane. Nathaniel's breathing slowed, and his color waned. At the foot of the hill, Annalisa laid him by the side of the road. Her shoulder sizzled and ached when she removed her shoe and stocking, and tied the silk around Nathaniel's pulsating leg.

"Oh God," he whimpered. "'Tis agony."

About a quarter-mile up the hill, minutemen gathered.

Is that Jack with George?

"Jack." Her voice rasped and cracked. "George." Annalisa peered at Nathaniel and slapped his face. His eyelids fluttered. "You're tempting the ethers of existence. You mustn't give in."

Nathaniel groaned. "Cav, where are we?" His once excitable eyes now held the vacant stare of death.

"We're on the other side of the neck, on the road to Cambridge. But you need a surgeon." She stood and her knees bent.

A few more yards of dragging Nathaniel uphill felt like miles. Annalisa again stood, but collapsed. Her legs were as weak as a babe's, and sharp pains surged through her shoulder. On her hands and knees, Annalisa crawled a few feet up the road.

"Jack. George."

When she looked behind her, Nathaniel's eyelids drooped. She crept back to him and slapped his face.

"Nathaniel. 'Tis not time to see Ebenezer. Stay with me." She had one chance to get them home alive. Through the pain, she curled her hands under his arms and tugged him toward the base of the hill, her body shaking with each step.

"George!" Her voice cleared through the hoarseness, but it was too much. She crumpled to the ground and Nathaniel slumped against her. The hard dirt road cradled her weary body, and she closed her eyes.

55

JACK
CAMBRIDGE, JUNE 17, 1775

J ACK SAT IN HIS uncle's dimly lit study and unbuckled his stock. It was far too warm for the fires to be lit, but nonetheless, they blazed. Hours had passed since he'd washed the grime of battle from his hands and face, though he remained in his torn and tattered silk suit.

Father paced. "You defied me." The candlelight cast a flickering shadow onto his grim countenance as he eyed Jack's uncle.

Lord Brunswick sat at his large, cherry wood desk. He crossed one leg. "This charade was highly unexpected of you, Jack. First the altercation at the ball, and now this. There are far more judicious ways to show your support—"

"I explicitly forbade you from engaging in battle since Concord," Father erupted.

Lord Brunswick lifted a hand. "Easy, John—"

"You put William Howlett in danger of being killed, as well as yourself." Father drove his fist onto the mantle. "You know Mr. Howlett is a Loyalist. He never would have forgiven such an act. You're lucky he's forgiven as much as he has. 'Tis one thing for George to join. Your cousin will do as he pleases. He's certainly got Bixby blood for that." He cleared his throat. "But your uncle is right. There are superior ways to show your support for the rebels. We've discussed your coming to Philadelphia."

"No." Jack met his father's gaze.

"No?"

"No, sir. I will stay here and join the army with George."

The vein on Father's forehead bulged. "You are my heir, and now your uncle's. You hold far greater responsibility than George."

Jack slid from his coat. "Sir, you have two other capable sons."

"Don't even speak of it," Father snapped. "You know as well as I, Oliver is far too conniving and ambitious to inherit the estates. He will squander everything. Andrew has not the fortitude."

Jack threw back the remainder of his brandy. The liquid burned his throat. "Then you condemn me to a life I care little for." The glass landed on the table with a clatter.

Lord Brunswick rested an elbow on the arm of his chair. "You've signed the papers—willingly, I might add—and now you must uphold that honor."

Father approached. "Our support is strong for the colonies to govern themselves independently. But we will not fight on the front lines. Your uncle in Parliament, and I in Congress. That is where we shall oppose King George, along with several other worthy gentlemen."

Jack stood. "I'm not a child. I won't be dictated to as our own king dictates to the colonies. Father, Uncle, I appreciate your generous offers, but I belong with a musket in my hand—and with Annalisa Howlett by my side." He turned to leave. "If you'll excuse me, I must check on her."

"'Tis out of the question." Father stopped him. "Child or no, you've responsibilities—"

"Miss Howlett is the proper choice, Jack," Lord Brunswick said.

Jack tightened his jaw. "Tell me, does his lordship find bravery and courage so condemning in a woman that he may refuse me the right to marry the woman I love?"

Lord Brunswick shifted in his chair. "Miss Annalisa is not the well-bred woman suitable for being your wife you presented her as. She's demonstrated this enough over the past two days. Society will not accept her."

"This is preposterous." Jack leaned across his uncle's desk. "Uncle, if being your heir means I cannot marry her, 'tis not worth it. Let me to the papers I signed. I'll toss them into the fire this instant."

Lord Brunswick rose from his chair. "I appreciate your frustration, but do be sensible. 'Tis only a marriage."

"*Only* a marriage? My lord, a marriage is for eternity. I don't take that promise as lightly as *the ton,* or apparently, your friends in Parliament do."

"Enough," Father said. "You may not throw around insults. Your nuptials will take place this November upon my return from Philadelphia. End of discussion."

Lord Brunswick frowned. "I am grieved to see you in such a state. Had I known you carried such fondness for this girl, and the disdain you place on Society, perhaps I would have taken better consideration of Oliver."

"Then do it, my lord," Jack said. "Offer your estate to

him. He will gladly accept, along with all the duties charged him—including a marriage to Jane Howlett."

"Insolent boy." Lord Brunswick's nostrils flared, and his face blazed in the candlelight. "Do you understand the implication of forfeiting your inheritance? You will be left with nothing. Do you understand? Nothing."

Father lifted a hand. "Peace, Brunswick." He faced Jack. "Your uncle is right. I understand your heart, Jack. But sometimes we must put reason first, hmm?" He peered over his spectacles as though he were delivering a verdict in court. "A rational mind is of utmost importance, and when matters of heart cloud our judgement, we are no longer able to hear the voice of reason."

"Father, please." Jack softened his voice and tamped away his pride. "I swear to you as a gentleman, if you allow me to wed Annalisa...I'll join you in Philadelphia."

Father's lips tightened. "I had given you my blessing, but that was before *Bunker Hill*." He spoke the word as though it would conjure the devil himself.

Lord Brunswick sighed. "She may have courage, but she lacks discretion and obedience. You cannot have a wife whose name is clouded in scandal. Society shall never forget what she has done."

Jack threw up his arms. "Society does not even know."

"There will be gossip, Jack," his father replied. "Don't even deny it."

Jack returned to the fire and leaned over it. The heat soaked into his face, lighting his spirit aflame. He spun around and eyed his father. "Then we'll elope."

"You wouldn't dare," Father hissed. "If you truly love Miss Annalisa as you say you do, you will give her up at once, and not further dishonor her with the scandal of an elopement. As a gentleman, you owe her at least that...if you love her."

"Of course, I love her." Jack's voice cracked with fatigue.

Father clasped his arm. "Prove to your uncle and me you're a man of honor. Marry Jane and keep our family—and the Howletts—unsullied."

Jack swallowed. It burned, but not as harshly as the brandy, or his father's words—some of which were true. He could hardly elope with Annalisa and cause her and her family more shame and ridicule.

But how can I marry her sister instead?

56

ANNALISA
CAMBRIDGE, JUNE 17, 1775

B ATHED AND IN A clean chemise, Annalisa lay in
bed, her shoulder bandaged and burning. In the dim,
wavering light, Abigail's hand smoothed her hair. Her
friend's rose perfume was a reprieve from the stench of
battle, but plagued her memory of the ball.

"I'm so sorry, Annie. I'll never again wag my tongue as
I did. You have my word. You had me so scared—and your
wound. I wish you had allowed Dr. Cook to look at it. I
daresay, had Uncle been able to procure a proper surgeon,
you would have, yes? This entire town is in disarray. Does
it hurt much? I can get Clara to bring you some tea—"

"My shoulder hurts only a little. And the thought of tea
churns my stomach."

"I see." Abigail paused, and silence spread between
them. "Why did you do it? Are you so unsatisfied with
your womanhood?"

"I had to find George and Jack."

"I know. You said that already." Abigail frowned.
"Well, I swear no one shall find out about it. My uncle

will make sure of it." She gave a tight-lipped smile. "He will come up with something clever to tell Society, I promise."

Society. Annalisa looked away. *I must look upon Bunker Hill with shame when I should be proud for showing such courage.*

The door creaked open and a man cleared his throat. "May I speak with Miss Annalisa...alone, please?"

Annalisa looked up. *Jack.*

Abigail turned. "Are you finished speaking with Uncle and Papa?"

He shifted his weight. "Quite."

"I'll return when he's finished. I promise." Abigail left the room and latched the door behind her.

Though he smiled, his eyes appeared heavy and burdened. "I am awed by your resilience." He sat beside her on the bed and smoothed the hair from her face. "Is your shoulder feeling any better?"

She reached for his hand. "I'm as well as can be."

"Good." He looked aside. "My God, this is too hard."

"What is?"

"I hate to bring this up in the light of what we've been through." He paused. "But we must discuss Jane."

"Yes. She mentioned the engagement."

Jack started to speak, but Nathaniel's bleeding leg flashed behind her eyes. She shook her head to chase away the image.

"Can we speak of it another time? I can hardly think without seeing brutality."

"Of course." Jack's gaze dropped, and she thought he might weep. "Your beautiful eyes have seen much today, such that I wish you could have never seen." He brushed

her cheek with his thumb. "And your delicate shoulder."
His hand slid down to graze her collarbone.

"You aren't cross with me?"

"No." Jack pulled away. "But there's nothing I can say
that will ease the pain of today."

"I know." Annalisa sat upright. "And I'm so sorry."

"Me, too."

She pulled him to her breast and held him. Her nose to
his head, she ran her fingers through his hair. He still
smelled of gunpowder and smoke. What she wouldn't do
to keep him beside her each night.

"I thought you left with George—I had to follow you,
I—" She choked on her words, hesitant to relay the truth.
"I had to be part of it, to show you I could do it."

When Jack lifted his head, his glassy eyes were rimmed
in red. "I know." He kissed her hand and held it to his
chest. "But my heart would have stopped today if yours
had."

"Then will you lie with me a moment?"

He slid behind her on the bed and wrapped an arm
about her. Her skin erupted in goosebumps under his
warm breath. They remained like that for several minutes,
then with one look over his shoulder, Jack stood.

"I won't trouble you any longer."

"Trouble me?" Annalisa pinched her bottom lip as he
advanced toward the door. "John Jackson."

He turned, his brows arched at the formal address.
"Dear heart, what is it?"

"I love you."

Jack rushed to her. "Annalisa." He leaned over her and
united his lips with hers. How soft, how gentle, and with
such loving warmth he kissed her.

But—is that the salty taste of his tears?

He pulled from her and wiped his eyes. "Sleep, my darling girl."

Annalisa held her gaze on him until the door latched shut.

ॐॐॐ

A SHRED OF MOONLIGHT SHONE THROUGH A GAP IN THE curtains. Abigail and Jane had long since joined her, and now slept. Annalisa kicked off the coverlet and turned to her right. A bolt of pain shot through her shoulder.

She tossed onto her left. A dull ache coursed through her body. With her knees curled to her chest, she blinked until the tears receded. It was futile tamping away the barbarity. Selfishly, she had put those she loved through panic and torment, all to follow Jack and George, all to prove her worth. But guilt trapped her far worse than any humiliation she'd endured at the hand of Oliver, or Lord Suffolk's Ball.

In the darkness, Annalisa sat upright. Her muscles burning, she turned toward Jane. Her sister's white silhouette glowed. She was so still, save for her slow, steady breath escaping and returning. In this silent moment, Jane's vulnerability shone through. She thrived in her womanhood; lived for Society, no matter their foolishness and judgment.

Annalisa hugged herself. All she saw and experienced today would remain with her until the end of her days—*the ultimate punishment*, as Mamma had put it. She exhaled the stale air from her lungs, and the guilt lifted for a moment. She'd made it to Bunker Hill, fought the Redcoats, survived, and rescued Nathaniel. Dr. Cook had saved his leg. These were acts of bravery Society would never acknowledge.

Her shoulder throbbed, and queasiness overtook. The musket round was still lodged inside.

George cannot know I was shot. He'll think me a fool. I must remove it without him knowing.

Annalisa rubbed her arms. Despite vigorous washing, the dried blood of others still flecked her skin. As quickly as pride had lifted her, despair dragged her to the deepest depths. A putrid bouquet of searing flesh and gunpowder still lingered within her nostrils. Grisly visions of men without limbs haunted the blackness behind her eyes.

She screamed into the dark. Drenched in cold sweat, Annalisa bolted upright in bed. She'd fallen back asleep.

The door flew open. "Little One?"

"Annalisa."

"Jack?"

"I'll handle this, Cousin," George whispered, and the door closed.

"Annie?" Jane's half-asleep voice trailed into noth-ingness.

Sweat trickled down Annalisa's breast. "George. I dreamt...of blood." Pain radiated from her shoulder through her chest.

"Hush." George knelt and set the chamberstick on the bedside table. He smoothed the hair from her face. "How is your shoulder?"

"'Tis nothing compared to the nightmares." She wiped her forehead. "I saw a man lose his head."

"Battle is full of horrors." George wiped her tears. "Today was far worse than Concord. You will be tormented by these memories until you can no longer remember."

She shivered at his words. "I'm proud I fought. I told you I could."

"Lie down." George held her hand as she shifted onto her left. "I'll remain until you sleep."

In the dancing light, she studied his sad frown. He was so handsome and strong. The best of them. If only he could find happiness—marry Abigail, have children, work at his tavern. All of this she wished for him, but her victuals told her he would soon leave them all.

"I love you, George."

"I love you too, Little One."

Annalisa glanced over his shoulder across the room at Jane and Abigail, who slept. "I'm sorry I never told you what Oliver did to me." Her voice broke, still hoarse from the smoke.

"I've never given you reason not to trust me."

"I know. But I was afraid your temper would get the best of you, and it did. You nearly killed Oliver at the ball."

"He's alive and well," George grumbled. "I admit I was a bit...daft. But you're my sister. I must defend your honor—"

"I'm nineteen. You needn't protect me. I daresay, I've shown I can defend myself."

His brows furrowed and she thought he might quit the room, but he remained, silent. When at last he spoke, his mouth curled. "How came you to join Stark?"

"I saw them at the junction in the road. I slipped among them."

"Your friend Nathaniel was asking for someone named Cav?"

"I called myself Cavendish. Benjamin Cavendish."

"Benjamin Cavendish. Have I heard it before?" He tapped his chin and considered it for some time.

Will he, too, reprimand me the same as Mamma and Papa?

George sighed. "I tried my best to dissuade you, but I suppose a part of me always suspected this would happen —though not quite so grave. You fought and saved a man's life, Annie, and you lived to tell the tale, mostly unscathed. Not even I can boast as few wounds as you." He shook his head. "While uncouth, I misjudged you, Little One. I'm remiss to say it...I'm impressed."

She exhaled, a sense of peace finally overcoming her. "Then I've done my duty, sir." Annalisa yawned and closed her eyes.

George kissed her forehead. "Get some sleep, Cav."

57

JACK
TOPSFIELD, JUNE 23, 1775

A T THE MEETINGHOUSE ON Sunday, Jack sat
beside Abigail in his family's pew, nearest the
pulpit. He studied Annalisa from across the room. Despite
the neck handkerchief positioned over her shoulder to
cover the bandage, she looked sun-kissed and beautiful—
and well recovered—as she sat beside George.

A week had passed since Bunker Hill and Lord
Suffolk's infamous ball, and he'd been in Topsfield four
days now. Annalisa and her parents had returned only
yesterday. While his father and uncle had contrived a tale
for her wound, it already was town's worst-kept secret.

He lifted his gaze to Jane. She sat between Mary and
Henry, as far from Annalisa and George as possible. Mrs.
Howlett must have confirmed the engagement to Annal-
isa. After the harvest, he'd have to call Jane his wife.

*But will she be satisfied marrying me when I already
proclaimed my love for her sister?* The situation was akin to a
Greek tragedy.

After the service ended, Jack followed his family

outside. A brisk morning breeze swept under his hat, cooling his face. Annalisa stood with her brothers beneath the church elm.

"Annie. You're looking well." Abigail left Jack's side and linked arms with her.

Mrs. Andrews loomed. "Miss Annalisa, what a scare. To have been assaulted on your way from the ball must have been terrifying. I knew it was too dangerous to go anywhere near Boston." Her chubby face glowed like a strawberry beneath her straw hat.

Annalisa's mouth formed a tight line. "Indeed, marm. But I was able to have my debut with higher society."

"I suppose that is good," Mrs. Andrews replied. "Tell me, do you have a cousin by the name of Cavend—"

"You must excuse us, Mrs. Andrews." She and Abigail turned and walked toward the common with George and William.

Jack hurried after them, but Miss Balch, Miss French, and Miss Shepard intercepted him. "Good-day, Mr. Perkins," they each said, giggling between curtsies.

He tipped his hat, then proceeded toward the common when his mother reached for his arm. "Jack, why don't you take Miss Howlett for a stroll."

"Mr. Perkins, are you courting Miss Howlett?" Mrs. Andrews eyed Jane with curiosity.

"They're engaged to be married, Mrs. Andrews." Mother beamed. "You'll see the banns shortly."

The burning in Jack's stomach reached his throat. Unable to smile, he offered Jane his arm and led her toward the common.

"I hope you don't mind I've worn this dress before."

Jane fanned her skirts. "But I thought you might like the color on me."

His mouth pressed into a tight smile.

"And once we're married, I'm sure to have many more fine dresses for our engagements with Society. You needn't worry about this old one—"

"Miss Howlett." Jack stopped and turned. "Are you quite happy accepting this arrangement knowing how I feel about your sister? Knowing how you feel about Ollie."

"My sister?" Jane glanced at the common, no doubt studying Annalisa in the distance. "Sir, love is so transient, is it not? You did fancy me once, yes?"

"Love? Transient?" He frowned. "I apologize, but you confuse love with dalliance. Have you entirely forgotten our intercourse at the ball?"

"I haven't." She lowered her gaze and smoothed her bodice. "But I'm certain I'll change your mind."

It was true, he'd fancied her, but that had been a silly, youthful infatuation. "I doubt that, Miss Howlett. I was coerced into this betrothal." He continued their walk.

"And you think this is easy for me?" Her face remained pleasant, but her words fixed his stride. "Think you I find particular pleasure in all of town knowing you're to wed me second to my younger sister, arranged or no? And I've no doubt bruised your brother's ego—"

"Then why not refuse the match with me? You can still marry Ollie—"

"No." She met his gaze. "You're to be the next Lord Brunswick. How could I refuse such a match?"

It was the advantage and title she wanted, not him. "Oliver could be the next Lord Perkins if I relinquish it to him. Would you be happy with that title, Miss Howlett?"

Jane's lips parted to speak but another voice entered his ears.

"What do you suppose happened between Jack and Annalisa?"

Miss Shepard's boisterous voice spoke with Miss French and Miss Balch. Jack staggered at the common's perimeter and pulled Jane with him behind a large oak.

"What are you doing?" Jane hissed.

He placed a finger over his lips. "Shh."

"You saw how they danced at the festival but a fort-night ago," Miss Shepard continued. "Now he courts Jane. Nay, I just heard from Mrs. Andrews he means to *marry* Jane."

Miss Balch snickered. "Jane was caught in the Howlett barn with Oliver."

"I suppose Jack and Jane aren't as well-bred as we supposed," Miss French replied tartly.

Miss Shepard said, "How awful for Miss Annalisa. Mrs. Andrews says Jack played upon Annie's heart like a spinet."

"La," Miss French exclaimed. "See, Lizzie? I knew Annalisa Howlett could never have married Jack Perkins. I always supposed he would marry Jane. Jack's the hand-somest man in the province, and Jane is far more beautiful than Annie. Beauty must stick together."

Jack balled his fists. *My poor Annalisa, disgraced. I can never forgive myself, and neither will she.*

He looked to Jane. "How can we endure this?"

Jane straightened her hat. "Jealousy is an ugly thing, sir." She glanced at the grouping of ladies. "I've endured theirs all my life. 'Tis the price of beauty. You should know this, being the handsome man you are." She eyed him carefully. "The gossip never fades, Mr. Perkins. You simply learn to tolerate it. As for Oliver—I shall quit him. We're in this together, you and I. I promise to never again betray your confidences."

☙✽❧

JACK SPENT A WEEK IN DISTRACTION BY SETTING UP HIS law office in town. When he'd endured George and Annalisa's silence long enough, he rode north to Portsmouth.

He stepped inside George's Black Water Inn. Several men read aloud from newspapers about Bunker Hill. They spouted proud words for their own New Hampshire-born Colonel John Stark and his campaign against the Royal Welch Fusiliers. A strange pride swept over him knowing his brave, darling girl had been among Stark's men.

George stood behind the wooden bar. He wore a clean black coat, his long obsidian hair tied in a queue as he wiped clean a mug. Behind him, shelves housed pewter tankards and plates, and bottles of wine, brandy, and port. He appeared very-much the established tavern owner.

"Cousin, a word, if you please."

George's emerald eyes glared then returned to his tankard.

"I've come all this way to speak with you. If you could give me a moment of your time—"

"You're turning into quite the doxie."

Jack leaned over the bar. "I had nothing to do with this engagement to Jane—"

"I'll be damned." George slammed the pewter cup upon the bar. "If you think that is the reason I've distanced myself from you, you truly know me not at all."

Jack lowered his head. "'Tis Ollie."

"A capital study." George set the mug on the shelf behind him. "Annie is my greatest happiness on that farm. She deserves nothing but goodness, and I'll be damned if a son of a bitch tries to take it from her—my mother and aunt included. I'm disgusted by it all—your engagement, Oliver's assault—but for you, the one other person in Topsfield I trust, to keep something like that from me?" His lip curled. "I'll not forget it."

Jack frowned. *When did I become such a cowardly fool?*

There was nothing he could say to atone for all he was accused of, but he had to try. "'Twas hardly my right to do, but you must know how much I care—how much I love—you and Annalisa. I suppose there's no way I can convey how sorry I am for betraying your trust."

George jeered. "I can protect Annie like no one else—"

"And she'll never stop needing her older brother."

"She used to need me." George rubbed his temples. "Perhaps now she doesn't. I keep forgetting she's a woman grown. Yet a woman unmarried. God help the gentleman who does. He'll need enough breeches for the both of them." George fell silent. "I will never understand a woman's heart. Devil knows the complicated matter between me and Abigail."

He held Jack's stare as if examining him in a court of law, though Jack knew his cousin had never stepped foot inside a courthouse. It mattered little; George was a brother who loved and protected his sister at all cost, and Jack could hardly fault him for it. He'd do the same for his own sisters.

George sighed. "Then you do love her. You must make amends. She's quite vexed, as you can imagine. I could show you her letters, but she'd probably have me given the modern punishment."

"Think you she'll receive me?"

"I'll do what I can to convince her." George held out his hand. "If there is one man in the province worthy of her, 'tis you, Cousin. Would that you could marry her."

"An elopement is the only way, and would further disgrace her. I can't bring myself to do that to her." Jack frowned. "I love her too much."

"It may be worthwhile to tarnish yourselves." George smirked. "You are both always welcome here." He grabbed two glasses and a bottle from the shelf behind him. He pulled out the cork with his teeth, poured rich amber brandy into each glass, and slid one before Jack. "Stay the night. 'Tis a long ride back to Topsfield in this heat." George lifted his drink. "To you and Annalisa—may you find a way to elope."

Jack chuckled and took the brandy. "I'll call on her tomorrow as soon as I arrive home."

58

ANNALISA
TOPSFIELD, JULY 1775

ANNALISA SAT BY THE basement pantry hearth with a basket of Quinnapin's herbs. Weary, and with shoulder throbbing, she sifted through the greenery and wondered how Nathaniel fared with his leg.

I can hardly visit him, wherever he is in New Hampshire. She set the basket down as a hot gust of summer air blew in from the pantry door. Jack entered.

"Miss Annalisa."

Her stomach coiled, and she stood.

"Good-day." Dizziness swirled her consciousness, spoiling her curtsy.

Jack rushed to her side and steadied her. "Are you poorly?"

She shrugged away his hands and sat. "Some days are better than others." Unable to remove the musket round, her wound had grown red and angry, leaving her winded and with night fevers.

"We must talk." He fiddled with his signet ring. "As you became aware, Jane and I are engaged to be married.

It was arranged by our mothers and settled upon by my—"

"I wish you'd have confirmed it sooner—that I wouldn't have had to hear it from my mamma after you left Brunswick House...while I was suffering from my—" She averted her gaze. "What more is there to say on the matter?"

"I tried to tell you that night—"

"I know."

Jack paced, rambling. "I tried to quit the arrangement, but my father and uncle have dictated I hold to it, else I lose both inheritances. I could never dishonor you with an elopement, but," he sighed, "believe me, this has been no easy decision—"

"You mean to follow through with it?" Her cheeks tingled. "You're agreeing to marry my sister? How long have you known about the engagement?"

"I found out before the ball—"

"Before the ball?" She turned from him and grazed the tip of the wooden busk nestled within her stays. "Did you know the day we spent in the oak?"

"No—"

"Then, when?"

"Two days—" He lowered his gaze. "I found out two days before the ball."

"Two days?" Annalisa cupped her mouth. She stood and paced before the unlit hearth, her shoulder burning with each step. "You knew that night in the carriage. Oh, what a fool I was. What a pitiable fool."

"Annalisa, please, you're no fool. 'Tis I who is the foo—"

"A fool? No, you're a scoundrel—like Oliver. I can't

even look at you, Jack Perkins. You're betrothed to my sister. I could have understood before all this happened between us—I did understand. Heaven knows I tried to quit you for her sake. I'd have done anything to keep her from marrying Oliver, so I suppose I should be glad for your betrothal, but I cannot." She clenched her fists. "Did you ever truly fancy me, or was I just some silly dalliance?"

"Yes, I...I mean no, you are not some dalliance."

Her anger bubbled to a head. "You made me believe I would share your life with you."

"I did—"

"You knew you were engaged that night in the carriage, yet you advanced upon me as though I were yours to have."

"I did—"

"At Lord Suffolk's Ball, you spoke as though you meant to marry me."

"I did—"

"You made me believe you loved me—"

"I do."

Annalisa froze at his admission. *He loves me?*

"I do, Annalisa. I may have done all these things, with only the best of intentions at heart, but my feelings for you are unchanged—"

"How can I believe another word from your unscrupulous tongue?" Tears spilled from her eyes, and she turned. "Know you what they are saying in town? The people are saying you've played upon my heart like a spinet." She wiped her eyes. "Now, I am even more shamed than when I fought at Bunker Hill, but nobody can know *that* noble deed, can they? Rather, I'm some tawdry whore who's bewitched her sister's betrothed."

Jack's face contorted. "Annalisa, you're no whore." He reached for her. "I love—"

"Don't touch me." She recoiled. "And don't you dare say it. Because I do not love you, John Jackson. Not anymore."

He stepped back as though she'd slapped him. "Please, if you would just listen—"

"Listen? I despise you." A piercing pain bolted down her side. "In fact, I wish we never were acquainted."

He pinched the bridge of his nose. "I can hardly blame you..." He cleared his throat. "I've committed things I wish could be undone, but I'll never regret our time together. I've meant every word—including the night in the coach—no matter the engagement. And I still do. Please, let me right these wrongs, Annalisa. There's a way for us to be together, if you would only listen and give us a chance—"

"For what? For me to be your mistress after you wed my sister? Poor wretch that I am. Neither a wife nor a best friend—simply a lover. Sounds like a whore to me."

"Hardly! No, Annalisa. I can't imagine my life without you. Please, listen to me. I—"

"I don't wish to set eyes upon you again." Shaking from heartache and fatigue, she quit the room, and left him staring after her.

༺✦༻

A SUFFOCATING HEAT SETTLED OVER THE FARM. EVEN Dane, Quinnapin, and Zeke sought refuge from the fields inside the barn with George, who'd just arrived from Portsmouth. Annalisa wheezed as she fed the hogs with Mary. It was difficult breathing in such humidity, and by noon, her heart galloped, her shoulder pounded, and her dizzy head dripped with sweat.

She and Mary scurried from the field and into the cool gloom of the pantry cellar to join Addy and Liza. There, Annalisa writhed and shifted to loosen her stays.

"Miss Annie, why d'ye dance like that?" Liza asked.

"I can't breathe in this heat." Annalisa picked up a basket of peas and placed it on the wooden table. Dyspneic, she rested a moment. Her wound dispelled a foul suppurate. Light fevers plagued her sleepless nights—not to mention the heartache of losing Jack. Now, her heart never slowed.

I must have dropsy, like my poor muse, Benjamin.

Mary shucked the last few peas from her basket. "At least 'tis twice as cool down here than in the kitchen."

Addy beamed. "Where I'm from, this heat is nothing." Her brown velvety face held a light sheen.

"Where is that?" Mary asked.

"Barbados. A place you've never seen, Miss Mary." Addy glanced at Liza, who grinned.

The Irish girl had been indentured to them for seven years by her aunt and uncle in New Hampshire. "We ne'er had heat like this in Ireland."

"Do you miss home?"

Liza nodded. "Aye."

"Of course, Miss Mary," Addy sighed. "Barbados was hot all the time. It did rain, but when the sun shone bright, it was like all the earth an' sea come to life."

"That sounds wonderful," Annalisa said. "I wish I could see it." A slight wheeze escaped her lips, followed by a wet cough.

Addy took Liza's basket of herbs, sorted through them, and tossed a few into the mortar.

Annalisa gripped the table. "Addy, I've been...feeling poorly." Lightheadedness overcame. "I've...been quite ill."

Her knees gave out and she collapsed to the floor.

59

GEORGE
TOPSFIELD, JULY 1775

ADDY RUSHED INTO THE barn. "Mr. George. Mr. Quinn, come quick. Miss Annie's fainted."

George threw off his leather apron and sprinted from the barn with Addy and Quinnapin. They burst into the basement pantry. Mary trembled in Liza's arms, both gaping at Annalisa, who lay on the stone floor. Her face, now ashy in complexion, shined with sweat.

Mary sputtered. "She was speaking to us one moment, and the next, she fainted."

George pulled Mary from Liza's pallid grasp. "Go upstairs with Mother and Jane."

Mary nodded and fled the basement.

Liza squatted beside Annalisa. "We were shellin' peas n' she collapsed, sir. She were tellin' us she be poorly, sir."

George and Quinnapin lifted Annalisa onto the kitchen bench. He felt Annalisa's forehead with the back of his hand. The surface was wet and fiery hot. He looked at Quinnapin. "She claimed a ball skimmed her shoulder at

Bunker Hill, but that was weeks ago. She'd refused the doctor's care in Cambridge."

Quinnapin's lips pursed. "I've seen this before. I bet she holds lead inside her."

George pulled the neck handkerchief from around her and tugged the bodice of her gown from her shoulder. A thick pus oozed from an opening in her right shoulder. He gagged and coughed against the stench.

A foreboding nausea rocked his victuals. The flesh pierced by the hole was inflamed. He felt something solid and round. "Well I'll be damned." He looked to Quinnapin. "You're right. The ball is still in there." His face burned.

She lied to me. Again.

George gritted his teeth. He should be angry, and he was, but such a wound could kill his most beloved sister.

What will I do if this claims her? 'Tis all my fault. I was foolish enough to indulge her curiosity, and now she's near-dead. But she's not dead, yet. There's still time. Still a chance.

"Addy, a cloth please. And call on Dr. Brown. She needs a bloodletting."

"No, no bloodletting." Quinnapin stepped between George and Annalisa. "You need herbs. And ointment. And where is the *wampum*? I blessed it to keep her safe."

"You mean this?" George reached into his pocket. "I found it in her room in Cambridge."

"Yes." Quinnapin tied the necklace around Annalisa's neck and whispered something George could not hear.

Addy handed George a clean linen towel. Gently, he wiped away the purulence. As the wound cleared of pus, he spied the ball embedded within semi-healed muscle, just to the right of the joint.

Quinnapin studied the wound. "This must come out, or she will die."

"Can you remove it?" George asked.

Quinnapin pressed around the hole, then placed a finger inside. "I need something small."

"We must get Dr. Brown," George said.

Quinnapin shook his head. "No." He looked to Addy. "Please get the smallest spoon."

Addy rushed upstairs.

"No doctor?" George crossed his arms. "Know you better medicine?"

"I do." Quinnapin's hand met his chest. "My father is our medicine man. You must trust me."

Addy returned with a child-sized pewter spoon. Before she handed it to Quinnapin, she held the rounded end into the fire. George's innards wrenched as he observed his sister. She lay unconscious and with shallow breaths.

He bit his cheek. "Yes. Of course. Please, help her any way you can."

Quinnapin pressed on Annalisa's shoulder and dug the tiny spoon into the opening.

Annalisa groaned.

With only two twists, the ball lifted to the surface. He removed the spoon from the wound, and with it, the bloodied musket round. He stood, holding it between two fingers.

"Lead." He handed the ball to George, then leaned his face near the wound. *"Mishquèsand auntau."* Quinnapin looked to Addy. "The Blood Spirit speaks. I need yarrow."

"Liza, grab the stiff goldenrod and buck brush, too," Addy said.

Liza plucked some plants from the dried garden

hanging above, and brought them to Addy with her mortar and pestle.

"Willow bark," Quinnapin added. He reached for some more dried plants and separated them into two piles. He tied one into a bundle and lit it in the fire. The bundle emitted a sweet, spiraling smoke that he swirled over Annalisa.

George's body tingled as Quinnapin chanted something in his native Wampanoag, some kind of sacred ritual George did not understand.

Should I even witness such magick?

The room stilled, as if frozen in time, and a gust of cool air swept across his face.

A spirit, perhaps? He shuddered with awe and turned from the scene.

His attention on Addy, she crushed and ground the selected items, then made a paste with some kind of bitter smelling herb oil. She stood by Annalisa and wiped the hole clean with a cloth dipped in boiling water. With skilled hands, she packed the wound and lay a piece of linen over it.

"Another cloth, Liza. Soaked in boiling water." Addy turned to George. "This needs to be changed until the skin heals, Mr. George. She will also need to drink Quinnapin's willow tea. It will help the fever."

George crossed his arms. "And she needn't a blood-letting?"

The herb bundle ceased to smoke and Quinnapin leaned over Annalisa, his long, black hair trailing over her face. Satisfied, he looked to George. "She will survive this."

George clasped Quinnapin's hands with gratitude and wonder. "Thank you, my friend." He wrapped Addy in a grateful embrace. "Both of you." He released the older woman and turned to Quinnapin. "Let's get her upstairs."

They lifted Annalisa from the table and carried her up the narrow, creaking stairs. Mary scrambled from the parlor and met them in the foyer.

"What's happened? Mamma's in hysterics."

"She kept a musket round in her shoulder." George shifted under Annalisa's weight. "We're bringing her to bed. Make sure no one disturbs her. Especially not Mother or Jane. Go and fetch some water from Addy and bring it up."

"Yes, sir." Mary shuffled behind him into the kitchen.

Once in his sisters' chamber, they lay Annalisa on the canopy bed.

"Thank you, Quinn. I knew not you were a healer, as well."

"I learned some from my father. When he dies, my sister will become medicine woman." Quinnapin placed a hand on George's shoulder. "Miss Anna is going to survive, but she needs harmony with herself, those around her, and the Creator. Each of us is responsible for our own health, and that includes our thoughts and actions, which have consequences. This trauma is a consequence of Miss Anna's actions. When harmony is set right, she will return to health."

George pondered this. "How right you are, my friend."

Quinnapin nodded. "She's special, George. Her Spirit is strong." He turned and left the room.

George sat beside Annalisa on the bed and wiped the hair from her forehead. "You foolish, proud woman."

His dearest sister; he'd felt a closeness to her from the

moment their mother had birthed her. He'd wished for a brother after Jane was born, but he got Annalisa instead.

Perhaps that is why she's the way she is. I treated her like the brother I'd always wanted...before William.

And even when William idolized his every word or movement, he sought Annalisa's company; her challenges, her devotion, her sisterly affection. When Jane reminded him of their different fathers, Annalisa never made him feel anything less than their full brother.

And now she lies here, nearer to death than...it should be me, not her.

He checked her pulse. It pounded. "Whatever were you thinking?"

The door creaked, and Mary entered with a pitcher of water and a tin cup. She paused before setting them on the bedtable. Her hazel eyes watered, and her bottom lip quivered.

"Is Annie going to die?"

"No." He kissed Mary's forehead then took the water from her and poured it into the cup. "Quinn assured me." George moved behind Annalisa on the bed and propped her up. With one hand, he opened her mouth. "Go ahead."

Mary's hands trembled as she trickled the water into Annalisa's mouth.

Annalisa gargled and sputtered, and her eyes slowly opened.

"Annie." Mary climbed onto the bed and held Annalisa's hand.

After several coughs, Annalisa cleared her throat. "I know not what came over me." She started to turn, then gripped her shoulder and winced.

"Drink." George gave her the cup, and she gulped the remainder of the water.

"What happened?" Her voice croaked.

"Addy and Quinnapin fixed your wound," Mary said. "And Quinnapin is making you some magick tea."

"Willow bark tea." George looked to his youngest sister. "Why don't you retrieve it?"

Mary sighed and left the room.

George slipped from behind Annalisa and guided her against the pillow. He knelt on the floor and held the ball for her to see. "Look what we found."

"Oh, God." She closed her eyes. "I'm so sorry, George."

Heat rose up his face. "You were shot and didn't tell me."

"I'm so sorry, I—"

"Your pride will be the death of you, Annalisa Howlett."

"I knew not what to do. I didn't want you and Jack to think me foolish."

He shoved the ball in front of her. "*This* is foolish."

"George, please—" Tears trickled down her cheeks.

Her distress softened him, and he withdrew his arm, tucking the ball into his fist. "Still think you don't need me?"

Addy and Liza entered with a steaming mug of tea and more herbs. Liza set the cup into Annalisa's trembling hands and looked on her with kind, grey eyes.

"Miss Annie, ye got a fever from that angry musket hole o' yers."

"Please don't be upset, Miss Annie," Addy said in her warm, smooth voice. "You fainted, and we had to get your brother and Quinnapin to see what were wrong. Quinnapin took it out hisself. This physick will make you heal."

George cleared his throat. "I've seen wounds like this kill men. Particularly those that keep their rounds." He hesitated, sensing her disquiet. "But you're lucky, it seems. Quinn said your spirit is strong."

Annalisa sipped the willow tea and grimaced. "I couldn't...I didn't know how to tell you. You were so disappointed—"

"My disappointment had gone. Until now." He paused. "Don't dare hide this sort of thing from me again."

"You're right." Annalisa coughed. "I do need you."

George gripped her hand. "I'll not chastise you like Mother, or William, or Jane. But you must trust me."

"And I can heal that hole, Miss Annie. It is my magick, remember?" Addy winked but frowned. "You are very sick. You must drink Quinnapin's tea."

Annalisa sipped from the cup. "Would that I could learn your magick physick, and Quinn's."

"You'll have to ask Quinn if he is willing to divulge such knowledge." George scratched behind his ear. Even at her worst, her curiosity reigned, though he'd witnessed something entirely inexplicable in the basement.

"I'll teach you what I know, Miss Annie." Addy looked to Liza. "But...you mustn't tell a soul."

"You have my solemn word." Annalisa reached for Addy and squeezed her hand.

"And ye mustn't tell nobody neither, sir." Liza stared at George.

He nodded, curious to also learn. "Mum's the word."

60

JACK
TOPSFIELD, JULY 1775

T HE WHISPERING WILLOW TAVERN held a
crowd of over twenty men. Jack and George sat at
their old table with Samuel and Quinnapin, and listened to
the townsmen. Spoken by nearly every man, murmurs of
General Washington's army in Cambridge commanded
Jack's attention.

"More flip?" Quinnapin's voice snapped him back.

Jack looked up from his mug. "No."

"Zounds." George slapped the table. "I'm only in town
for three days. Drink."

Jack finished his tankard.

Samuel guffawed and smacked his back. "There's a
proper lad."

"Another round," Quinnapin shouted.

The potboy, Master Herrick, attended with a steaming
pitcher of flip.

Jack sipped the bitter, earthy liquid. "Abigail received a
letter from Lord Essex today."

"That plum." George grunted and lifted the tankard to

his lips. "Did she say what he wrote?"

"He means to call."

"She won't accept him." George finished his flip. "She told me she'd wait for me."

"I hope you're right."

"I know Abby. She loves me." George poured himself another from the pitcher. "But you and Annie—you might still try and make things work."

"I tried to speak with her about eloping but I doubt she'll agree to it—"

"Shut it, Perkins." Samuel sat back and picked his teeth with a fork. "What be the worst of it? Ye lose the benefaction to yer da's an' uncle's estates—which, if I recall, ye prefer t' relinquish t' Ollie anyhow—"

"Not prefer." Jack shuddered. "Ollie would make a terrible lord."

Samuel shrugged. "No matter. Ye still be a lawyer, a respectable trade with a proper income. It might not be what yer used to, but 'tis somethin'. Annalisa's already at risk o' bein' shunned by Society because of Bunker Hill rumors. What's one more blunder?"

Jack chuckled dryly. "Yes, I'll ask Annalisa—who now despises me—to elope. She'll further tarnish her reputation, and ruin her family. But none of that shall matter because I'll make us rich as a country lawyer somewhere in New Hampshire."

Samuel dropped his fork. "Be yer own man, Perkins. Stand up to yer da n' uncle fer the woman ye love. I only suggest not all hope be lost. They might not be agreeable options, but they're there."

"I tried to speak with her, but she would not listen."

"Cousin." George squeezed Jack's shoulder. "Annie's as

stubborn as I am. You'll need to catch her when she must listen."

"Must you marry at all?" Quinnapin asked. "George refuses to marry until the war is through."

"I've thought about postponing everything, Quinn, but the clause in my uncle's paperwork includes me '*taking a wife of upstanding character*' before the year is out." Jack shook his head. "Some unreasonable, antiquated request on behalf of his Earldom."

Quinnapin frowned. "I suppose an elopement is only disagreeable in that you'll forfeit everything." He eyed George. "But it would be better than marrying Miss Howlett and having to forever look upon Miss Anna, the woman you love, as your *sister*."

They all groaned.

Jack cringed and ran a hand over his face. "You're right. I'm shamed by how I've behaved through all this. I suppose pleasing others is quite a difficult lesson to unlearn."

"That be settled." Samuel's fist landed upon the table. "Howlett, since ye have a fine lady waitin' fer ye here, when do we join Washington an' his Twenty-third Continental Regiment?"

George smirked. "You mean our Second Massachusetts Bay Provincial?"

"Aye." Samuel grinned with pride. "Ours be the first in th' Continental Army."

"I'll enlist when Mr. J does." Quinnapin winked.

"No, Quinn. If you wish to, you should join. Especially if your primary employer plans to." Jack smirked and nodded toward George.

Quinnapin laughed then shook his head. "I will, but I'm marrying soon."

"Marrying?" George nearly spilled his tankard. "You never told me thus!"

Quinnapin smiled. "Weetamoo. She's already agreed to being a camp-follower."

"Congratulations, Quinn." Jack's mouth curled with regret. "You know I would join if I could."

"You can," George replied.

"If I convince Annalisa to elope, I won't leave her."

"Fair enough." George finished his drink. "But I suspect she'd want you to."

"Then 'tis decided." Samuel slid from the table. "Howlett an' I ride t' Cambridge t' join the new Twenty-third Continental Regiment."

"Aye, just give me until after Mr. Hooper's dinner party in Danvers." George peered into his empty cup. "Annie's been unwell, and I must ensure Elisha has what he needs to run the Black Water in my absence."

"Unwell?" Jack's stomach tightened. "Should I go to her?"

"No, not yet," Quinn replied.

George hesitated. "She ate something...made her sick."

"Then we leave end o' August," Samuel said. "Ye can attend th' dinner party, an' Howlett can make sure Anna has recovered from her spoilt fish puddin'."

George refilled his mug and toasted Samuel. "August it is."

61

ANNALISA
DANVERS, AUGUST 1775

A NNALISA STEPPED INTO THE white-paneled
assembly room at Mr. Hooper's summer home in
Danvers, the air redolent of orange blossom and musk.
Handel's *Water Music* had never before induced such palpa-
tions within Annalisa's breast, but the familiar notes were
now a bittersweet reminder of Lord Suffolk's Ball. The
past month had been harrowing, but she was well enough
—thanks to Quinnapin and Addy—to attend tonight's
dinner party. Though her shoulder and heart still ached,
she hadn't much choice in the matter. Mamma insisted she
attend to redeem herself, much to her reluctance.

"There." Abigail nodded toward a tall window at the
far side of the room. "Lord Essex. We danced at least
thrice at Suffolk's Ball."

The viscount stood erect in a gold embroidered pink
suit in ditto. Annalisa fisted her cold hands until the blood
returned, then glanced behind her. Her parents stood
against the wall with Lord and Lady Perkins, watching.

If only Jack and Jane weren't here tonight, too.

"Think you Lord Essex will approach?" Abigail's gaze lingered on George. "He wrote. He means to call."

"I can't see why he wouldn't. But what of George?"

"I promised I would wait for him." Abigail fumbled with her reticule. "But I must make my papa think otherwise."

"Quite." She understood Abigail's plight, and in many ways sympathized, but in this crowded room, Annalisa focused on her shoulder. She adjusted the muslin neck handkerchief over her scar. "There is still much gossip about how I was wounded."

Addy's poultice and Quinnapin's tea had worked true magick. In a month's time, the skin had mostly filled in, leaving a pink divot that would only continue to heal. She could never repay them for such kindness and wisdom— particularly what Quinnapin offered to her in herbal teachings and the medicine wheel.

Annalisa grazed the *wampum* at her throat. Never again would she remove it. In addition to the Wampanoag talisman, she tucked her musket round from Bunker Hill into her pocket, a reminder for when her courage must remain hidden.

"No one will suspect anything if you act as though nothing happened." Abigail grinned. "Now, let's look a bit more confident, yes? Chin up, shoulders back, and smile."

Annalisa followed Abigail's command and stood tall. Not a very trying task. She was already one of the tallest— if not, the tallest—women in the room.

Jack escorted Jane toward them, and George approached with a glass of wine.

"Each time I leave my inn for an evening with aristocracy, I wonder why." George looked about with a critical eye. "I told myself Suffolk's Ball would be my last."

Jane's face remained neutral. "Not everyone had a disagreeable time on Tory Row."

Jack peered at Annalisa. "I suppose we're all servants to Society now."

She diverted her gaze. Jack's spineless cowardice was the reason they couldn't be together. *Perhaps it is for the better.*

Yet, her heart trembled.

"Miss Perkins."

They all turned at the address, and Abigail curtsied. "My lord."

Lord Essex grinned and his chin divot deepened. "Miss Annalisa, I see you're healing quite well from that—assault —after Suffolk's Ball."

"Yes, my lord." Annalisa glowered. "Though, nothing smarts quite as much as the British victory at Bunker Hill."

"Annalisa," Jane hissed.

George laughed. "It seems not even a rotten Bloody-back can keep my sister from experiencing Society, my lord."

Knowing George's disdain for gentry, Annalisa bit her cheek to keep from giggling.

Lord Essex adjusted his coat. "Miss Perkins, would you honor me with the first two dances?"

"Of course, my lord." Abigail cast a side-long glance at George, and proceeded to the set with Lord Essex. Of course, Jane and Jack followed.

Alone with George, Annalisa regarded him. "Here we are, again."

"Soldiers in a sea of pomp." He lifted his glass to hers and they saluted. "I can't imagine you'd like to dance."

"No," Annalisa snickered. "I forgo the minuet from now until I die."

He guffawed. "I suppose it would be hard for you to dance, now that you've fought in battle."

"How do you mean?"

"You've a taste for war, Little One. I suspect it will be difficult to ignore. With Washington's recruitment and his army surrounding Boston, we've much to consider."

"We?" Annalisa set her hand on her waist. "You'll hardly allow me to enlist, if that is what you mean."

"No." George pursed his lips. "But *I* might."

"And who will run the Black Water if you're in the army?"

"Elisha. And perhaps William, if I coax him enough."

"A fair trade, I suppose." She frowned, wishing he'd asked her to join him.

When the first two dances ended, Jack approached and held out his hand. "Miss Annalisa, would you do me the honor?"

"I'd rather burn in embers."

"Annie," George rumbled.

She turned from them, but Jack held her wrist. "Please. We must talk. I've written you a dozen times—"

"And the letters will continue to burn as well. Please unhand me."

"Not until you listen to my proposition."

"Annie, go," George said. "Hear what he has to say."

She huffed and reluctantly followed Jack to a table of desserts tucked against the wainscoting.

"Rum cake?" He gestured to the delectable treat.

She folded her arms. "You can't be serious."

"Play along, follow me." Jack paused. "Rum cake?"

She rolled her eyes. "Yes, please."

He handed her a plate with a piece of golden sponge, then slipped out a door beside the dessert table. Annalisa looked around, saw no one watching, and followed.

Jack stood in the vacant hall. "This way."

He led her down the corridor and into an empty room, and latched the door. Three great windows lined the adjacent wall. Beyond them, the sky was dark. Two candles flashed light upon several bookcases.

Mr. Hooper's library.

Annalisa set down her plate atop a shiny, wooden desk. "What is it you want?"

Jack turned with urgency. "Elope with me."

Her shock subsided, then laughter overtook. "I beg your pardon?"

"You never let me speak, Annalisa." He frowned. "While an elopement would be disagreeable, 'tis better than any alternative. I know I can endure such disgrace, but it was never my right to assume the same of you."

She scoffed and paced the room. "You come here with your betrothed, then ask me to elope when you had said you could not further sully my name with an elopement. Why did you not say so sooner? My heart cannot handle these charades." She faced him. "Do you love me, Jack? Enough that you will forsake your inheritances and ruin both our families' reputations?"

He advanced with a determined countenance and took up her hands. "I do."

Her heart swelled, but her mind halted all feeling. "I

want to believe you." She pulled from him. "I only wish you asked me sooner, after Bunker Hill."

"I was a fool, trying to do the right thing. But so long as you're willing to partake in the madness that might end up being our lives, I'm ready to take the reins. I swear—I promise you, Annalisa—I will never forsake you. I will do whatever you ask of me, no matter." He sighed. "That includes me walking out of this room, if you never again wish to speak to me."

She softened from the love and devotion in his eyes. "And where would we go—if I agree, of course. In all your madness, have you considered a place?"

He grinned crookedly. "North, to Portsmouth. There's a lovely town near there, right by the sea, called New Castle. Your brother can run his inn, I can set up a law office." He gazed into her eyes. "It would be modest, but none of that matters, so long as I have you. And you're happy."

New Castle. She knew the place, remembering the Portsmouth powder alarm. The candor in his eyes told her she could trust him. Truly, she'd never doubted his love, and now he meant to secure their fate.

If only I hadn't been so stubborn.

Annalisa bit her lip to hide her cracking smile. "What else do you see in this future?"

"A house facing the ocean. And children. Plenty of them."

"How many will we have?"

"Four boys and five girls."

"Nine children?" She laughed. "You plan on keeping me quite busy."

"Only if 'tis the life you want." Jack took her hands and

kissed them. "Because none of this means anything if 'tis not what you want."

Her sisters would be ruined and her parents would disown her, but the real segregation had only just begun; war with Britain threatened separation between Mother Country and the colonies. Jack would be distracted, perhaps he would enlist.

Will he continue to indulge my curiosity, and my political voice after marriage? And what of my dear muse, Benjamin Cavendish?

Now that she'd been mostly healed, she too, could try to enlist in Washington's army.

Annalisa plunged her hand into her pocket to feel the Bunker Hill musket. Her shoulder twinged, and the *wampum* warmed at her neck. She'd risen to meet her fate as a militiaman, and in many ways, succeeded. This was her chance at another kind of happiness.

There has never been a man more understanding, more deserving of me than Jack Perkins.

"I'll oblige."

Jack's smile dimpled. "Is that a hearty consent to my daft plan?"

Annalisa nodded, unable to contain her smile.

He clutched her hands. "You agree to marry me?"

"Yes, I do."

He lifted her and spun around, and his handsome face glowed with delight. "Praise God!" When he set her down, Jack rested his forehead to hers. "May I?"

"You'd better."

Their lips touched, tenderly at first, then bonded tighter, tasting of earthy pipe tobacco. Jack wrapped his arms about her, his scent of amber surrounding her. His famished kisses devoured her as though he'd been starved for too long. Her appetite equaling his, she tugged his coat from his shoulders.

Jack flung it to the floor and backed her into the bookcase. His mouth trailed down her neck. She reached up, tugged his hair from its tie, and ran her fingers through his long, glossy locks.

"Annalisa, this past month has been agony."

"'Tis been agony for me, too."

"Never again shall I leave you." His lips swept her collarbone, and he pulled away her neck handkerchief. He slipped the sleeve of her gown from her shoulder and stopped. His fingers grazed the healing hole. "Is this from Bunker Hill?"

"It is." Annalisa licked her swollen lips. "But I am mostly recovered."

"My God, this is why you fell ill." He cupped her face. "Annalisa, I had no idea the injury was so serious."

"I hid it from everyone. Including George. I was a fool to keep it from him." She searched for his gaze. "And you."

"This could have claimed you."

"Let us not dwell on it. Thanks to Quinn and Addy, I am well."

Jack kissed her. "I could marry no other." His tongue entered her mouth with a sultry promise of pleasure. He gathered her skirts in one hand, and the memory of that night in the carriage house roused her.

"You remember well how to please me."

"How could I forget?"

His soft lips showered her with velvet kisses, and she shivered, the culmination of his efforts mere moments away when the door to the library opened with a crash.

62

ANNALISA
DANVERS, AUGUST 1775

"*Z*OUNDS! I SHOULD HAVE knocked."

Annalisa and Jack thrust apart.

"My God, George." Jack panted and righted his breeches.

Annalisa fixed her petticoats and yanked up her stockings. Her brother's deep chortle rumbled as he latched the door.

"I have to say, of all the positions I expected to find you in, this was hardly it." George smirked. "Happy to see you've reconciled."

Annalisa's face warmed. "Please, forget what you saw."

Jack tied back his hair. "Why have you come for us?"

"You're missed." George approached the desk and picked up the plate of cake. "Abigail and I contrived some excuse for why you've been missing, but Princess Jane has started to question." He dug the fork prongs into the soft sponge and shoveled it into his mouth.

Annalisa positioned her neck handkerchief over her

wound and sniffed Jack's perfume on her. "It matters not. We're going to elope."

"You stubborn minx, you've finally listened." George laughed. "Pray tell, when?"

Jack kissed her hand. "Tonight. Let's leave at once."

"Tonight?" Annalisa gasped. "I'm not ready to leave now."

Jack's brows creased. "It must be before the harvest, my love."

"I can hardly abandon my family so soon. And my shoulder still heals. We've time, yet."

"You must make haste, Annie." George finished the cake and tossed the plate and fork upon the desk with a rattle.

"September," Jack said. "We can wait no longer."

৩২৯৪

TWO DAYS LATER, ANNALISA SAT IN THE DINING ROOM with her family, breakfasting. The morning sun streamed into the room, reflecting off Annalisa's plate. The sulfur of boiled eggs reminded her of the gunpowder from Bunker Hill, turning her stomach sour. Nonetheless, her heart filled with Jack.

"Janey, you were simply elegant at Mr. Hooper's dinner. I've thought of nothing else." Mamma peeled an egg. "And I heard from Lady Perkins that Lord Essex may make an offer to Abigail." Mamma looked to Mary. "Young miss, you'll do well to admire Janey and Miss Abigail. Most advantageous marriages."

Annalisa chewed her lip and studied George. He stared into a mugful of cider.

"If Abigail marries Lord Essex, Janey, you will have a most esteemed brother-in-law." Mamma scraped soft, yellow butter across her toast. "I can hardly imagine it. What weddings there will be come autumn. Janey and Jack —Lord Brunswick's heir—and Abigail and Lord Essex."

Jane fixed her gaze on a piece of dry toast. Her face looked paler than usual, with a hint of green.

"Lord Essex hasn't proposed yet, Mamma." Annalisa searched for George's gaze. "Please do not assume he will."

"Nonsense. Lady Perkins believes he will, and my nerves tell me he will—and my nerves are always right, are they not, Mr. Howlett?"

Papa peered up from his newspaper. "Quite, madam."

"Aye, and she would do well to marry such a man." George set down his cider. "With Washington recruiting for his army, who can say what other dandy prats may be left to marry?"

"Fie, George," Mamma hissed. "What do I care for that brutish traitor? Vulgar talk for breakfast."

"Mother, Lord Essex is a Whig, a supporter of the rebellion," William added. "As is Lord Perkins."

"Must you all rebuke me?" Mamma huffed. "Jack Perkins will inherit two estates. Lord Essex is a viscount, and a gentleman. Don't you agree, Mr. Howlett?"

Papa set down his newspaper. "Lord Perkins is a reasonable man. I see no reason for him to refuse the viscount, no matter his politics."

Papa's indifference and Mamma's ambitions agitated Annalisa's stomach. She pushed away her plate of food.

Poor Abigail. We are all pawns in Society's grand chess game.

Mamma regarded Jane. "We've much to prepare for tonight, Janey my dear."

"What is happening tonight?" Mary asked.

"Jack Perkins is spending the night with Janey in a bundle bag."

"What?" Annalisa glared at Jane. "Did you orchestrate this?"

George choked on his drink. "That old tradition?"

"A bundle bag." William snickered.

"Hush, the lot of you. I think 'tis a fine tradition," Mamma said. "I would have bundled with your Papa had I been a maiden before our wedding—"

"All you that in your beds do lie, turn to your wives and occupy. And when that you have done your best, turn arse to arse, and take your rest." George howled.

Annalisa glowered. "'Tis not funny."

Mamma's icy glare froze the room. "George Bixby Howlett, enough of your vulgarities."

"Come, Annie." George stood, the chair squealing behind him. "Let's find the canvas sack."

Annalisa followed him from the dining room and outside, but rather than pursue him into the barn, she ran through the fields to the ancient oak.

Beneath the great canopy of leaves and heavy boughs, she paced then sat, then paced some more until she decided to climb into the tree. By the time she reached her perch where the trunk widened and the limbs flattened, George discovered her.

"I knew you'd be here. I think this will do." He held up the canvas sack he found in the barn and pulled on the stitching. "We'll make sure Jane can't rip it open."

"This is foul news. What will I do if Jane strums him? And Lord Essex wishes to wed Abigail—George, we should all leave this place. Life as a soldier would be far simpler. I can endure being a man. I can, I swear it to you. Please let me enlist with you and Jack, and we can bring Quinn and his new wife, and Abigail—"

"Zounds. Enough." George threw the sack up at her and she caught it. "After that wound, never again will I see you dressed in men's clothing. Ben Cavendish is dead." He pointed his finger. "Jack loves you. If you can't accept that by now, perhaps you should abandon your plans and let him be noozed to Jane."

"Fie." She bunched up the bag and flung it back down at him. "Shut your potato trap and give your tongue a holiday. Benjamin Cavendish is not dead." Her elbows dug into her thighs. It had been two months since she'd donned and abandoned his breeches. And she'd have to keep her desire to enlist at bay if she eloped with Jack.

"Don't you tell me to shut it, young miss." George narrowed his eyes. "You think I want any of this to happen?"

"I know."

"I'm hardly concerned about that viscount plum. I trust Abby will refuse him." He tossed the sack to the ground and climbed into the tree, where he sat beside her. "And 'tis not Jack you have to worry about." George wrapped his arm about her. "Jane looks poorly this morning. I wouldn't be certain she'd try to break him free. And if she did—it takes two people to strum, Annie."

She rested her head on his shoulder. "I need only get through tonight."

"Aye." George kissed her forehead. "We'll get through it, like we always do. I wouldn't have our sleepless nights in the pantry to look forward to if it wasn't for old Cav and his tomfoolery at Bunker Hill."

She sighed, relieved she'd have his company through another sleepless night—an additional consequence from Bunker Hill to haunt her.

❧ 63 ❧

JACK
TOPSFIELD, AUGUST 1775

J ACK DIDN'T DARE BREATHE as he knocked on the Howlett door. *How am I to endure a night bundled beside Jane? I'll have no problem thwarting her, but what of my Annalisa?*

The door opened and Liza greeted him, her round face without expression. "Mr. Perkins, do come in."

The purple twilight cast wide shadows across the pine floors before him. He stepped over the threshold and handed Liza his hat.

"Thank you kindly, Miss."

George appeared from the hall. "Perkins, you made it."

Jack groaned. "Aye, and not a moment too early."

When Liza had gone, George leaned in close. "You and Annie should have left town."

"It was only this morning my mother told me about tonight—I had no idea Jane would request to bundle." He ran a hand over his face. "There was no time to gather my things, let alone ride here to collect Annalisa." He hesitated. "We should have left after Mr. Hooper's dinner."

"Hindsight gives foresight," George grumbled. "Come —we're assembled in the drawing room."

Jack followed his cousin from the foyer, and Annalisa's rich alto reciting poetry, floated down the hall.

Upon seeing him, she stopped. "Mr. Perkins."

Mrs. Howlett smiled. "So good of you to join us tonight." She looked to Annalisa. "Is the bundle bag prepared?"

"Yes, marm." Annalisa closed her book. "'Tis in my bedchamber."

Mrs. Howlett nodded. "Good. Mr. Perkins, you are welcome to use the girls' room to ready yourself. When you're in the bag, do ring, and I will stitch you in."

"Indeed." Jack followed Jane from the drawing room and up the stairs. He'd never seen the bedchamber Annalisa shared with her sisters.

Jane opened the door. The air smelled of fresh, delicate lilac, and honeyed lavender. Candles flickered in their sconces upon white walls with blue painted molding. At the far end of the room stood a large canopy bed with blue toile curtains.

"I'll step out and let you freshen up," Jane said.

"Thank you, Miss Howlett."

"Call me Jane." She lingered then kissed his cheek. "We are to be husband and wife."

Jack remained still until she closed the door, then sat on the bed. He held his head in his hands.

"Lord, forgive me."

A whiff of lilac caught his attention. He placed his nose to the pillow beside him.

Annalisa.

Holding the pillow, he inhaled her scent again. Jack

rose, removed his coat, and placed it over a chair by the escritoire. A blank piece of paper beckoned. Quickly, he scribbled a note to Annalisa and tucked the folded page into her pillow. Surely, she would take it with her tonight.

"Mr. Perkins?" Annalisa's muffled voice sounded from the hall.

He opened the door. They were alone but wouldn't be for long. As soon as the door latched behind her, he pulled her close and buried his face in her hair.

"I am so sorry. I had no idea until this afternoon. If only I could have stolen us away tonight…"

She pressed her face to his chest. "What terrible conspirators we are."

"I can steal us away tonight."

Her head jerked. "Tonight?"

"Yes. After Jane falls asleep, I'll cut myself free of the sack and escape with you. You only have to meet me at the oak—"

"'Tis too risky. If we're caught, the repercussions would be far worse."

Jack lifted her chin. "No one will keep me from you. I promise."

"I believe you." Annalisa held his gaze for a moment, then returned her attention to the door. "Jane and Mamma are coming."

He slipped off his shoes, stockings, and waistcoat, and snuck inside the canvas sack atop the bed. It smelled of hay. He must have wrinkled his nose, because Annalisa's face blushed.

"I tried to air it out." She leaned down to kiss him, but the door opened. Her gaze darted to the seams. "I think this needs a better stitch."

Jane, already in her bedclothes, glided toward them. She handed Annalisa a needle and thread.

"Oh, dear." Jane pulled at the sides. "Best you tighten it. We wouldn't want to tempt our charming gentleman, would we?"

Annalisa lowered her gaze. "Mamma is coming. She will tighten it."

"You should start on it." Jane returned to the looking glass and combed her long, dark hair. Her complexion was only a shade or two lighter than her linen shift. She looked like an apparition.

Annalisa took the needle and stitched him into the sack.

Jack winced. "Ouch."

"I'm so sorry."

"'Twas a jest." He chuckled.

"You mischievous cur."

"Annie." Jane spun around and drifted to the bed to observe Annalisa's fingers as the needle poked in and out of the canvas. "You used a backstitch, I hope."

"Of course. But Mamma will reinforce it." Annalisa looped and tied the thread, then leaned in and ripped the ends with her teeth. She lingered just long enough to flood him with lilac. "I'll retrieve Mamma." She slid from the bed, grabbed her pillow, and opened the door. "I bid you both good-night."

After Mrs. Howlett had strengthened Annalisa's needlework, Jane crawled beneath the coverlet and closed the bedcurtains. In the darkness, Jack remained silent and motionless.

"Jack."

"Yes?"

Jane snuggled closer to him.

Lavender. This is the wrong scent, the wrong girl beside me.

"Shall I loosen the stitching? Annalisa's backstitch is weak, and Mamma's is only moderately better."

"I should think not, Miss Howlett. I have no intention of getting you in the family way."

"We're to marry. Surely it wouldn't matter if you strummed me now, or later."

"Then you mean to honor me with the dignity deserving of a bride."

Jane lowered her face beside his, her lips grazing his ear. "It must be important for you to wed a virgin. I couldn't possibly take that from you."

He turned his head from her. "Your claims of virtue make no difference in how I feel, Miss Howlett. We both know you are no virgin."

"And these are the loving words of my betrothed." She crawled on top of him and crossed her arms. "You don't mean to refuse me because of my sister, do you?"

"It would make little difference, wouldn't it?"

"Then you don't deny it."

"Deny what?" Jack asked.

"That you still prefer Annalisa."

"I love Annalisa. And it seems you prefer Oliver."

"Preferred," Jane huffed. "I'm devoted to you, and you alone."

"Yet you are not devoted to your sister—"

"I could not help my attraction to Oliver. And my sister made claims I felt to be incongruous with his nature." Her face bore the tale of betrayal. "Perhaps I should not have been so quick to dismiss her story."

"Then you must apologize to Annalisa." Jack shifted

beneath her weight. "But I'll neither confirm nor deny your accusations. I'm unaccustomed to curtain lectures."

"I'm in no position to reprimand you," Jane said. "I only wish for you to return my love with greater conviction. Is that too much to ask?"

Guilt bubbled up, drowning him. "You're right, Miss Howlett, you are deserving of love. But it shan't be me who gives it to you."

"I've told you once before, I'd support you in all of your Patriot endeavors." Jane's gaze turned from considerate longing to hunger. "It is hard for me to be here with you like this. A woman also has desires. And you did fancy me before."

Jack frowned. "I'm sure you do, but let us leave it to the imagination."

She pouted. "If it pleases you."

"It does. Good-night."

Suddenly, her lips met his. His mouth tightened and he craned his neck.

"Miss Howlett, stop."

Jane doffed her shift, revealing voluptuously round, white breasts and a narrow waist. She leaned down and pressed herself against him. Jack closed his eyes and shuffled onto his left side.

"It can't be all bad, can it?" Jane slipped onto her side, so they were again face-to-face. She glided one hand down the front of the bundle bag and caressed the outside of the sack. "Since the night of the corn husking when first you kissed me, I've wondered what you might be like in your lifted state." She massaged him. "Surely, you've imagined the same of me. You must like what you see. I can free your hands to explore."

Jack tucked his chin to his chest. At this rate, Jane would have him out of the bag in minutes—or perhaps just his phallus.

Is she bold enough to cut a hole in the canvas to expose me? With enough coaxing, my pego is sure to deliver what she wishes. Can I force myself to remain flaccid?

Of course, I can.

His dearest Annalisa was just down the hall. Sickened, he rolled away from Jane.

She pulled at the seams on the bag. "You're rather cheeky this evening, Mr. Perkins. I promise you'll enjoy me."

"Miss Howlett, enough. I'm in no mood for this sort of cajoling. Cannot you be content sleeping by my side? Rest your head upon my chest if you must, but that is all."

Jane sat back on her heels and for a moment, he thought she would burst to tears. "Why must you refuse me? Am I so repulsive to you?"

"No." Jack paused, a stream of remorse surfacing. "You're a lovely woman. But I am in love with your sister."

"I'm flattered by your honesty, and I admire your scruples." She inched toward him. "But I will change your mind. And please you tonight, I shall."

64

GEORGE
TOPSFIELD, AUGUST 1775

G EORGE SAT WITH ANNALISA by the dying fire of the basement pantry. Though first light was near, silver rays from the full moon spilled through the lone window. Neither he, nor she, had been able to sleep—a loathsome consequence they shared since Bunker Hill. But tonight, he felt particularly rueful; he meant to leave town with Samuel, and Jack was upstairs with Jane.

I should have told Annalisa sooner than now.

She flipped through her 'physick diary'. She'd written down each herb, root, and plant Addy and Quinnapin used in their poultices and teas, detailed every receipt and nature of its function, and memorized Quinnapin's medicine wheel. She'd done this meticulously for weeks.

Perhaps she wishes to be a healer if she cannot be a solider.

George handed her a pamphlet.

Annalisa looked up. "What's this?"

"Washington still recruits."

"I know." She glowered. "I wish I could join."

"Think not of it." He reached for her trembling hand.

"Soon you and Jack will be gone from here and you'll begin life anew."

Annalisa nodded, but said nothing.

The weight of his journey to Cambridge pressed on him. "My inheritance afforded me quite a bit. And the Black Water Inn has been rather prosperous."

"It has. Why do you speak of it?"

"I want you and Jack to run the tavern for me. At least until he's well-established."

She set aside her notes. "You mean it?"

"Aye. I want you to have the best life you can." He forced away a chill. "Jack's family is wealthy, but once he leaves with you, he won't be. 'Twill take time for him to start a new law practice. 'Tis all I can do to offer you solace..."

She tilted her head. "What for?"

"I'm leaving." George shifted in his seat. "At dawn. For Cambridge." A beat of silence passed between them. "I've made arrangements with Samuel to enlist."

"I always suspected you would." Her eyes grew wide. "What about Abigail? What if Lord Essex proposes?"

"She'll refuse. She promised she'd wait for me."

Annalisa frowned. "What will I do without you?"

He howled. "This coming from the doxie who told me she no longer needs me."

She pushed his shoulder. "You know I was foolish for speaking thus."

"'Tis what I must do. I've never believed in anything so strongly, Little One." He held her hands. "I cannot promise I'll return soon, but I daresay I have the most honed eye of any of man in town." He chuckled. "Save for you."

Mischief gleamed in her eyes. "Then take me with you. I know Jack will go, too."

"I've no doubt you'd fight fearlessly as Benjamin Cavendish—but we both know what would happen if you're discovered."

"I was a convincing man at Bunker Hill—"

"Save for your morbid flux. I saw your breeches. Thank God they were also stained with Nathaniel's blood."

She colored. "I'll fashion something to prevent that from happening again. No one will discover me in Washington's army. I swear it. George, after I elope, Jack and I will have nothing. My name is already shrouded in rumors. What is one more scrap of gossip?"

"You are marrying Jack. You should resign to that fate —and that scrap of gossip. Not one of war and battles. Leave that to me."

"But we are at war. The colony is in shambles—like us." She rolled the musket round between her fingers. "I've always wished to marry Jack. I dreamt it when first we met. But I always imagined our reverend would marry us. I never thought to be with him we'd have to elope, that I'd have to ruin our family—and Mary's chances of marrying well."

"Life is rarely what we think it should be."

"So I'm learning." She gazed into the fire for several moments. "If I join the army with you, I'll be strong and fearless. You and Jack needn't protect me."

"No. You must stay here and heal. That wound won't get any better without Quinn and Addy's physick."

"I'm well enough." She touched her shoulder and rotated her arm. "And I have my physick diary."

He tightened his jaw. "Please accept my gift. Jack will

be a fine, devoted husband, but I must be convinced you'll be well. If you love me, take it."

Annalisa clasped her hands. "I do love you. More than anyone else in this world." She lifted her gaze and held his stare. "I promise. I'll accept."

"Good." George stood, lifting her alongside him. He held her tight. "You must write once you've made it to Portsmouth. Elisha will know to expect you." He kissed her forehead. "Be a decent mort while I'm gone. But not too good. Jack's too handsome to keep you from his bed much longer, and I want to return to plenty of nieces and nephews."

Annalisa tittered into his chest. "I promise."

Beyond the window, first light shone. Annalisa followed him to the pantry door. "Write as soon as you can."

"I will." With a final kiss to her cheek, he took off to the barn.

His fowling piece and cartridge box hung from nails. Bixby in particular, held an ethereal glow in the deep, blue light. All else remained tranquil. He lifted the weapon and cartridge box, slung them over his shoulder, and gathered his haversack.

With his hat cocked right and his spatterdashes buttoned, he mounted Frederick and rode from his family's secluded farm. Samuel was waiting for him at the Willow, but he had one final destination before town.

65

ANNALISA
TOPSFIELD, AUGUST 1775

M AMMA THREW DOWN HER napkin. "George has gone and done what?"

Annalisa set her fork beside her plate—she couldn't eat anything, anyway—and rubbed her temples. Her head and heart ached. "He's left to enlist with the army."

"What about his inn? And your papa? And the farm? Has he no sense of propriety? No consideration for this family? Poor Elisha must burden himself at that tavern, and William and Henry must trouble themselves with his responsibilities. That willful, ungrateful boy. He is no son of mine!"

Annalisa peered at Mary beside her, then across the table at Jack, who sat next to Jane. Her sister searched for his gaze, but he focused on a half-eaten boiled egg.

"Papa has Zeke, Dane, and Quinn to help on the farm. He should hardly miss George." Annalisa touched her mother's arm. "George was a minuteman, and as a man of four and twenty, you cannot blame him for such an act."

Mamma jerked her arm. "An act of treachery. He

knows well enough your papa is loyal to King George, yet he joins with those rebels. And what of your scruples, Annalisa Howlett? You had the chance to stop him, and you let him go."

"Me? Why should I? He's a man grown." She turned to her sisters, both silent around the table. Neither of them met her anxious stare.

Mamma bared her teeth. "You're as guilty as he."

"Mamma." Mary's small voice finally broke the tension. "It is his duty."

"Hush, Mary." Jane met Mamma's glare. "Please, go rest this morning, Mamma. Your nerves have overcome you."

"But there's the flax—"

"Mary and I will finish the spinning." Jane smiled sweetly.

Jack's eyes filled with sincerity. "Mrs. Howlett, your feelings are shared by many at this table, but George's principles are unwavering, and to be respected."

Mamma's mouth pressed into a firm, thin line. "Mr. Perkins, I'm quite vexed this morning. Do excuse my absence. Surely you can understand my heart is in disarray."

"Get some rest, ma'am," he said, unaffected. "'Tis well-deserved."

With a huff, Mamma quit the dining room, her rose perfume gusting as she passed through the door. Annalisa respired and looked to Jane, who nibbled a piece of toast.

"Thank you for reassuring Mamma."

Jane's nose wrinkled. "'Tis the least I can offer after you allowed George to leave. His actions taint the rest of us as treasonous rebels. How little you care for our family's reputation."

Jack cleared his throat. "Miss Howlett, that is hardly the case—"

"I'll not take these abuses." Her fury boiling, Annalisa stood. "Excuse me."

She rushed from the dining room and barged through the front door, slamming it behind her. The barn called to her, and a need to fire Bixby. When she went to take the fowler from its holding, it was gone.

Of course, it was gone. Bixby was gone because George was gone. Annalisa slumped into the sweet-smelling hay. If only he were here, he could have saved her from Jane's and Mamma's abuses with his witty vulgarities. Now, she was alone.

"All will be well, Annie. Please don't cry."

She lifted her head. Her thirteen-year-old brother, Henry, stood in the doorway. He entered the barn and sat beside her in the hay. She hadn't heard Papa return with her brothers.

"We all miss George." Henry wiped her tears. "It was a shock to find him gone this morning."

"Is Papa angry?"

"He was. But I think he's more saddened—he feels like this war might tear our family apart."

"Might? It already has." She picked hay from her skirts. "I know not how to be without him, Henry. George was always by my side—even when he was gone to Portsmouth, I always knew he'd return home."

"I know." He held her hand. "But now you have Will and me."

"And me."

Annalisa and Henry turned.

Jack stood in the barn doorway. "May I speak privately with Miss Annalisa?"

"Of course." Henry rose and dusted off his breeches. "I'll be with Will and Mary, placating Mother, no doubt." He smiled warmly and quit the barn.

When he'd been gone at least five minutes, Jack offered his arm. "Care to join me in a turn about the farm?"

She lifted from the hay and brushed clean her skirts. "And if Jane sees?"

"It shan't matter much longer. Let's to the oak." With a crooked grin, he added, "Perhaps we can climb out of view to talk."

Annalisa took his arm, wondering what had passed between him and Jane last night. They left the musty barn and stepped into the warm August day.

"I'm mortified by Mamma's display at breakfast."

"Don't be. I understand her perfectly well. Though I wonder how she can be so accepting of my family, knowing we're Patriot—save for Ollie." He shook his head. "In every way, my brother would be a better match for Jane."

"Everyone is blinded by your inheritance. 'Tis every middlin' girl's dream to marry advantageously."

"And do you, too, share this dream?"

"I'm eloping with you. Does it seem like I care about becoming the next Lady Perkins or Lady Brunswick?"

He grinned and they continued toward the sprawling, ancient tree.

When they reached the refuge of their old oak, he faced her and took up her hands. "We must leave immediately."

Her chest pinched. Now she, too, would abandon her family, so soon after George.

Jack chose a branch facing the woods, away from her farmhouse. He stepped onto the bough and held out a hand. Annalisa grabbed it and lifted beside him. They continued up another two limbs until they reached the trunk's wide cove between boughs. Jack settled into the tree and pulled her to him. They sat, legs entwined, while he traced his thumb across her knuckles.

"How quickly could you be ready?"

"With my family grieving George? Tonight, I suppose."

"His absence does make this harder." Jack's mouth curled. "And my father's written. He returns from Philadelphia in a fortnight."

"Should we wait until he's home and settled, and my family is recovered from George?"

"There will never be an easy time." He kissed her hand. "If you can be ready tonight, I will come for you after midnight."

"Will we make it to Portsmouth straightaway?"

"There's a new tavern in Newburyport. We can stay there the night before finishing our journey."

Annalisa bit her lip, forcing back tears. "Part of me doesn't want to do this, Jack—leave my family, and ruin my sisters." She wiped her eyes. "But then I think of the alternative—you marrying Jane—and a part of me dies within."

He brushed her cheek, his thumb lingering over the scar beneath her right eye. "I know." Cradling her in his arms, he stroked her hair. "I don't want this, either. But what choice have we? If this is the only way, so be it."

Annalisa rested her head against his chest. The late

summer cicadas buzzed against the thrumming of Jack's heart. "What passed between you and Jane last night?"

He rubbed his face. "She tried to force herself on me."

"No." Annalisa pulled away.

He reached for her. "I swear on my honor as a gentleman, nothing became of it."

She trembled at his soft touch, and his eyes full of gentle candor. "I believe you. How could I elope with you if I did not?"

Jack gave a sad smile. "It pains me to think you might believe me capable of strumming Jane."

"'Tis not you I distrust. Jane's charmed nearly every man in town—including your brother—without remorse."

"I am tempted by no one except you, dear heart." His gaze drifted toward her bosom. "Pray tell, do you still wear the busk? Or did that, too, turn to ash when you burned my letters?"

Carved from the very tree in which they sat, she lifted the wooden piece from her stays. "I daresay, I kept my feelings for you secret, far better than you."

He kissed her. "I can't wait to call you my wife."

"Then let's not wait." Annalisa pulled him closer, the heat of his body radiating. "My family may grieve me along with George in one, swift blow. Let's leave now. I need nothing, save you."

"Leave? Pray, tell, where do you intend to go?"

The familiar voice echoed into the branches of the oak, and Annalisa and Jack froze in place.

✤ 66 ✤

JACK
TOPSFIELD, AUGUST 1775

JACK PEERED DOWN. MARY Howlett stared up at them, her head cocked with curiosity.

"Annie, why are you up there with Jack?"

"Mary, hush." Annalisa pulled from him. "Speak not another word." She scrambled down the branches and Jack followed, landing beside them with a thud.

Jack crossed his arms. "Please, Miss Mary, tell us what you heard."

"Only that you were leaving." Her face scrunched with melancholy. "Do you intend to bring George home?"

"No, Miss Mary. We cannot bring George home. I was telling your sister I mean to travel to New H—"

"Newburyport," Annalisa said. "He wishes to find new shoe buckles for his wedding. I offered to help."

Mary squinted dubiously. "I saw you up there, too, Annie. I'm no fool."

The thirteen-year-old was more astute than he'd thought.

I wonder what else she's observed these past several years.

Annalisa cupped her sister's shoulders. "I'll be honest with you." She glanced at him. "Jack and I are in love, and we mean to elope. But you mustn't tell anyone, do you understand?"

"I always knew you loved each other." Mary looked at the house. "But I think Jane suspects. She was out here as well."

Jack tensed. "By this tree?"

"No. She was looking for you, and Henry said you were walking around the farm. I said I'd find you. I assumed you'd be by the oak."

"Why?" Annalisa asked.

Mary snickered. "If I wished to steal away with the man I loved, this is where I'd go."

Annalisa gasped. "Mary Howlett."

"Clever girl." Jack laughed. "I apologize for discrediting you, Miss Mary."

The girl's grin faded into a frown. "But with George gone, I'm going to lose you, too, Annie?"

"It won't be forever." She hugged her sister. "But Jack cannot marry Jane."

Mary sniffled. "Please, don't leave today. I can hardly stand it that George left, and Mamma's in disarray."

Annalisa wiped her sister's tears, and Jack softened. "I suppose we could delay."

❦

LATE-SEPTEMBER, 1775

Three weeks had passed since Mary Howlett discovered them in the oak, but the stretch had given Jack ample time to plan. He sat in his room, meticulously organizing each document he'd need for their journey to Portsmouth. They were leaving tonight.

"Jack, darling, where are you?" Mother called.

He hid the papers and fled his bedchamber, down the steps, and into the parlor. Father had returned from Philadelphia, and sat in his chair. Jack hadn't heard the horses, or even the front door open. A cloud of tobacco smoke hovered about Father's head as though he'd never left.

Jack sat in the chair across from him. "My apologies, sir." He eyed Abigail and Susan between Ollie and Andrew on the sofa.

"'Tis no matter." Father pulled at his pipe. "Jack, you look well. I spoke much of you in Congress. As did Adams."

Jack's thoughts shifted to George and Samuel, now with Washington's Continental Army; his only solace that he would soon be in New Hampshire with Annalisa.

"Adams was quite pleased to hear of your inheriting Brunswick's estate. As was Jefferson."

Oliver crossed one leg. "A waste."

Father peered up for only a moment. "Mr. Jefferson is eager to make your acquaintance."

Abigail rolled her eyes. "I think Jack would make a lovely captain in General Washington's army."

"The army is no place for a gentleman such as your brother." Father set down his pipe. "And he knows this full well. Jack has learned his lesson from Bunker Hill."

"But General Washington—is he not a gentleman?" Abigail asked.

"General Washington is a commander, my dear. 'Tis entirely different than firing in the front lines as a private," Father replied. "But yes, he boasts some of the best manners of any man I've known."

"Yet he is a general." Abigail smoothed her skirts. "Could not you buy Jack a commission as an officer?"

"Abby." Jack grimaced at the entitlement of such a prospect.

Father scowled. "Young lady, you're awfully persistent this evening. I'll not entertain this conversation further. Jack is implicit in my wishes, and so I expect the same of you, hmm?"

"Yes, Papa."

His father picked up his pipe and drew from it without success, then set the piece on the table beside him. "I learned from Mr. Hancock that Lord Essex has formed quite an attachment for a particular young lady." Father eyed Abigail. "It seems he plans on taking a wife."

"Who, sir?" Andrew asked.

Father beamed. "Our Abigail, of course."

Jack and Abigail held each other's stare. They said in unison, "He does?"

"More wonderful news." Mother clasped her hands.

Abigail clutched her bodice as though she might faint. "No. I could not possibly marry such a man."

"Nonsense, my dear." Father stood and crossed the room to Abigail. He lifted her hand with tender reverence. "He is deserving of you. And with an inheritance of twenty-thousand pounds, I could give you up to no less."

"Twenty-thousand pounds?" Abigail cried. "Is that all this is, Papa? A transaction for my love?"

"My dear, of course not. You must be well-cared for, and Essex is just the man."

Jack stood. "Lord Essex is hardly the man Abigail wishes to marry. Surely, he will steal her away to England. Is that what you want, sir?"

"Oh, I could never leave this town for England," Abigail wailed.

"Nonsense." Oliver threw up his hands. "Essex is exactly the sort of man Abigail must marry. He is a proper Englishman of noble blood and birth—a peer, and member of Parliament."

"You Loyalist dog," Jack shouted. "You care nothing for Abigail's happiness, only for how your allegiances appear to Society. Father is Patriot. As am I. And as far as I understand, so is Abigail. She cannot marry a man who will hide her away in England, Whig or no."

"Enough." Father's forehead vein throbbed. "Cannot you both alleviate your grievances? I am home but an hour and you're at each other's throats like wild beasts." He sat in his chair and took up his brandy. "I'll not hear another word." He eyed Abigail. "Young lady, I shall give my hearty consent to the gentleman, and you will accept him."

Jack held Abigail as she sobbed against his chest.

"He is well-bred, of good society, and boasts an open mind to this rebellion. I could not have made a better match myself." Father shuffled in his chair, irritated. "Bette, please console your daughter, for I cannot understand why she grieves."

Mother stood, pulled Abigail from Jack, and led her from the parlor.

"Now." Father set down his brandy. "I'd like to hear your good news, Jack."

Unnerved, Jack cocked his head. "Sir?" He glanced at Oliver, whose interest had also piqued.

Father held back a smile. "I believe congratulations are in order. I heard it from your mother the moment I walked in the door. Jane is with child."

Jack's eyes rounded, Oliver smirked, and they said, "She is?"

67

ANNALISA
TOPSFIELD, LATE SEPTEMBER 1775

ANNALISA FOLDED HER FAVORITE petticoat and tucked it into George's old haversack, followed by her poetry book with notes on Benjamin Cavendish, and her physick diary. She wavered, deliberating on whether or not to pack her breeches. Her time in the Danvers militia felt like a lifetime ago, but she could hardly consider joining another after marriage. And tonight, she and Jack would ride to George's tavern, where tomorrow, she'd be a wife—something she'd never imagined of herself.

"Where are you headed?"

Startled, she looked up. Jane leaned in the doorway of their bedchamber.

"Nowhere."

"You fold your favorite petticoat around your favorite books and claim you're headed nowhere?" Jane clicked her tongue. "Come now, tell me the truth."

"You wish for the truth?" Annalisa sat on her heels. "I'll not trust you again."

"I can hardly blame you. But put yourself in my position for a moment, please. I've been offered the marriage of a lifetime, Annie. Would you refuse if you were me?"

"But you would rather marry Oliver. Admit it."

Jane pushed into the bedchamber. "I know you love Jack. But you can hardly take him from me. You're still at the heart of much gossip—which, by the way, you've dragged Jack and me along with you."

Incensed, Annalisa stood. "You're in my way." She slung the haversack over her shoulder. "I wish to get down the stairs."

"No." Jane blocked the doorway. "Not until you tell me where you're going."

"You're a fool to think Jack would marry you when he loves me."

Jane crossed her arms. "He doesn't love you if he's agreed to marry me."

"He didn't agree," Annalisa snapped.

"He did agree. And he does love me." Jane placed a hand over her belly. "Jack loves me so well, he got me with child."

Annalisa ground her teeth. "And you say I lie."

"I'd not lie about something like this." Jane's face softened. "I don't wish for you to hurt any longer. Please accept this—we will be married."

Annalisa burned with fury. She shoved passed Jane and into the hallway. "You're a callous fool to think I would believe something so ridiculous. That is Oliver's child, and you know it."

Jane gripped Annalisa's shoulder and pulled her from the stairs. Annalisa winced at the pain but quickly dug her nails into Jane's wrists.

"Let go of me." Her shoulder throbbed with each movement, but she outclassed Jane in strength. Her sister wouldn't last long, especially not while they teetered atop the stairs.

"Then I am a pitiable fool." Jane's eyes welled.

Annalisa relaxed at Jane's sudden change in demeanor. "Why do speak thus?"

"Because you know the truth." Jane seized Annalisa's shoulder tighter.

"Stop it, you're hurting me. Stop and we can talk about it—"

"No." Jane's beautiful face flushed a dark shade of rose, and a rogue tear fell from her desperate eyes. "I told Mamma the babe was Jack's. She would disown me if she knew I lay with Oliver."

"That is untrue."

"It *is* true."

"Let me go. We can find a way to tell Mamma. You can marry Oliver instead. You do love him, don't you?"

"I do, but I cannot."

"Whyever not?"

"I must marry Jack so I can save my reputation," Jane pleaded.

"Reputation be damned," Annalisa cried. "What of mine? Think you I care for it when so much else is at stake? Be reasonable, Jane!"

"What's happening up there?" Mamma called from the parlor.

"No," Jane hissed.

"Yes, you must tell Oliver."

A shadow of desperation fell upon Jane's face. "Then I'll do what I must." Suddenly, her grasp loosened.

"Jane, no!"

Her sister tumbled down the stairs and landed with a thud at Mamma's feet.

Mamma screeched. "Janey! My sweet, dearest girl. Mary, quick. Get your brothers."

Dizzy with guilt and anger, Annalisa sank to her knees. William and Henry hurried to the bottom of the stairs with Mary.

William knelt beside Jane and slapped her cheek. "Janey, wake up."

Jane's eyes fluttered, and she clung to her stomach with a groan.

"Henry, help me lift her," William said.

Together, they carried Jane up the stairs. Annalisa's body stung with fear as her sister's ghostly face passed her.

"Fetch Addy," Mamma called to Mary as she ran up after them. When she reached the top, she glared at Annalisa. "What happened?"

"Jane threw herself down." Annalisa trembled. "I swear, Mamma. She says she's with child—"

Mamma's hand flew across her face. "She is with child, you fool."

Mamma knew and hid this from me? The sting of betrayal hurt worse than her smarting cheek.

"Get out of my sight." Mamma disappeared into the bedchamber as Addy scurried up the stairs.

"Should we call Dr. Brown, marm?"

Annalisa followed Addy into the room. Jane lay atop their bed, her hands clutching her belly. Blood spotted her skirts.

"Or, I have a tea, marm." Addy's voice lowered. "It may get her through the worst of it until the babe passes."

"Yes, Mamma," Jane sobbed. "Please."

"No," Mamma cried. "You will not lose this child. This babe will secure your marriage, Janey."

Addy placed a cloth to Jane's forehead. "All will be well, Miss Jane."

Mamma turned to Annalisa, her glacial eyes rimmed in red. "Tell William to call on Dr. Brown. We need him urgently."

"Yea, marm." Annalisa backed out of the room. Her stomach crumpled into knots. With the door latched behind her, she leaned against it for a moment to compose herself.

Mamma wished to use Jane's pregnancy to guarantee Jane's marriage to Jack.

Disgusted, she ran down the stairs and found William in the kitchen. He fled the house before she had time to say good-bye. Annalisa hastened through the kitchen, into the foyer, and ended in the parlor. Mary sat at the loom.

"Knew you about this?"

Mary lifted her gaze. "I know too much, Annie."

"Help me convince Jane to tell Mamma she carries Oliver's child."

Her sister remained silent, gloomy.

"Mary, please."

"What difference will I make?"

"If Jane tells the truth about who the father is, she can marry Oliver instead." Annalisa forced away her shudder. All she'd done to keep Jane from marrying the scoundrel, until this very summer, now vanished into a desperate wish for Jane to marry him.

George was right. Life is rarely what we think it should be.

"Then, Jack and I may marry here in town, legitimately. I don't wish to elope, Mary."

"And if Jane refuses, what shall I tell Mamma when she realizes you've gone?"

"Tell her I went to Boston with Abigail and Jack...to find George."

Mary held her stare. "If I help you, you must tell me where you are truly headed."

Annalisa hesitated. "George's tavern."

☙❧

THAT EVENING, ANNALISA SNUCK WITH MARY INTO their bedchamber. Twilight faded to dark beyond the casement, and a lone chamberstick fluttered golden light from the desk. Jane, who lay in the canopied bed they shared, opened one eye then the other.

"Please leave me."

"We know you are resting, but 'tis good news from Dr. Brown." Mary slid onto the bed and held Jane's hand.

"He saved my pregnancy. How can this be good news?" Jane turned from them.

"Then you did mean to miscarry." Annalisa hid her discontent. "Please, tell Oliver. You must make this right by the Perkins family, and ours. Do not falsify who fathered this babe. 'Tis not correct. Nor is it honorable."

Jane grimaced and they helped prop the pillows behind her.

"'Twas a mistake I made." Jane sniffled. "I fancied Oliver, and it near killed me when I learned what he did to you, Annie. I was satisfied to marry Jack after I heard of his inheritance from Lord Brunswick, but that was after I lay with Oliver—and missed my flux. How could I ever tell Mamma the truth? Or Jack?"

"Jack will know the child is not his, Jane." Annalisa stroked her sister's hair.

"'Tis no matter, now." Jane turned her head. "You must both think me a monster to have done something so selfish."

"No, Janey." Mary reached for her hand. "We love you."

"Jane, I love you, too." Annalisa continued to smooth Jane's hair. "No matter our quarrels. I want what is best for you and your babe—my niece or nephew. What Oliver did to me was deplorable, but perhaps he will make you a proper husband." She sucked in a breath, then exhaled. "I'm willing to put it behind me. For you. He does love you —he always has. And I know Papa would be happy for you to marry him. For you to be a Loyalist's wife would be far better than the wife of a Patriot."

Jane reached for Annalisa. "'Tis so you may marry your Patriot. Is it not? So you may become the next Lady Brunswick?"

"I care not for the titles, Jane. I know that distresses you." Annalisa bit her lip. "But don't I deserve to be happy, too? And as much as I detest Oliver, he has a right to father his child."

Jane was silent for some time. "I cannot." She held her face. "Everything I've worked towards, my lessons, my reputation...will be ruined. I could never face Society again."

68

ANNALISA
NEWBURYPORT, LATE SEPTEMBER 1775

T HAT NIGHT, LIGHTNING STREAKED, thunder cracked, and rain spattered against the casement. Annalisa turned on her side to stare into the blackness. Another flash illuminated the bedchamber. Her sisters lay asleep beside her, the bedcurtains drawn on one side. Another deep roll of thunder shook the house. Annalisa rose and pulled on her dress. She lit a paper spill from one of the embers in the fireplace and took it to the candle in the window.

A soft glow bathed the room in warm light, a beacon for Jack. She peered at Jane's sleeping face.

How innocent and carefree she looks in slumber.

Poor Mary beside her now bore the brunt of their poor decisions. Leaving was hardly easy, but she'd given Jane the chance to atone. With one final look at her sisters, Annalisa grabbed her haversack and tiptoed from the bedchamber.

She paced the basement pantry, her spirit heavy with

guilt. Outside, rain pummeled against the house and fallen leaves like small stones. The clock chimed two.

Will Jack still come? Perhaps he heard of Jane's pregnancy and decided against the elopement.

She turned to the stairs but glanced out the window once more. Lantern light flickered off the droplets of water.

Jack.

Annalisa grabbed her haversack and hurried from the basement, into the storm. The drenching rain cooled her body as she ran toward him.

He dashed from the path, splashing through small puddles in the grass. Water dribbled from his hat and landed on the tip of his nose. Lightning streaked across the sky, and thunder boomed.

Jack embraced her. "I'm sorry I'm late. We must make haste."

He helped her onto his horse, and she wrapped her arms about his waist. When they met the lane, her being quaked. The safe, narrow road that led to home.

My home no more.

Annalisa thrust her face into his wet cloak and closed her eyes.

AN HOUR ON HORSEBACK, THEY FINALLY REACHED Newburyport and the Old Port Inn. The downpour had lightened to a drizzle.

"Let's rest here," Jack said. "We'll at least have a dry, warm bed till daybreak."

Inside the inn, Jack opened the door to their room. He

set the chamberstick atop a desk by the window, and tossed off his sopping hat and cloak. With a smile, he went to her and cupped her face.

"Here at last." He bonded his lips with hers. "When we wake, we'll straightaway to Portsmouth, and I may call you Mrs. Perkins."

"Will they recognize us without a marriage banns?"

"Yes. A reverend will marry us. 'Tis still a marriage without the banns."

"And our license?"

"I've taken care of it."

Annalisa dropped her haversack and wrapped her arms about him. Jack's scent of amber roused her as he untied her soggy, wool cloak. It fell to the floor. She staggered backward until she reached the bed, and toppled on it under his weight.

Jack pressed himself against her, his mouth searching every inch of her face and neck. "It may be precipitous, but I may call you Mrs. Perkins now, if you like."

"It pleases me to hear that."

He lifted her skirts, and slid his hand against her thigh. "Then Mrs. Perkins, shall we consummate this common-law marriage?" Jack's mouth glided over her leg with tenderness.

She bit her lip in an attempt to ignore her gnawing culpability. "If you so wish."

Jack sat upright. An apologetic look melted away his desire. "Forgive my haste. I mean not to advance upon you like this if you are unwilling before we wed."

"No, 'tis not that." Annalisa sat up and shivered. "I do want you." The rain had seeped through her clothes and dampened her shift beneath her stays.

The lust in his eyes faded to longing, and he ran a hand over his face. "You must wish to discuss Jane."

"Yes."

"On my honor as a gentleman, I swear we never strummed."

"I believe you—"

"Thank heavens." Jack reached for her, but she pulled away.

"But no one else shall, unless she rescinds her claim."

His brows furrowed. "Pray tell, is she truly with child?"

"So says Dr. Brown."

"Zounds." His fist pounded the bed. "I'd prayed my father was wrong."

She jumped, startled by his reply. "But 'tis Oliver's child."

"Yes, and I've confronted him." He rubbed the back of his neck.

"Will he marry her?"

"Only if she is willing to break our engagement."

"Jane said she wouldn't risk her reputation." Annalisa heated with anger. "She was in our barn with Oliver in June, and 'tis now September. Dr. Brown says she is three months pregnant. You spent the night with her a three weeks ago. Anyone who knows anything about pregnancy will recognize 'tis a lie. Jane realized she was with child then arranged the bundling. 'Twas all a ruse to guarantee your wedding—"

"It guarantees nothing. We're here, now." Jack reached for her the yearning returned to his eyes. "And tomorrow, I truly can call you my wife."

She pulled her hand from his. "Jack..."

"What is it?" He edged closer.

"I cannot."

His face distorted as though she'd punched his gut. "You cannot marry me?"

"No."

"Why?" His thumb swept her cheek. "Annalisa—"

"Don't you see? Now you *must* marry Jane."

He narrowed his eyes. "And raise my brother's son as my own? 'Tis not my responsibility to rectify Oliver's misdeeds."

"But she needs a husband."

"Please, no."

"Jack, you must."

"You're not in your right mind." His face pinked, and he stood from the bed. "You're asking me to marry Jane?"

"Yes. She's with child, and you are still her betrothed."

"How can I live with Jane as my wife?" He hastened toward her. "How can I call you *sister* when you are so much more to me?"

She recoiled at his words. "I know not."

"Do you realize what you're asking of me?" His tone sharp, she could tell he was angry. "Is this what you want, Annalisa?"

"Fie." She threw up her hands. "None of this is what I want. I desire to marry you at home in town, not run away and shame my family. I want your family to prefer me to Jane, and I wish Oliver never assaulted me all those years ago so I could feel good about my sister carrying his child. I wish the province wasn't at war. None of this is what I'd envisioned for any of us. But now we're faced with something too great we can't escape. Jane is my sister. She is pregnant with no husband...because the father is a scoundrel." She glared at him. "But you're not a scoundrel,

Jack. You are the most honorable man I know. Will you do the decent thing and marry my sister?"

His lips grew taut. "Then you love me no longer?"

"That is hardly the case."

"Then tell me you love me, Annalisa."

She quaked under the weight of her own conscience. Of course, she loved him. She loved him with every breath she took. But no profession of love could alter the fate that had aligned so poorly against them.

"What difference would it make?"

"Perhaps you would rather marry another," he said coldly.

"Another?" She huffed and jumped from the bed. "Now it seems *you're* not in your right mind. Whyever should you think that?"

He turned and pulled on his frock coat. "If you will not marry me, why not someone else?"

"I'm refusing to marry you because of Jane. It has nothing to do with my feelings."

"What of *my* feelings, Annalisa? Have you once considered them?"

The gravity of his words crushed her. "Of course, I have. But our feelings matter not. We are bound by integrity. Are we not?"

"I am bound to *you*." Jack peered out the casement. Already, dark blue light glowed from beyond the shutter. He went to his belongings and threw on his cloak, followed by his cocked hat. "'Tis first light." When he faced her again, his eyes appeared hollow. "Come. Gather your things so I may take you home."

She crossed arms. "No."

"No?" His brow arched.

"Will not you fight for me until I've protested enough? Will not you fight me until the sun has risen so you may drag me to Portsmouth? Will not you argue with me about this until I've conceded and may call you *husband*?"

Jack's gaze softened, but Annalisa suspected he was still cross with her, perhaps even as conflicted as she. Desperate, she lay on her side, away from him, and waited. Several moments passed in silence until his voice surrounded her.

"It seems nothing I say or do pleases you." Jack's footsteps creaked behind her, but the bed never shifted under his weight.

His breath extinguished the candle, leaving them both in darkness.

Annalisa clenched her eyes shut. At least he hadn't taken her home.

69

JACK
PORTSMOUTH, LATE SEPTEMBER 1775

J ACK'S NECK AND BACK panged as he turned. Annalisa slept in the four-posted bed, her back to him. He pulled out his pocket watch.

Noon!

They should have been on the road hours ago. He stood, rinsed his face and mouth in the washbasin, and combed the knots from his hair. When he'd finished, he returned to the bed to find Annalisa still in soundless repose.

He ached at their quarrel last night. He'd never considered he would refuse to lie beside her. Jack crawled onto the bed, edged closer to her, and brushed her hair from her neck. He touched his lips to her nape. She smelled pleasantly of rain and earth.

Annalisa's eyes fluttered open and she faced him.

He nuzzled the side of her face. "I'm so sorry for the way we fell asleep."

"I am, too."

"Shall I take you home? Your family will be anxious—"

"No." Annalisa bit her lip. "I thought about Jane all night. I offered her the opportunity to make right, and she refused. We deserve to be happy, Jack."

He sat upright and pulled her forward. When she reached the edge of the bed, Jack took her hands and knelt on one knee. He held out a sapphire ring, the gold band etched with leaves.

"Marry me, my wonderful, darling girl."

Her mouth parted and the corners upturned. "I dare-say, I shall."

Jack's broad smile dimpled his cheeks, and he placed the ring upon her finger. He kissed her hands, then stood and drew his love to her feet. "'Tis already half-noon. We must make haste."

"Half-noon?" Annalisa pulled her hands from his and rummaged through her belongings. She removed a blue quilted petticoat and with a sheepish grin, said, "Mind you turning while I dress? You can't see the bride before she's ready."

He chuckled. "Let me take our things, and I'll meet you downstairs."

In the musty tavern, Jack ordered a pint of ale and a hard-boiled egg while he waited. As the potboy served other patrons, he wondered if Elisha still knew to expect them. Jack peeked at his pocket watch. They were already several hours late.

Annalisa stepped into the room and each man lifted his head from his tankard or newspaper.

Jack stood, the chair scraping behind him. "You look radiant." He turned to the room. "This brave young lady has agreed to marry me today."

An eruption of applause drowned out his beating heart as he approached her.

Annalisa held out her skirts. "I've not worn this dress since our first Strawberry Festival."

Jack marveled at the white chintz printed with dozens of blue cornflowers, green leaves, and vines. Her loveliness brought a halt to his breath, with or without the sentimental dress.

"Let's to the stagecoach. We should arrive by three. Samuel's uncle lives in Portsmouth. He's agreed to marry us."

Annalisa's face lit up. "Samuel's uncle?"

"Aye," Jack laughed. "He's the reverend."

❦

THEY ARRIVED AT GEORGE'S BLACK WATER INN several hours later than he'd anticipated. Relieved, but still somewhat eager, Jack helped Annalisa from the coach, and ushered her inside.

Elisha waved. "You've made it." He offered them the key to their room. "I was beginning to worry of your delay. Your guests are waiting."

Annalisa turned to Jack. "Our guests?"

"One more surprise for you, dear heart." Jack led her up the stairs to the bedchamber at the end of the hall.

"This is the largest room. George told me before he left he was reserving it for General Washington." She laughed. "I can hardly imagine a man of his importance ever visiting this place."

"There may be a more worthy man inside." Jack

winked, unlocked, and unlatched the door. There stood two men, one much taller than the other.

Annalisa shrieked and hurried inside. Jack stepped in behind her and closed the door. She flung her arms around George.

"Little One." George lifted her up and spun her around as he had the day they reunited in Boston.

"Oh, George, I've missed you."

He set her down and studied her thoughtfully, swiping his thumb beneath her right eye. "I wouldn't miss this for anything. Not even Washington or Henry Knox could keep me."

Jack smiled. "Thank you, Cousin."

"Took you long enough." George eyed Samuel's uncle. "My victualing office is rumbling. Elisha's made sure we have enough pies to feed fifty men."

Reverend Wildes shifted uneasily and adjusted his black frock coat. "We feared you would not make it."

"Yesterday was terrible," Annalisa said. "Jane threw herself down the stairs and Mamma was in hysterics—"

"You never told me thus." Jack's breathing staggered.

Concern swamped George's tired face. "Is she well?"

"She's well enough, but I can hardly bring myself to say what caused her madness."

Reverend Wildes cleared his throat. "Well, we have our bride, and we have our bridegroom." He turned to George. "And our witness." He opened his Book of Common Prayer. "Shall we begin?"

◈

"A TOAST," GEORGE BELLOWED, HIS EYES GLASSY AFTER six pints of ale. He tore into a mince-filled pie, chewed voraciously, and swallowed. "I must make the first coach to Boston in the morning—which is in a few hours. Make it worth my while, Perkins."

"Easy, Mr. Howlett." Elisha winked at Jack as he refilled George's tankard.

"I'll oblige." Jack stood and lifted his glass of brandy. "To appease you, dear cousin—or shall I say, Brother." He regarded Annalisa lovingly. "Let us honor my courageous wife, who was devoted enough to marry me today but daft enough to love me from first we met. It seems the hazel-nuts in the fire at our first corn husking knew better than I, and though I jested and called you my wife that same night, know I have loved you since the massacre—the day you donned breeches and pummeled stones at His Majesty's men; our first Strawberry Festival, when we gazed at the stars and fireflies overtook the common—I knew there was no other lass fit to be my wife. Though I may have taken my time in getting us here today, I pray I always give you a reason to look upon me with those affec-tionate, emerald eyes, and give you reason to be proud to call me 'husband.'" He lifted his dram of brandy. "To Mrs. Perkins.'"

The room cheered. "To Mrs. Perkins."

"Sluice your gob, rogues," George bellowed.

Two gentlemen played *Flowers of Edinburgh* on their fiddles, and Annalisa beamed the widest smile Jack had ever seen. She finished her madeira then pulled him in for a kiss.

"Fond memories of our first year together in Topsfield. You must remember our dance at the Strawberry Festival.

I daresay, I have reason now to give you a venerable smile." Annalisa traced the buttons on his coat and looked up with desire. "Pray tell, when shall we return to the bedchamber and you make me a wife?"

Jack grinned, the anticipation of consummating their marriage now within reach. "We could go now—"

"After this dance." George shoved them to the middle of the room.

The smoky tavern sweltered, and Jack tossed off his coat and loosened his cravat. Surrounded by a dozen red-faced, clapping patrons, he took up Annalisa's hands. They turned about the room, and the tavern revolved in circles. But Jack focused on his lovely wife, her cheeks glowing, her countenance jovial. He laughed, his face aching from endless joy.

The tavern door opened and a reprieve of crisp, autumn air inundated the room. Jack turned toward the entrance. William rushed inside, his face linen white.

His agitated stare found Annalisa. "Annie. George?" A look of confusion sprawled across his face.

"Well I'll be damned," George guffawed. *"Wilhelmina!"*

"Will, what is it?" Annalisa's grip on Jack's hands loosened.

"Jane's gone."

70

ANNALISA
LATE SEPTEMBER 1775

A NNALISA RAN TO WILLIAM and gripped his trembling hands. "Jane's left?"

"Aye. She told Mother she was calling on Miss Perley, but never returned." William addressed Jack. "My father went to your house for help and found your parents in an uproar—that you had gone. Now Oliver is missing. We think Jane fled with him."

"The reptile," George muttered.

"Did Ollie indicate to anyone where they meant to go?" Jack asked.

"No." William fumbled with his coat. "But now my father knows Annie lied about traveling with you and Abigail to find George."

"What are these stories?" George roared. "I came here to witness Jack marry Annie. Otherwise, I'm indisposed to help. I must return to General Washington by morning."

William frowned. "Mother is bedridden, taken ill by two fallen daughters. Poor Mary is tending to her as though she's dying. But worst is Father. I've never seen him so incensed." His anxious blue eyes pleaded with whomever would hear him. "I know not what else to do."

"We will help," Annalisa said. "But how did you know to find me here?"

"Mary. And Father bade me find you."

"The devil she did," George rumbled.

"She didn't want to tell, but I knew if you came home, you could save Mother from hysterics and Father from madness."

"Me?" Annalisa's chest constricted. "Mamma has always loved Jane better."

"It matters not." William shifted his gaze between Annalisa and Jack. "Mother needs you. We all need you."

"'Tis unlike Oliver to elope." Jack fixed his cravat. "I know my brother and he's selfish. He'd never do anything to taint his reputation. I bet they haven't wed and will return."

"Jack, we must go." Annalisa turned to George. "Will you help search?"

George crossed his arms. "I have an obligation to General Washington."

She reached for him. "I know you loathe Oliver, but you must at least try."

He grunted. "If what Jack says is true, they should return to Topsfield, which would make any search of mine futile."

"Oh, please." William seized George's shoulders.

George sighed. "I suppose I can scour Dorchester Heights, but 'tis the last place the scoundrel would go. The Continentals have surrounded Boston. Not a Loyalist remains."

Annalisa wrapped her arms around George. "Thank you."

He kissed her forehead. "Anything for you, Little One."

☷☷☷

SHORTLY AFTER MIDNIGHT, JACK, WILLIAM, AND Annalisa rode up the narrow lane. Sore from the long ride on horseback, she followed her brother and husband into the farmhouse. Angry shouts echoed from the parlor. Mamma and Papa stood red-faced in the firelight. Beside them, Lord and Lady Perkins appeared similarly agitated.

"Oh, William, you've found them. Thank God." Mamma hurried to Annalisa and promptly slapped her. "You stole away with your sister's betrothed while she is with child. You malicious, selfish girl."

Annalisa held her smarting face, and Jack pulled her into his arms. "Mrs. Howlett, peace. Allow me to explain."

"Annalisa Howlett, I'll not be taken for a fool." Papa's coffee eyes appeared black and menacing. "Did you or did you not elope with this traitorous rebel?" He gestured to Jack as though he were a villain, rather than the formidable son of their dear, old friends. "This...*gentleman* who is engaged to your sister, and who has gotten her with child."

"Papa, 'tis not true." Annalisa pulled from Jack's arms. "Jane doesn't carry Jack's child."

Mamma hissed, "You lie."

"No, Mother." William braced himself. "Jane lied."

"Mr. Howlett, sir." Though his jaw firmed, Jack maintained an air of calm. "Oliver got Jane with child." He reached for Annalisa's hand and squeezed. "And I am in love with Annalisa. I always have been."

"You'll not marry my daughter without my consent." Papa returned his distress to Lord Perkins. "Engagement, pregnancy, or no, I've already lost one daughter to your sons. I'll not lose another." He pulled Annalisa from Jack and thrust her toward Mamma.

"No, please." Annalisa rubbed her arms as Mamma held her. "Papa, please listen to me."

"I'd never defile Miss Jane, sir, nor Miss Annalisa," Jack said. "You have my word as a gentleman—"

"A gentleman, say you?" Papa sneered.

"Jack is honorable—and he is my husband," Annalisa cried. She held out her hand to show the sapphire ring. "He'd never do anything to our family. You know him. You know the Perkins are a goodly family, no matter the rebellion!"

Lady Perkins gasped. "My mother's ring. Jack, I knew not you took it."

"Annalisa!" Mamma's grip tightened on her shoulder. The healed wound throbbed, and Annalisa thrust her hand into her pocket and fingered the musket round.

I am strong, with or without my breeches.

Papa's distress colored his tawny face. "Your husband? Then you did marry, and without the banns. You have breached my confidences for the final time. First 'twas Bunker Hill. Now this."

"Mr. Howlett, come. We are old friends." Lord Perkins sounded less like a magistrate and more like a diplomat.

Papa shook his head. "Perkins, I cannot forgive this. My daughters are shamed because of your sons, the well-bred gentlemen they are."

"This is most distressing." Lord Perkins paced by the fire. "Most distressing, indeed. My sons are worthy of your daughters—perhaps too worthy."

"Too worthy?" Papa threw up his hands. "One has gotten my eldest daughter with child, the other convinced my younger daughter to elope."

Lord Perkins puffed out his chest, but Jack hastened toward his father and tugged his arm. "Father, please."

Lord Perkins lowered his shoulders. "Let's not allow this war, elopement, or pregnancy divide our families and friendships." He adjusted his spectacles. "If Jane is with child by Oliver, then she is with the rightful father and should marry him outright. I'll not deny the propriety in that." He observed Jack with sudden sorrow. "My dear boy, I only regret I had not blessed this match sooner."

The front door opened, and George stepped inside with Jane and Oliver. "I believe you were looking for these two."

"Jane." Annalisa cupped her mouth as Oliver escorted her sister into the parlor.

"Georgie, you've come back, and with my Janey." Mamma left Annalisa and embraced Jane. "Thank heavens you've come home." She turned and smiled remorsefully at Annalisa. "All of you."

"Enough. She's hardly innocent." Papa's arms crossed. "Young lady, pray tell, have you married this man as decency dictates?"

Jane's decorous stare shifted between her family and the Perkins, seemingly unaware of the altercation, yet not entirely ignorant as to why both families assembled at so late an hour.

She placed a delicate hand over her stomach. "Mr. Oliver and I had much to discuss."

Oliver stepped forward, smug as ever. "Mr. Howlett, Father, I apologize for taking Miss Howlett away for so long, but she's returned safely, and with her virtues intact—"

"Her virtue intact? 'Tis no thanks to George you've been returned home." Annalisa's blood boiled. No longer needing the cloak of her breeches, she swung her fist across Oliver's face. "My sister is with child, you arrogant fool. Your child!"

George's deep laughter filled the room and Mamma screeched.

"Lord in heaven, Jack." Oliver held his cheek. "Control your wife. If you can even call her thus." He peered at Jane as if to admit she'd told him about their elopement. "Scandalous gossip travels fast in a small town."

"Never." Jack grinned. "My wife shall strike a scoundrel as she pleases. 'Tis about time she assaulted you as I have, and George." He kissed Annalisa's hand, then faced Jane. "And 'twas by your admission, Miss Howlett, you falsely gave claim to me."

Jane lowered her stare. "I apologize, sir."

When her sister's gaze lifted, Annalisa detected a small smirk at the corner of her feline lips. *Is Jane pleased by this retribution?*

Jane continued, "But we were engaged, sir, and I knew not what else to do."

"Perhaps tell the truth?" William snapped.

"I acted brashly." Jane smoothed her skirts. "I pray you may all forgive my foolishness. Annie, 'twas wrong of me, and I have learned my lesson well."

Annalisa reached for Jane and embraced her. "You are forgiven."

When she pulled away, Oliver tucked Jane's hand under his arm. "Miss Howlett has agreed to marry me."

Mamma's face relaxed. "Oh, my Janey. I was so worried about your health and the unborn babe." She looked to Lady Perkins, hopeful. "But we shall have a wedding after all."

"I suppose I'm relieved to hear it." Papa regarded Lord Perkins and held out his hand.

Lord Perkins shook it. "I look forward to the nuptials, Howlett."

Lady Perkins faced Jack with somber eyes. "Your uncle will be most distressed to hear of your elopement."

Oliver smirked, despite the swelling beneath his left eye. "Seems I'll be inheriting Uncle's estate."

"I gladly give it to you." Jack held Annalisa's hand. "My wife cares little for titles."

❦

JACK, GEORGE, AND ANNALISA STEPPED OUTSIDE, INTO the brisk September night.

"Where did you find them?" Jack asked.

"I was barely outside Newburyport when I stopped to make water at the Old Port Inn, and discovered them." George guffawed. "Oliver nearly shite through his teeth when he saw me. I had no trouble at all in threatening them to return."

Annalisa hugged him. "I'm saddened you must leave."

"I am, too." He kissed the top of her head. "But seeing you strike Oliver was worth every second of my time away from the army. I know not whether I can continue calling you 'Little One.'"

"I haven't been little since I was ten. Why stop now?"

George snickered. "Fair enough, Little One. Now go, enjoy your wedding night." He pushed her from his embrace and thrust her into Jack's arms. *"All you that in your beds do lie, turn to your wives and occupy. And when that you have done your best, turn arse to arse, and take your rest."* His guffaw echoed into the night as he rushed to his horse. "I'll write when I return to the Heights." He mounted Frederick, and galloped away down the narrow lane.

71

ANNALISA
TOPSFIELD, LATE SEPTEMBER 1775

JACK CARRIED ANNALISA OVER the threshold of his bedchamber and sat her on his canopied bed. The room smelled redolent of amber, mingled with woodsmoke. She kicked off her shoes, still shaken from the encounter at her house.

"I cannot believe I struck Oliver."

Jack laughed. "He is deserving of it." He reached for her hand. "Pray tell, does it hurt?"

She made a fist. "Only a little."

He kissed each knuckle. "Better?"

"Yes."

Jack stripped from his coat and placed it over the back of his desk chair. When he returned to her, he lowered his gaze in faint embarrassment. "In all my haste to marry you, I regret we must live with my family until our house is built. You need only tell me where you wish to live."

"'Tis no consolation." She ran her hand over his fine, silk coverlet. "For all the times I've been inside this house, I'm glad to finally see your bedchamber."

"And sit upon my bed?" He winked.

She trembled with nervous exhilaration. "And share it with you."

"Dear heart, you share far more than that." He slid behind her on the bed and closed the bedcurtains, leaving only a view of the fire. His fingers glided down her arm and he rested his chin on her shoulder.

"I once thought myself unworthy of such affections. Particularly from you, sir."

"It is an honor to share my life with you. Since living with Adams and his wife, I've coveted their marriage, their friendship. I wish for nothing more from my future wife. I daresay, you give that all to me and more, and so I promise to always treat you as my equal, truly, that I may seek your counsel in all things, no matter the importance, or triviality." He studied her, his thumb trailing across her hand. "Annalisa, I hope you find comfort confiding in me..."

Her confidence bolstered at his fine words. "I do have a secret for you."

His brow lifted curiously, and his cheek dimpled. "Do tell, Mrs. Perkins."

"The day I scarred my cheek, Addy told me I'd find a man to marry someday. I didn't believe her. I never wanted to embrace womanhood, I never wished to marry. Then I met you, and dreamed of the day you would notice me before Jane. Now, I sit here as your wife, and find myself yearning for something I never thought I wanted for myself."

His hand brushed a piece of her hair from her face and he smiled. "Tell me, Mrs. Perkins."

"A child."

Jack slid closer, his voice husky in her ear. "It would be

my delight to give you a child." His lips brushed her cheek then moved to her mouth. He pulled the pins from her bodice, opening the dress and exposing her stays. His hand slid down and untied her petticoats. Annalisa tossed the garments to the floor. In only her shift and stays, she marveled at how little she feared being undressed before him.

Her fingers unbuttoned his waistcoat, then unwound the fine silk from his neck. He slid his arms from the waistcoat and threw it aside with his neckpiece. The shirt opened to reveal soft tufts of light brown hair. He pulled her between his legs and slowly unlaced her stays. His lips swept her neck, down her shoulder, and finally her upper back.

Annalisa's skin goosepimpled. The looser her bindings, the quicker her heart beat and the deeper she inhaled. Jack lifted the stays over her head then discarded his own shirt. Beneath the light array of hair, his chest was muscular, his ridged stomach flat, and his fitted breeches clung to his hips. Annalisa reached out to touch him, but hesitated.

Jack placed her hand over his heart. "My heart only beats for you, Annie."

Her breath caught. It was the first time he'd ever called her thus. She remembered how she'd longed to hear him call her by her nickname, to be so close to him as to share such a simple familiarity.

He fused his mouth to hers and lay her on her back. His hand glided up her leg, sliding her shift above her thighs. Jack knelt between her legs and untied the ribbons holding up her stockings. He rolled one down. Then, the other. Holding her leg, his lips touched her right ankle and skimmed up her calf, to her knee, then her thigh.

Heat flushed her face. He meant to tip the velvet. Annalisa rested her head against the pillow and closed her eyes, accepting the softness of his mouth. For a moment, he peered up and smiled. At his tender look, her knees fell apart. Each flick and swirl of his tongue was a novel sensation, quite different from the pleasure he'd given her with his hand.

She reached for him and his body glided over hers, and she felt the arousal beneath his breeches. Jack untied her shift. The neckline widened to expose her shoulders and breasts. He grazed her collarbone and returned one hand to the space between her legs.

"You tease and taunt like the flirt you are."

"Me? A flirt?" He gave a handsome pout and pulled at the buttons on his breeches until the flap exposed him. He slipped the breeches from his hips, kicked them away, and crawled on top of her. "I love you ardently." Jack's lips bonded to hers, and he slowly pushed into her.

She tightened her grip on his arms. He must have felt her tense at the pain because his hands curled up to her face, and his kisses softened. Annalisa eased him into her, and hoped tonight, he would get her with child. The thought warmed her, as she couldn't imagine loving him any more than she already did. But for him to create a child with her—such a miracle could only intensify her love and devotion.

A sensation of utter joy coursed through her, and she held him tight, wishing they could remain entwined forever. His mouth found her breasts and Annalisa wrapped her legs about him, pushing him deeper until she let go in ecstasy.

He stiffened and moaned her name, his body quaked,

then relaxed. For several moments, he remained atop her, kissing her before rolling onto his side.

"My heart. My dearest heart." His breath burst in quick, shallow movements. "How have we kept such intimate pleasure from each other for so long?"

Annalisa grinned and slid her fingers over his chest. "I know not, but I daresay, you will strum me again quite soon."

He laughed. "Tonight?"

"If you're able."

Jack glanced down and chewed his lip. "Give me a quarter hour."

⊗❧⊗

ANNALISA OPENED HER EYES. JACK WAS PROPPED ON ONE arm, smiling.

Startled, she asked, "How long have you been awake?"

"Not long. I've found particular delight in watching my wife sleep, even if only for a little while."

She threw a hand over her face. "I must look haggard."

Jack chuckled. "You look well-loved. Pray tell, are you well? Are you sore?"

"I am a bit."

"That will improve the more we're intimate." He slid onto his back and tucked his hands beneath his head.

Annalisa curled up beside him and rested upon his chest. "'Tis like a dream. I've not slept a wink since Bunker Hill."

"I pray those memories fade to nothing." He kissed her head and slid an arm around her. "I'll to my father today and sign the documents I must. I imagine Oliver is quite ready to inherit my titles."

"New Castle." Annalisa sat up.

Jack peered at her. "New Castle?"

"'Tis where I want to build our house."

"You've given it thought?"

"Yes. 'Tis what you said in Mr. Hooper's library. I went to New Castle when I was visiting George's inn. The sea air, the ocean—I want all of that for us."

"You're sure?"

"Yes."

His cheeks dimpled. "'Tis done." He kissed her again then stared up at the canopy. "You give me a life to look forward to when this war's over."

Annalisa twirled his long, chestnut hair about her finger. "How do you mean?"

He sat up. "Once there is peace, I see our future so clearly. Our house by the sea, my law office, our fifteen children running about—"

"Fifteen?"

Jack snickered. "Judging by last night's performance, it will be at least fifteen." As quickly as he'd laughed, he sobered. "But I know not how long it will be till then. Annie, I must go to Philadelphia with my father. 'Twas a promise I made him."

"I thought you wished to join George in the army."

"I can hardly enlist with the Continentals now that I have you." He pulled her close. "The thought of leaving for Philadelphia is hard enough. But to endanger myself in battle is something I cannot do. I promised you before Concord I would be safe. By some miracle, we both survived Bunker Hill. Annie, I will die keeping that promise. I have you to think of." He glanced down and placed his hand to her belly. "Our family to think of."

Her body tingled.

If I were him, I would join the army without question.

She chewed her cheek. She, too, had a family to consider.

Jack swung his legs over the side of the bed, stood, and pulled his clothes off the floor. He grinned impishly. "Are you ready to confirm to all of town we've been married?"

"'Tis Sunday." She sat on the edge of the bed and admired his physique.

I'm the one who learned what's beneath those breeches.

She smirked to herself. "The meetinghouse will be full." Annalisa slipped into her shift. "I can hardly wait to see Hannah French, Fannie Shepard, and Lizzie Balch's faces."

72

ANNALISA
TOPSFIELD, LATE SEPTEMBER 1775

ANNALISA GRIPPED JACK'S ARM. The new minister, Reverend Cleaveland, gave a tedious sermon, which left her longing for George's droll whispers. But now, she sat with Jack and his family in their pew box beside the pulpit. When the meeting ended, Jack led her outside, where everyone gathered on the common.

"Miss Annali—I mean, Mrs. Perkins—congratulations," Fannie Shepard said.

Annalisa smiled. "Thank you, Fannie."

Lizzie smirked. "I knew my fortune was right."

"I cannot believe you eloped." Hannah stuck her nose in the air. "I daresay, you're lucky the town—and Reverend Cleaveland—have chosen to recognize your marriage."

Annalisa scowled. "I beg your pardon?"

"Hannah." Abigail approached. "You'd do well to mind yourself. My brother and Annalisa will always be welcome here in town, no matter your thoughts on the propriety of their marriage."

Jack kissed Annalisa's hand. "I only regret I could not

declare myself to Annie before our entire town. But I stand beside her, now and always, as the happiest of men."

"How wonderful to hear." Martha Perley clasped her hands. "You two make a lovely pair. Pray tell, where will you live?"

"I believe I can help that." David Perkins, the town treasurer, ambled toward them with Captain Stephen Perkins of the militia.

"There's a house near the grist mill, Jack, that belongs in our family," David said. "'Tis vacant and within walking distance to Stephen, and is only a mile or two down the lane from your families. I'd be much obliged for you to live there until you are ready to build."

An expression of earnest surprise colored Jack's face. "Sir, that is far too generous."

"'Tis the least we can do." Stephen cupped his shoulder. "You saved my life at Concord. I can hardly repay you for it."

"Then how can I refuse?" Jack shook their hands. "Thank you, sirs."

"I know that house, sir." Annalisa looked to Jack. "It would be close to home. I could see my family often."

"What luck," Martha said. "I should very much like to visit you both."

Hannah French, with red face, promptly excused herself. The others quickly followed.

EARLY NOVEMBER 1775

Since Jack's untimely departure to Philadelphia with Lord Perkins at the beginning of October, Annalisa spent much of her time in the kitchen of their rented two-story house with Quinnapin's new wife, Weetamoo. With its large central chimney and saltbox roof, it was easy to stay warm on these brisk November days.

"Annie, are you sure you've enough firewood?" William settled into the chair nearest the hearth and warmed his hands. He and Quinnapin had been chopping wood since dawn.

"I'm sure." Annalisa sat back in her seat. "You've been too good to me since Jack left."

"I can imagine how you miss him. He'll return from Congress soon, then you may travel to Portsmouth."

"How fares George's inn? I'm meant to travel thither next week."

"'Tis making plenty of money," William replied.

The front door knocker rapped, and Papa entered the kitchen holding a large iron pot. "Addy sent venison soup and corncakes."

"God love Addy." Annalisa stood, ready to take the pot from him, but Papa stopped her.

"Daughter, allow me." Papa set the pot onto the crane and swung it into the hearth. "I heard from a tiny bird the Lord hath sent you a gift." He eyed her stomach for a brief moment and a twinkle returned to his eyes. It was the first time he'd looked pleased since her elopement.

Annalisa smiled. "I told Mamma not to tell anyone until I was further along."

"Is it true?" William rose from his chair.

"It is."

"Then I'll have more nieces and nephews in the coming year than I thought." William laughed. "Jane is looking quite round."

There again came a rapping upon the door.

Papa turned. "You need a housekeeper." He left the kitchen and soon returned with Stephen Perkins and his wife, Eunice. They carried blankets and pillows in a large basket, and a small bookshelf.

"We come bearing more furnishings for you, Dear." Eunice's smile appeared wide on her thin face.

"You're too generous, marm." Annalisa kissed her cheek.

Eunice set the basket on the wooden kitchen table. "We know how difficult it is furnishing a home, and with Jack gone, you need all the more help."

Annalisa ran a hand over the fine woven coverlet. "'Tis beautiful and will keep us warm this winter. Thank you."

When they'd all left, Annalisa returned to her chair by the kitchen hearth. A gust of cold air whistled down the chimney, flaring the flames. She shuddered, poked the burning logs, and swung the kettle into the fire.

"Would you like some coffee, Mrs. P?" Weetamoo asked.

Annalisa jumped, startled. "I've got the kettle on, now. Addy made us venison soup and corncakes." She stood, retrieved two bowls, and ladled the soup. "Please, bring some to Quinn."

Weetamoo gave a pleasant smile. "Thank you, Mrs. P."

No sooner had she done this than did the knocker sound at the front door. Weetamoo started for the door, but Annalisa motioned for her to stop.

"I'll get it. Go eat with Quinn, dear friend." Annalisa hurried into the foyer and opened the door.

Abigail stood, teeth chattering.

"Annie." Abigail rushed inside and flung her arms about Annalisa's neck. "I've missed you so much."

They held each other for a moment, then Annalisa drew herself away. "'Tis only been a week." She laughed. "Let me take your cloak."

"No housekeeper yet?" Abigail handed it to Annalisa, and she hung it beside the door.

"No, not yet, but Weetamoo has been helping me learn to cook. She's been teaching me receipts she learned from an Agawam woman. I like to think my grandmother would be glad for me to learn them." She led Abigail into the kitchen. "I sense you're nervous about the wedding. How goes Lord Essex?"

Abigail smoothed her skirts and sat upon the wooden kitchen bench. "I fear the wedding will be too extravagant. He places far too much meaning on little details I'm sure to hardly notice."

"Jane will notice. And Oliver." Annalisa sat in her chair by the hearth and studied her friend's vacant stare. When she lifted her gaze, Annalisa saw Abigail's eyes were red-rimmed. "Have you been crying?"

"I have." Abigail stood from the kitchen bench and paced. She paused before the fire to adjust a pewter plate upon the mantle.

"Abby, what is it?"

"Lord Essex is a fine man, a gentleman who would never wish to hurt me, but I am always thinking of your fantastical brother." She turned and reached for Annalisa. "I promised to wait for him."

"I know." Annalisa frowned, her spirit heavy for George. "Did you write to him?"

"No...I know not what to say."

"Then I'll do it. He deserves to know."

"You're right. But you must know I never chose Lord Essex over him. My Papa chose for me, and I couldn't refuse. I wish I had followed George to Boston."

"George would never have allowed it of you. He would have insisted you stay behind. To keep you safe."

Her friend's lips quivered. "Yes. How right you are. Now, when he returns, I'll be married. He will loathe me."

"I'll write to him that it was beyond your control." Annalisa stood, and brushed a piece of her friend's hair from her face. "Chin up, shoulders back." She quoted Abigail from the dinner at Mr. Hooper's, though George's wisdom echoed in her mind: *life is rarely what we think it should be.*

Abigail fidgeted with her hands. "I am grieved we must leave for England."

"Of that, I am most distressed. But you will return next year, will you not?"

"Yes. And probably with several children in tow."

Annalisa giggled. "'Tis nine months for a child, Abby. You'll hardly have several if you're gone a twelvemonth."

Abigail smirked. "How are you?" She eyed Annalisa's stomach. "My mamma said you've missed your monthlies."

Annalisa ground her teeth. She'd told Mamma in confidence; now, it seemed her entire family knew. "My stomach has been sour since Jack left for Philadelphia."

"You miss him terribly."

"I do. But it shan't be long before he returns. I daresay,

he'll be home for the weddings. I only hope he'll be here when the child is born."

"That is eight months from now." Abigail held her hand. "But I see your worry. I lament mothers who are missing their husbands and sons to the army and must raise their children alone."

Annalisa remembered she had water boiling. She reached for a towel and pulled the crane holding the cast iron kettle from the flame.

Abigail cocked her head. "Tea?"

"Coffee. My husband may have dumped tea into the harbor...it suffices to say, we don't keep tea in this house."

73

JACK
TOPSFIELD, DECEMBER 1775

J ACK TROTTED HIS HORSE down the narrow
lane. He'd left Philadelphia with Father a week ago,
but this last mile to Annalisa was the longest of the
journey. Round the bend in the road, his humble saltbox
stood etched against the purple twilight. Smoke spiraled
from the chimney and candles danced in the first-floor
window. His heart quivered. It had been months since he'd
last held his wife.

When he'd stabled his horse and greeted Quinn, he
trudged through the snow to the front door. The iron
lantern glowed amidst the cold. He knocked playfully.

The door creaked open. "Jack."

"Dear heart." His wife's lilac perfume flooded him as
he hoisted her up and spun her in circles. When he set her
down inside the foyer, he kissed her.

"Welcome home, Mr. Perkins." Addy curtsied. "Miss
Annie bade me let her open the door."

"Miss Addy, a wondrous surprise." Jack hugged their

beloved housekeeper then returned his attention to Annalisa. "What plagues you, love? You look weary."

"I've a letter from George." She led him into the kitchen, lifted the page from the wooden table, and handed him the note.

BOSTON

NOVEMBER 1775

DEAREST LITTLE ONE,

I WRITE TO INFORM YOU I WILL BE ABSENT FROM NEW-ENGLAND THESE NEXT FEW MONTHS AS I JOURNEY TO FORT TICONDEROGA WITH HENRY KNOX. THIS IS ALL I CAN SAY OF THE EXPEDITION, BUT KNOW I THINK OF YOU OFTEN, AND LOOK FORWARD TO WHEN WE SHALL MEETE AGAIN. THANK YOU FOR TELLING ME ABOUT ABIGAIL'S ENGAGEMENT. I KNOW SHE IS HARDLY TO BLAME, BUT I'VE NEVER KNOWNE SUCH DESPAIRE. SINCE WE LAST CORRESPONDED, ABIGAIL'S AGREED TO KEEP WRITING TO ME FROM ENGLAND. MORE INFORMATION TO COME.

YOU'RE ALWAYS IN MY HEART. PLEASE GIVE JACK MY REGARDS.

YOURS &C,

G

"THEN HE IS IN NEW YORK." JACK FOLDED THE LETTER. "And with Henry Knox, no less." He chuckled. "I remember on Pope Night when George kissed Lucy Flucker. I heard Knox has since married Lucy."

Annalisa did not laugh. "He is far from us now. And

we're losing Abigail." She paced by the kitchen table, clutching her stomach. "Would that I could join him."

"He will be safe." Jack set the note on the table and intercepted her pacing. "And you are meant to be here." He placed a hand to her stomach. "You carry our child."

"I do not." She held her face and sank to the floor. "I would've written..."

Jack knelt beside her. "Pray tell, whatever do you mean?"

"I lost the child." She heaved. "I bled for days at the end of November. If not for Addy, and Weetamoo, and Quinn, I might have died."

His cheeks numbed, and he rocked her in his arms. Jack buried his face in her hair and blinked away the heaviness behind his eyes as Annalisa sobbed against his chest.

When he'd composed himself, he said, "'Twas the first one. And you're alive and well. We shall make another. I promise." He kissed her head and smoothed her hair. "'Tis my fault. I've been absent from this house, our bed, for too long."

She pulled from him. "I was so certain of this child."

He swiped his thumb across her cheek. "I know."

They remained on the wooden floor until soup splashed over the pot, landing in the fire with a sizzle. Jack lifted his wife to her feet.

"Let me serve the soup." He turned to the fire and paused. "Where is the ladle?"

Annalisa smiled. "To your left."

"Ah, there in front of me." Jack chuckled and ladled the savory pumpkin soup into two bowls, and sat across from her. How quiet and simple this new life of theirs was. Jack reached for her hand, the firelight flickering upon her wet, ruddy cheeks. "Are you ready for tomorrow's nuptials?"

"I am. But I'm more interested to hear what befell you in Philadelphia at Congress."

"Of course, you are." Jack winked. "We formed the Committee of Secret Correspondence."

Her eyes rounded and she glanced about the room. She leaned closer, and nearly spilled her soup. "Is it a spy ring?"

"Dear heart, no, but you seem eager to join one." He laughed. "It is a committee where we are dedicated to corresponding to our friends in Britain, and other countries...notably, France." Jack hesitated. "I've been appointed to join—I've a contact in Paris, a Monsieur Beauregard."

"Say something to me in French."

"*Je t'aime ma chérie, et je ferai trembler tes jambes toute la nuit.*"

Annalisa smirked. "Is that so?"

He warmed, and knew his cheeks burned fiery red. "Then you recall more of your French lessons than I'd hoped."

She giggled. "Jane was a slave to my education, but I understood not a word of what you said." Annalisa stood and walked around the table to sit on his lap. "But if it means you'll take me to bed tonight, I most heartily consent."

THE ASSEMBLY ROOM OF MR. HOOPER'S HOUSE IN Danvers pummeled Jack with memories of the night he'd proposed their elopement. Yet everything smelled of musk and lavender, which was reminiscent of Lord Suffolk's Ball—and Annalisa's escape to Bunker Hill. How quickly those memories turned from perfume to gunpowder. He bristled. They'd all been lucky to have escaped alive that day.

Mrs. Howlett, escorted by William, intercepted their walk toward Abigail and Lord Essex.

"Oh, Jack, Annie. I pray Janey finds in Oliver what you've found in each other. I worry a bit. They can both be a little...self-indulgent." Mrs. Howlett squeezed Jack's hand. "I was wrong to have tried to arrange that marriage between you and Janey."

"All is as it should be, ma'am." Jack bowed.

"You should be proud, Mamma." Annalisa slid her arm around his. "It seems I've found myself a gentleman of Society, too."

"How wrong I was to have condemned you." Mrs. Howlett kissed the scar beneath Annalisa's cheek. "By your leave, Mr. and Mrs. Perkins."

Mrs. Howlett disappeared into the crowd with William as Abigail and Lord Essex advanced toward them. Annalisa dipped into a curtsy and Jack bowed.

Jack kissed his sister's hand. "Our congratulations."

In her cream and silver *robe a la français* gown, Abigail looked every bit the new Lady Essex, yet, he felt consternation she could not marry George. *I wonder if she, too, resents this day.*

"Mr. Perkins, I hear your uncle and father have reconsidered several things about the estates since your marriage. 'Tis truly no business of mine, but," Lord Essex leaned in, "it would be better to have an ally such as yourself than your Tory brother."

Jack shifted uneasily. "I'd rather have Annalisa beside me and not a shilling to my name."

"That is bold indeed, sir. In choosing love, you are braver than most men." Lord Essex bowed. "It is an honor to call you my brother."

"Likewise, my lord."

"I only regret we must leave for England so soon, my lord." Abigail sighed. "I would do anything to have Annie and Jack with me."

Lord Essex winked. "Perhaps if Brunswick comes to his senses, Mr. and Mrs. Perkins may not be far behind us, my dear." He bowed again. "By your leave."

Annalisa called after Abigail, "Abby, whatever does he mean?"

Abigail blew her a kiss, and continued to cross the room with Lord Essex.

Annalisa turned toward Jack and squeezed his hand. "Is there something you're keeping from me?"

He started to answer, but Oliver and Jane loomed. The joint wedding seemed to put them in high spirits. Jane got every lavish detail of Lord Essex's opulent taste, and Oliver had all the important guests he felt he deserved.

Jack shook his brother's hand.

"My thanks to you, Brother." Oliver smirked. "Were it not for your untimely elopement, I daresay, this day might not have been ours. And your inheritance would still be yours."

"Ollie." Jane's rosy cheeks bloomed. "Not today."

"Janey, you look beautiful. And I can hardly wait to meet this little one." Annalisa touched Jane's swelling belly.

Jane covered Annalisa's hand with hers. "I daresay you'll always be the 'Little One' in our family."

Lord Brunswick entered their circle with Aunt Catherine. "Ollie, congratulations are in order." He shook Oliver's hand and kissed Jane's. "Simply stunning, my dear."

Aunt Catherine glowed. "I marvel at your glorious youth."

Lord Brunswick locked eyes with Jack. "Mr. and Mrs. Perkins, my congratulations to you as well. I am mighty impressed. Mighty impressed, indeed. Jack, your work in Congress is something to be proud of. And Adams' nomination of General Washington as commander in chief—astounding. I anticipate what he can do for this new Continental Army. But this Committee of Secret Correspondence. We must speak further on the matter."

Jack started. "Of course, Uncle. Whenever it best suits you."

Lord Brunswick crossed his arms. "I wish I could convince Ollie here to attend Congress with you and your father."

Oliver smoothed the sleeves of his silk frock coat. "It is not within my principles to partake in treasonous meetings that oppose our rightful king, Uncle."

"Indeed." Lord Brunswick jutted his chin. "Jack, a private word, if I may."

"Sir." Jack left Annalisa with Jane, Oliver, and Aunt Catherine. He followed his uncle from the assembly room, down the hall, and into Mr. Hooper's library. He bit his tongue, remembering the last time he'd been in this room.

Lord Brunswick faced him with imperative need. "Jack, I insist you remain my heir apparent."

"Sir." Jack's jaw dropped. "Are you certain?"

"I am." Lord Brunswick set a hand to his hip. "Oliver has demonstrated a litany of character flaws I truly disdain. As to the matter of your wife," he sucked in a breath, "...she is a fine, hearty, courageous woman who I hope will give me a second chance at knowing her. I'll be the first to admit I was wrong. That is termed humbly admitting fault. A lesson your brother should wish to learn."

"Sir, I'm flattered. Must I tell Oliver of your decision, sir?"

"Nay." Lord Brunswick held up his hand. "I'll relay the news to him. There's no need to spoil the poor lad's wedding night." He held out his hand, and Jack shook it. "To my heir apparent."

When they re-entered the assembly room, Annalisa glided to his side with Mother, Father, and Aunt Catherine.

"Perkins, I present to you my heir apparent." Lord Brunswick gestured to Jack.

Father raised his brows. "Then you've reconsidered."

"I have. All you told me of Congress has impressed me. And if Jack's to be nominated to go to France, he will require my support."

"France?" Annalisa gasped. "Mean you to leave me again so soon?"

"Young love." Lord Brunswick laughed. "Leave you? My dear, you should spend this winter season brushing up on your French."

The room suddenly felt warm and stuffy, and Jack adjusted his stock. "My thanks to you, Lord Brunswick, Aunt Catherine." He bowed. "Father, Mother, we'll see you on Sunday."

Jack led Annalisa from the group. When they reached the edge of the room, she faced him.

"What is all of this talk of France? Have you agreed to something without first speaking with me?"

"No, of course not. It may be months before Congress decides. But I promise, you will be the first to hear of it."

She bit her lip, then cracked a smile. "I'd better be."

74

ANNALISA
TOPSFIELD, DECEMBER 1775

T HE CHAISE WHEELS JUDDERED along the frozen, narrow lane. With the newly fallen snow, it was just wide enough for the two horses to pass. Quinnapin and the other stable-hand stored away the chaise in the small carriage house, and Jack brought the horses into the barn. Annalisa waited on the front step of their house. The sun had set, and early stars dotted the eastern sky. It had been a wondrous two days celebrating Abigail and Jane, but George's absence lingered like a fire that had been banked overnight. He was gone to New York. Until his return, she could only anticipate his letters.

The cold air slipped into her chest, and she wrapped her cloak about her. The regulars still occupied Boston, and she'd seen how they'd fought at Bunker Hill. They would be hard-pressed to give in to Washington and his new army. But still, there was hope.

A deep curiosity settled over her as more stars brightened the void. A great unknown sprawled before her. While it was uncomfortable and terrifying, she reveled in the mystery. The future was sure to offer countless obstacles, but she would share them all with Jack beside her—the companion she was so afraid to acquire, the gentleman her mother believed she could never attract, the husband Society deemed her unworthy of; the man who found her his equal.

Jack emerged from the stable and trudged up the shoveled path. His breath emerged in small white puffs. "Shall we retire within, Mrs. Perkins?" His cheeks dimpled.

Annalisa returned his smile. "Yes. We shall."

He opened the door and led her inside.

"Welcome home, Mr. and Mrs. Perkins." Addy's mouth widened with a wonderful grin that filled Annalisa with the warmth of her childhood; the same smile that had comforted her the day she'd scarred her face; the same smile that had reassured her the first day she'd gotten the morbid flux. Addy was more mother to her than her own.

Annalisa pulled her into an embrace until Addy said, "Come now, let's get you out of your chilled riding clothes and into the kitchen. A nice fire's goin'."

Addy took Annalisa and Jack's riding coats, then disappeared down the hall.

Before the blazing kitchen hearth, Jack reached for Annalisa and tugged her into his arms. "With my uncle's inheritance, we can now afford to stay here in Topsfield and build a summer home in New Castle. Imagine our summers by the sea..."

"I'd love that very much."

They remained in an embrace, warming one another, when Annalisa spoke into his chest. "I hope you realize if you're summoned to France, I'll be joining you."

"I should hope so. But could you endure crossing the Atlantic with just me for company?"

"Well, when you put it like that..." She pulled from him. "I may reconsider."

Jack arched a brow. "Is that so?" He reached for her, but she dodged him and scurried around the table. He chased after and finally caught her, lifting her into the air. They twirled and laughed, and the world spun, as it had the night they danced on the common, and the day they married.

Thud.

"What was that?" Jack set her down.

A small, lead musket round rolled toward the hearth.

"My ball. From Bunker Hill." She scooped it up and held it in her palm. "I take it with me wherever I go. To remind me."

"I've a surprise for you." Jack quit the kitchen and left the house for several minutes.

Annalisa stood by the hearth, examining her musket round. Some of the grooves still held the rusty remnants of dried blood.

When Jack returned, a gust of cold air blew in from the outside. He sauntered into the kitchen with Quinnapin, and a musket. It looked new, but she couldn't be certain. Annalisa crossed in front of the fire to where he stood.

"Wuneekeesuq," Annalisa greeted Quinnapin.

He smiled. *"Wuneekeesuq,* Mrs. P."

"Quinn and I had this made for you, my rebel rogue." Jack offered her the musket.

She held the weapon. It's cool steel and smooth, walnut stock felt like Bixby, the first time she'd wielded a firelock.

She turned to Quinnapin. "Thank you, my friend." Her throat tightened as she faced her husband. "Jack." She blinked away her tears. "How well you love me."

Jack closed his hand over hers as she clutched the musket and pressed his forehead to hers. He smelled familiarly of amber and pipe tobacco, and he hummed *Flowers of Edinburgh*. The warmth of his touch filled her with ease.

"Someday, we'll have a remarkable story to tell our grandchildren."

THANK YOU

Thank you for reading *Muskets and Minuets*.

Please consider leaving a review. Reviews not only help other readers to find new books but they also let readers know which books may end up being their favorites!

GLOSSARY OF 18TH-CENTURY & NEW ENGLAND VOCABULARY

ABRAMS: men/gentlemen

BAGPIPE: fellatio

BANNS: (marriage banns) an announcement of impending marriage

BAWDY BASKET(S): a lady or group of ladies

BEAR-GARDEN JAW: rude or vulgar language

BENEFIT OF CLERGY: avoiding the death penalty as a Christian by pleading benefit of clergy; one would be branded on the thumb with the letter of their crime: F for felon, M for murder, T for theft; this was so the benefit could not be claimed more than once.

BLOODYBACK: redcoat in His Majesty's Army

BUNDLEBAG/BUNDLING: an old New England tradition in which parents would arrange courting couples to spend the night together. The gentleman would be sewn into a canvas sack to prevent copulation prior to marriage. Other times, a long wooden board was placed between the couple.

CHRISTMASTIDE: the twelve days of Christmas, beginning on December 25th and ending on Twelfth Night, Epiphany, January 6th. (Sometimes the dates observed are Dec. 24th – Jan. 5th) Christmas itself was rarely celebrated in New England.

COCK ROBIN: a soft, easy fellow

CURTAIN LECTURE: an instance of a woman reprimanding her husband in private

DANDY PRAT: an insignificant or trifling fellow

DILBERRIES: excrement stuck to the hairs of one's arse (dingleberries in modern terms)

DISGUISED: drunk

DOXIE(S): lady/ladies

DRESSED TO THE NIINES: dressed to perfection

FIE: used to express outrage or disgust.

FLIP: tavern drink made of rum, ale, molasses, and eggs,

then beaten with a hot fire poker to create a nice froth, topped off with grated nutmeg. Each tavern had their own version of flip.

FOWLING PIECE/FOWLER/FIRELOCK: Smooth bore flintlock, muzzle-loading gun, used primarily to hunt fowl. Was typical household weapon in New England.

GO OFF: to orgasm

HOOPS (see *panniers*): undergarments worn beneath ladies' petticoats to give wide skirt appears classic to the 18th century

INTERCOURSE: conversation

GREEN GOWN (to give someone): to have sex with a woman in the grass

GOLLUMPUS: a large, clumsy fellow

JERRYCUMMUMBLE: to shake or tumble about

LA: expression of surprise

LEAPING OVER THE SWORD: a military marriage

LET-GO: to orgasm

LOBSTER/LOBSTERBACK: redcoat in the His Majesty's Army

LOOKING GLASS: mirror

MARM: ma'am

MORT(S): lady/ladies

MUSKET: smoothbore barrel, muzzle-loading gun. Less accurate but was usually used within the military because of quicker loading and the ability to attach bayonet.

NECESSARY: bathroom/loo/privy/outhouse

NOOZED: married, hanged

OWL IN AN IVY BUSH: said of a person who wears a large, frizzed wig

SPATTERDASHES: made of wool, leather, or linen, they covered a man's leg from mid-shin to top of the foot. Worn by military, sporting, or working men for warmth.

SPILL: a piece of rolled wood or paper used to light a fire

PANNIERS (see *hoops*): these were worn beneath a lady's petticoats to give the wide, 18th century skirt silhouette

PEGO: a man's penis

PHYSICK: medicine

PLUM: a fortune of £100,000 or someone with such fortune.

POMMADE: hair grease used with powder to create desired hairstyles

PUK-WUDJIE (various spelling): translating literally to 'Person of the wilderness'. Little people of the forest in Wampanoag folklore who are mischievous in nature.

RECEIPT: recipe, old spelling

ROGUE: men/gentlemen

REMEDY CRITCH: a bowl/chamber pot, usually porce-lain, in which to urinate

RUN GOODS (to take): virginity, or, to take one's virginity

SHENEWEMEDY: some historians believe it is Tops-field's name, according to the Agawam, meaning 'the pleasant place by the flowing waters'. Some believe it was how the Agawam pronounced Topsfield's first colonial name of New Meadows. It was changed to Topsfield in 1648, and the town incorporated in 1650.

SHITTING THROUGH THE TEETH: vomiting

SHUT YOUR POTATO TRAP AND GIVE YOUR TONGUE A HOLIDAY: to shut up

SLUICE YOUR GOB: to take a hearty drink

STAYS (pair of): whale-boned corset that gives conical

shape to torso that is classic to the 18th century woman's silhouette

STRUM: to have sexual intercourse

SUIT IN DITTO: a man's suit where all pieces (breeches, coat, and waistcoat) are of the same color and fabric

SQUEEZE CRAB: a sour-looking, shriveled, diminutive fellow

TIP THE VELVET: to put one's tongue in a woman's mouth, or cunnilingus

VICTUALING OFFICE/VICTUALS: stomach

WHIP JACKETS: men

WHOLE NINE YARDS: clothing took nine yards to make; to be the whole nine yards meant your outfit was cut of the same nine yards of dyed fabric, which meant everything matched perfectly; sometimes dyes differed.

WRAPPED UP IN WARM FLANNEL: drunk with spiritous liquors

ZOUNDS: an exclamation of surprise or indignation

Casting Shadows (Casting Shadows #1) by Dziyana Taylor

Queen of All (The Jena Cycle #1) by Anya Leigh Josephs

ABOUT THE AUTHOR

A born and bred New Englander, Lindsey hails from the North Shore of Boston. A member of the Topsfield Historical Society and the Historical Novel Society, she forged her love for writing with her intrigue for colonial America by writing her debut novel, *Muskets and Minuets*. When she's not attending historical reenactments or spouting off facts about Boston, she's nursing patients back to health in the ICU.